Elizabeth E. Proctor

In the Cool of the Day

Books by Susan Ertz

Novels

MADAME CLAIRE

NINA

AFTERNOON

NOW EAST, NOW WEST

THE GALAXY

JULIAN PROBERT

THE PROSELYTE

NOW WE SET OUT

WOMAN ALIVE

NO HEARTS TO BREAK

ONE FIGHT MORE

ANGER IN THE SKY

MARY HALLAM

THE PRODIGAL HEART

INVITATION TO FOLLY

CHARMED CIRCLE

IN THE COOL OF THE DAY

Short Stories

FACE TO FACE

BIG FROGS AND LITTLE FROGS

For Children

BLACK, WHITE AND CAROLINE

In the Cool
of the Day

Susan Ertz

HARPER & BROTHERS PUBLISHERS
New York

Library of Congress catalog card number: 60-13440

In the Cool of the Day

I

HE had had five full days in New York, which had meant five late nights with few sleep-filled hours, and though he had never been there before those five days and nights had given him the keys of the city. If he had been leaving again at once he would still have been possessed of things indelible, of memories almost as solid, as tactile, as the streets and buildings themselves. No one could now tell Murray Logan anything about New York that he couldn't get out of a guidebook. The unique flavor of the place was his. Meetings between a city and a traveler, he thought, were private affairs and incommunicable. Paris, Rome, Athens—they had come to no ripening at all until he had set foot in them; then came the sudden complex flowering.

There was no one to whom he particularly wished to explain or describe the impressions he had derived from his days in New York; fortunately, for he would have found it too difficult unless he had confined himself to the trite and obvious. Like his own existence, it did not lend itself to decoding. He saw his whole life as painfully unsharable, and though he knew that in any life there was a flow of thought and feeling that was as secret as the flow of sap in a tree, he himself felt weighed down by his self-imposed exclusiveness. Self-imposed or fate-imposed; he did not know which.

Now he was possessing himself as far as he was able of the state of Connecticut during a drive from Greenwich station to Sam Bonner's house eight miles away. Till then it had been a shape sometimes seen on a map, and anything he had read or imagined about it was being smoothly effaced by the inevitable yet unanticipated look of things—as—they—are.

The outskirts of Greenwich, the graceful elms, handsome houses, green lawns and fine roads made their impression, and he formed the mental comment that all this, surely, was too rich for a mere publisher. Then he remembered that Sam Bonner had married a rich woman. Woman? Girl? He had no idea in what category to place her, nor could he remember, if he had ever heard, how long Sam had been married. Three years? Four years? It might even be as much as five or six, with time slipping away like water through the fingers. Other members of the firm had said she was rich. It was all he knew of her.

It was early April, and the only color, apart from the returning green of the lawns, was the yellow of the forsythia fountains which played everywhere—in gardens, along the road, at road junctions. It was obviously a much-loved thing and for a month or more, he supposed, people could look on these spouting yellow arabesques and rejoice, as he was rejoicing now. The happiness to be derived from such sights was the one valid happiness he knew. The only one not to be mistrusted.

It was certainly, hereabouts, a rich community, much addicted to imposing white houses in the Colonial style, with pillared fronts and green shutters. They were now passing what appeared to be large estates and from time to time the

2

driver, an elderly colored man who said he had previously driven for Sam's father, would point out the home of some wealthy executive, well known, no doubt, to the world of American business.

"That's the residence of Mr. Sherborn Masters, president of the South Bay Oil Company. They're a lovely family, yes sir. Miss Sheila Masters she takes prizes jumping in the New York Horse Show." And again, "This here's the residence of Mr. Julius Gottschalk. He's from out West. Copper. He's sure a mighty rich man, yes sir. Owns a yacht, too, and a fine place in the Bahamas."

He noted that this soft-voiced gray-haired man spoke of these people with pride, the pride of one who had himself been nourished and given security by just such men, whose fortunes were bound up with theirs. He no doubt owned a car, lived well and envied no one. A dark and happy satellite.

Soon the country grew less tame; stretches of woodland appeared and acres of marshy ground where great green tropical-looking leaves were unfurling out of the earth. "Skunk cabbage," the chauffeur said. "Smells bad but looks real pretty."

The woods were thick with young growth. He hadn't seen any fully grown trees anywhere except planted along the roads or standing on private lawns. But the young woods had an innocent charm; he thought he must have known such woods as a child. They struck a chord of memory in him.

"There's the gates of Mr. Sam's house down on the left," the driver presently said. " 'Runnybrook' they call it. There's a brook runs right through the place. Mr. Sam dammed it up last year and made a lake. Yes, sir, here we are."

The only member of the American side of Atlantic House he had not yet seen on this brief visit—apart from Sam's father, who had been seriously ill—was Sam himself, for he had been staying at home recovering from a heavy cold. Sam had rung him up from the country the morning he'd arrived

3

and could scarcely make himself heard, being almost voice-less. It was a whole year since Sam had been in London, but they'd seen a good deal of each other at that time, for although Murray was not then a member of the board, Sam had twice selected him to accompany him to Paris as his self-taught French was fairly fluent and Sam's atrocious. The second time they had spent several days there and had between them managed to "tie up" a shy French novelist who spoke not a word of English and had been approached without success by many publishers for his English translation rights. Now that he was on the point of seeing Sam again, by a common but curious trick of memory he became vividly alive to him. He could even feel in anticipation the clasp of that large warm cushiony hand. He wondered a little at the strength of his own liking for Sam, and still more at the thought of Sam's liking for him. He was sure that his promotion to the London board owed quite as much to Sam's partisanship as to two recent occurrences: the death of one member and the retire-ment of another. He could tell himself, as he often did, that he was where he was thanks to Sam's friendship and to a series of flukes, one of them being the fact that Charles Kendrick's wife was his own mother's cousin, and Charles had given him his chance eighteen years ago to please his wife—though he had had no cause to regret it. Anyway, there was not a great deal in it to feed his self-esteem, a commodity of which he had little.

The car turned in through white gates and he could now see Sam's house through the lightly sketched, unleafed trees. It extended its considerable length upon a rise of smooth lawn and, though more modest than many they had passed, looked capable of providing hospitality of a generous sort. Upon its somewhat *House Beautiful* front, Murray's mind now superimposed the picture of his own home, a semi-detached "villa" halfway between Morden and Wimbledon. When people asked him where he lived he said Wimbledon, but in fact it was in Morden. He was unashamed. In no other way, he believed, could he ever alter the situation of his house.

The garden of Sam's home was pleasantly landscaped, and here too forsythia made its brilliant display and was even trained prettily over the front door. Near the house he saw a red tricycle which he supposed belonged to a visitor's child, for Sam had told him he had no children. As they reached the house the chauffeur gave a loud blast on the horn, saying apologetically as he got out to open the car door, "Mr. Sam's orders, sir. He likes to know when folks arrive."

That it had had the desired effect was soon evident, for Sam himself promptly opened the front door, a cocktail glass in his left hand, his right held out in welcome.

"Well, well, here you are," he said, and Murray's hand was enveloped in that familiar clasp. "This is great. Gordon got you here in fine time. It's good to see you. Leave your dispatch case right here in the hall. We'll deal with what's in it after lunch. Where's Mary?" And he gave a loud, uninhibited shout. "Mary! Where are you?"

A middle-aged woman wearing black ran through a door at the back of the square hall.

"I'm so sorry, Mr. Sam," she said breathlessly. "I was right out in the garden when I heard the horn, looking for that Seth. I can't find him anywhere. How are you, Mr. Logan? We're glad to have you here. Give me your hat and coat and I'll hang them up for you. My! It's pretty cold still, isn't it?" She took his hat and coat and then said in a bustling, slightly monitory way, "Lunch'll be ready in half an hour, you know, Mr. Sam. I promised Maggie I'd remind you in case you strolled down to the lake or anything."

"Now that's all over, come in and have a drink," Sam said, with the air of a man ridding himself of feminine fuss, and he led the way into a long cheerful white-painted room. It had well-filled bookshelves between the windows all down the

5

outer wall, and books were lying about on tables and on the floor beside the armchair Sam had been sitting in. Green plants flourished here and there in the almost tropical warmth, and a wood fire was burning in the big open fireplace. "Mary's the housekeeper here," Sam said. "She pretty near runs this place and everybody in it. She's quite a character if you know what I mean. Sit down and tell me what you'll have."

"First of all, tell me how you're feeling?" Murray asked.

"Oh, fine, fine. Cold's just about gone. I'll be back at the office tomorrow."

"Good," Murray said. "I've missed you, in spite of the fact that they've all been wonderfully kind to me." He was letting his eyes rove now. "Hello! Isn't that a Grandma Moses over the mantelpiece?"

He knew it was because he'd had a Christmas card from Sam which was a reproduction of that very painting.

"Yeah," Sam said. "I've got another one upstairs in the bedroom, too. I'm crazy about the old girl. What'll you have?"

"A martini, if that's what I see in the jug." Murray answered. "What a delightful house this is. It seems to me perfect." He felt curiously at home in it, curiously at ease, and it and Sam's presence in it gave him a feeling of well-being and satisfaction. The thought of a new personality, that of Sam's wife, presently intruding on them, irked him.

"I like it," Sam said, and his voice had melancholy overtones. "I like it fine. Help yourself to some of the fixings."

He indicated a tray on which were celery, sliced carrots, mayonnaise and cheese biscuits.

Murray saw that Sam had been putting on weight—too much weight. He was not tall, and was so broad-shouldered that it was almost a deformity. Now he was on the way to becoming a fat man, the fate of many an ex-football player. The rough tweeds he wore made him look still bulkier, but he moved lightly and there was nothing clumsy about him. His blue eyes were young, lively and innocent, with the innocence of a good child, and his half-humorous, half-deprecatory expression was peculiarly his own. It was as if he'd just been caught doing something comically self-revealing but was prepared to brazen it out. His slightly plaintive way of speaking also was a thing specially belonging to his personality, as were his childish mouth that seemed not to have altered since boyhood, his thick, arched eyebrows and his abundant reddish-brown hair. Murray found everything about Sam likable, endearing; he was one of the very few people he felt a comfortable affection for. He even felt an added affection for him now because of the absurd and artlessly vulgar tie he wore. A thing he envied Sam was his ability to make a kind of cult of his personality, which included at times an amiable buffoonery, though anyone who failed to see what lay beneath it would be unwise. Sam was very far indeed from being a fool.

"Did you have time to read your Sunday papers on the train?" Sam presently asked. "There's a good review in *The Times* of Pybus' book on China. It ought to help it along."

"I'm afraid I was too busy looking out of the window," Murray said. "Besides, the train was so hot it made me drowsy."

"Must have given you a thirst," Sam said. "Drink up and have another. I'm going to."

As Sam filled their glasses again Murray said, "They tell me your father is making a wonderful recovery. I'm so very glad to hear it."

"Oh, yes, poor old boy, he's getting along, he's getting along. They all say he's doing fine. You know how damn cheerful they always sound, as if they were putting on an act. God! I hope I die before it happens to me."

"But why?" Murray asked. "He *is* recovering, isn't he? Don't they say he'll be back at the office soon?"

"Yes, he'll be back, but for how long? You know as well as I do, Murray, and Charles Kendrick knows it too, that what he's had is his notice to quit. To quit for good and all.

Once I've had notice to quit I hope I go, and go fast. What sort of life is it, knowing what's waiting for you around the next corner?"

"But don't we all know it," Murray asked him, "as soon as we know we're mortal? You really have a horror of death, haven't you, Sam? I remember you told me so in Paris. It was the night you took me to the Lido. You spoke about it while those girls in their feathers and net tights were dancing."

"That's what made me think of it, I guess," Sam said. "And I guess that's why we like to look at those beautiful healthy young animals, kicking up their heels. They make death seem so damn far away. Yeah, it haunts me all right. You've heard of people who live with a skull on their tables. Well, that's me. The damn thing never stops grinning at me. And it not only grins, it ticks, like a clock. Ticks the time away." He half emptied his glass. "Oh, I guess I'm no different from most, it's just that I admit what other people won't admit. The thought of death scares the daylights out of me. Not only for myself; for people I love. Let's talk about something else. Want me to tell you, Murray, the happiest thing I can recall? The thing that gives me a warm sort of glow whenever I think of it?"

Murray, smiling under his clipped mustache, keeping his eyes on Sam, said yes, he would like to hear it.

"Well, I'll tell you. It's the picture I've got in mind of those two lads, my dad, a young Rhodes scholar, and your Charles Kendrick, standing on that little bridge over the Isis, plotting the whole damn thing. Building up Atlantic House in their minds. Solemnly swearing they'd make a go of it. Do you know what I did when I was in England last year? I never told anybody. I went up to Oxford and stood on that same little bridge just for sentiment's sake. Well, I don't care; it was pretty fine, it was pretty fine."

"It was pretty fine," Murray agreed, and he was touched

8

by the picture evoked of Sam standing on the bridge looking back into a past long before he was born, and looking back with tenderness. "And now that you've filled up our glasses again we can drink their healths. You've made me feel sentimental too."

"To those two lads," Sam said, raising the glass which he had quickly replenished.

"To those two lads," Murray echoed, and wondered why a feeling of embarrassment invariably accompanied such moments. Sam's eyes, he now saw, were glistening with tears. What ailed him? he wondered. Something more than his father's illness, something more than this backward look and these memories? It would seem so. No doubt he would learn, sooner or later.

"One of Dad's worries, just after his coronary," Sam said, blinking unashamedly, "was the fear that he might never get to England again. I kept telling him it was all hooey. He ought to try and get over this summer if the doctors will let him. You tell him so, will you? You'll be seeing him, I hope."

"I want to, of course, if he feels like seeing me," Murray answered, and in fact it was an errand with which Charles Kendrick had particularly charged him, saying, "Go and see for yourself how he is. I get so many conflicting reports."

"Of course he'll want to see you. I'll ring him up later this afternoon and tell him you're coming. What about tomorrow? Say at five-thirty or six. Would that suit you? He's only supposed to have one visitor at a time, so I won't go with you."

"That would suit me perfectly," Murray said, but he had a nervous feeling that the meeting with the head of the firm might be something of an ordeal. He had to remind himself that he was no longer a part of the staff but a member of the board.

"O.K., that's settled then. He's got a nurse there, and she won't let you stay long, but he'll be glad to see you. You

9

know, Murray, we were all pleased as hell here when Charles promoted you to the board. It's been a long time and you got there the hard way, without being passed over anybody's head. I was damn glad."

"Yes," Murray said, "I'm glad of that too, but as you say, it took a long time. I'm thirty-seven. Charles wasn't going to let anyone say that he was promoting me because I was his wife's cousin's son."

"I guess nobody would ever have thought that."

"As you probably know, I went straight from school into the office." It was very rarely that Murray talked about himself, even about matters that were not of a private kind, but to talk about himself to Sam, and after two martinis, was just possible. "I've regretted ever since that I never went to a university—any sort of university—but I felt it would be wasting precious time, and there wasn't the money. My parents lived on four hundred pounds a year."

"You're no worse off for not going," Sam said comfortably. "Don't have it on your mind."

As Murray well knew, Sam's years at Yale were near and dear to him. That the fame he had won as halfback was a source of pride from which he would always draw a warm satisfaction. He smiled at Sam, but decided not to remind him of these facts.

"Tell me about Charles's wife," Sam then said. "I used to see her quite a lot in the old days, but nowadays she never appears at any of his parties. Is she a little bit funny in the head?"

"I wouldn't say so," Murray told him. "A trifle eccentric, perhaps."

"I guess she's eccentric all right," Sam said. "Anyhow, she scared me off Celia. I liked Celia a lot at one time—oh, I guess that was about fourteen years ago when I was over there during the war. How many dogs does she keep in the house?"

"I'm not sure. I haven't been there just lately. I should think five or six."

"Isn't that plain hell for Charles?"

"He never says so. He's devoted to her. She only started keeping dogs after Celia married and went to Canada."

"Took half a dozen of 'em to fill her place, that's something," Sam said.

Murray glanced at his watch while Sam was helping himself to some of the "fixings" and saw that it was close on one. He had expected every moment to see Sam's wife come into the room. Now he supposed she wouldn't appear until lunch was announced. He was on the point of inquiring about her when Sam abruptly asked, not looking directly at him: "By the way, how's that boy of yours? Martin his name is, isn't it?"

"Yes, Martin. He's well, thanks; he's with Sibyl and my mother."

"Good," Sam said with forced heartiness. "Glad to hear he's all right." He didn't ask about Sibyl, whom he had never met, and Murray was grateful to him for not asking. "Finish your drink," he urged, "and have another. I'm going to. Look, the jug's nearly a quarter full."

"Not for me, Sam, thanks. They're pretty strong. Stronger than I'm used to."

"Well, I'll have another even if you don't." He filled his glass and then emptied it quickly as he heard footsteps crossing the hall. (Here she is at last, Murray thought.)

But it was Mary, the housekeeper, who opened the door and said, "Lunch is quite ready, Mr. Sam."

"Good," Sam said, getting to his feet. "Just in time to keep us from having one too many. Come on, Murray. You must be hungry."

Murray followed him across the hall, which, he now noticed, was quaintly papered and furnished with pieces of old pine furniture—early American, he guessed. The dining room was

11

on the other side of the hall. It was a room of ample size, painted a bright yellow, with Chinese flower paintings on the walls. But what chiefly interested Murray was the fact that the oval table was laid for only two. The fact that Sam had neither referred to nor explained his wife's nonappearance puzzled him. He decided that to go on ignoring the absence of the lady of the house was hardly possible or polite, and that he must speak of it now or not speak of it at all.

"Is your wife away, Sam?" he asked, feeling for the first time since he had been in America some of the social awkwardness he too often felt in his own country.

"Yeah," Sam said as he unfolded his napkin and spread it on his knees. "She's away. Been away quite a time." He squared his shoulders, looked at Murray and said with a change of voice, "How's Dick Bayliss?"

"Very well indeed," Murray answered, telling himself that when in doubt the best policy was to keep one's mouth shut. "He's pleased as Punch just now because he persuaded Charles much against his will to publish So Short a Lease and it's already sold about forty thousand."

"Bound to," Sam replied. "Bound to. Tell Charles from me that he must be slipping. We're getting it out here next month. It ought to do damn well."

Gordon came in then wearing a white coat and white cotton gloves and served them with shrimp cocktails. As soon as he had left the room again Sam said—and he seemed to gather up all his resolution to say it: "You may as well know, I guess. I'm pretty well out of my mind about Christine. Just six weeks ago yesterday she got nervy and restless and said she'd got to get away. I'd half promised to take her somewhere, maybe to Virginia Hot Springs, but with Dad so ill I couldn't. So she went to Mexico to see her sister. All by herself, too. She stayed there about three weeks and then came back, but she didn't come back here. Now she writes to me from somewhere in New York that she doesn't know when she's coming back and maybe the answer is never. That's all for now. I'll tell you more later."

"I'm terribly sorry," Murray said. "Sorrier than I can say. Wouldn't you rather not talk about it? There's no need . . ."

"I'd rather talk," Sam said, "but not now, with Gordon coming in and out. I'll talk later." He passed a big bandanna handkerchief over his face and put it back in his pocket. "Tell me what you've got in that dispatch case out there. Anything that's liable to hit the jackpot? I wish we did better with English novels. Not like the good old days of Atlantic House when we couldn't get along without 'em, but I guess we've been saying that for some years now. This publishing business has got me pretty worried, Murray. I don't like what's going on. What people here want to read today is novels that tell them how filthy rotten life in America is and how most of us are perverts or, if we're not actually perverts, that we're full of every sort of nastiness; then they all have a good wallow and beg for more. I tell you the more mud and muck that can be crammed into a novel these days the higher it gets in the best-seller lists. Advice to young writers who want to succeed ought to be 'make 'em long and make 'em dirty.' That's the formula."

A year ago, Murray remembered, when they were in Paris together, he'd taken more or less that line himself and Sam had then defended what he called "a good old down-to-earth realism." He wasn't going to take the opposite view now just for the sake of argument, though he knew Sam enjoyed arguments.

"Oh well," he said, "one's got to remember there are fashions in these things. There's a vogue now for the ugly, but it'll pass."

"It can't pass too soon for me," Sam said. "I'm pretty sick of the whole business. The wheel's gone full circle, I guess, all the way from 'Sex is sin, keep away from it,' to 'Sex is

13

dirt, let's all go play in it.' If you ask me, both points of view are pretty damn vulgar and silly, but the newer one's the worst. I tell you I've just about had my fill of it."

"I've brought you an Australian novel that I think you'll like," Murray said. "We're really excited about it. It's something quite out of the common run."

"Well, we like Aussies," Sam answered, "but it'll have to be good. It'll have to have impact," he said, and Murray was glad to see that his eyes were now amused and ironical. "It'll have to be significant. Boy! It'll have to have involvement and even commitment. Has it got all that?"

"We think it's got just about everything," Murray said, smiling at him. "Charles is going all out for it."

"Well, if you were to twist my arm," Sam remarked, "I'd have to admit that the firm could do with a few home runs just about now."

"It could," Murray agreed, though it hurt him to have to admit it. "It could."

"God!" Sam exclaimed. "Pray that we don't have a recession. Pray hard."

"Aren't you taking a rather too gloomy view of things?" Murray asked.

"Wouldn't you," Sam retorted, "if your dad had had a bad coronary, if the firm wasn't showing what it ought to show in the way of profits, and if on top of all that your wife had walked out on you?"

Before Murray could make a reply, and he had no idea what reply he would have made, Gordon returned to take away the first course and to serve chicken à la Maryland, a mixed green salad and cheese. He had no sooner closed the door again than Sam clapped a hand to his forehead and cried: "Listen, Murray! I'm the biggest fool in Christendom. Say, ignore what I've just said, will you? Put it right out of your mind. I'm not forgetting what you've been through. Hell! Nothing as bad as that has happened to me yet."

14

"It's all right, Sam," Murray said, and his lips felt stiff and dry. "We all have to take it sooner or later, I suppose. My troubles came early. Don't worry about what you said. It's all some time ago now."

"Well, relax," Sam pleaded earnestly. "For God's sake, relax. Let's both relax. What do you think of this wine, boy? I'll tell you where it comes from. It comes from New York State. I think it's pretty good."

"It's fresh and delicate," Murray said, tasting. "I don't like a full-bodied white wine. I couldn't have made a guess, of course, as to what it was."

"It comes from New York State, and it ought to be a lot better known than it is."

"I don't know much about wine," Murray told him, "but I like this very much. I didn't even know New York State produced any wine."

"Well, it does," Sam answered. "You've got a lot to learn about this country, yet, boy." And he spoke with affection.

II ✍

Murray could feel that Sam wanted to talk about his trouble, that the pressure of it was too great to be borne by him unshared, and when they were back in the living room again drinking their coffee, he said, to help him, "Does anyone else know about this, Sam?"

He was wondering, even as he asked the question, how far he could rely on his own tact, now that he was upon such perilous ground. He was neither a giver nor a receiver of confidences and would have preferred to be told nothing of Sam's present dilemma. He thought that if he had so much as seen Sam's wife it would have been easier for both of them.

"Nobody outside the family knows," Sam answered, and his plaintive voice, which usually accorded so oddly and even comically with his words, now perfectly suited what he had to say. "That is, only Dad and Christine's sister Marietta. And just in case things come out right—a pretty slim chance, I guess—I don't want anybody to know. In the meantime I'm just about going crazy. She's in New York somewhere, I don't

16

even know where. Dad doesn't know either; she goes to see him sometimes, but she hasn't told him where she is. She says she doesn't want to see me till she's made up her mind, for good and all, what she's going to do. God! I just don't know how I'm going to stand it. I just don't know."

He rubbed both hands over his face and hair, bending his head as he did so; then he looked up at Murray again with a look so utterly miserable and despondent that Murray was moved to say: "Don't despair, Sam. It can all come right yet. Perhaps she just wants to be alone for a while. There are people who have to be alone sometimes, who have to get right away from everybody. I know, I'm one of them." And he thought with pity how difficult it was and always had been for a fat man, especially one wearing an absurd tie with rocks and mermaids on it, to convey even the most deeply felt grief.

"Not Americans," Sam said gloomily. "If Americans are unhappy they have to tell people. Americans are gregarious as hell, happy or miserable. Well, I guess that isn't true of Christine, but it's the first time she's ever done such a thing —cut herself off from me and from her home. Oh, if I thought it was nothing more than her wanting to be alone for a while, that would be O.K. But it's a whole lot more than that. I'd better tell you about her. For one thing, Murray, she's never had more than a few days at a time of feeling really well in her whole life, and certainly not since we've been married. The family had a pretty hard time keeping her alive, what with one thing and another. She had t.b. when she was a kid. She had a lobectomy when she was fourteen and another, a partial one, when she was eighteen. I guess it was one of the things that made me love her, her being so delicate and unlike all the others. But right now it's a lot more than just poor health. She's got into a funny sort of mental state. Our doctor here, Tom Luscombe—he was at Yale with me—he's pretty nearly as worried about her as I am. He's been sending her to specialists, and this winter she was a couple of weeks at the Presbyterian Hospital, getting a thorough checkup, but they didn't find anything wrong with her that we didn't know about before. Then Tom persuaded her to go to a psychoanalyst, but she had a couple of sessions with him and refused to have any more. Now she won't see Tom at all. She won't see her own mother if it comes to that—Mrs. Gellert thinks she's still in Mexico—but maybe you can't blame her for not seeing Mrs. Gellert. She's pretty terrific." He broke off and then said with a look of embarrassment, almost of shame, "Last year Mrs. Gellert was voted America's best-dressed woman. Maybe that'll give you the idea."

It did and it didn't, for Murray was trying to form some sort of outline of Christine, and it eluded him. Never having known anyone who resembled her, the fact that her mother had been voted America's best-dressed woman merely added one more unexpected and bizarre element.

"Anyhow," Sam went on, without waiting for any reply, "maybe you knew and maybe you didn't, Christine is Raymond Gellert's daughter. The old man died about a year after we were married and left Mrs. Gellert and the two girls very well off. It was a great pity he died. He was only just sixty, and he and I got along fine. I liked him a lot—I don't know if the name means anything to you."

"I connect it rather vaguely," Murray said, some faint memory having stirred in his mind, "with things like deep freezes and TV sets and electrical appliances generally. Is that right?"

"It's right as far as it goes," Sam answered. "Well, as I was saying, Mrs. Gellert's pretty terrific and Christine just can't stand up to her. She never could. That's why she won't see her. I guess Marietta feels the same, but she lives in Mexico now, out of Mrs. Gellert's way. She eloped when she was eighteen with a guy that kept a garage at Darien. The marriage didn't last, of course. Then she married a rancher from

18

Wyoming, but that didn't last either. She's just got her second divorce now, and she's bought herself a house at Cuernavaca."

He stopped to light a cigarette and Murray asked, "Is Mrs. Gellert the sort of woman who interferes in her daughters' marriages?"

"I don't think you could say she interferes exactly," Sam said, "but what she does do is this: she distills a subtle kind of poison that you aren't even conscious of till the damage is done. Boy! That woman's fallout is really something lethal. She only has to be in this house an hour before I begin feeling I ought to have on a gas mask. Oddly enough, Mr. Gellert always seemed to get along all right with her, or he managed to give the impression he did. He was loyal as hell. If you ask me, he was a pretty gallant sort of person and I don't blame him for a single thing, unless it's for marrying her in the first place, and I can't even grumble about that as it produced Christine.

"But I'll tell you something else, Murray. The way she brought up those two girls—well, maybe a really good novelist could describe it—Mauriac or somebody like that. I can't. You wouldn't believe it was possible in the United States today, but those girls never met any men if Mrs. Gellert could help it. She was jealous as hell. In her way I believe she was fond of the old man, but he couldn't take late nights or parties, and they were just what she longed for. Besides that, of course, he held the purse strings. As soon as he died she cut loose. Both the girls were out of the way by then, and she was still young enough to do the things she'd always wanted to do. Well, she's doing them, all right. Within the last three years or so she's become the most talked-about woman in New York.

"You see, going back a little, if she couldn't get around much on account of Mr. Gellert, she was determined that the girls shouldn't either. After Marietta ran away she made Christine's poor health an excuse to keep her right at home and supervise every breath she drew. Christine never went

19

back to school after that first lobectomy at fourteen, and she'd had only about a year's schooling before that. Until she was nearly eighteen she had a French governess, and then an English governess, but after that she had to educate herself as best she could. If you want to know, I think she made a pretty good job of it, too. I guess reading was the only pleasure she had. I'll tell you now how we met. It's quite a story. You know Brentano's, on Fifth Avenue?"

"I do," Murray said. "I was in there yesterday morning with Jim Hancock."

"All right. Here's the story. Six years ago last month I was in Brentano's talking to the head buyer, and as I came out of his office and was leaving the shop I saw this delicate-looking girl standing by a counter holding a list of books as long as your arm. She had a nurse with her, in uniform. It was soon after that second operation on her lung and she wasn't allowed out alone. She'd come up to New York for the day from their place in the country. It just happened that I overheard her trying to explain to the salesman about a book she wanted —it was a book on Greece that we'd published a few years back and it was out of print. So I spoke to her and introduced myself. I said we'd got some copies of the book in the office and if she'd allow me I'd send her one. I did send it and she wrote and thanked me for it. She said that if I was ever up that way—their place 'Summerhays' was about ten miles from here; it's sold now—maybe I'd call or come to lunch.

"Of course I made a point of going one Sunday quite soon after that, and that's how it all began. The minute I saw her in Brentano's that day I knew I was going to want to marry her. When I saw her again that Sunday I was still more certain of it—more certain than I'd ever been of anything in my life. I knew I simply had to marry her. Mrs. Gellert did her best to freeze me out. The way she looked at me that day you might have thought I was just another guy from the filling station, but I could see that Mr. Gellert liked me and I knew that whatever happened I was going to marry Christine if it took me the rest of my life. At times it looked as though it might, too, but in the end Mrs. Gellert decided she might as well give in. The funny thing was that in a way I think she wanted to get Christine off her hands, but she couldn't bear the thought that she might be going to be happy, maybe happier than she was. Anyhow, Christine and the old man together were too much for her, though Christine would never have been able to put up the fight she did if she'd had to do it alone. I guess, too, the truth was that by that time Christine knew she'd got to get away or take an overdose of sleeping tablets. She'd had just about as much of Mrs. Gellert as she could take. I may as well admit that."

There was an uncomfortable pause, uncomfortable for Murray because he felt he ought to say to Sam that he was sure it wasn't that, but any words he formed in his own mind seemed to him fatuous. He said presently, to break the silence, "She's never been to England, has she, since you've been married?"

"Who? Christine? Only on our honeymoon." The bitterness was gone now from Sam's voice. "And that's quite a story, too. We spent most of the time in Scotland because Christine had been to England with her parents once and she'd never seen Scotland. We spent quite a while traveling around. I don't suppose you remember, or maybe you never even heard about it, but we finally landed up in Edinburgh. You know that station hotel there? Of course you do. God! I'll never forget it as long as I live. It had suddenly turned rainy and cold. Why is it that cold in the summer's so much harder to bear than cold in the winter? Maybe one's blood gets thin. Anyhow, it was too much for Christine. We were planning to spend a couple of nights there and then go to London when she suddenly went down with pneumonia. It was a virus pneumonia and they took her straight off to the hospital. For over three weeks I don't think I left her bedside except to go back to the hotel

21

to try and get some sleep. Christine said afterwards that she only pulled through because I made her. Yes, I guess I made her get better. I got so close to her, Murray, that I didn't know which of us was which. Do you know what I mean? I honestly didn't. Sometimes it seemed to be me lying there with Christine sitting by the bed. Maybe it doesn't often happen but when it does it's a kind of fusion, and with me it was total. When I wasn't with her I wasn't whole. I wasn't anybody. It's still like that with me. Just at times, at brief moments, I've thought it might be like that with her, but most of the time I guess she's miles away from me. It takes the heart right out of me when it's like that. Sometimes I've wondered if she doesn't hate me for not letting her die there in Edinburgh. She was quite ready to die. She used to open her eyes sometimes and look at me and say, 'Am I still here? I thought the journey was over.' But I can't live without her, and that's the truth. I can't. These last weeks have been absolute hell, and it's getting worse. I don't know what I'll do if she doesn't come back."

He pulled the bandanna handkerchief out of his pocket and Murray looked away. He had been so imaginatively caught up in what Sam was telling him that he could almost feel it as something that had happened to himself.

"I seem to remember," he said, to give Sam time to get himself in hand, "that Charles flew up to Edinburgh in a great hurry. I think I was in Manchester at the time, at the printing works. Of course I'd never met you then."

"Yeah," Sam said, wiping his eyes and then putting the handkerchief away. "Charles came up to see if he could help, and Mrs. Gellert flew over, and Mr. Gellert wanted to come too, but he wasn't well enough. We came home by ourselves on the Queen Mary. Mrs. Gellert went on over to Paris to see the dress shows and buy clothes, and that suited us fine. There wasn't a soul on the boat we knew and Christine used to lie all day looking at the sea and getting stronger. Those

22

were about the five best days I ever spent. They were completely happy. But when we got home again, back to this house—Mr. Gellert had given it to us as a wedding present and we'd furnished it and got it all ready—she seemed to lose heart. Maybe it was too great an effort to take things up again after she'd so nearly died. We had Mary and Gordon and Maggie—she's Gordon's wife—but still it seemed as if it was all too much for her. Oh, there have been times when she's seemed contented enough and pretty well, and at those times I'm walking on air, but then she'd get ill again, or depressed, and maybe I'd fuss over her too much. Anyhow, for some time before she left she was getting terribly restless and nothing seemed to go right. She tried to pretend it wasn't so, but I could see that things were getting too much for her. She was like a woman trying to push some enormous weight up a hill. About six weeks ago the crisis came. It was a sort of attack—I don't know how else to describe it—an attack of utter desperation, almost frenzy. It wasn't hysteria, she's never been hysterical, thank God; no matter how bad things are with her she keeps some hold on herself, but she seemed to have got to the very end, the very edge of something pretty terrible. She was like an animal in a trap, imploring with its eyes to be let out. It nearly killed me. There was nothing for it but to let her do the one thing she wanted to do—to get away, and by herself. So she went down to Mexico. Most of the time she was staying with her sister, but part of the time she was alone in a hotel. Well, now she's in New York, and as I told you I don't know where. Nobody knows where. She's rung me up from time to time to let me know she's all right, and that's all, except to tell me she doesn't know yet if she's ever coming back. If she doesn't come back I can't take it, Murray, I can't."

"You'll find you can, Sam," Murray said. "If you must, you can. Believe me, I know."

"Well, I know one thing," Sam said, heaving himself out of his chair. "I want some brandy. How about you?"

23

"No, thanks, not for me."

"For me then, I guess."

He went to the door and shouted, "Mary!"

She appeared very quickly, wearing a coat over her black dress and ready to go out. Sam told her what he wanted. She was back again shortly with a decanter and two glasses and she put the tray on a small table beside Sam's chair. Murray noticed that without putting the tray down noisily, she put it down with a certain emphasis expressive of nonapproval, and he noticed it because he lived with two women who might have done the same thing in the same way. He was used to seeing simple acts performed with special meaning.

Then she said stiffly, looking out the window, "That dog isn't back yet, Mr. Sam."

"Don't worry," Sam said. "Gordon knows where he is. He's over at the Sheldons'. They've got that collie bitch there and she's collecting all the dogs in the place."

"That's what Gordon thinks," she replied with tartness. "Well, he isn't there. I've been to look."

"Oh, he's hanging around the place somewhere, hiding from you, I guess. You know how smart he is. Just don't worry."

"I'm sick with worry," she said. "Mrs. Sam would never forgive us if anything happened to that dog. I'm scared he'll be run over."

"Old Seth? He's much too smart. Don't give it a thought."

"Will you be wanting anything else?" she asked, and she bore heavily on the word "else."

"Not a thing, thanks."

"Well, I guess I'll go for a walk now, and maybe I'll see somebody who's seen Seth." And she left them, closing the door behind her.

"They all think I drink too much," Sam said, with a look expressing both sorrow and embarrassment. At the same time he poured himself a generous helping of brandy.

24

"And do you agree with them?" Murray asked.

"Well, it's worry," Sam answered. "A worried American is pretty apt to be a hard-drinking American. I'm putting on weight, too. A lot of weight. I'd be all right if Christine came back. I'm not naturally what you'd call a hard drinker and never was. Besides, we've already got one alcoholic in the family—my Uncle Tom."

With pity and some pain Murray was thinking how difficult it was to approach close to someone in trouble, even to someone one liked as much as he liked Sam. Sam's trouble put a distance between them, a distance that was made by awkwardness, by the inability of the listener to offer any sort of help. He felt empty-handed, inadequate, and it seemed to him that nothing he could say, never even having seen Christine, could have the slightest validity. He saw Sam's marriage as on the way to total disaster, and the reasons for it would be as difficult to sort out as the coils and writhings of snakes in a pit. All he could possibly do would be to try to take Sam's mind off it for a short time. He put a hand on Sam's shoulder, and then got up to get his briefcase. He took from it a bulky manuscript.

"Here's that Australian novel I spoke of, Sam," he said. He proffered it to Sam, who took it and weighed it in both hands, with a look of dismay.

"Well over six hundred pages, I'd guess," Sam said, responding to Murray's obvious wish to get him onto some other topic. He opened it and glanced at the last page. "Six-seventy-five. It had better be good. Can't you persuade him to cut it down?"

"No," Murray told him. "We've tried. And anyhow, when you've read it, as I hope you will, you'll see he's right not to cut it down."

"All right," Sam said. "I'll start reading it tonight if you really want me to. Maybe it'll help to keep my mind off other things. What's that one?" as he saw Murray about to bring out another manuscript.

"It's Herman Colesfoot's latest."

"Put it away. We only sold three thousand of his last one. Not enough to cover the advertising."

About an hour later they put on their coats, as there was a chilly wind blowing, and went out into the garden. The air was full of the growing smell of spring, earthy and propitious, deeply welcome after the chill odorlessness of winter. Murray paused to look at a big American robin briskly extracting a worm out of the lawn and devouring it.

"How do they find them?" he asked. "If we wanted a worm we'd have to dig for it."

"I don't know," Sam answered. "I never thought about it. Maybe they hear them. I just wouldn't know."

"Who owns the red tricycle?" Murray then asked. "Has Gordon any children?"

"No, only two grown-up daughters, married and living in Harlem," Sam replied. "This belongs to a kid from next door. He's over here about half the time. Christine's fond of him, and he keeps coming over to ask when she'll be back. He's probably out with Mary now. Well, come and look at the lake I made last fall and see the ducks; then I guess it'll be time for Gordon to take you to the station. Too bad you can't stay to supper, but as you're dining with the Brinkermans I'll have to let you go."

Wallace Brinkerman was head of the sales department and Murray had met him only once. He thought how much he would have preferred to stay with Sam, and then told himself that if he were staying he'd have to hear a good deal more, probably, about Christine, and he found it all rather painful. He could not imagine himself, in any circumstances at all, talking about Sibyl as Sam had talked about his wife. It might have been better if he could, but he had never found it possible to lift the lid on the ugly circumstances of his married life, nor could he imagine what words he would have used to describe what he left each morning and returned to each evening, and in what domestic climate he spent his weekends. He lived too much enclosed within his personal drama to be able to translate it into speech or at least into speech that he could feel bore any relation to the truth. He did not know from what angle he ought to view his own life, nor did he know where he stood in relation to it. He could not have said with certainty whether his childhood and boyhood had been happy or wretched, for it presented at different times two entirely different aspects to him, one pleasant to look back upon, the other the very reverse of pleasant. Atlantic House alone gave back to him a clear reflection of himself; clearer still now that he could see himself as a part of the executive body of a well-known firm of publishers, a director among other directors. This was a simple fact that could be stated in simple words, and it was the only picture of himself he was willing that other eyes should see. All the rest was like a looking glass that had been shattered, each small broken fragment reflecting some part of his existence but never to be brought together into a picture having meaning and coherence.

They followed a path under slender bare trees and presently the small lake lay quietly gleaming in front of them. The utterly reposeful thing, he thought, the example to be held before the eyes of strained, taut, anxious human beings, the very symbol of rest, of equilibrium, of something perfectly at peace with itself. He was so charmed by the scene that he pitied Sam for being able to find no satisfaction in it. At least, he thought, in his own case home and circumstances, both unlovely, suited each other. Here there was cruel discrepancy.

The lake did not look new. It seemed to possess the landscape and it was hard to believe that these reflections, these lights and gleams and shadows had been caused by the hand of man, by the simple damming of a small stream six months ago. Here Sam could feel himself a creator. The serene sheet of pale blue under a veiled and diffident sun was unruffled, the

27

trees seeming to gather up and hold the wind high in their gently swaying tops.

There must have been forty or more ducks on the lake, swimming, diving or peacefully floating and quacking. That sound was all that was needed to perfect the scene.

"I made it for Christine," Sam told him. "She used to say she'd sit here and read and watch the ducks. What the hell's the good of it now I don't know, except that I like to hear them."

To leave all this, Murray thought, trying to imagine it his —to leave the pleasant house with its friendliness and space and comfort; to leave Mary and Gordon and Maggie, that excellent cook; to leave the books, the dog Seth who had not returned—had he gone straying because his mistress had been absent so long?—the neighbors' child, who, it seemed, could not keep away—surely Sam's wife must have hate in her heart for Sam or, if not hate, the spreading canker of indifference, of boredom, of not-loving. If there had been another man, Sam would have had the honesty and courage to say so. It was certainly not that.

He was not sure he liked the outline of Christine's character as it emerged from Sam's talk, though she appeared to be victim rather than victor, and emotionally if not always rationally Murray was on the side of all victims, even those who victimized themselves. She was no doubt the victim of poor health, of a terrible mother, of a marriage that had not come up to her expectations. How perverse she was, how much the author of her own and Sam's sorrows he could not guess. Perversity there must be, and perhaps some cruelty with it. Wasn't it probably true that she had married to escape from an unbearable situation and, having once escaped, wasn't she now ready to escape again at no matter what cost to Sam? He broke a silence to ask, "What's that little chap over there by the log? The lonely one?"

"That? Oh, that's a blue-winged teal—wait a minute, what's

his other name? Anas discors—he's the only one I've got. I must get a mate for him. When I started stocking this lake, I got interested in the subject of wild ducks and so did Christine. We learned all their Latin names. But I've forgotten most of them now. The rest are mostly mallards, except for a couple of pairs of mandarins, and the pintails. Here come some pintails now. I ought to have remembered to bring down some bread. I love the noise ducks make. Listen. Don't you get the feeling, with that sound in your ears, that nothing bad can happen? 'Everything's fine,' they seem to say. 'We're happy, everybody's happy.' I love the little liars."

Going back in the train, Murray wished he had been able to say something comforting to Sam, even something that would have expressed his liking for him, though this, he was sure, Sam knew. But comfort was the rarest of commodities. When he had needed it himself he had found none; never the needed word or look, nor in his heart had he expected to find it. All that he had found was a way of withdrawing himself from where his pain burned most fiercely, as one draws back from too hot a fire, and little by little, over the years, to put himself beyond the reach of further disaster, something to be achieved only by deliberate and watchful noninvolvement. This had become more than a habit, it had become a way of life, even giving him at times a certain wry pleasure.

But Sam in his ordeal, he thought, was showing the greater courage. He was giving his pain the run of his whole heart and mind, letting it consume him, with no attempt to immunize himself. And in Sam's case there was no element of guilt, of blame, nothing to give the hand of the torturer, grief, an added skill. He was sure that Sam had done—would always do —the very best he could.

III 🖋

MURRAY had too recently been made a director of the firm to have had the opportunity of meeting Frederick Bonner on anything like equal terms. He had shaken hands with him and exchanged "good mornings" on meeting him in the London office during his twice-yearly visits, and had talked briefly to him at the cocktail parties Charles Kendrick sometimes gave for him. His knowledge of Frederick Bonner, however, was extensive, for Charles Kendrick loved to tell anecdotes about their time at Oxford together or stories culled here and there from their long and close association. He always described him as an incurable romantic, or the last of the romantics. It was as a romantic young man of twenty-four, a Rhodes scholar at Oxford, that he had conceived the idea of founding an Anglo-American publishing house and had gone with it to his best friend, Charles Kendrick, also at Christ Church. Murray had heard Charles say, laughingly, that Frederick Bonner had then been, and had remained, almost embarrassingly sentimental about the subject, always dear to his heart, of Anglo-American friendship.

"His time at Oxford" he remembered Charles Kendrick saying, "was so full of pure happiness that he chose to sit down there in his room at Christ Church and remain there —figuratively speaking—for the rest of his life."

It was well known that he had made a romantic marriage, and had eloped with a pretty, red-haired girl from Philadelphia whose father considered the young man's prospects insufficiently sound. Within a year a wealthy uncle in California had died leaving everything to his nephew, and Frederick Bonner was able to go quickly ahead with the founding of Atlantic House. For Charles Kendrick the financing of the London branch was very much more difficult, but with Frederick Bonner's financial help and the backing of a newspaper syndicate it was brought about, and before they were much over thirty they had succeeded in doing what they had planned. Founded in 1921, Atlantic House had had its ups and downs, but it had survived the depression of the early thirties and the Second World War, though the London premises had been obliterated by bombing in 1940 and thousands of books destroyed.

Murray, driving in a taxi to Frederick Bonner's house in the East Sixties, wondered, as he had wondered many times of late, what vital force seemed to be ebbing out of it. Nobody in the firm had admitted this in his hearing until Sam had admitted it the day before. It was holding its own, but little more. Frederick Bonner's heart attack had been like a sharp earth tremor, boding no good at a time when shocks elsewhere had brought about the fall of longer established firms. But if it was true that the firm was at present somewhat in the doldrums, there was always the possibility that some large body of readers, in spite of TV and a slackening of mental muscles, might feel a new hunger for books or that some section of the public which had never felt the need of books might now demand them. There were too, of course, amalgamations that might be made, and one was even now under discussion. But Frederick Bonner, boundlessly optimistic, had so far refused to listen to any such proposals. He was, as everyone knew, in love with Atlantic House and wanted no changes. He was in love with everything and everyone concerned in it from the office boys up. As soon as anyone joined the firm, in whatever capacity, he or she was given a halo that might vary in size but not in effulgence. He made the health and well-being of the staff his personal concern. At eleven o'clock each morning, following a custom that went back more than thirty years, a gong sounded loudly throughout the premises, whereupon, winter or summer, every window was thrown open and every employee stood as close to one as he or she could get and inhaled slowly and deeply twenty times. Even Frederick Bonner himself obeyed the gong, though rather than subject a visitor to a cold blast, he would excuse himself and go into his secretary's room next door. He liked to feel that the members of the firm, and the authors as well, were all together a big, happy family. All this was agreeably idiosyncratic, and that it persisted into the harsh and competitive world of the 1950's was thought by some to be a pleasing anachronism and by others to be merely absurd.

The taxi took him with swift bursts of speed and sudden stops to Frederick Bonner's brownstone house between Park and Lexington avenues. Most of its neighbors had long since been given new faces and had had the high, ugly front steps removed, but Mr. Bonner preferred to go on living, without any changes, in the house in which his beloved wife had died, and which had once belonged to his father, Cornelius Bonner, head of the old printing firm of Bonner and Klee.

It was common knowledge that after his wife's death Mr. Bonner had taken his younger brother Tom, a confirmed alcoholic, to live with him, giving him and his male nurse the

32

top floor of the house. Now as Murray got out of the taxi he involuntarily glanced upward, half expecting to see a head at a window.

Even without being aware of the existence of "poor Tom," the visitor might feel, he thought, a lowering of the spirits. The house seemed to look out of its windows with a gaze full of gloomy resignation, contrasting most oddly with the happy and confident nature of its owner.

The door was opened by a middle-aged nurse wearing out-door uniform. She spoke with a Scotch accent and looked robust and competent.

"If you're Mr. Logan," she said, "he's expecting you and you can go straight up. He's already got one visitor, but he's so much better it doesn't matter. I'm just off to the drugstore to get some things he wants."

"And where do I go?" Murray asked her.

She pointed upward. "He's in his library; right overhead. Front room, one flight up."

He laid his hat and overcoat on a hall chair and went up the stairs. The walls were papered with some dark and durable stuff, called, he thought, Lincrusta, but the colored prints that were hung in the hall and up the stairs were old and rare, and all of them were scenes in and about London and Oxford. On the upper landing he paused in front of a closed door, heard Frederick Bonner's voice and knocked. At an unexpectedly hearty "Come right in" he entered the room.

He saw his host sitting in the window that looked on the street, a plaid rug over his knees. Opposite him a large, much-worn easy chair with sagging seat awaited the latest visitor. The visitor who had preceded him sat on a sofa toward the back of the room, and he guessed that she had just vacated the empty chair in the window. The lights had not yet been lit and the books that lined the walls almost from floor to ceiling tended to darken it still further, but he could see that

33

she was sitting with her legs under her and her body at ease against the cushions. He did no more than glance at her as he went forward to take Mr. Bonner's hand.

And here, he thought, as he had always thought whenever he had seen Frederick Bonner, is masculine beauty. A full, round, roughly graying head, a face that was more than handsome; that was of antique design, with deep and expressive and benevolent lines, and the finest pair of eyes and eyebrows that Murray knew of, excepting only those modeled by Michelangelo. It was a splendid head for bronze or marble, a truly noble head, and when, as now, Frederick Bonner was seated, he looked his remarkable best. Standing—and it was almost the only way in which Sam resembled him—he lacked the needed height to carry that splendid headpiece as it should have been carried.

"I'm so very happy to see you, sir," Murray said, and was surprised at the emotion he felt. "And especially to see you looking so well."

"Oh, I'm fine, fine," Mr. Bonner said, and his handclasp was as strong as ever. "They all tell me they're pleased with me, and I propose to believe them. I'm only ashamed of giving them such a scare. Murray—I do call you Murray, don't I?—look behind you and you'll see my daughter-in-law, Christine. Christine, this is Murray Logan from the London office. I'm delighted to see him here."

Murray went toward the half-reclining figure in the shadows, and the young woman offered him her hand without otherwise stirring. As he took it he kicked one of her shoes which she had placed on the floor beside the sofa. They both ignored it and she said "How do you do?" and smiled a little. He went back to Mr. Bonner with a picture in his mind of a too-thin body in a red woolen dress, but he had looked into a face in which he knew he would have seen, if he had dared to look longer, simple, effortless charm, without artifice. He had now seen, at any rate, what Sam was breaking

34

his heart for. He felt nothing but resentment toward her, certain that she had made of her fragility a coward's weapon, a sort of Gorgon shield behind which she could shelter, and balk and confuse the man who so greatly loved her.

It was long after the stir and dissensions of the Suez affair had died down, but it was much in Frederick Bonner's mind and he had questions to ask about it and much to say, with troubled sincerity. True to form, he stoutly defended the British government's action against all critics, past and present, and he opened the subject without delay, explaining that it was a long time since he had been able to talk to somebody "from over your way."

"Many of us in England think our action was unjustifiable," Murray said. "In fact I can't remember anything that divided the country as that did."

"Well, in my opinion," Mr. Bonner said, "the British government is usually discovered to have been right in the long run. Thanks to our interference I look for a situation in the Middle East that's going to be too hot to handle. Your government was prepared to destroy the egg out of which World War III is all too likely to be hatched. It looks to me as if it were hatching now."

Murray, who had been greatly troubled about the whole affair, said something about the importance "of keeping our hands clean," but Mr. Bonner brushed this aside.

"It was a time for action," he said. "A time for action. It needs a kind of genius for a man in a responsible position to perceive such times when they come, and to go forward courageously."

Sam's wife took no part in the discussion but Murray felt that she was watching and listening and that she would have been glad if the conversation had taken another turn. Mr. Bonner did not, it appeared, think highly of the present administration in Washington, nor did he trust the State Department, keeping his harshest criticisms for its head. At last

Murray succeeded in bringing the talk around to Charles Kendrick—Mr. Bonner was unique in calling him "Charlie" —and Mr. Bonner presently leaned forward and put a hand on Murray's knee.

"That was fine, my boy, their making you a member of the board. I want to congratulate you, and the firm too. I was mighty pleased when it happened. I ought to have written to say so, and I would have done so but just about that time I had this bit of trouble and I'm only just getting around to writing letters again. So I hope you'll forgive me."

Murray made an appropriate reply, adding that thanks to his promotion he was now making his first visit to America and enjoying every moment of it.

"I hope they're all looking after you well," Mr. Bonner said. "I hear Jim Hancock is taking you down to Washington. When do you go?"

"Tomorrow," Murray told him. "We'll spend one night there. I'd hate to go back without seeing it."

"You'll like Washington, but you must try to put out of your mind while you're there the total lack of any constructive policy emerging or likely to emerge for the next few years from that seat of government. See as much as you can. Don't fail to see the Lincoln Memorial, Rock Creek Park and the National Gallery. And when you get back," he added, "come and tell me about it."

"I'll do that, sir, if I may."

Then suddenly from the shadows Mrs. Sam Bonner spoke. "Have you ever been to Greece, Mr. Logan?" she asked.

He replied, turning toward her, "Yes, I have. I took a holiday there last year, for the first time. It was the best holiday I ever had. I long to go back again."

"How did you go? What did you do? Tell me."

Murray was always drawn to anyone who said, "Tell me." It was as if a rope had been thrown to him in the choppy sea of social intercourse. If someone said "Tell me," he knew

36

he would have something to say that they wanted to hear. He almost regretted that it was Christine Bonner who now said it. He wanted to keep his disapproval of her intact.

"I went by boat," he said. "A slow cargo boat that went from Venice down the Adriatic coast, stopping at every port of any size and ending up at Piraeus. I stayed in Athens for a while and then went to some of the places I've always wanted to see: Olympia, Corinth, Delphi, and Mycenae. All that I could see in the time. I traveled by bus, by train, and a good deal on foot."

"Did you go alone?" she asked.

"Yes. I prefer that. Especially," he added, "as I was traveling 'hard.' No luxuries, no cars, no good hotels. Just sleeping at inns or, some nights, out of doors in my sleeping bag."

"Was it very 'hard'?"

"Not too much so. Or, I didn't find it so. The weather was perfect. I took my holiday early, in May."

"Did it come up to your expectations?"

He answered, with feeling, "It made nonsense of all my imaginings; it was far beyond anything I could have imagined."

She got up from the sofa abruptly, put her feet into her shoes, one of which she had to grope for under the sofa, and went to a nearby table from which she took a large book. She then came toward him, paused to switch on a reading lamp, and before he could guess what she meant to do she knelt down beside his chair and laid the book on his knees. Frederick Bonner gave an amused and indulgent chuckle.

"I guessed she was leading up to that," he said.

"Look, Mr. Logan," she said. "I do want you to look at this. I brought it here a few days ago to show to Frederick."

Murray was instantly reminded of the way a dog or perhaps a child will suddenly and unexpectedly "take to" a visitor or a stranger, showing a flattering liking and interest, often forcing owner or parent to say, "Don't let him (or her) make a nuisance of himself." There was precisely this quick and unlooked-for expression of trust and liking displayed. He even drew his knees aside a little so that she might not inadvertently lean against them.

She opened the book at its title page, laid her hand on it and said, regarding him with a clear and friendly look, "I've been trying to persuade Frederick to have this translated here, and then publish it. It was sent to me from Paris. It's a book on Greece by a young Frenchman who also did the illustrations. I think they're enchanting. Let me show you some."

She turned the pages and her head with its smooth, light-brown hair was close to his.

"They're gouaches," she said. "Look, isn't this lovely?"

She was showing him a scene painted from very near Delphi, looking down toward the Gulf of Itea, down over the gentle gray-green flood of olive groves that sweep in, almost from the gulf itself, inland, to wash the very feet of the hills on which Delphi stands. He was moved; a sort of shiver of delight ran up his spine.

"But I've stood in this very place!" he exclaimed. "It's one of the loveliest sights in the world. I've stood just here, just here exactly, again and again, trying to remember every detail of it."

"You've actually been there," she said softly. She looked into his face with a searching, probing look he was soon to know well; probing and also appealing.

"As a matter of fact," Murray said, wishing now to make less of it, "everyone who goes to Greece goes there. Not, of course, that that detracts from its beauty."

"My wife and I went there in 1928," Mr. Bonner said. "We were on a cruise. I agree with you, Murray, it's a thing one never forgets. Are you by any chance a classical scholar?"

Murray answered that no, alas! he wasn't. He'd had no chance to be. "All I know about Greece and Rome," he said, "I've had to teach myself, by reading everything about them I could find time for."

"I imagine you've found time for Gibbon then," Mr. Bonner said. "I've just read *Decline and Fall* right through for the third time. It helped me through this period as nothing else could have done."

"I started with Gibbon," Murray said. "Then of course I got to know the Greeks and Romans themselves. Only in translation, unfortunately."

Christine lightly touched his arm. "Look," she said, and she was the importunate child, demanding the visitor's attention. "Look at this one, of Olympia. You went there too. Isn't it lovely? I'd like to buy the originals, only of course they won't be for sale. Frederick, I do wish you'd publish this book."

"No, dear," he said. "No, I'm afraid it would cost a very great deal and sell at the most about a thousand copies. To please you I've had it gone into very thoroughly by both Wallace Brinkerman and Jim Hancock. Some more adventurous publisher might do it, but not Atlantic House."

"What would it cost?" she persisted. "I'd far rather invest money in a work of art like this than see it invested in copper or oil."

"No, dear," he said, and his look was indulgent, as if he were speaking to a loved but difficult child. "No, I couldn't let you do that. Buy the original paintings if you like, and if they're for sale. At least you'd get pleasure out of them."

She sighed and turned her head toward Murray again. "It isn't fair. I'm not allowed to do what I like with the money my father left to me. Now look at this one."

She showed him a painting of the Parthenon, wet after a downpour. Large puddles reflected the columns, and all about were broken things: broken reflections, pieces of broken marble, rubble, and above these stood the serene temple itself, its color made warmer in tone by the rain. Clouds were breaking, and both puddles and sky were jeweled with blue. They both looked silently at the picture, and then she closed the book, pushed it onto a nearby table and got to her feet.

"Did you go to Marathon?" she asked. "Did you see Sparta? No, you had no time, I suppose."

"Perhaps next time," he said.

"Next time," she repeated, and gave him one of those looks which seemed to make a private meeting place, though for what purpose she wished to make one he did not know. She then turned to Mr. Bonner: "I ought to go now, Frederick. I've stayed more than an hour. And I expect you and Mr. Logan will want to talk shop. Not that I don't like listening to your sort of shop, I do, but I ought to go."

"No, no, not yet," Mr. Bonner almost pleaded, his handsome, strongly masculine head upturned to her. "Murray must have been talking shop ever since he's been here." It was plain that he did not want to lose her, would contrive, if he could, to keep her there longer. Murray surmised that when she left the house Mr. Bonner knew no more than Sam knew where she went, and that he wanted to keep her there not only for his own sake but for Sam's. "Besides," he added, "no one's allowed to talk shop to me until next week."

"It would be less exciting for you than politics," she said, smiling down at him, and then bending she brushed his forehead with her cheek.

"Wait, dear," he urged, taking her hand. "Miss Puddock will be back soon, and then Murray can take you wherever you want to go."

With a fugitive smile that seemed to be at some thought of her own, she replied, "Oh, I can take myself." Still with her hand in Mr. Bonner's she stood leaning lightly against the side of his chair. Murray noticed that the only ornament she wore was a gold bracelet hung with coins which lightly tinkled and clashed when she moved her arm. She looked toward him and said, as if some recognition of the fact that he was a stranger was due: "I often wonder what it's like to be in New York for the first time. It's the only city I know well—it's the place where I was born—but I'm never quite

40

sure what I feel about it. I only know I don't want to live in it—or die in it either."

Murray could have wished as she stood there with her hand in Mr. Bonner's that she possessed less of the simplicity and easy naturalness that so attracted him to her. And, thinking of Sam and his misery, he felt a sudden desire to hurt her if he could, to pierce that gentle armor. What right had she so effortlessly to make a friend of him, to assume that he was ready to be a friend and not an enemy?

"I'm enjoying it immensely, of course," he answered. "But what I've enjoyed most of all since I've been here was my visit to Runnybrook yesterday. I'm only sorry you weren't there too."

She flashed him a quick look before turning away, as if she had perceived in an instant that the meeting ground could also become a battle ground. As soon as Murray had spoken he knew he had spoken with the crass boldness of a diffident man. A less diffident man, less actuated by nervous promptings, would have refrained. (Yet why, he asked himself, seeking his own justification, should he be expected to know what the real situation was between her and Sam?) He was immediately aware, all the same, that he had said the very thing most likely to break up the smooth ordinariness of this meeting, and now that it was said all that had been open and gently candid in her face was wiped away. Her look became preoccupied and, for him at any rate, blank.

She went to a chair and took from the back of it a short fur coat, into which she slipped her arms before Murray could move to make at least the gesture of helping her. Then she replied to him with calculated indifference, "I didn't know you'd been there."

In a silence she went back to Mr. Bonner's chair, and as if by her action she wanted to put "finis" to that uncomfortable exchange of words, bent to kiss his cheek.

41

"Now I really am going, Frederick. Don't bother to ring for Mrs. Shaw. I'd rather let myself out."

But at the door which Murray, contrite now, went to open for her, her way was blocked by the nurse, who had just returned, her arms full of parcels. For the diversion her arrival made, Murray was grateful.

"Going, both of you?" she asked cheerfully. "Well, perhaps it's time. I must give Mr. Bonner his medicine now."

"In that case," Murray said, moving quickly to Mr. Bonner's chair, "I'll say good-by too. May I really come and see you again, sir, before I go back?"

"Please, my boy, please come again," Mr. Bonner urged. Clearly he had accepted Murray's words as having been spoken in complete ignorance of the facts. "If you were staying till next week, you'd see me back in the office again, thank heaven. It's three months since I was there."

Christine had paused to speak to Miss Puddock, but now she turned and waved her hand to Mr. Bonner before going out of the room and down the stairs. Murray, as if he now feared nothing so much as losing her, hurried after her, catching up with her on the landing. An elderly woman with a mop of coarse white hair was in the hall below collecting some letters. She went to open the front door for them, while Murray hastily picked up his hat and coat from the chair and prepared to follow Christine.

"Thank you, Mrs. Shaw," Christine said. "Tell me, are you quite well again?"

"I'm better," the old woman replied, "but I shan't feel real well till that Miss Puddock takes herself off. I asked her to wait a second and take these letters up to Mr. Bonner, but would she? Not her. I hate that tribe. It's lucky I've got nothing to do with the one on the top floor."

"Well, it won't be long now," Christine told her. "It's only till Sunday, you know."

"Praise be to God!" the woman exclaimed.

As they reached the bottom of the steps, Christine said without any trace of awkwardness, "If you've had as much to do with nurses as I have you'll know that when they enter a house peace flies out the window, though it's no fault of theirs." And she went on, before he could answer that he had indeed had much to do with nurses, "I've got my car here. I'll take you wherever you want to go. It's that Jaguar just down the street."

The thought of that delicate girl driving a car in New York astonished him. It was totally unexpected and seemed to him wholly and even startlingly out of character.

"You're very kind," he said, concealing his surprise. "If you're sure it isn't too far out of your way." He told her where he was staying.

"It wouldn't matter where it was," she said. "I've nothing to do at the moment and I love driving. When's your next engagement?"

"At about seven, at the Hancocks'," he told her.

"Oh, yes, Frederick told me and I'd forgotten. I hear it's to be a cocktail and supper party combined. You won't have to change, so there's time for a drive through the park if you'd like that."

"I'd like it very much," he said, and he guessed that Sam knew nothing about the gray and gleaming car which she had parked a hundred yards down the street, out of sight of Mr. Bonner's windows.

IV ✍

He got into the front seat beside her, noticing as he did so that the car not only looked but smelled as if it were fresh from the salesroom. He had never in his life owned anything but secondhand cars, and he thought it a smell he was never likely to become very familiar with. They had to make a detour before turning toward Fifth Avenue, and she handled the car easily and competently. He kept glancing at her profile, which he now clearly saw for the first time, and found it altogether charming, with pleasing irregularities. Her lips were apart, as if she were about to speak; it seemed in fact as though speech hovered just behind them waiting to become audible. But she did not speak until after they had reached and entered the park, when they at once became part of a fast-moving flood of cars all headed uptown at the day's end. She was not at all disconcerted by it but seemed used to it and drove at the same speed as all the rest. She knew very well what she was about. Then her first words startled him and sent the blood to his face.

"So you wanted to see how I'd react," she said, but she spoke quietly, even gently. "That's why you spoke of going to Runnybrook."

He gave no sign of being embarrassed and, though his heightened color might have given him away, she did not turn her head to look at him, nor was there enough light left to have betrayed him.

"I spoke of it," he answered, "because I enjoyed my day there and wanted to tell you so."

"I'm not deceived," she answered, but still there was no hint of anger in her voice. "Sam talked to you. He talked to you, didn't he?"

"Talked to me?"

"You know quite well what I mean. He *told* you, didn't he?"

Honesty, he thought, was all that was left to him. "Yes," he admitted. "Sam did talk to me."

There was a moment's silence, and then she said, "At least don't despise me until you know a little more. Not that Sam wouldn't be entirely loyal, I know he always would, whatever I'd done. But I can guess what your opinion of me is likely to be."

"Despise you?" he cried, recoiling from the very word he might himself have used, in his own mind, earlier. "What right would I have to do that? Or what reason?"

"You might have had reason," she answered. And then she said, and he could not doubt her complete honesty, "I'm so desperately sorry about it all. I do so wish I could make Sam as happy as he deserves to be."

However sincere this might be, he did not intend to be won over, though there was danger of it. Once again, as when she had laid the book on his knees, she had reduced the distance between them to nothing at all. He replied a little stiffly, feeling less confident than he sounded: "Presumably you can. All that Sam wants is to have you back again." As she made no reply, he went on with caution, "Unless I'm a good deal mistaken, so far you've burnt none of your boats."

A laugh broke from her, as if it were out of her control.

"Boats?" she asked. "I've got no boats to burn. What boats do you imagine there are? I'm just what you see—a young woman with poor health, a good deal of useless money, and this car I bought, greatly daring, two weeks ago. By the way, I hope you aren't nervous. I've been taking driving lessons every day for nearly a month now."

"I'm not in the least nervous," he said. "You drive very well. So the problem isn't a complicated one. You *could* go back tomorrow?"

"Yes," she answered. "I *could* go back tomorrow. It's as simple as that—or I suppose it looks as simple as that to you." And then she burst out, as though in frustration and despair, "Oh, how can I hope to explain to you all that's involved in it?"

He replied quickly, prompted by the feeling that he was being taken by a strong current in a direction full of rocks and rapids: "I think it would be very foolish to attempt it."

"The curious thing is," she said with complete conviction, "that I want to. In fact I think I must."

She let this drop and waited to see what effect it had, and he did not know how to answer unless he answered her brusquely, for he had no wish to be involved further than he was involved, which was already too far for his liking.

"I can understand that, I think," and he was coolly matter-of-fact. "It's quite common—the wish to confide in someone you'll never see again. The completely impersonal ear."

"I want to," she said without emphasis and without resentment, "because I believe you're fond of Sam and capable of understanding both him and me. And because I think you might be able to help before it's too late."

He was still intent on noninvolvement. "That must apply, surely, to a good many people," he told her. "To your father-in-law, for one."

"I think you know perfectly well," she answered, "that Frederick is the last person I could discuss it with at the present time. Or at any time. He's very fond of me, as you may have guessed, but Sam is his only son, all he has. Sam's happiness means everything to him, and the fact that I don't feel I can go back to him as things are distresses him terribly."

He knew he had deserved her reproof. What she needed and had evidently not found was dispassionate judgment, dispassionate advice which might possibly throw some light on her own situation and bring some order where there was confusion. But he felt a deep reluctance to allow her to confide in him. He was Sam's friend and she seemed to ignore the fact that he was most probably comfortably biased in Sam's favor. And, too, if she put into words all that threatened her marriage, it would only build up and strengthen her own case. She would parade before his eyes all her reasons for finding life with Sam unsatisfactory, dressing them up in stronger colors than they merited and gaining conviction from her own presentation of what, to her, were the facts. He had no wish whatever to assist in this. In spite of her undeniable attraction, he was not sure that he even liked her.

"I think it would be a mistake to discuss it with me," he said, fending her off as best he could. "I'm Sam's friend, too much on his side. And I can't help feeling that things are more apt to end well for him if too many words aren't spoken."

And I know what I'm talking about, he thought. I know how truth can be buried and utterly lost sight of on a dumping ground of words, words, words.

She made no answer to this. She looked straight ahead, giving the impression, almost, that she had not been listening. He felt certain that he had not turned her aside from her purpose, that she was bent on ending what probably was for her a long and lonely silence. Behind those cunningly curved and parted lips the words he did not want to hear

47

waited to be spoken. Then abruptly, without preamble, they came.

"They made me go to a psychoanalyst," she began, and now she seemed to have become merely a vehicle for what had to be said. "I couldn't go on with it. I couldn't. It isn't in me to be able to undress—mentally—at so much an hour. I detest it and I'm afraid of it. It may be good for some people, it certainly isn't good for me. If you've never had anything to do with it, leave it alone." Now her lips moved sharply, painfully, as if she were holding back tears. "All this labeling and ticketing of emotional states—it's become a fashion here, a craze, and it's undermining more characters than it's building up. In the cities people are going rotten with it. What's the good of this organized introspection when there's nothing to see inside that gives one any satisfaction to look at? What's the good of turning people into doubting, self-conscious introverts? Oh, I'm not talking about the really twisted minds. That's a different matter. But people like me—what I need and need badly is to talk to a civilized, rational person like yourself, you especially because you know Sam and he likes you and might listen to you, and because you're outside it all. Since my father died I have no one, no one at all. I'm not given to confiding in women friends, and besides, I have hardly any. I'm going through a state of torturing uncertainty that keeps me awake night after night. And I know only too well what it must be doing to Sam. Now are you afraid to hear what I've got to say? You've listened to Sam. Now won't you listen to me?"

He saw that the time had come to throw aside his doubts and reluctance. If she were making a mistake in thinking he could help her, it was useless to tell her so.

"Yes," he said. "Of course I'll listen. Please say anything you want to say. I doubt very much that I can be of any help —I haven't handled my own life with conspicuous skill—but at least I can try."

48

She was turning into another road, one that took them toward the west, where a glow in the sky, apricot-colored, lingered as a painted background to glittering towers.

"Now, of course, I feel miserably shy," she said. "But you've agreed to listen and I feel like a bird who sees the cage door opening. I'm going to talk to you as if Sam hadn't told you anything.

"You see, first of all, I've never known what it's like not to have to consider my health, or have it considered all the time by other people, and oh! so boringly. I'm not a hypochondriac, I'm simply stating a fact. I had a lobectomy when I was fourteen, and another, smaller one when I was eighteen. I've had frequent bronchial attacks, and I've had pneumonia twice. Naturally my heart has suffered from all this, but not disastrously, and it may improve. But what I expect, what I demand, is that Sam should look on me as expendable. To let me live while I do live. To use me up, or let me use myself up. He isn't willing to do that, and that's the core of our whole problem. It's my quarrel with him. He even refuses to take the risk of letting me try to have a child. Well, I'm sick and tired of it all. Tired of the sort of life he makes me live. Can't you, won't you try to convince him that I'm at least as expendable as any young man who goes to war? It's all I ask. I asked it when I told him I'd marry him. I made it a condition of our marrying. He promised. Then he went back on his promise. I find it hard to forgive him. It's no use your saying, as I suppose you'll feel you have to say, 'But he loves you.' I know that. I know it only too well."

"I won't say it," Murray answered. "It's too obvious. Please go on."

"You see he's killing me, stifling me with his care and protectiveness. It's nothing but death in life, and I'd prefer death. It's cruel of me to say this to Sam, but I've had to say it, I've been driven into saying it. In fact I've told him so often that he's stopped his ears. I married him because I thought he was unselfish enough to spend me, not to hoard me. Well, he's a miser, he's a miser! I found that out on the very night of our marriage. He was afraid to consummate it until long afterwards, and then only with every caution and precaution. And this still goes on. You see, I'm past caring what I say, only for pity's sake don't look at me while I say it. Our doctor, his old Yale friend Tom Luscombe, has convinced him because he wants to be convinced, that if I have a child I'll die. I've been sent to gynecologists, of course, and they agree that there's a risk. Well, who cares about that? I want to *live*, and Sam wants me to stay safely in prison for the rest of my days."

She was driving slowly now, and close to the grass verge. Murray saw that her eyes were full of tears ready to overflow. She took one hand from the wheel, fumbled for a handkerchief in her bag, wiped the tears away, and then went on again at her previous pace. He waited for her to speak again.

"So now," she presently said, "you've heard the words you were so reluctant to hear. The fact that they're spoken can't make things worse than they were before and might just possibly make them better. You can forget what I've said or you can see Sam and tell him he's driven me away with his intolerable care and goodness. Or what he is pleased to think is goodness."

"Be fair," Murray protested. "Any decent man would feel the same in Sam's place."

"I don't believe it," she cried, "I don't believe it. Not all decent men would be so lacking in—oh, what word do I want?—in sagacity. That's why I made up my mind to speak to you this afternoon. I think you have more wisdom than Sam, though Sam might have it if it concerned anybody but me. Besides, you're not entirely a stranger, you know. Sam talked about you quite a lot when he got back from London last year."

50

Genuinely surprised, Murray asked, "Did he? Did he really?"

"Yes, he did. We'll come back to that later. Now I've got more to tell you. Because I so nearly died on our honeymoon —I expect you've heard about that—he's afraid to let me travel, afraid to let me out of his sight without someone to keep an eye on me. You must have seen our housekeeper yesterday, Mary Doyle. She used to be a trained nurse, and she nursed my mother-in-law until she died. She's devoted to me and in some ways she's worse than Sam. Between them they've decided that I must be in bed before ten, and I'm not allowed up till noon. The only holiday Sam ever takes is in the winter, when we go to Florida. We stay in a luxury hotel with plenty of doctors within call. I loathe such places. Don't you see, Sam's turned himself into a fussy old woman for my sake? He's playing the father in *The Barretts of Wimpole Street*, and I'm an Elizabeth Barrett without any genius, without even any talents that I can put to use. And," she added, with a touch of sad irony, "without a Browning, either. If it hadn't been for him, I don't think Elizabeth Barrett could have kept sane, and I'm not at all certain that I can."

He thought she had come to the end of what she had to tell him, and he felt it was time he spoke. "I understand it all better now. But don't you think . . ."

She broke in, not ready yet for his comments: "Well, this year, early in March, by making one scene after another, I got him to let me go to Mexico, and alone, to stay with my sister. He telephoned to us every single day, chiefly to tell my sister what I needed and what she ought to do. So I left and went by myself to a hotel, just to get away from those telephone calls. Unless Sam will stop all this, I can't go back to him. I'll live my own life. It may be short, but it will be more to my liking."

He was now in no doubt at all that this was a young woman

51

of strong will and that the need to alter the conditions of her life was imperative. She must have chafed intolerably under Sam's benign but restrictive rule. Her face as he saw it under the lamps was sharpened with purpose, the poise of her head was strained. He asked quietly, "And what would you do if you did leave Sam?"

"Oh," she cried, "first of all travel, travel. Why not? I'm starved for strange places and people. I've been once to London, once to Scotland and once to Paris—shopping with my mother. Now I've seen a little—not much—of Mexico. The rest of the world I only know from books. And even if I couldn't travel I could live alone and get up when I liked and go to bed when I liked. That would be something."

This last childish outburst decided him; he must do his best for her. But she'd all along avoided, it seemed to him, the very core of the whole matter. He couldn't allow her to go on avoiding it. He offered up a prayer that he might not blunder.

"Even if Sam could be persuaded to treat you as if you were a perfectly healthy woman," he asked, "would that solve everything? Wouldn't it still be true that you don't love him and never have loved him?"

At his question she did at last relax that strained and painful tension. She sat at the driving wheel more easily, as if she had been relieved of some burden. "You were bound to ask me that," she said. "I'm glad you did."

"You're not of course obliged to answer," he told her, and in fact he dreaded an answer on which all his hopes for Sam's happiness might founder.

They had been returning, though he was hardly aware of it. the way they had come, and now, ahead of them through the skeleton trees, he saw the lighted giants closely grouped, shouldering each other against a twilight sky of almost royal blue. A beautiful, yet, he thought, strangely unreassuring sight—even, to him at that moment, somehow terrible. In all those myriad lighted and overheated rooms, piled tier on tier, how many men and women were content with their lives, happily mated, not straining away from each other or one straining away from the other? There, he couldn't doubt, repeated countless times, hideously multiplied, were himself and Sibyl, Christine and Sam, come up through millions of years from the mud of a pond for no better purpose it would seem than to make each other wretched; their lives soon to be snuffed out without any better purpose—or any purpose at all—made discernible to them. No, he thought, there is nothing in that sight to reassure her or me.

"I began all this," she said, after a moment's silence, "so it's only fair that I should answer you as truthfully as I can. I liked Sam from the very first, I liked him and trusted him— anybody would. I was deeply touched that he was willing —well, more than willing, determined—to take the risk of marrying me. I was so watched and guarded, I'd spent so much time as an invalid that Sam's was my first proposal, though when I met him I was nearly twenty-three. I'm very fond of him—please understand that I am very fond of him, that I love him as a human being. But I ought to admit that I married him chiefly to get away from my mother, and in the hope of living a life that would be tolerable to me. It sounds utterly selfish, doesn't it? But at least remember that I was ready to give Sam everything I had, even though I didn't love him as a woman hopes to love the man she marries. I was ready to give him everything, even my life, and he wouldn't take what I offered. He promised to, and he broke his promises. So it hasn't turned out as it ought to have done. All the same—and this is what you must bear in mind, please —I could go back to him and make him reasonably happy *on my own terms*. But he must honestly accept those terms, and abide by them. Or else I go for good."

"I'd better know what those terms are, hadn't I," Murray asked, "if I'm to talk to Sam?"

She recited her needs so promptly that he knew they must be always in the forefront of her mind. "He must let me try to have a child. If I don't succeed in having a child, he must let me travel a reasonable amount, alone if he can't go with me. I must be allowed to get up when I please and go to bed when I please. I'd promise to be sensible about this. I am not to be watched by Mary or by anyone. If I'm ill, it's to be accepted as an inevitable part of my life. All the fuss and care and medical attention I've had haven't prevented illnesses. Surely those are reasonable terms, aren't they?"

"But isn't it possible for you to see him and tell him all this yourself?" he asked, making a final attempt to relieve himself of this awkward duty.

"Don't you understand?" she cried, and she did not disguise her impatience. "I've told him these things a hundred times. And if I were to see him now, after this long absence —well, you know yourself how emotional Sam is—he'd only break down. It wouldn't be any use. Letters are no good either. I've tried that. I gave him a written ultimatum once, and signed it in my own blood—I pricked my finger to do it. It was silly, I know, but I hoped it might impress him—but he just tore it up and in the end we were both in tears and things were no better at all. If I were to see him now I couldn't talk to him. He can't keep his hands off me. It's hopeless."

"You've chosen a poor ambassador," Murray said.

"Sam has confidence in you," she said. "He likes you. I believe he'll listen to you."

It was quite possibly true, he thought, and how odd that it should be true!

"How much has he told you about me?" he asked, prompted by a sudden curiosity to know how much Sam knew.

She glanced toward him quickly, and then her eyes went back to the road ahead.

"He told me about that accident," she said, "and about your wife."

54

"And about the boy?"

"As much as he knew," she said.

"So we're quite old friends." He could not keep the bitterness out of his voice. She was already aware, then, of the bleakness of his life. But how had Sam known? Not through him. Through Charles, perhaps. This had puzzled him yesterday, too.

"He didn't find it out from me," he said. "I don't talk about myself."

"Is that a little gibe at me?" she asked. "Because I have talked about myself?"

"Good God, no!" he exclaimed. "It's just that I can't."

"Why not? Perhaps you ought to try."

"Why not? I suppose because I feel that nothing about my private life could possibly interest or profit anybody."

She was silent. When she spoke again it was to say, quietly, "I suppose you ought to be looking at the Hudson. We've come to Riverside Drive now, and here it is. It's a great river, and higher up it's very beautiful."

He looked at the river silently but made no comment.

"I'll be seeing Sam tonight at the Hancocks'," he told her. "Shall I talk to him afterwards?"

"Yes, do," she urged him. "Please do. And please try to keep him from drinking too much. I'm afraid he is drinking too much."

"This suspense is the worst thing for him," he told her.

"Not quite the worst. He still has hope. Oh," she cried, "it's terrible to love too much. If you love someone as Sam loves me you live too dangerously."

"Yes," he agreed. "Sooner or later one's got to learn non-attachment. Thank heaven, I've learnt it now."

"Then we're alike there," she said, almost with eagerness. "I've been too near death too often to be afraid of it, or to be afraid of losing anything I have."

"One learns to loosen one's hold," he said. "To slacken, like

55

a swimmer who knows he can never reach the shore. Who knows damn well there isn't even a shore to reach."

"You're very unhappy," she said. "Aren't you?"

He felt a sudden revulsion against himself and against his own words. Against the self-pity she had betrayed him into expressing. He said, almost with harshness, "Now you see why I don't talk about myself. When I do I say things I hate myself for saying. What I've just said isn't even true. I like my work, my life is perfectly tolerable. As tolerable, I expect, as most people's."

"You really needn't have said all that," she told him, in soft reproof. "Now I ought to take you back. At least you can say you've seen the Hudson."

"I don't think I can," he said. "I've hardly looked at it. If I'm going to act as intermediary between you and Sam I'll have to report progress. Can I see you when I get back from Washington?"

"Yes," she said. "Of course. It had better be the next day. Could you take me to lunch on Friday?"

"Certainly. Where?"

"There's a French restaurant Sam used to take me to," she answered. "Its walls are lined with old wine bottles, and the food is very good, and it's peaceful."

He took out his little diary and wrote down the name and address.

"Hadn't you better tell me where you're staying?" he asked. "If anything happened to prevent my coming I wouldn't know how to let you know."

"What could prevent it?"

"I might be taken ill. I might be run over."

"You won't of course tell Sam."

"Naturally I won't. But let's hope it needn't be a secret much longer."

"All right," she said. "I'm at the St. Regis under another

name. I wouldn't have put it past Sam to sit down with the telephone book and ring up every hotel in New York. He probably has. You'll have to ask for Mrs. Charles Darnay." She laughed. "You see, I'd just been rereading *A Tale of Two Cities* and it was the first name that came to my mind."

"It sounds an innocent sort of double life," he remarked.

"It couldn't be more innocent," she said. "Except for Frederick, and my driving teacher, you're the first man I've talked to since I came back from Mexico. And even at my sister's I hardly spoke to a man. She's been going through a crisis too, though a different sort. She's had a temporary surfeit of both husbands and lovers. But I suspect she's only biding her time."

"Resting?" he suggested.

"Yes, resting: I'm very fond of her, even though we're completely different. Our chief bond is that when we were girls we were both unhappy, and we both loved my father and did not love my mother."

They must be nearing the street where the Hancocks lived, Murray thought, and there was one thing more he wanted to know.

"What do they all think?" he asked. "About you and Sam, I mean. The Hancocks and all the other people in the firm?"

"Oh," she said, "they know I went to Mexico. I suppose they think I'm still there. I haven't seen anybody. And as I don't want to risk being seen now, I'll just drop you at the corner, two blocks away. You'll have to get out quickly, and we needn't say good-by. May I call you Murray?"

"Yes, of course."

"You know my name's Christine. We're nearly there. I just want you to tell me one thing, now that you know what you know. Do you honestly think there's a reasonable hope that it would work—my going back to Sam, if I did go?"

"I think," he said carefully, "that the success of the whole thing depends more on Sam than on you. He'll have to try terribly hard. He'll have to treat you and think of you in a wholly new way. It won't be easy for him."

"No," she said. "I know that. It won't be easy. And you must tell him so. But you still think there's a hope? You think it's worth trying? Is it unfair of me to make you commit yourself? I don't want to put too much on you, but I do want your honest answer. And if there's a note of doubt in it, I shall hear it."

"I think it's more than just worth a try," he answered, and now he knew he was making himself responsible for too much. "I think you're morally obliged to try it. Does that sound priggish?"

"Yes," she said. "It does, but it's true. I know it's true. All right. Provided Sam will give you the promises and the assurances I need, I'll consider going back. I think you'd better get out here."

She was already slowing up and before the car stopped he had the door open.

"I'll do my very best," he said.

"You can tell Sam about the Jaguar," she called out.

She drove on quickly and he watched as the car turned a corner and vanished from his sight. She had gone, but there was little diminution of his awareness of her. Her personality, he thought, was too permeable for his comfort. He had known her for an hour and he knew it would be impossible to forget her.

He walked on slowly toward the Hancocks' apartment house. It looked like all the others, but it had a bright red awning at the entrance, and the awning reached almost to the edge of the pavement. He was reluctant to arrive, though he knew it was time. He wanted to go over that conversation in the car. Did she guess how exacting her terms were? What she required of Sam was that he should begin to love her in an entirely new way. To succeed he would have to teach himself, hour by hour, day by day, to adopt a wholly new attitude, he would have to watch himself at every turn. By the time he reached the red awning he was convinced that Sam would fail, that he was doomed to tragedy, and he felt a sharp pity for him. He did not find Sam's state of mind concerning Christine at all difficult to understand. He saw that Sam was not only this young woman's husband and lover, he was her father, mother and brother as well, and in addition to all that he looked upon himself as her resident medical adviser. A relationship so total, so all-inclusive, might well become—and had become—all-engrossing to him and intolerable to her.

His own feelings about her were now lit by several certainties. He found her very decidedly likable. He would leave it there, for the present. She possessed a curious power of attachment. He was certain, also, that though she had for him, and clearly for Sam and probably, therefore, for most of the men she met, a very strong sexual attraction, she appeared to have no wish at all to exploit it, to use it as a means to any desired ends. Yes, he felt the attraction, undeniably, but he told himself that in spite of it he had no wish to draw nearer to her physically. Instead he felt a powerful longing to know more of that complex of thoughts and memories of which she was compounded; to draw closer to the ego which inhabited her, and even perhaps—and this was something new to him—to reveal to her something of his own. This innocent desire, he was certain, did not lessen his usefulness as a go-between, if useful he might be. The thought of restoring her to Sam's bed, he found, did not at all disquiet him. There was, it was true, a certain incongruity about it, for there was something of Caliban in Sam's make-up which her fragility accentuated. But that was not his affair, and love, even mere liking, took no account of such things. If he could help Sam to get back at least his chance of happiness he would gladly do everything he could.

In spite of this, a sense of deprivation remained. What it

59

amounted to was that he felt he had lost, or was about to lose, something he had never had, but might conceivably have had, had fate been kinder.

Well, he had better take his mind off all this, and the next few hours should help him. In dealing with a situation so fluid, so delicate, be it important or unimportant, it was never desirable to think out too carefully in advance the words to be spoken or even the attitude to be taken up. He would leave that to the moment and whatever wisdom the moment might bring.

As he got out of the lift at the seventh floor there came from an open door the high, confused roar, like nothing but itself, of a cocktail party in full swing. For a moment he felt daunted. It was partly the feeling that he wanted to keep his memories of that drive and that talk intact a little longer and partly the feeling that any party that was going as well as this one seemed to be could not possibly require his presence. He had to remind himself that it was, after all, being given in his honor, and that he was already late.

V

It was, as Christine had predicted, a cocktail party and buffet supper combined. Some of the guests were only holding drinks in their hands, some had put their drinks down within reach and were coping with plates of cold food, while others, luckier, were sitting down with their drinks on the floor beside them and their plates on their knees. The scene, as he entered, suddenly struck Murray as comic, rather like one of those drawings in *The New Yorker*. A few drinks would be needed to remove the conviction that this was a very odd way for human beings to conduct themselves.

He was later than he should have been, and he looked hurriedly about him for his host or hostess. At their first meeting, a few nights ago, Mrs. Hancock had told him to call her Bess, and he was searching the crowd for Bess or Jim when he saw her pushing her way toward him. Thanks to her height she had already seen him.

"You're late," she cried gaily. "Don't you know you're the guest of honor? I've been looking for you this last half hour.

Come and get a drink before I start introducing you around."

She was quite six feet tall, built on a generous scale and at the very peak of her queenly good looks. She was wearing the plainest of black dresses which showed, with cunning boldness, a great deal of splendidly maternal bosom, and Murray found it hard to keep his eyes from straying to it. (Nor, he supposed, was there really any reason why he should.) Like many women of opulent build, she had neat ankles and small hands and feet. Her complexion was clear and healthy, and her blue eyes full of bonhomie. Murray, who had accompanied her and Jim to a night club, had observed that she was capable of drinking a good deal more than he was while retaining unimpaired her serene good humor and vivacity.

"Couldn't I just stay here and talk to you for a while?" he asked, almost loving her for being familiar to him. She had put a drink into his hand and they were standing close together in a comparatively quiet little backwater at the end of a buffet table. He could see another table similarly laden, through the open folding doors, in the next room.

"Well, just for a few minutes. Don't tell me you're feeling antisocial, because really this is no moment for it. I've just about run myself ragged getting together all the literary tycoons in New York. You're here for a purpose, my boy, and don't you forget it."

"I'll be good," Murray said. "I'm sorry I was late, but it was unavoidable. By the way, what's this you've given me to drink?"

"That? It's bourbon-on-the-rocks. It's the best drink in the long run. Why, don't you like it?"

"I like it very much. I just wanted to know so that at some point in the long run I could ask for another."

"Now you're getting into the spirit of the thing." She called to someone Murray could not see, "Pete! Come here, Pete, I want you."

62

A boy of about fifteen cautiously pushed his way through the crowd holding a brimming glass in each hand.

"This is Peter, my eldest," she said. "Pete, this is Mr. Murray Logan from the London office. If I'm not around, just you keep an eye on him and see he has everything he wants. He's our guest of honor."

"I know," the boy said. Murray looked at his agreeably ingenuous face and marveled that a fifteen-year-old could keep that open, freckled farm-boy countenance in a city like New York. "I was just taking these to Mr. Reinhold," Pete added, "but I guess he can wait a minute."

"What," his mother asked, "both glasses?"

"No, the other's for whoever he's talking to. I don't know his name."

"What's your chosen drink on these occasions?" Murray asked him.

"Me? Oh, I only drink Coke," the boy answered. "I don't go for hard liquor. Say, Mom, I'm going to the movies soon. Can I have some lobster salad before I go?"

"Of course, darling. Help yourself to anything you want. Who are you going with?"

"Mr. Cromarty," Pete answered. He gave his mother a most engaging grin and said, "He invited me. He said, 'Come on, Pete, let's get the hell out of here and take in a movie.' So I said that was O.K. if you didn't mind, and I was pretty sure you wouldn't."

"Well, I don't," she said, "and you can just tell young Bill Cromarty that he won't even be missed. But he's got to bring you back by ten, do you hear?"

"Sure, Mom, I hear," the boy said. "Now I'd better get this drink to Mr. Reinhold or he'll start hollering for me. 'Bye, Mr. Logan. Be seeing you, I guess."

Bess's eyes, full of maternal love, followed Pete until he was lost to view, then she turned and looked at Murray.

63

"I know all English people think all American children are horribly badly brought up," she said, with the slight defensiveness Murray was now growing used to hearing, when Americans spoke of British opinion, "but honestly, Murray, that's one of the best boys in the world, if I do say it myself."

"I believe you," he told her. "And may I please be dissociated from any such crude and unfair generalizations?"

"All right," she said. "All the same, I wish our kids didn't use slang so much. It's the only vocabulary they've got. I guess it's the only vocabulary of about eighty per cent of the American people, including myself."

She broke off to welcome some newcomers, and Murray observed that she kissed them all, even putting her arms about some of them and pressing them to that splendid bosom. She turned back to him to say, "Come along now, it's time I started introducing you around."

"All right," said Murray, still loath to move. "But first I wish you'd tell me why so many women here manage to look like duchesses. I mean the way duchesses ought to look."

"Well, just let me tell you something," Bess replied. "We don't feel like duchesses. It's no good looking like one if you can't behave like one, and for that you need a cook and a butler and all the rest of it. I prepared all this," she said, indicating both buffet tables with a sweep of her arm. "I was at it all day yesterday and all day today, and with a toddler pulling at my skirts, too."

"It's a miracle," he said.

"I'll bet your wife does it. Unless of course you're a millionaire, and I guess you aren't."

"No," he told her, "she doesn't. We don't live in London and we don't entertain."

There was no time for more because Jim Hancock discovered them and made his way to Murray's side.

"Look," he said to Bess, "you've been monopolizing him.

Come on, Murray, you've got to circulate. Say, Bess, this is terrific. How many invitations did you send out?"

"Only about seventy," she said. "Though there seem to be twice that number here. Off you go, Murray—but have supper with me later. Here come some new arrivals."

She raised a goddess's white arm to welcome them, and Murray observed, amused, that they got the same treatment as the last ones, kisses and warm embraces. He let himself be guided here and there by Jim Hancock, who seemed bent on skimming off the cream for him, for he introduced him chiefly to people whose names, as a popular weekly would have put it, made news. With Jim Hancock he found it all easy and agreeable enough. He never slurred over a name, and if he thought Murray was in doubt as to who the person was to whom he was being introduced, offered brief and rapid explanations. "Howard Purviss, Murray, is the new president of the Garfield Press, and I don't need to tell you what a fine, go-ahead firm the Garfield Press is. Now that Howard's in the presidential chair, we expect to see things happen." And, "Bill, this is Murray Logan from the London office. First time over here. Murray, this is Bill, otherwise William Kane Hofer, who ought to be a lot better known in England than he is. You and Charles Kendrick ought to put your heads together over this. Here, Bill, your glass is empty." He took it out of his hand. "Back in a minute."

"No English publisher will look at me," the young man said, smiling pleasantly through thick-lensed glasses, "and I'm quite unknown over there, except that I once gave a talk on poetry for the BBC. My latest novel was offered to you and rejected with such Old World courtesy that it nearly brought tears to my eyes."

"That must have been Charles Kendrick himself," Murray said. "He's famous for it. Address the next one to me, personally, will you? Then I'll bring it to Charles's attention. If Jim says you're good, I believe him. Give us another chance."

"I'll do that," Hofer said. "The next one's more than half finished. I think it's going to be all right. Maybe you'll really like it."

At the end of an hour and a half Bess came for him and took him away to have supper. He had been plied with bourbons-on-the-rocks, but either in spite or because of them he now longed for nothing so much as a place to sit down. The crowd seemed not to have thinned out at all. Bess was still looking like a big, freshly opened rose, not even as yet full blown, but she, no doubt, had had recourse to her dressing table. When he remarked that she looked as if the party had just begun, she said, "Well, the truth is I adore parties, even my own, and I'm glad to say we have them pretty often, though not always as big as this. Now come and sit here. Beatrice is going to bring us something to eat. You must be starving."

He asked if Beatrice was the pretty, self-possessed colored girl he'd seen carrying trays of food and drinks.

"Yes, that's Beatrice. Whenever we give parties she comes and lends a hand. Did I say *lends* it? Ha! Ha! She hires it out at about a dollar a minute. Would you believe it, that girl owns a Citroën! Yes, sir, a common American car wasn't good enough for her, she had to have a French one, and I bet it's parked right outside the front door. She's a friend of the janitor's and he gives her special privileges. Why, Murray, if that girl said she couldn't get here without a helicopter I guess we'd have to see that she got one."

Beatrice presently brought them two well-filled plates, and supplied them with knives, forks and napkins. Bess surveyed the plates quickly.

"Beatrice, you haven't given Mr. Logan any of the Virginia ham. He's from England, and I want him to have a couple of good big slices. And plenty of brandied peaches."

66

"Sure," Beatrice said, with a wide smile in which there was charm and coquetry. "Guess he's never et any ham like our ham. I'll bring it right away."

"If there are any more late-comers," Bess said to him, "I just won't see them. Isn't this cozy? Funny how cozy you can be in the midst of a mob. Have you talked to Sam this evening?"

"I had a few words with him," Murray said. "There was no time for more. But I'll be seeing him later, I expect."

"He looks terrible, doesn't he?" Bess said. "Jim and I are really worried about him. For one thing, he took an awful knock when Frederick had that heart attack. He just adores his father. Then he let Christine go off to Mexico without him because he didn't like to leave Frederick, and I guess she's still there. That must be worrying him too, because it's the first time she's ever been away by herself since they were married. She's delicate, you know. You see, Sam is one of those people—well, when Sam loves somebody he loves them. Period. Christine is the sun in poor old Sam's sky. Anyhow, even if she was back she wouldn't be here because she never does go to cocktail parties. It's a pity you haven't met Christine. I admit she's a puzzle to me. Jim thinks he's got her taped. He says she's a coldhearted, selfish little so-and-so. Well, I think he's wrong about her. I don't know what she is, but I feel sure she isn't that."

"I hope not, for Sam's sake," Murray said with caution.

"Well, whatever she is, he's absolutely nuts about her," Bess said. "If she'd been a normally healthy woman I don't believe he'd have loved her half so much. He's just like a dear old hen with one chick. Sam and Frederick aren't a bit alike except in one thing—they're utterly devoted to the people they love. Well, that's all right, lots of us are that way, but they get positively fanatical. Poor Frederick was like that about Sam's mother. Nobody thought he'd survive her death, but I guess he went on living for Sam and for Atlantic House. They're a couple of romantics, all right, but you know, Murray, most people are so damn cynical nowadays it's a blessed relief."

"You aren't," he said.

"Me? Oh, I'm just a great big softie," she answered. "So is Jim, if it comes to that, though you'd never think it with that face that looks as though it ought to belong to Mephistopheles. Actually he's the kindest man in the world, if you want to know."

"I do know," Murray said.

"I'm a lucky woman, all right," she said. "This lobster salad is heaven, isn't it? As you haven't said a word about it, I thought I might as well."

"Look at my plate," he answered. "As for the ham, it's the best I've ever eaten. Did you cook it?"

"I certainly did. Look. I'll send you a Virginia ham for Christmas, and I'll give you the recipe for cooking it, so you can give it to your wife."

"No, no," he protested, "you're much too generous. Please don't do that. What on earth could I send you in return that you could possibly want?"

She cried indignantly, "Who wants anything in return? Who ever said anything about sending something in return? I never heard of such a thing."

He hastened to placate her. "It isn't that; I doubt if my wife could make a success of it. She isn't fond of cooking, to tell you the truth."

"Who does cook then?"

"Oh, she cooks when she has to. Most of the time my mother does it. And I often lend a hand."

"Does your wife write or paint or something? Or has she got a job?"

"No, it isn't that. Some women seem to enjoy cooking. Others don't. Now we're going to be interrupted," he added, as a woman nearly as large as Bess but far less lovely came

68

toward them. He was not sorry, for Bess's directness and her friendly curiosity were difficult to parry. He got up and offered the newcomer his chair.

"Why, Mirabelle!" Bess exclaimed, but this time there were neither kisses nor embraces. "I haven't seen you all evening. When did you get here?"

"Half an hour ago," the woman said, "but I saw you were in a huddle with the best-looking man in the room and didn't like to interrupt."

"Well, now that you have," Bess said genially, "you'd better meet him. He's Murray Logan, from the London side of Atlantic House. Murray, this is Mirabelle Codrington, who writes under the name of Mirabelle Hollis. She's just published a book called *The Sex Life of the Victorians*. It made me want to go right back about eighty years."

Murray had put aside his plate and now lighted a cigarette. Miss Hollis was already supplied with one, and with a bourbon-on-the-rocks. She said she preferred not to eat anything. She was slimming.

"Tell me about the book," he said. "Who published it?"

"The Garfield Press," she told him. "Frankly, Atlantic House turned it down. Now I guess they're sorry. It's been on the nonfiction best-seller list for the last three months."

She spoke aggressively, clearly airing a grievance. She was florid, much made up, and was wearing a tight-fitting cocktail dress of peacock-blue satin; over her yellow hair was a diamanté veil.

"Oh, well," Bess said, "you know why we had to turn it down, don't you? Mr. Bonner and Sam and Jim all wanted to keep their illusions about the Victorians. You stripped the poor things right down to the skin."

"Do you know how much time I spent in your British Museum Reading Room?" Miss Hollis asked Murray, looking up at him and ignoring Bess's remark. "Well, let me tell you I just about lived there for four months. I asked one of the attendants one day if they couldn't put up a camp bed for me and would you believe it he thought I was serious? He actually did. He said, 'Sorry, madam, I'm afraid that would be quite against the rules.'" She gave an exaggerated rendering of an English voice and accent. "Anyhow, when I got out of that place at the end of the day I used to start looking around for a hansom cab. I honestly did. How long are you going to be in New York?"

"Not very long. Only a few more days unfortunately."

"Say, Bess, why don't I give a party for him?" Miss Hollis asked. "Listen, Murray, I've got a penthouse right in the heart of Greenwich Village. I'd just love to give a party for you. Just tell me which evening would suit you. What about Thursday night? I'd say he'd get a real bang out of one of my parties, wouldn't you, Bess?"

"He certainly would," Bess agreed, "but the fact is, Mirabelle, we've got the poor man tied up for every hour of every day before he leaves. He's got to go to Washington tomorrow with Jim. So I guess this will just have to be hail and farewell, and maybe you can give a party for him next time he comes."

"I'll surely do that," Miss Hollis said, but she looked, as far as was possible for a lady of such physical exuberance, deflated. "I oughtn't to like Britishers," she went on, "but I do. I was married to one once. He was my first husband. We lived in Kensington. Say, do you know what that man used to do? He used to go every day of his life and sail a boat on the Round Pond. You know, in Kensington Gardens. Off he'd go with that sailboat under his arm, carrying a long stick with a sort of hook on the end, and he and another guy, who I guess must have been crazy too, used to have boat races there. They'd run around that pond like a couple of loony kids, and when the boats came in on the wrong tack or something, they'd poke them off with those long sticks. Did you ever hear of anything like that?"

"I've heard of worse hobbies," Murray told her.

70

"So have I," Bess said. "A girl friend of mine was married to a man whose hobby was—no, I guess I'd better not say. But I can tell you, you got off lightly, Mirabelle."

"Well, I got off all right," Miss Hollis said, "but it wasn't easy. They don't seem to know what mental cruelty is on your side of the water, so I had to make myself the guilty party. I had to come home and take up with another guy before he'd agree to divorce me."

Then Sam joined them, shook hands with Miss Hollis, averting his eyes as he did so, and told Murray he had simply got to talk to him.

"God!" he exclaimed as they moved off, "how did that female get in here? Bess hates the sight of her. I'll bet she gate-crashed. Listen, Murray, I've just this minute been talking to Dad on the phone, and now I've got to talk to you."

"Well, I want to talk to you," Murray said. "Where can we go?"

"The party's pretty near over," Sam replied, "and Jim says we can go into his study if we want to and lock the door. It's this way. Follow me."

A couple who had felt the need of being alone had got there first, but on Sam's arrival they took note of his angry frown and removed themselves.

"All we want now," Sam said, looking about him, "is two glasses and a bottle of bourbon and some ice."

"Don't bother to get anything for me, Sam," Murray said.

"Well, for me then, I guess. Hold the fort. I'll be back in a jiffy."

It was a small room, full of books, and there was a big leather-covered writing table and two armchairs. One wall was covered with photographs, most of them signed, and Murray amused himself looking at them. Sam presently returned with what he had gone for but he had brought two glasses, and in spite of Murray's protests he filled one for him.

"Sit down," he said, first locking the door and then taking

one of the easy chairs himself. "Dad told me that Christine was there today. Why didn't you tell me? I've been bursting to talk to you for the last half hour. So now you've seen her. I guess you didn't get a chance to talk to her, did you?"

"Yes, I did," Murray said. He resolved to keep back as little as possible. "I did, and I've been bursting to talk to you too. We left the house together, and she took me for a drive through the park in her new Jaguar."

"In her—what?" cried Sam. He could hardly have been more amazed if Murray had told him she'd taken him for a trip in her new jet plane. He seized the arms of his chair as if he were about to push himself out of it, and his astonishment —must it always be so with a fat man? Murray wondered— was comical.

"Don't be alarmed," Murray said, smiling at him. "It's all right. She's bought a Jaguar and she drives it perfectly. I was nearly as surprised as you are, after what you'd told me. She took me through the park and then over to Riverside Drive, if that's what it's called. Anyway, I saw the Hudson."

Sam was speechless, and his eyes stared. He reached out and added more bourbon to his glass, and his hand was shaking. He drank it down hastily. Then he said: "Once I tried to teach her to drive. That was about four years back. At the end of it she got out of the car so faint and trembling she nearly fell. I had to help her into the house. I pretty nearly had to carry her."

"Well, husbands are notoriously bad teachers," Murray said. "Anyway, she's been taking lessons from an instructor, and now she drives as if she'd been doing it all her life." He paused, waiting for the right words, the right approach, and then plunged before too many approaches suggested themselves. "She talked quite freely to me, Sam. As freely as you did. She guessed, as soon as I told her I'd spent Sunday with you at Runnybrook, that you'd most probably talked to me,

72

so I admitted that you had. It seemed to me best to be frank."

"Good God!" cried Sam. "Can you remember everything she said?"

"Yes," Murray answered, "I think I can. I've got a pretty good memory for conversations, and I've cultivated it because it often comes in very useful."

Some of Christine's more intimate confidences he omitted, but he let Sam have all the rest as nearly as he could word for word. Sam listened, biting his nails in agonized suspense. Then, like a boy who has often been scolded, he would remember and thrust his hand into his pocket, but he never took his eyes off Murray's, and when he had finished he sat back in his chair looking exhausted, and for a moment he closed his eyes. Then he opened them and sat upright again, but he half emptied another glass of bourbon-on-the-rocks before speaking.

"I pretty well knew she'd say all that if she said anything," he told Murray, and his voice sounded terribly weary. "She wants me to agree to let her commit suicide. That's what it all amounts to. She wants me to give her the green light. Well, I vowed to love and cherish her. They all tell me that if I can just keep her ticking over for five, maybe ten years she may outgrow most of what's wrong with her. That's my job in life. To give Christine a future. Any man who loved her as I love her would want to do the same." He tapped his knee with his fist. "She's just got to be patient. I keep on telling her, she's just got to be patient."

"She won't be patient any longer," Murray said. "That much is absolutely certain. You'll lose her, Sam, make no mistake about it. She means every word she said. You'll lose her. You nearly lost her this time. And if I may speak frankly, I think you'll deserve to lose her."

Sam put his head in his hands and groaned. Then he looked up and said: "Can't you see that she's only got to be patient?

73

Can't you see that her whole life, her whole future, is at stake? God! The girl's only twenty-nine. She's got her life ahead of her. If I do what she wants, it'll be murder."

"I think you've got to face it," Murray said. "I think you've got to take that risk. In fact I can't see that you have any choice, unless you want her to leave you altogether. You've got the chance now of being happy with her for a time, anyway, and it's a chance you'd better take, in my opinion. And remember, Sam, in matters of this sort there are a lot of factors you can't be sure of. Isn't it just possible that if she feels less supervised, feels that she's leading a freer and more normal life, her general health may improve?" He felt ashamed to be saying the things he had to say; ashamed to be talking like a man who knew how to manage his own life and the lives of others. "Anyway, it seems to me a chance you've got to take. She's desperate. She's worried and unhappy and uncertain, and that can't be good for her. Also, remember, she's financially independent. She can simply refuse to go back to you. She's quite free to try the experiment of living the way she wants to live. You couldn't stop her. No one could stop her. There'd be nothing you could do."

"No," Sam agreed, deeply despondent. "There'd be nothing I could do."

"Well, then, don't hesitate. Agree to her terms. It seems to me that she's got a better chance of living if she stays in her own home with you to love her and take reasonable care of her—I repeat, *reasonable* care—than she would have if she were living apart from you. I gather she's not on very happy terms with her mother—"

"God, no!" Sam interrupted. "How could she be?"

"And though she seems fond of her sister she obviously has no intention of living with her. She'd be pretty much alone, wouldn't she?"

"Yes," Sam said. "She's never had a lot of friends. She'd be pretty much alone."

"Well, then," Murray pleaded, "for heaven's sake, Sam, agree to her terms, and keep to them. Above all, keep to them." And he added, this time choosing his words with care, "I've only met Christine once, but I was with her for something over an hour. She seems to me well worth making the effort for."

Sam looked up at him, and tears welled into his eyes. It was the moment, Murray felt, to drive home what he had still to say.

"Don't imagine I think it's going to be easy," he said, as Sam pulled out his handkerchief. "I don't think that for a moment. I know it's going to be damned hard. You'll have to watch yourself the whole time."

The next instant Sam had broken into painful sobs. Murray guessed that they were caused partly by the inexpressible relief of knowing that he might get Christine back again and partly by the apprehension that in getting her back he would be shortening a life that meant everything to him. At last he wiped his face, and after a childish sniff or two controlled himself and looked at Murray shamefaced. His tears seemed to have washed some of the blue from his eyes.

"I guess you think I'm nothing but a big crybaby," he said. "But you can tell Christine she's won. Tell her I agree to everything. Every single thing. Do you get me, Murray? Everything she asks. No reservations."

"I'll tell her," Murray said, "I'll tell her, no reservations."

"Pretty soon," Sam said, and he was looking a good deal less miserable. "When all this is over, maybe I'll be a man again. I just don't know how to thank you, Murray. No one's ever done so much for me. And I mean that. And I'm not going to forget it either. If we hadn't both talked to you, I guess it would all have finished up on the rocks. And that would have finished me. Now I've made promises I'd no right to make, I've promised to do what I believe is absolutely dead wrong, but as you've made me see, maybe some good may come out of it. I'll pray that it will. I'll pray hard."

"I'm thankful things have turned out as they have," Murray said. "I'm certain it's going to be for the better. I'm certain of it."

"God!" Sam suddenly exclaimed. "Think of that girl buying a Jag and learning to drive it herself." He shook his head. "I'd never have believed it if you hadn't said you'd seen it and been in it." He put out a hand toward the bottle of bourbon, and then withdrew it again. "No," he said, "I guess I've had enough of that stuff to last me a long time."

Murray got up. "I think we ought to go, Sam, it must be getting late."

Sam stood up too. "O.K.," he said, "let's go, but I can't go back in there again. Just you go in and give Bess a big kiss for us both, will you? And tell her we're off to bed."

He unlocked the door and, a little unsteadily, tiptoed out into the hall and toward the front door. There was still the sound of voices, but more subdued now, and Murray saw that there were perhaps thirty late-stayers who seemed to have settled down to talk, and who looked as if they were going to be difficult to dislodge. He went straight up to Bess.

"Oh," she cried, disappointed, "I thought that when everybody else had gone, you and Sam and Jim and I could have taken our hair down and had a lovely time. Must you really go, darling?"

"I really must. Forgive me, Bess, but I'm not used to so many late nights. Thank you for everything. It was a wonderful party."

"Well, tell Sam he's a mean old four-flusher, and see that he goes straight home to bed. I thought he was looking terrible."

"I will," Murray said. "Did Pete get back by ten?"

"On the stroke," she replied. "Didn't I tell you he was a good boy? Thank you, darling, for remembering to ask." She kissed him warmly. "Good-by, God bless you! Don't stop to talk to Jim. I'll tell him. He's gone into a huddle with some of the boys. Good night."

Sam was waiting for him down below, by the entrance. As they left the building they met a searching, buffeting wind, and a half-moon was hiding and then briefly revealing its face. The wind, though cold, was welcome, and the air seemed fresh from the sea. They walked for a while, then hailed a taxi and drove first to Murray's hotel. As they neared it Murray asked Sam, a little perfunctorily, if he wouldn't come in for a drink.

"No, thanks," Sam said, "I don't need a drink now. Listen, when you see Christine on Friday, just ask her when she's coming, will you? Get her to give you the day, and the hour, if you can. I want to alert the household. I want to get everything ready for her. Maybe she'd ring me up at home on Friday night. Do you think she'd do that?"

"I'll ask her," Murray said. "I think she's sure to." And then, picturing Runnybrook and what she would be going back to, it suddenly entered his mind to ask about the dog. Had he come back yet? No, Sam said, but he wasn't seriously worried. After all, it was spring. And if Seth had been run over, he'd have heard, because his address was on his collar.

Sam got out of the taxi to say good night and took Murray's hand, holding it with great solemnity. "Just remember," he said, "you're my friend for life. Don't you ever forget it."

He turned quickly and got back into the taxi, and the last Murray saw of him was his back view, rather like the hind quarters of a bear.

He went up to his room, his mind still dwelling on Sam with affection. He felt very wide awake and more consciously alive than he had felt for a long time. It was not the bourbon he had drunk. It was the feeling that—for a diffident man wholly unused to being asked for, and giving, advice on other people's problems, especially on such private and personal problems—he had not done badly. Also, to his surprise, he found that on the whole he had enjoyed the party. There had been an unbuttoned ease about it all which had taken away his shyness; what he regarded as his social inadequacy. Even Mirabelle's pounce, though happily frustrated, had not been unenjoyable. Of course her referring to him as the best-looking man in the room had been utter nonsense. And as he remembered Bess's splendidly maternal bosom he could have wished to lay his head on it. She was the same, if not quite to everybody, to nearly everybody, but he loved her for letting him have his full share of her bountiful kindness. She had done him good. He thought that a few more weeks of American life would do him still more good, but there were not many days left, and he regretted it.

Now there was his biweekly air-mail letter to be written home, and he overcame his reluctance and sat down to write it before going to bed. No letter written by him to Sibyl ever conveyed anything but formalities and, he well knew, banalities. The very act of writing to her seemed to seal up his thoughts. He was performing nothing more nor less than a duty:

Dear Sibyl:

I hope you have been receiving my letters regularly. Sometimes I have found it quite hard to get a moment to myself. I have been kept very busy, and one never goes to bed until pretty late. However, I have found it all very interesting and enjoyable. Tomorrow I go by air to Washington with Jim Hancock and we will be spending the night there. I am looking forward to seeing Washington very much.

I went today to call on Mr. Frederick Bonner who, I am glad to say, is making good progress. There is no doubt that it was a very severe heart attack. He hopes to be back in the office next week.

This is a fascinating city and unlike any other, I should think. The height of the buildings takes one's breath away, even though one has seen them so often in photographs. I'm bringing you some gloves and stockings that I bought on Madison Avenue—in rather a hurry, I'm afraid—and a blouse for Mother. Perhaps you can buy equally good ones in London, or even in Morden, but I wanted you to have something from New York.

There are not many signs of spring here yet and it is still quite cold. I hope all is well there. I may write again before I leave, perhaps a line from Washington, but unless my plane is late I should be with you by lunchtime on Sunday.

My love to you all,
Murray

It was an air-mail letter and there was fortunately no room for more. She would read it to his mother, probably, as they sat at breakfast in the kitchen "nook," the boy between them. He could picture the scene in every detail. His mother would feed the boy spoonful by spoonful before having her own breakfast. She had no uncertainties about her place in the household. She knew she was indispensable, and this knowledge was like the steady wind that fills the sails of a boat and carries it onward. Sibyl, her shining blond hair elaborately waved and dressed, would be wrapped, as was her custom, in the shabby dressing gown that he had bought for her seven years ago when she was in the hospital; a constant reminder, if any reminder were needed, of that terrible time. After the dishes were washed, Sibyl would dress, get out the old Morris Minor and drive to the shops to do the marketing while her mother-in-law took the boy for his walk. Sibyl never went, if she could avoid it, to shops where she was not already known, and when talking to the people who served her would keep her eyes on theirs, dreading that their eyes might be lowered as far as her scarred mouth and chin and neck. When this did happen, she would instantly be aware of it and would suffer a lacerating pain over which she had no power. He knew that it was the same today as when she had looked at herself for the first time in the hospital. He had been there, standing beside the bed, when the nurse, at Sibyl's insisting that she would wait no longer, that she would get out of bed and find a looking glass for herself, brought her a hand mirror.

He sealed up the letter—thinking how much better they made air-mail letters in America—and took it along to the letter chute beside the elevators. The act of writing it and then seeing it drop out of his hand, knowing how soon it would be dropped into the slot of the front door of "Southview." Bingham Road, Morden, brought his home and the people in it still more closely to him, so that no distance at all seemed to divide them. He felt as though he were about to kiss his mother's downy, drooping cheek, look into the boy's room to see that he was asleep—what were his dreams?—and then go to the room he shared with Sibyl. He had not got the solace, the haven, of a dressing room, where he could go when the tensions between them, or one of her restless nights, made it a sorely needed thing. He had often calculated that only another five hundred a year would have made a move to a larger house possible. And even then, who, except himself, would benefit from the move? It would only put a heavier burden on the two women.

He remembered that Christine had said, before they had left Frederick Bonner that evening, that she did not want to die in New York. He too had strong feelings about where he did not want to die. He did not want to die in Southview, in that bed beside Sibyl's, where he had had hideous nights, too hideous ever to be forgotten.

With any luck at all, he sometimes told himself, he would die in a hospital bed where others had died before him and where others would die after him. This made death seem an impersonal thing, a thing merely inherited, handed on, and he could accept it without dread. But if he could have chosen he would have liked to die and be buried in Greece on a small headland near Delphi beside some vineyards overlooking the sea. He sometimes thought that this would be the nearest thing to a home that he could ever hope for. It had even become a goal, though a fanciful one. When he had first seen the place he had thought—as some men might have thought it the perfect site for a house—that he would like his body to lie just there, to become a part of the soil. He recognized the absurdity of wanting that superb view, yet could not quite rid himself of the thought that his adoration for the beauty of that particular spot might draw him back to it, that some feeling, thinking part of himself would rejoice that he was there.

VI ✐

Iᴛ seemed that they were all worried about Sam. They all knew he was drinking too much, and guessed that Christine's continued absence was the cause of it. Jim Hancock began to talk about it almost as soon as the plane had got off the ground, and Murray was driven to awkward evasions.

"Poor old Sam," Jim Hancock said, speaking from the inner core of his own comfortable married state, "he hasn't got the wife he deserves. I don't know her what I'd call well, none of us do, but I'd say he couldn't have done much worse for himself if he'd tried. If she isn't sick, he's scared she's going to be. She never goes anywhere with him, never even turns up at Bess's parties, though I guess that's his doing as much as hers, because he thinks cocktail parties are bad for her. All the same I get the impression that she wants him to give up publishing because she's rich, and go wandering around Europe with her. I've no time for that young woman. Perhaps you remember, though it was all quite a while ago now, that he took her to Scotland on their honeymoon and she nearly died there."

"Yes, that I do know," Murray said, as Jim seemed to wait for a reply.

"Well, not unnaturally he's in no hurry to take her abroad again. I wish she'd settle down to being what she is—an invalid—then we'd all know where we were with her."

"Isn't she rather young for that?" Murray suggested.

"I suppose I sound pretty unfeeling," said Jim, "but I'm thinking of Sam's good more than hers. It seems to me she's using her poor health as a weapon, and Sam is so tenderhearted and so devoted to her he just can't stand up to her. She can play hell with him if she feels like it, and I suspect she's doing that right now."

"What is her background?" Murray asked, feeling hypocritical, but willing to let Jim shed as much light on it as he could.

"Background? Rich, indulgent father, terrible mother, socially ambitious, completely selfish and jealous as hell of both her daughters. Sam has told me that himself. Oddly enough, there's a piece about her in one of those big glossy women's magazines this month. Bess happened to see it at her hairdresser's. It describes her wonderful clothes, her apartment in the Waldorf Towers, and how she's remade her life since her husband's death. I'll say she has! I saw her not so long ago when I was lunching at the Colony with Arthur Reinhold. She had three men with her, all of them the sort of types you'd expect, and when the waiter presented the bill she signed it without even looking at it. I guess she'll marry again, and that'll take her more out of Sam's life. Not that he sees more of her than he can help. Personally I'd as soon marry Messalina, but some poor fish is going to get the hook in his guts, one of these days."

"It doesn't sound as though she'd be very helpful as a mother-in-law," Murray said, and now he wanted to talk about something else because Jim's summing up of Christine's character was so palpably incorrect and ill-informed that he did not want to hear more of it.

"She'd be as much help in a situation like that as a live boa constrictor," Jim said.

Then Murray made haste to change the subject by saying, "By the way, did Sam say anything about a book I gave him to read last Sunday, when I was lunching with him at Runnybrook? It's an Australian novel we're going to publish in the autumn, and I'm hoping you'll be interested in it over here. It's quite remarkable."

"I've got it in the office," Jim Hancock said. "I haven't had time to look at it yet, but I'm going to read it right away. Sam thought a lot of it."

"There'll be plenty of good stuff coming out of Australia soon," Murray told him.

"There will," Jim Hancock agreed, "and we're interested in it. You know, Murray, I often wish we were as young as Australia is. I kind of envy them. We've lost the freshness and spontaneity of youth here—and before our time—and there isn't the kind of ripeness there ought to be to take its place. A kind of decay has set in, the kind that's becoming only to old countries, and it's got me worried. We don't wear it well. You haven't been here long enough to know what I mean. I'm hoping something will give us back—oh, not our innocence, of course, there's no recovering that commodity—but the kind of wisdom we'd acquired along about the turn of the century, and before. Somewhere soon after that we got our noses to the wrong scent, like a lot of silly hounds after the wrong quarry. I guess the smell of money was too powerful."

"What could start the hounds on another scent?" Murray asked. "A religious revival?"

"God, no. There isn't a hope of it. And that isn't the way I want it to be, either. No, something based solidly on simple, decent ethics. The ones that can be proved to work, and always have worked, and always will. I'm not a religious man. I mean I don't have anything to do with organized religions. They've overproliferated and in my view they've messed up the whole business. No, I guess the only hope is in the scientists, especially the astronomers; they may find out something that'll make sense of the whole thing. I won't live to see it, but Pete may. At the rate things are moving now it's not impossible. You've got a boy about Pete's age, haven't you?"

Murray thought that if he could be granted one wish it would be that people might never know he had a son. Feeling the old pain from the old unhealable wound, he said, "No; Martin's younger. He's thirteen. He's backward. I don't know why I should tell you this, but it's worse than mere backwardness. He'll never be any better. When you say that the astronomers may be able to make sense of the whole thing, can they ever make sense of that, I wonder?"

"God, I'm sorry!" Jim exclaimed. "God, that's tough!"

After a moment, Murray said, "Well, that's that. Forget it. It's something I never speak of."

"And is he the only one?"

"The only one," Murray repeated.

He looked out of the window at the thick gray cloud layer that screened the earth from them and thought that if another plane should shoot up out of it and collide with them he, personally, would not have a single regret.

Yes, he discovered a second later, he would have one. He would be sorry, very sorry, to miss lunch on Friday. He wanted to do what he could to bring Sam and Christine together again.

The next day he told Jim he was amazed that the same country could produce two cities as unlike as New York and Washington. They were returning in a taxi from the National Gallery, through which Jim had conducted him too quickly but very knowledgeably, to keep a luncheon engagement at the Mayflower Hotel, after which they were to catch a plane back to New York.

"Don't make any mistake," Jim said, "this country can

produce anything it likes in the way of contrasts and anomalies. Damn it, it can produce *anything*. Yesterday in the plane I was talking like a misanthropic old crank. I'm fanatical about this country, if you want to know; that's why I care so damn much about the direction we're moving in. I'm just crazy about this country, and I want to make that quite clear."

"Well, I'm in love with Washington," Murray said.

"You're meant to be. Everybody's meant to be. It's my fault that I'd rather live in New York. If I live in a city, it's got to be a city, with all the vices and wickednesses and advantages and wonders that a great city usually has. One of these days, of course, Bess and I are going to live on a farm; a small farm in Virginia, or Maryland. That's after we've finished educating the kids. I'm hoping I can pull out and retire when I'm about fifty-five." He smiled, and when he smiled his big-featured, lean and sardonic face was highly attractive. "Then I'll settle down and never read a damn thing I don't want to read. Do you look forward to that as much as I do? I guess all publishers do."

"I don't know," Murray said. "I have no plans at all for the future," and it was true that he had none. It was wiser to live from day to day.

"Are you going to see the old man again?" Jim presently asked.

"Yes. I told Sam I'd look in on him at six this afternoon."

"Good. He'll like that. He'll tell you what sort of an administration we've got down here."

"I've heard something of that already," Murray told him, smiling.

"Well, he's a grand old boy, and I hope he lives to be a hundred. Not that Sam won't make a good president when the time comes—unless that young woman finishes him off first —but I couldn't bear to see the old man go. He and Charles Kendrick are a fine team. It's no fault of theirs if the firm isn't on the up-and-up. It's just one of those things, like a man suddenly getting sick for no reason the doctors can see. All the same, I think we're on the turn now, and I'm not usually what you'd call an optimist. You tell them that when you get home. Tell them we all feel here that we're on the turn."

"Sam doesn't seem to think so," Murray said.

"Sam's got too much on his mind," Jim replied. "He'll think differently as soon as his domestic affairs shake down a little—if they ever do."

And that, Murray thought, is very much in my hands. Perhaps altogether in my hands. And this seemed to him a most extraordinary thing.

When he saw Christine the next day at the restaurant, she did not look the same to him, and he found this disconcerting. He had seen her before only in Frederick Bonner's dimly lighted library, and then out of doors in the twilight and in the intermittent light of street lamps. Now as he saw her waiting for him at a table against the wall he was at once aware of her apartness from the people about her, and more aware of her attraction. Her face was almost colorless, and she was hardly at all made up, only her lips were touched with a faint red. Except for the light-brown hair which she wore coiled at the back of the head and the chestnut-brown eyes, it was not unlike a small Greek head in marble, finely poised on the slender neck. She was hatless as before and today she was wearing a neat black suit with a thin white embroidered blouse showing under it. The white blouse, like the forsythia bushes, he thought, tentatively proclaimed the approach of spring. He wondered how long it would take him to feel as much at his ease with her as he had felt when he had got out of her car near the Hancocks' apartment and how much ground had meanwhile been lost. He had been delayed at the office by a meeting which had started late and he hoped she had not been waiting long. There was a place for him beside her and this he was glad to see as now he need not confront her yet, need not turn his head to look at her until he wished to.

He apologized for being late.

"I wasn't worried," she said, smiling at him. "As no message came for Mrs. Darnay, I presumed that all was well."

"Have you, in a way, enjoyed your incognito?" he asked her.

She answered with her usual candor. "I suppose it wasn't unenjoyable. At least I felt adventurous, and it was like living in someone else's skin. I began to know a lot about Mrs. Darnay." She picked up the huge menu. "There's so much to talk about, shall we get this out of the way first? I suggest hors d'oeuvres, which are very good here, and then their special chicken dish with spring vegetables. Unless you'd rather have steak."

"No, thank you," he said, and he was in no doubt about this. "I've had steak in some form every day since I've been here. Chicken would be perfect."

"And to drink?" she inquired, laying down the menu. "I only have one cocktail a day, and that's before dinner, but please say what you'd like."

"I'd like some white wine with lunch, if that's agreeable to you."

"It's just what I'd like too."

"And," he told her, "this is going to be my lunch. May we settle that now?"

"No, no," she objected. "You're a visitor, and as I can't entertain you in my own home, for reasons you know, you must let me entertain you here."

He saw that she was determined to have her way, and she ordered the lunch and the wine. He wondered if, when the bill came, she would sign it without looking at it, as her mother had done, and felt ashamed of the thought. In everything she was and did she would be totally unlike that fabulous woman.

As soon as the waiter had left them, she turned and looked at him. Her whole face was an interrogation, he thought, and her lips were parted as if she were about to speak, but he knew she was waiting for him to speak, and that he had better not pause to choose his words.

"I had that talk with Sam," he began. "We went into Jim Hancock's library when the party was nearly over, and Sam locked the door so we shouldn't be disturbed. I'm going to tell you everything he said. I think I can give it to you word for word almost. That's comparatively easy. What won't be so easy is to convey to you how deeply moved he was. But perhaps you can imagine all that."

She nodded her head without speaking, and all the time he was talking her eyes never left his face. He got the impression that she hardly breathed, so silent and still was she and so intent on what he was telling her. She must have known that Sam would promise anything to get her back, and that he had really little to tell her that was not an old story. The new element in it was what he himself could supply. What she would want to know, what she would have to know, would be whether or not he felt any reliance could be placed in Sam's promises. Upon him rested the responsibility of persuading her that if she went back things would be different. In fact he felt sure that what she waited for with wide-eyed intentness was his assurance, and that everything hung upon his power to convince her of Sam's utter surrender, his total capitulation.

As he talked, she seemed to guard her expression and he could not guess from it what she was feeling. She never once interrupted him to ask a question or make a comment, but waited until he had given her his report. Then she went straight to the core of the matter. Leaning nearer to him she laid a hand on his sleeve; not lightly, he could feel the grip of her fingers on his arm.

"Tell me this," she said, her eyes earnestly searching his, and he knew how much depended on his reply. "Did you get the impression that Sam means to keep his promises this time? Is he honestly and truly determined to keep them?"

He put all the conviction he could into his answer. "Yes,"

he said unequivocally. "I'm absolutely certain that he not only honestly intends to keep them, but that he can and will keep them. I have no doubt of it."

"No doubt?" she asked. "No doubt at all?" Her hand still gripped his forearm, just above the wrist. "Because I can't go through this again. And neither can he. It would break us both. Do you know how hard it's going to be for him to keep these promises?"

"I do know. I repeat, I'm sure he can and will."

She took her hand away, but she still watched his face. "Then you believe," and she said it sadly, "that people can change themselves?"

"Up to a point, yes."

"But not very far? Never quite far enough?"

"It's a matter of will, I suppose. Some have strong wills, some haven't. I would say that Sam has."

"Well, he hasn't," she said. "What he has got is great tenacity and stubbornness." Then she asked, "Could you change yourself? Could you?"

"I might," he said, "with sufficient incentive. And that's what Sam has; a very powerful incentive."

She gave him another searching look, then looked away. There was a moment of silence before she asked, "Did you remember to tell him about the Jaguar?"

"I did, and he was absolutely astounded. The fact that you were driving it quite happily about New York, and alone, was almost more than he could credit."

"I hoped you'd remember to tell him," she said. "I bought it to prove to him that I'm capable of doing more than he thinks, but then I couldn't see how best to let him know. My meeting you at Frederick's was providential."

"You call the meeting providential," he said, and he was choosing his words carefully. "I take that to mean that it has accomplished something."

She was not ready, it appeared, to reply to that all-im-

90

portant question. She was not yet ready to commit herself. She took up her cup of black coffee and held it between both hands, staring across at the opposite wall.

"Tell me," she said, and he thought she must have been visualizing her life at Runnybrook, weighing this against that in her communion with herself, "when you were there on Sunday did you see my dear dog Seth?"

He told her that Seth had been missing and saw her expression change swiftly to one of acute anxiety. He said that Mary Doyle had been out searching for him.

"Had Sam done anything about it?" she asked. "Had he told the police? He's never strayed before. I've had him for five years, ever since he was a puppy. He's never strayed."

"No, Sam didn't seem unduly worried. He assumed that he was in attendance on a certain lady at one of your neighbors' houses."

"Oh, that bitch at the Sheldons', I suppose. They never look after her properly. But that's no distance away at all. Surely they would have gone there to look for him."

"Mary Doyle had been there more than once, but he wasn't to be seen. Sam thought he was probably hiding."

"Oh, no, oh, no!" she cried; and her calm had gone. "He wasn't there, I'm sure of it. But where can he be?" Her distress was great, and he had no comfort to give her. "He must have taken to straying because I've been away so long. You see, he's devoted to me. When I'm ill they have to drag him out of my room; sometimes, big though he is, they have to carry him out. Didn't Sam say anything about him the other night at the Hancocks'?"

"We were talking about other things," Murray reminded her, but she missed the irony, or ignored it. "However," he went on, "as he was taking me to my hotel in the taxi, I asked him if the dog had come back yet. He said no, he hadn't, but that he wasn't greatly worried because if he'd been run over he'd have heard."

"That was two days ago," she said. "What can have happened to him?" She was pressing her hands together nervously. "Sam ought to have told the police at once. Why didn't he, I wonder?"

"Perhaps he has, by now," Murray answered.

After a moment's silence she said, "This has changed everything."

He made no comment, but he had received a shock. A distaste was gathering in his mind like mist rising. She looked at him swiftly and she must have known what he was thinking, for she said, with an appeal in her eyes, "You see now how much I need a child, don't you?"

She spoke with emotion, with deep sincerity, and the nebulous dislike was dispelled, but he still found it impossible to do more than nod his head. He waited.

"Will Sam be at his office this afternoon?" she asked.

"Yes. I'm seeing him there at three-thirty."

"Then will you please tell him that I'm coming home?"

Again he couldn't immediately answer. He was greatly puzzled and concerned by the turn things had taken. A new factor had been introduced and he was not happy about it. It was a small and totally unexpected factor and, while he could not call it an altogether frivolous one, it was one that should not have been there at all. He felt cheated of a victory that he thought he had earned, for if victory there was it was the dog Seth's. And not only that, the whole issue was now confused and confounded. He wondered if Sam would even care if he knew. He was getting her back. That would be enough for him.

And, he thought, suppose that in the end her going back to Sam should prove to have been a mistake? Suppose it only resulted in greater unhappiness for both of them? Mightn't I be glad to be relieved of the sole responsibility for it? He resolved not even to put the question that was inevitably on

92

the tip of his tongue: Had you made up your mind to go back before we spoke of Seth? He would rather not know.

She was looking at him, waiting for his answer.

"Yes," he said, "I'll tell him that."

"And will you tell him that I'll drive myself home, and that I'll be there in time for dinner?"

He said he would.

Her mind was still very much on the dog. "I can't understand why Sam didn't notify the police at once. He's a red setter, a beautiful dog. He might have been stolen." She sighed. "I hoped that once I'd made up my mind either to go back, or never to go back, I'd begin to sleep again. I've had dreadful nights, and I try not to take sleeping tablets, I've had to take so many in my life. But if Seth is still missing . . . Do you ever lie awake for hours, until daylight comes?"

"I've done plenty of that in the past. I don't now."

"It's queer, isn't it," she said, "how one dreads lying awake? After all, sleep is a little death, a foretaste of death, and life is so short you'd think we'd be glad of a few extra hours of consciousness. But it's a consciousness that isn't any good to us. No good at all. At least it's never been to me." She broke off. "Murray, tell me about those nights when you couldn't sleep. You seem to have come so close to Sam and me because of all this that I feel I know you well, intimately almost, and yet I don't really know anything about you. I want you to tell me something about your life, past and present. I want you to let me share it a little. Is that stupid of me, to ask? Is it impertinent even? If you say it's impossible for you to tell me, I'll never, never ask again. I'd be on one side of a wall and you'd be on the other. But please, please, don't let it be like that. It matters very much to me."

"Why?" he asked, astonished. "How can it matter?" But he knew instantly that the moment had come when he could talk to someone. He was on the edge of an experience en-

93

tirely new to him. He knew he could talk to this particular young woman, Sam's wife, and to no one else, and that he was going to do just that.

"Why?" she echoed. "Because I want you for a friend. I have very few friends. My life hasn't been like other people's. I want you to let me inside that private enclosure you live in. There's plenty of time." She looked at his wrist watch. "We have over an hour, and they never hurry you here. It's peaceful, and the lights aren't too bright. Don't choose your words or stop to think. Just tell me."

She had once again moved closer to him, but it was a closeness that had nothing to do with her body, which had not moved at all. It was not a physical closeness, and he was sure it never would be. He was sure, too, that he would never want it to be.

"Begin from the beginning," she said. "Begin from where you began. Where were you born? Who were your father and mother? Begin there."

VII

HE began there. His father was a poor country curate, or, as he explained to her, assistant to the minister in a small town in Wigtownshire, but he had abandoned the Scots Kirk to embrace Anglicanism and had moved to London with his young wife and baby son at the age of twenty-seven. It was a daring and even rash undertaking, as he was without friends or influence. After a period of instruction and probation, he was fortunate enough to be offered a curacy in a small village named King's Baddeley in the heart of Somerset. There the little family settled down in lodgings, and as soon as he was old enough Murray was sent to the village school with about twenty other children. His father, like many a convert before him, adopted his chosen faith with narrow fanaticism and lived for nothing but his religion. His earnestness and devotion attracted the notice of the bishop with whom he talked when he was on his diocesan visits, and on the death of the local vicar, an old man of nearly ninety, he was given the living which brought with it three hundred pounds a year. As he had been receiving two as curate, this seemed like affluence. The vicarage was large, inconvenient and damp, but it was better than lodgings and they moved into it, if not with enthusiasm, at least with satisfaction, enthusiasm being an emotion indulged in by the new vicar only in the matter of saving souls and by his wife not at all, though she was earnestly dutiful. The boy, Murray, was taught to make himself useful about the house. At the age of six he cleaned all the shoes, blacked the grates, ran errands, and kept his father's bicycle immaculate and shining. The parish was widely scattered, though small, and when Murray was eight a subscription was started by the parishioners as a result of which Mr. Logan was presented with a small and ancient Ford car and taught to drive it. This was a day that Murray never forgot. His pride in his father's ownership of a car was great, and when he was told that it would be his duty to keep it free from mud in winter and dust in summer he thought himself fortunate. It did not dawn upon him until he was nearly ten, and mixed more with other boys, that his life was wholly made up of school, work and sleep. He had never, even, had a holiday, for during the school vacations more work was found for him about the house.

"You're to be a good boy and help your mother and me," his father would say. "Don't forget, it costs us a lot to keep you, and it will cost us more and more as you grow older. Your mother and I will do what we can, but never forget that you must do your share."

He did his share, and more, and when his tenth birthday drew near, his father said, with unexpected indulgence, that he might ask for something he wanted, and if it was within reason he should have it. He asked to be taken to the sea. This caused some consternation, but his mother persuaded his father that the request was reasonable and that the journey could and should be undertaken. Fortunately, his birthday fell in August, when holidays could be considered, and it was decided that they should write for lodgings in Minehead and drive there in the car.

The boy's joy at the idea of a holiday by the sea, which he had never seen, kept him from sleeping the night before, and during the sixty-mile drive to the Bristol Channel he was sick with excitement. He was not feeling well, but not for anything in the world would he have said so. They reached their lodgings—two rooms in a hideously ugly gray stone house well away from the sea, not even within sight of it—without mishap. His burning desire was to get to the sea before they could discover that he was not well and put him to bed. As soon as they had unpacked and put the car into an unused garage, the three of them started sedately down to the sea front, but Murray presently raced ahead, his parents calling out admonishments and following as quickly as they could.

He was never to forget what he saw. The tide was out; there were nothing but vast brown mud flats stretching almost to the horizon. The disappointment was more than the boy could bear. He flung himself down on the sand and burst into uncontrollable sobbing. Where were the racing, white-edged, curling waves he had seen in pictures, where was the vast blue expanse his imagination had conjured up? He was heartbroken. They scolded him and reasoned with him by turns, explaining that the tide was out and would in a few hours come in again, but he was inconsolable. At last they realized that there was more the matter with him than his disillusionment, great though this was. He had a fever. He was put to bed and was there for three weeks with a severe attack of measles. When he was well enough he was taken down to the sea once more, but the tide was out again. Mr. Logan could not wait for its return. They set off and drove back to King's Baddeley.

His mother, conscientious and hard-working, entirely absorbed in the affairs of the parish and in helping her husband, had little time to devote to her son. She was what was called in those days well-connected, and had a cousin of her own age who had married a young publisher in London. She rarely spoke of this couple, and expected nothing from them, but two years later the cousin and her husband came to spend a week at a country house not many miles away and stopped at the vicarage for tea. This was an important day in Murray's life. The shy and awkward boy was brought in and introduced. He saw a handsome, friendly man of about thirty-five who immediately charmed him. He had never seen any-one like him, nor, though she interested him far less, had he ever seen anyone like his wife, who was dressed in good country tweeds and talked incessantly and amusingly. Even then he recognized her as someone out of the ordinary and totally unlike his humble, hard-worked mother.

But it was Mr. Kendrick who entirely won him. He called the boy over to him, put an arm about him and said, "Now, what's to be done with this lad when he leaves school? Why don't you send him up to London? He can come into the office if he likes. How about that, my boy? Would you like a job in a publisher's office? My wife will find a room for you when the time comes, and keep an eye on you. What do you say?"

"Oh, I'd like to, sir. Thank you. I don't want to stay here."

"It's the first I've heard of it," said his father, with a frown-ing glance at him. "The fact is, Mr. Kendrick, I've always hoped my son would follow in my footsteps, but I'm bound to say he shows no sign of it yet. What is certain is that he'll have to earn his living. Are you serious, now?"

"Of course I'm serious," said the smiling man, glancing first at his watch and then at his wife. "Send him along. That'll be in about five years, I take it. Lily and I will keep an eye on him, I promise you. Now it's time we were on our way."

"I never thought," his mother said as they all stood up,

98

"that he could look to you for anything, and that's the truth. I feel no claim upon you, none at all, even though your wife and I are cousins. My husband and I ask for nothing except from the Lord, but if you mean what you say . . ."

"Of course he means what he says, Maud," Mrs. Kendrick told her, as she pulled on her gloves. "Don't be so suspicious. It would be nice to have the boy in the firm. We've no son, and who knows . . . ? If he does well, anything may happen. I think he's going to look a little like your brother Daniel. You know I was fond of Daniel when we were children."

"Let's hope the resemblance stops there," Mrs. Logan said. "Daniel was no credit to his family."

"Oh, come now, Maud! What's the harm in going on the stage? The sad thing was that he simply hadn't it in him to be a good enough actor. Do you remember, I sent you a little obituary notice from *The Times* when he died?"

"I do," Mrs. Logan said. "It was kind of you, Lily. I doubt I didn't answer your letter, but I'm no letter writer."

As the years passed without Murray's showing the smallest desire to enter the church, and as no other opening offered itself, it was agreed that if Mr. Kendrick was still of the same mind he should go to London on leaving school. His parents dreaded it, not because the separation would be particularly painful to them but because of the dangers and temptations that would lie in the boy's path. Then a timely letter came from Mr. Kendrick's secretary, saying that although Mr. Kendrick was at present abroad he had not forgotten his promise and had asked her to get in touch with Mr. and Mrs. Logan about sending their son to London. This seemed to clinch the matter. Murray, on his own initiative, answered the letter as best he could. He said he was greatly looking forward to being employed by Mr. Kendrick and would gladly accept any job in Atlantic House however small. He asked if he might start work as soon as the summer vacation began.

99

A room was found for him in a young people's hostel in Bloomsbury within walking distance of the office, and Mrs. Kendrick sent him his fare to London.

"I can't tell you," Murray said at this point, "how thankfully I left King's Baddeley. I don't know if I was actually unhappy at home, but there was nothing there that I needed, and in retrospect I know that I must have been anything but happy. At any rate, the world was opening for me, and that train journey to London, by myself, was pure ecstasy. That ecstasy completely left me when I found myself at the office. I had outgrown my clothes, I was a shy, awkward boy with an unsatisfactory complexion, and I must have looked pretty unpromising material. However, there I was. I didn't see Charles Kendrick for several days, but when I did he was very friendly and encouraging. Mrs. Kendrick—later on I called her Aunt Lily—bought a new suit for me, and some shirts and shoes and underwear, but however hard they tried—and they did try—they couldn't overcome my terrible shyness and awkwardness. They seemed to me almost a different human species from myself or anyone I'd known.

"There was another boy in the office, just senior to me, who also belonged to that different and superior order of human beings. He was everything I wasn't, and he made fun of me from the start. I soon began to hate him, and he undermined any confidence in myself that I might have acquired. For the next few years he made it impossible for me to feel happy during office hours; in fact he made my life wretched. Perhaps he didn't even realize the effect he had on me. I never spoke of it to a soul, and a good deal of it was probably caused by my own jealousy. I loathed him and at the same time I deeply envied him. How I envied him! His name was Tom Remenham. He was a happy extrovert, good-looking, with money to spend, and exceedingly popular with everybody, especially women and girls. He joined up in 1940, and died of malnutrition in a German prison camp in 1944. Since then I've never envied anyone."

When he was about eighteen the Kendricks began asking him to the house to meet other young people, and he saw a certain amount of their two lively daughters, Celia and Veronica, but his inability to throw off his shyness became a burden to them. If they teased him, his feelings were hurt; if they refrained and kept their teasing for other young men, he felt left out. He gradually stopped accepting invitations from them, partly because all social activities, however informal and friendly, only increased his self-criticism and his feelings of inadequacy, and partly because he could not afford to return hospitality. The most he could ever offer was a visit to the movies, and so many other young men were offering visits to the movies, or to theaters and dinners as well, that he soon dropped out altogether. And all too often Tom Remenham was there, highlighting the differences between them by his gaiety and casual charm. He knew that only at the Kendricks' house was he likely to meet the sort of young people he supposed he should want to meet, but the effort was too great and too unrewarding. He made a few friends at the hostel, but no intimates, and he kept much to himself. It was at that time that books began to be really important to him and reading his one solace. Then he was called up.

He chose the army and went through his training in Scotland. It was the land of his birth, and though he felt no more at home there than in London, at least the rough and impersonal give-and-take of army life was good for him and he liked it. If he were socially inadequate, no one knew or cared. He was among all sorts, and no demands of the kind he dreaded were made on him. He got on well, and spent his leaves, when he could, in Somerset. He liked his father no better, but got on more easily than before with his mother, and she now began to show him some of the affection she had earlier withheld. He knew even then that it was too late, that she could never make up to him for what he had been deprived of as a child. What he enjoyed most was the lovely Somerset countryside and the woods that had been his delight as a boy. He found that his pleasure in them had increased rather than diminished.

He had not begun his training until after Dunkirk, and he remained in England until the Middle East campaign was under way. He was in Cyrenaica by February, 1941, and later was with the Eighth Army when it was forced to evacuate Bir Hacheim. He was wounded in the shoulder and ill with dysentery and spent many weeks in hospital in Alexandria. By the time he was passed as fit once more, El Alamein was won, and he did not see active service again until he was sent to Sicily. After desperately hard fighting in and around Messina he was taken ill once more, this time with malaria, and was invalided home.

When he got out of hospital he went down to King's Baddeley to find his father dying of cancer. He had not been told; his mother had wished to spare him because of his own illness, and he arrived just in time to speak a few words to his father and to help and comfort his mother. He promised her that he would make a home for her in or near London as soon as the war was over. Together they put the vicarage in order for its new tenants and he was able to stay long enough to see her settled in lodgings in the village.

But there was no question of his rejoining the Eighth Army in Italy. He had recurring bouts of malaria, was badly underweight and couldn't get his strength back. Finally he was invalided out of the army, and after a short period of convalescence by the sea, near Eastbourne, he went back to the office and to his job. But it was not the same office. The old premises had been completely destroyed in 1940, and after occupying temporary quarters for a while Atlantic House was now situated in a business block completed in 1938 just off Hanover Square. It was all much more commodious and there wasn't a dark corner anywhere, but he badly missed the old house in Bloomsbury with its charming doorway and beautiful windows, and the fine paneled room that used to be Charles Kendrick's office.

They were all glad to see him back, though they looked a little anxiously at his yellow face and the way his prewar suits hung on him. It was about this time that he remembered first meeting Sam, who was still in uniform—he understood that it was something to do with intelligence—though their acquaintance did not ripen until much later.

He had found a room for himself in a Bloomsbury boarding-house. It was a long way from the office, but he had got used to Bloomsbury and knew his way about in it. He had been there only a few weeks when he narrowly escaped death or injury from a flying bomb which killed the landlady and her husband and wounded half a dozen of his fellow lodgers. It happened at five o'clock in the morning. As soon as he had recovered from the shock of the explosion and the noise of falling plaster and tinkling glass, he remembered the tall blonde girl he had several times noticed in the dining room, whose bedroom was just across the hall from his own. He put on his dressing gown and went to see how she had fared. He found her door locked, but was able to break it open. She was in bed with a great deal of the plaster ceiling on top of her, but except for a cut on the head, which was not serious, she was unhurt. As soon as he had freed her from the fallen plaster he found he had to deal with an attack of hysterics, but he soothed and quieted her, wrapped her in a blanket and got her down the stairs. Neighbors were already on the spot with pots of tea, and rescue workers followed. He helped them to find and carry out the bodies of the land-lady and her husband, who had been sleeping in a room built onto the back of the house.

When he went later to look for the blonde girl, he found

103

that she was in her room packing her clothes. Her head was bandaged, but she was now perfectly calm and entirely recovered. She told him her name was Sibyl Wray, and he told her his name.

"I've only been here two weeks," she said, "and now this has happened. We'll have to find some other rooms today. We can't stay here. Let's go together and look for somewhere to live. I'm sorry about that attack of hysterics or whatever it was. It wasn't a bit like me."

Her assumption that they would take rooms in the same house did not at all displease him, nor did the fact that she was inclined to turn to him as if she had no one else in the world to depend on. She soon told him that in fact she hardly knew a soul in London. She came from Staffordshire, where she had been working in a munitions factory, but had decided to come to London when a friend wrote that she could get her a job at the Air Ministry. She had learned typing and shorthand and was delighted at the idea of working in London.

"But my friend got married a few days ago and left, so I'm all alone. I'm only in the typing pool at the Air Ministry now, but I'm hoping to get a better job later on."

They packed their suitcases and went out to find rooms. That afternoon they moved into a boarding house in Kensington, but in order that there should be no hitch, they booked their rooms separately and moved in an hour apart.

"We don't want people thinking anything," she said.

It was not long before she told him that her mother was the sister of Lord Holford, of Holford in Staffordshire.

"The family name is Craddick," she said. "We've been in Staffordshire for hundreds of years."

She had a remarkable head of golden hair, of which she was extremely proud, and he thought her beautiful. She had, he supposed, what people called "race." Her features were coldly regular, her hands and feet slender, and she carried herself well. Her father was dead, her mother had remarried, and she had a young brother who was a midshipman with the China fleet. Murray wished she had not got an uncle who was a peer; it seemed to put her at a distance from him. But certainly, if distance there were, it was not she who made it. She seemed bent on dispensing with distance of any sort. She confessed that she had been longing to know him ever since she first saw him in the dining room. He looked, she said with a laugh, so pale and interesting.

"And you had been longing to know me," she said. "I saw you looking at me. It seems as though we were meant to meet, doesn't it? I mean, even without the flying bomb."

Whether or not they were meant to meet, their circumstances, the dangerous days they lived in, and their youth and aloneness drew them close. She was only nineteen, though her assured manner and her disposition to lead rather than follow made her seem older. He was in no position, as yet, to marry, though when it became plain to him, as it soon did, that they were bound to become lovers, he made up his mind to ask Charles Kendrick to increase his pay, so that at least the possibility of marriage might not be too remote. To his great relief, Charles Kendrick agreed without demur.

When he told Sibyl that he was in love with her and wanted to marry her someday, they had already gone pretty far in the way of embraces and kisses. Now she flung herself into his arms with such ardor that he lost his self-control completely, and they went to her room for the first time. To his surprise he found that not only was she not a virgin but that she was prepared for just such an eventuality.

"Don't be so foolish, darling," she protested when they talked about this afterwards. "Surely you aren't going to be angry with me simply because you're not the first? I was engaged to a very nice boy at home. He was in the navy, and he was drowned last year when his ship was torpedoed. There's only been him and now you, and I love you a thousand times more than I loved him. And if you think this is the

105

moment to stop and argue, believe me I don't." And she drew him back into her arms with frantic strength.

He took up the argument again later. "But why didn't you tell me?"

"Have you told me about all the girls you've been to bed with?"

"No, I thought you were too young and innocent."

"Well, now you know better, darling, so you can tell me everything."

When he had sketched all this in, briefly, to Christine, she said, "I suppose she was the right sort of girl for you, in a way, at that period of your life, but you didn't marry her, did you?"

"Yes," he said, "I did. I'm still married to her."

"I see," she said. "Now go on with the story."

When Murray told Charles Kendrick that he was engaged, he advised him not to be in a hurry to marry.

"Like most other publishing firms, we're lucky to have survived the war," he said, "and the loss of about eighty thousand books hasn't helped. I'm afraid your recent increase in salary will have to do you for some time. Tell me who the young woman is."

Murray told him, adding, a little reluctantly but with the hope that Charles Kendrick might think better of his plans, that her uncle was Lord Holford, of Holford in Staffordshire. "They're an old Staffordshire family," he said.

"I never heard of him," Charles Kendrick replied, "though that's nothing against him. Is he prepared to help his niece in any way? Or is she already provided for?"

"I don't think she has any money of her own," Murray told him. "Her father died some years ago, her mother isn't at all well off, and there's a young son in the navy. Sibyl has a job in the Air Ministry, and I think she'd rather like to go on with it after we're married."

"Well, that seems to be common practice these days,"

Charles Kendrick said. "They all want to go on with their jobs until nature intervenes and they start having babies. Would you like to bring her to Sunday night supper one evening? We're usually by ourselves then."

Veronica had married and was living in Bristol. Celia had a war job at Cheltenham. As he accepted the invitation he was thankful that neither of them would be there. And then, with a kind of premonition that neither Charles Kendrick nor Aunt Lily would care much for Sibyl, he said, "I'm afraid, sir, my mind is made up. About marrying, I mean. I'd like to get married quite soon."

"Well, well," Charles Kendrick said with good humor, "I never supposed you'd listen to my advice, though I still wish you wouldn't be in a hurry. Well, bring her next Sunday night. We shall look forward to seeing you both. Oh, by the way, over on that shelf behind you you'll find the latest edition of *Who's Who*. Would it interest you to know just who and what her uncle is? If so, would you bring it to me?"

Murray, without replying, got up and took the fat red volume from its shelf. He gave it to Charles Kendrick, who soon found what he was looking for.

"Ah," he said, "here he is. I'll read it to you. 'Holford, third Baron, created 1908, of Holford, Staffordshire. Ralph Percival de Saulnes Craddick. Born 12 May 1890, son of Second Baron and Constance Ethel Gomshall, elder daughter of the late Colonel W. Watkins Gomshall, Royal Army Medical Corps. Succeeded father in 1931. Educated Haileybury and Wadham College, Oxford. No heir. Address, 24 Creech Lane, Holford. Club, Royal Automobile.' Well, he doesn't seem to have had much of a career, and I shouldn't think there was a great deal of money there. I suppose the family property has had to go. Poor chap. Let me see, he'll be fifty-five now."

"I wonder why his grandfather was made a baron?" Murray said. "I asked Sibyl, but she didn't seem to know."

107

"I might make a guess. They were handing out titles pretty freely in those days. He may have given generous help to the Liberal party, who must have needed it. There were two general elections in that year."

"I'm always astonished at your memory, sir."

"Ah, well, I was brought up a Liberal, and I had a Liberal grandfather who was a friend of Gladstone's. Those were the great days of the Liberal party. I'm a Tory now. What are you, my boy?"

"I think I shall start by voting Labour," Murray said.

Charles Kendrick got up and put a hand on his shoulder. "All young men should vote Labour till they learn better," he said, with the teasing look and smile that were so like Celia's. "As you go out, will you tell Miss Thompson that I'm ready for her?"

He felt that his premonition was all too correct that Sunday night at supper in Onslow Square. Charles Kendrick and Aunt Lily, who was tall and stooped noticeably and had clever, hooded eyes, both did their best, but he knew them well enough to know that they were trying to like Sibyl and not succeeding at all. Quite unfairly he was inclined to attribute this to the fact that Sibyl was just a girl living on her own and working in a typing pool, but he only half believed it. They simply didn't take to her, and he was puzzled to know why. She asserted herself rather more than she need have done, but they ought to have known that such a meeting was bound to be an ordeal for her and that she was sure to be nervous.

A few days later Charles Kendrick sent for him to speak about quite a different matter—to ask him, in fact, to move from the office where he then was, to share Dick Bayliss's office—but he took the opportunity to say to him, "What a wonderful head of hair your Miss Wray has. She's really quite striking looking." He moved some papers on his desk and then said, "I want to tell you, my boy, that if all goes

108

well there's no reason why you shouldn't one day hold a responsible position in the firm. If that happens, you'll need a wife who can help you in all sorts of ways. Do you think Miss Wray is likely to be that sort of wife? You're young, and you're related to me by marriage, so I feel I can speak to you in this avuncular fashion. I've nothing whatever against Miss Wray, but I still feel you ought to take your time and think the matter over well. Lily feels as I do. We wish you wouldn't hurry things."

"I can only repeat, sir, that my mind is quite made up," Murray replied, "and so is Sibyl's. We want to marry as soon as possible. I assure you I have given a lot of thought to it."

"In that case," Charles Kendrick said, "I'll say no more."

VIII ✐

EVEN then, Murray knew that what he had said in Charles Kendrick's office that day was not entirely true. He had been having second thoughts, especially in the early morning hours after he had slipped back to his own room; but because of the relations between them, now habitual and, he admitted to himself, deeply enjoyable, he could not possibly take a backward step nor contemplate for a moment "letting Sibyl down." Most of the time he was happy with her, but the moments when she dismayed him by the unpredictable things she said and by her sudden outbreaks of violent temper were increasing and inevitably led to quarrels.

He had told her from the beginning that if they married and had a home he must ask his mother to come and live with them, and at first she had accepted the idea with considerable grace and good nature, but one Sunday when they were returning from a walk she said belligerently, "If I've got to have your mother in the house she'll have to do all the cooking and housework. Two in the kitchen is one too many. I shall keep my job and be out all day. It would drive me crazy to be cooped up with an old woman."

"Sibyl, Sibyl," he protested, "why be so violent about it? When you see her you won't think of her as an old woman, and of course she'll help in any way she can."

"She'll just interfere," Sibyl said angrily, "and of course she'll always take your side."

"Let's hope she won't have to take sides," he said, and he drew Sibyl's arm through his as they walked. "Let's hope that when we're married we'll understand each other better and there won't be any quarrels."

"If she's there, there are bound to be, and you'd better face it. I've never pretended to be a saint."

He was determined to keep his temper and reason with her calmly. "I'm very sorry, darling," he said, "but I must at least ask her to come and live with us. She's terribly alone. It's possible she won't come, but I must give her the chance."

"You're so wonderfully considerate to everyone but me," she said bitterly, and this angered him by its total unfairness. They were at the door of their boardinghouse and he went upstairs without another word. She followed him up to his room, which was on the floor above hers, and said, shutting and locking the door behind her, "Look. We'd better have this out, and have it out now."

It ended as so many of their quarrels ended, and as always she was quickly soothed and placated, even promising that she would never bring up the subject again. Lying in his arms she said, "It's only like this that I'm sure of you."

"Sure of me?" he repeated, astonished. "What have I ever done or said to make you think you couldn't be sure of me?"

"It's Charles Kendrick," she told him, "and Aunt Lily, as you call her. They'll get you away from me if they can. But when we're like this I know you'll never want to leave me. We're too happy together."

He realized then that she knew what he had hoped she didn't know—that they had not liked her. He knew that she deeply resented it and them. He kissed her and comforted her, but his doubts made his heart heavy.

"Once we're married," he said, "you'll see. Things will be different."

They were married in June at a small church in Kensington, and Sibyl wore white and carried a bunch of lilies. She looked beautiful and even saintly as she walked up the aisle on the arm of her stepfather, a builder from Stoke-on-Trent. Her mother, now Mrs. Folsom, seemed the very antithesis of her daughter, for she was small, highly nervous and inclined to keep herself in the background. Her only resemblance to Sibyl was that her features were fine and regular and she must once have been very pretty, though she now gave the impression of only wanting to escape notice and of having accepted defeat at the hands of fate a long time ago. Murray liked her and wondered what combination of circumstances had led her to marry the florid, down-to-earth, unprepossessing Folsom. Her brother, Lord Holford, had been asked to give his niece away, but sent a telegram to say that ill-health prevented his coming to London. The telegram with its brief refusal and the word "congratulations" was all he sent. No present, no check was forthcoming. Mrs. Folsom did her best and gave the young people a box of household linen belonging to the Craddick family and what was left of old china bearing the family crest. Charles Kendrick and his wife gave them a check for fifty pounds and a set of chairs. Murray's mother was there, a sturdy little countrywoman with a fresh color and reddish hair that had not yet turned gray. She was to spend a few days in Onslow Square before returning to Somerset. Murray decided to say nothing to her about coming to live with them until they knew where they would make their home.

112

They went to the coast of Cornwall for their honeymoon and were gone ten days, and during that time Sibyl was considerate and loving. He longed to say to her, "If you were always like this, how happy we could be," but he well knew that such words would precipitate the flare-up he longed to avoid. When they returned to London and to their work they took a bedroom and sitting room in a house in Kensington that called itself a "private hotel," a contradiction in terms which always struck Murray as comic. Sibyl was delighted with the sitting room and would have been content to have stayed on indefinitely. She rearranged the furniture and kept fresh flowers in the window. She couldn't see, she said, why they should want anything better. But Murray longed for a home. He had spent ten years in lodgings and even though he had never lived as comfortably as now he hated the meals in the dining room, which was full of nodding white heads and couples who rarely spoke to each other. Nor could he speak in ordinary tones to Sibyl without being overheard. He wanted his own front door, he said, he wanted privacy.

It was Sibyl who eventually found the house in Morden. It was near the house of her best friend, the girl who had got her the job at the Air Ministry and was now married to a man named Humphries. Murray liked them both and thought it would be a good thing for Sibyl to be near people she knew. They furnished the house slowly and with caution and Sibyl showed taste and good sense in the things she bought. She had lately been taken out of the typing pool and had become one of two secretaries allotted to a fairly senior official. She gave up her job therefore with a good deal of reluctance when they moved into their new home, making it clear to Murray that she was sacrificing an interesting career and a good salary to keep house for him. She was mollified when they received a letter from Mrs. Logan thanking them for offering her a home but saying that she felt she could never leave King's Baddeley and her husband's grave.

"Well, that's one blessing," Sibyl remarked, "but kindly don't forget that I was willing to have her."

Murray's life was now at least dappled, stippled with happiness. Living with Sibyl was sour-sweet, he could never be sure of peace for long, but one thing at least gave him entire satisfaction. She was now beginning to read, and he was thankful because he often brought manuscripts back from the office to read in the evenings. She read, it was true, only such novels as the girl at the local library chose to give her, but he was hopeful that her taste would develop and mature in time. He had long been ashamed of the barrenness of his knowledge and instead of reading the papers as he traveled to and from the office by underground he was now reading Gibbon. Charles Kendrick, a good classical scholar, offered him anything he wanted from his own library.

When Sibyl told him she was going to have a baby he felt an almost overwhelming thankfulness and joy. What more, he asked himself, had he to wish for? His marriage was proving, if not as happy as he could wish, at least as happy as most people's; he liked his work and was doing well, he was able to pay his way, his health had greatly improved, and now he was to be a father. It was the best moment of his life and he asked Sibyl to go with him to church that Sunday—a thing they were not in the habit of doing—to offer thanks for these blessings.

She said it would be hypocritical and silly, and flouted the idea.

"You know very well I don't believe in all that. I got married in a church because I wanted to wear a white wedding dress, and registry office weddings are ugly, but I don't see why we need go to church just because I'm going to have a baby. So far as I know, there's nothing supernatural about it."

114

He was deeply hurt by her refusal and his happiness was temporarily snuffed out, but he went alone, and when he came back she tried to make up for her intransigeance by bright amiability, but it was a long time before he could put the incident out of his mind.

During the early weeks of her pregnancy he came home one evening, called out to her, and receiving no reply, went up to their bedroom. He found her sitting at her dressing table holding her hand mirror and she turned on him a face of wild distress.

"Look at me! I've come all out in spots. Is it something I've eaten, or have I caught some horrible disease? Just look at me!"

He looked at her, saw the reddish spots and patches and noted that she looked hot and flushed. He took her temperature and found it was just over a hundred.

"Not too bad," he said, "but I suppose it might be measles. Have you ever had measles?"

"Yes," she said, "and you ought to remember, because I've told you how ill I was. So it can't be measles. Perhaps it's scarlet fever. My throat hurts." She put a hand up to her neck glands.

"I'll ring up the doctor," he said. They had no telephone then and he had to go down the street a little way to the Humphries' house. The doctor said he would come at once. By the time he arrived she was in a state of terror.

"I've got diphtheria or scarlet fever," she announced, her blue eyes staring.

"Nonsense, my dear girl," the doctor said. "Let me have a look at you. Have you had measles?"

"Yes, when I was eight. That's why I know it's diphtheria. My throat hurts."

"Suppose you let me diagnose it," the doctor said. He was a young man with the forcefulness and authority of someone double his age. She had taken a dislike to him at their first meeting. He looked inside her mouth, took her temperature and felt her neck glands. "When did this rash appear?"

"I noticed it first about an hour ago. I was waiting for my husband to come home."

"Have you been exposed to German measles?"

"Not that I'm aware of. But I do stand in rationing queues and travel in buses, heaven knows."

He looked at Murray.

"It's German measles," he said. "I'd like her to go straight to bed."

"But what on earth for?" Sibyl demanded. "If it really is German measles, then it's nothing to make a fuss about."

"I think you had better let me be the judge of that," the doctor said. He snapped his case shut. "I'll call tomorrow, to see if there are any fresh symptoms, but I don't think there will be. And now, Mrs. Logan, do as I tell you, please, and get into bed."

She looked at him with deep suspicion.

"You think it's diphtheria or you wouldn't send me to bed. Besides, how can I go to bed? I've got my husband's dinner to get."

"Sibyl, that's absurd," Murray protested. "You know perfectly well I can look after myself."

"It's the first I've heard of it," she said. "I gave up a good job to look after you."

The doctor turned to Murray again. "Please see that she goes to bed at once," he said, and left the room. Murray followed him downstairs, and the doctor beckoned him into the living room.

"Of course you'll say nothing of this to your wife," he said, "but I think it only right to tell you that, although one doesn't regard German measles as at all serious as a rule, in your wife's case it takes on rather a different aspect."

"Why is that?" Murray asked, puzzled.

116

"Because she's in the early stages of her pregnancy, and German measles at this point might have some effect upon the child. Might, I repeat. I trust it won't, but there is that slight danger. I want her to be quiet and stay in bed for three days. It will probably be a light attack, but it will do her no harm to rest. Keep what I've told you entirely to yourself, of course. We don't want her worrying about it."

Murray's hands had gone damply cold, and he stook looking at the doctor stricken and appalled. He nerved himself to ask, "In what way could the child be affected?"

"There's no need to be alarmed," the doctor told him. "The chances are against anything going wrong, but if you want an answer to your question, I'll give it. Occasionally there's some damage to the child's eyes, or even heart, or brain. The risk is small, but all the same it's unfortunate that it should have happened now. I'll bring something in the morning for her to take. Not that she needs anything, but she may like a bottle of medicine by the bed. People do, I find."

"Isn't there some injection you could give her?" Murray asked. He longed to hear of anything that might offer some security.

"If I'd known she'd been exposed to German measles, I'd have given her injections at once, but it's useless at this point. Just keep her warm and in bed till the attack is over."

"I'll do my best," Murray said. When the doctor had gone he stood for a minute under the harsh light in the little hall with anguish in his heart. Why should this have happened to Sibyl and to him? He thought of the many pregnant girls and young women to be seen in an hour's walk about Morden. The suburb had been described as one of London's bedrooms, and he had once jokingly remarked that this was obvious. These young women, he had often thought, looked calmly confident; there seemed to him to be something pleasingly animal about them, something serene and almost mindless.

117

He had longed for the time when Sibyl would be one of them. He wondered if the doctor, who was after all only thirty or so, had been right to warn him and so rob him of his peace of mind for just over seven months. Then he heard Sibyl calling to him.

"What was all the talk about? You'd better tell me."

He answered as he went up the stairs. "Oh, he was just talking about your confinement. I'm very glad he's arranged for you to go to the hospital in Wimbledon. Now get into bed. I'll bring you up some soup or whatever you want."

"Soup will do. There are a couple of tins in the larder. What are you going to have? I was going to warm up some stew for you, and cook some potatoes."

"I don't care what I have," he said. "I'm not hungry."

The months went slowly by, and as the time drew near, Mrs. Logan—warmly welcomed at this point by Sibyl—came up from Somerset and was installed in the spare bedroom. A small room opening off theirs had been fitted up as a nursery.

"If it's a boy," Sibyl announced one day, "I'm going to call him Martin. If it's a girl I've decided on Penelope."

"Am I to have no say in it at all?" Murray asked, but he spoke mildly because it was best not to irritate her in any way, and also because nothing mattered to him now but that the child should be born perfectly normal.

She retorted, "Well, who's having the worst of it all? You or me?"

"Just as you like," he said. "I've no objection to either name."

The blow when it fell was a far greater tragedy for him than for her. He thought that what Sibyl felt was chiefly shame; shame and humiliation. Why should they, of all people, have had a mentally defective child? When the probable cause of it was explained to her, she scoffed at the whole idea. Dr. Burrows was too young and inexperienced to know what he was talking about. Who ever heard of such a thing? She called it an old wives' tale. It had been the lightest of attacks, she hadn't even felt ill. Gradually her attitude toward the disaster hardened and became clear. Somehow it must be Murray's fault. Somehow he was to blame. As the child grew older, there was no doubt whom he resembled. He had Murray's dark hair and gray eyes. He bore no resemblance to anyone in her family, who were all, she frequently pointed out, pure Saxon types—fair-haired and blue-eyed. At some point she had learned from Mrs. Logan, who enjoyed talking about her childhood in Scotland, that there had been a great-aunt who had chosen to dress like a man and had even succeeded, for a time, in joining the army.

What she made no effort to hide was the fact that she was repelled by the child. There was now no question of Mrs. Logan's returning to King's Baddeley. Her place was there, and in fact she dedicated herself to her task and lavished upon the boy all the affection she had withheld from her own son. Gradually a kind of understanding seemed to grow between them, and when the child began to make ugly, unintelligible sounds, she was able to guess their meaning. Murray was deeply thankful that she was there. Nowadays there was little wish on his part, or indeed on Sibyl's, for privacy. Their relations were going from bad to worse. Moreover, they had decided to have no more children, and Sibyl considered that abstention was less trouble than precaution. Emotionally she seemed to have gone into complete reverse. She was quite ready to put an end to what, previously, she could not have too much of. Murray often wondered, but without caring greatly, if she had found a lover. It seemed likely enough; she had lost none of her good looks, and she had plenty of time on her hands.

When the boy was six, Murray bought a small, secondhand car, and both he and Sibyl learned to drive it. She took such pleasure in the car that he felt it was an extravagance that had been well worth while, and soon Surrey and Sussex began to unfold their beauties to them. Sibyl even showed an enthusiasm for picnics, and when the moment came to halt for lunch after climbing some narrow chalk road to the top of the Downs or at the edge of a wood, she took complete control, arranged where everyone was to sit and handed round the food like a dictatorial governess. It was easier to let her have her way, but sometimes Murray would stroll away from the two women and the vacant stare of the child to lie alone in the sun, wondering why his life had gone so wrong.

"And now," he told Christine, "I come to the ugliest and most shameful part of my story. I can never forgive myself for what happened. Apart from Sibyl and myself, and now you, not a soul knows what really did happen. Perhaps my telling you will help to lighten the burden a little. If you can bear to listen, I'll take that chance."

She had been sitting very still, completely absorbed in what he had been telling her. Now she turned toward him with an impulsive little movement as if to come closer to him or to show him how close to him she already was.

"You must tell me," she said. "Whatever it is, I want to hear it."

One Sunday in early spring they went for a picnic with the Humphries and their two children. Mrs. Logan stayed at home with Martin, who had a slight cold. It was his birthday, but in any case, it was not a day that was ever celebrated. The two cars kept fairly close together, as Murray and Sibyl were to guide the party to a certain fold in the Downs, where they could be sure of shelter from the wind. Sibyl was driving. She preferred driving to being driven and Murray was glad to let her as her suggestions and criticisms when he was driving were hard to bear. The day had begun badly and they had left the house with jangling nerves. Sibyl

120

had lost her temper with the boy and had shaken him roughly. When Murray remonstrated, he was the next victim of her anger. He made up his mind to stay at home, but just then the Humphries arrived and wouldn't hear of going without him. He tried to persuade Sibyl to go in the other car, and let Edna or one of the children go with him, but she refused. They set off, unable to speak a word to each other for some miles. Then Murray said, "Let's not spoil the whole day. I'm sorry I was angry with you, but you must admit I had cause to be."

"All right," she said, with one of her sudden changes from fury to amiability. "I'll admit you had cause, and I'm sorry."

Grateful for peace he said, "Then let's forget it."

Having made her apology, she now said the one thing best calculated to hurt him. "All the same, I can't feel the least affection for the child. One day he'll have to be sent away. I won't be able to endure having him in the house much longer."

Keeping a tight hold on himself he said, "Let's not discuss that now, Sibyl. You know how I feel about it. I could never consent to his being sent to a home. Never."

"It's no good your saying 'never' to me," she answered, and her voice had begun to tremble with anger. "You're out all day. There aren't many women who could have put up with living with a mother-in-law and a half-witted child as long as I've done. One day, I warn you, I'll come to the end of my endurance."

"And then what?" he asked, knowing the folly of asking it.

"Then they'll both have to go; or I go."

"For God's sake, Sibyl, have you no heart at all?"

Ready now to lash out, she cried, "Don't talk to me about having a heart. Whose fault is it, anyhow? Your mother told me about that great-aunt of yours who pretended to be a man. They had to shut her up for a time. It's in your family."

They had never before come so near to mutual hate. Beyond caution now, he said, "And what about your uncle, Lord Holford, who ought to be shut up and isn't?"

What followed followed with lightning quickness. She turned and hit him in the face, and he, unable to control an instantaneous reflex, hit back, striking her shoulder hard enough to hurt her under her cotton dress. She gave a loud, hysterical scream that he was never to forget and took both hands off the wheel. The car plunged off the road before he could right it and struck a telegraph pole.

"I'll spare you the details," he said. "It happened just outside a small town in Surrey. The Humphries got us to the local hospital. Sibyl had been pitched through the shattered windscreen and her face and neck were terribly cut. Her head, luckily, was protected by a woolen scarf. I only had broken ribs and a dislocated arm. She was in the hospital for six months. Everything was done for her that could be done; she was treated by one of our best plastic surgeons, but in spite of all they could do she was badly scarred. She'd always been so proud of her good looks. Now there's little left of them but her beautiful hair. If I had gone on refusing to let the boy be sent away I'm quite sure she would have left me. Probably there was another man. I could never be certain. But that's all over for her. She has a morbid dread of being seen. She'll never leave me now, and needless to say, I couldn't possibly leave her. I was entirely to blame for the accident. The curious thing is that she has never, as far as I know, told anyone what really happened. It was a fairly old car, and it was assumed that something had gone wrong with the steering. Though I don't greatly care now, I am certain she has never spoken of it to a living soul."

He paused and seemed to be looking down at her hand, which was lying near him on the table, and at the bracelet with its coins. Then he went on: "She's a more intelligent woman than she was. She reads more, and with more discrimination, but we talk very little, and it's like living with a coldly reticent stranger. Watching television takes up a good deal of her time, but even then she doesn't watch just anything that comes. She picks and chooses. I don't know what's in her mind. She never tells me. I suppose she must hate me; I'm sure she does. Well, there's my life. There's nothing to be done, and there's nothing to look forward to, except that I hope to get back to Greece at least once more before I die." And for the first time since he had begun his story, he turned his head and looked directly at her and smiled. She did not answer his smile.

"But it's a terrible story," she said in a low voice. "It's terrible. You make me ashamed of being unhappy, with all that I have, and with Sam's goodness and devotion. You make me utterly ashamed."

"You mustn't feel ashamed," he said. "It's all relative, and you can't measure unhappiness. I ought to be able to find compensation somewhere, and if I can't it's my own fault, but I haven't been able to. I've only got my work. I am happy in that, luckily. Well, I suppose it was all easily avoidable. I should have listened to Charles."

"It was too late then," she said. "And don't look back and say 'Here is where I went wrong.' It only adds to the pain. I'm not sure you can even learn very much from looking back because circumstances are never quite the same." She sighed, and then she once more put her hand on his sleeve and gently drew back the cuff to see his watch. "You ought to go, I'm afraid. I've been oblivious to time and to everything but what you were telling me."

She now noticed that the waiter had brought the bill and that it was lying folded on a plate at her elbow. She put down some dollar bills and caught the waiter's eye. When he brought her the change she waved it away. "We've kept you so long," she said, with a little smile of apology.

They got up with reluctance. They both looked round them at the now almost empty restaurant with its walls lined with dusty wine bottles and its calculated air of a bistro gone up in the world.

"We'll always remember this," she said. "Won't we?"

"You know I will," he answered, and added, "a miracle has happened to me here."

Their eyes met with complete understanding. Outside, the bright day dazzled and the busy world seemed not to belong to them. They stood on the pavement a little irresolutely, feeling that once they had parted a thousand things would come between them.

"I don't want to say good-by," she told him sadly. "I wish I could be sure of seeing you again." And then she said, "They keep reminding us that we live in an atomic age, and that anything may happen. It doesn't worry me much, does it you?"

"Hardly at all," he replied.

"So you feel the same. I suppose it's because personal problems are so much closer to our hearts. I suppose if we had children . . ." She realized what she had said and broke off in some confusion.

In the bright light he thought she looked frail and tired.

"Let me get you a taxi," he said. "Or did you come in the car?"

"No. It's impossible to park it here. I'll walk. I've been so deep in your world it will take me some time to get back into this one again. And after that," she added, "I must pack."

"Please try to be happy," he pleaded, and he took her hand. "Please try. That house, that lake, the ducks, couldn't you . . . ?" He found he couldn't finish what he wanted to say.

She smiled a little and glanced away. Then she turned to him with a look of sudden decision.

"Do you mind if I write to you sometimes? To the office? I want to, if you'll let me."

"Oh, do!" he said. "Do!"

She gave him a look in which he saw a liking that was

124

almost tangible, like a present to be felt and weighed in the hand. It was a look in which there was something young, ardent and devoted, something intensely loyal and even school-girlish. It warmed and touched him, and he wished there were some way of keeping her there longer, of tasting and enjoying this for at least a few minutes more, but she turned abruptly, without a good-by, and walked away. A moment later he hailed a passing taxi which overtook her, so that he saw her once again. She walked lightly, with a straight back and shoulders, and the sun caught her light-brown hair and glinted on the gold bracelet which had slipped down over her black glove. All the way to the office his thoughts were wholly taken up with her. He did not feel that she belonged, in a sense, any-where, and it would have been hard to place her. She was not typically American in speech or manner. She had had too many foreign governesses, he supposed, and had been able to take too little part in the life around her. She had read so much that she had read herself out of the boundaries of any one country. He guessed that she was even more alone than he was. He had Atlantic House. She had her books, her home, which she seemed to regard half as prison, half as sanatorium, and the heavy obligation that had been laid upon her to be happy with a good man she did not love but who loved her inordinately.

He guessed that she had been happy for a time as Mrs. Charles Darnay, in whose skin she would probably have liked to stay longer. Now she had shed the adventure on which she had embarked and it was largely his doing. He and the dog Seth could divide that responsibility between them. One thing was made plain to him on that drive to the office, and that was that he could not now think, with any satisfaction at all, of her meeting with Sam and of the taking up of her life with him again. But this would pass; what would remain would be the extraordinary relief the opening up of his own life to her had been. As long as he lived he would be grateful to her for that, and if his sense of gratitude and wonder were so great as to amount to love for her, after all, this love was for Mrs. Charles Darnay, a woman Sam had not even met. Someday he might pursue his acquaintance with Mrs. Sam Bonner, but that was something that time would deal with. For Mrs. Sam Bonner's sake he hoped with all his heart that the dog Seth was home again.

IX

HE felt himself to be so changed that it was surprising to find Southview no different, except that the front lawn looked the worse for his absence, thrown into shaggy contrast by the trim lawns on either side. The grass had begun its spring growth before he left, and Sibyl had said she would get someone in to cut it, but had obviously not done so. Since the accident, she said, pushing a lawn mower hurt her back. The privet hedge had put out all its new leaves and needed trimming. The garden, at any rate, had missed him.

He had gone straight to the office from the airport and had spent a few hours there, part of the time in Charles's office telling him about his trip.

"You look all the better for it," Charles had said, sitting back in his chair with the completely easy and affable manner which suggested to his visitors that nothing ever worried him. "The first trip to America is like one's first love affair—it's with you for life."

Murray said, smiling, "My mind feels like Pandora's box

in reverse. Instead of being opened to let everything out, it's been opened to let everything in. It struck me while I was there that it's the first country I've been to where a guidebook would be a useless encumbrance. What you need to know, any taxi driver can tell you, and will. The country simply takes you in and envelops you, and it's just a matter of using your eyes from then on."

"I'm glad you felt like that," Charles said. "I was pretty sure you would. My only quarrel with Dick Bayliss is his inability to enjoy himself when he's over there. He merely becomes irritated and irritable. It's a curious flaw in his character. Now tell me about the big boss. How was he? How did he strike you?"

He lived it over again in talking to Charles and it was hard to recall how frightened he had been of him in the days of his apprenticeship. Looking at him now he thought, as he had often thought before, that if ever a man had been born to be a publisher Charles had been. And yet they all half suspected that he was toying with the idea of going into politics, though nothing had been said. His reason for not taking this step, Murray assumed, was his great affection for Frederick Bonner, and as long as he lived it was unlikely that he would take it. Nevertheless, it was rumored that Charles felt he had served his time as a publisher and would have liked a political career before he was too old. He had held responsible government posts during the war when Atlantic House had been put out of production by bombing, and it would not be surprising if he wanted to re-enter these fields. The newspaper syndicate that had originally put up the money for Atlantic House (London) had been taken over by another newspaper syndicate, and the head of this group was showing so much interest in the firm's affairs as to suggest that he would like the chairmanship himself. But to Murray the very thought of the firm's losing Charles was wholly distressing.

128

He often thought that if he could have chosen a father he would have chosen Charles.

He had a certain way of holding his head, a certain way of speaking that suggested fastidiousness, but this was not at all exaggerated and his manner was affable even when his words were most pointed. He made no show whatever of the fact that he was a first-rate classical scholar and never talked to Murray on anything but easy and equal terms. He had a pleasing and clever face, clean shaven and healthy, with an agreeable tan winter and summer, due, he readily admitted, to the constant use of an electric lamp and not to out-of-door life, for which he had no use at all. He would rarely leave London. "I can see all the trees I want to see out of my own front windows in Onslow Square," he said. The house he had lived in for so many years had been turned into flats like the other houses in the square, and he occupied two of these flats, the one on the ground floor—since both the girls had left home—being chiefly occupied by the dogs. No one who saw him and his wife, "Aunt Lily," together could fail to be amused by the contrast. Aunt Lily was a bluestocking, passionately interested in music and in experiments with extra-sensory perception, being gifted in both these directions herself. Her stooping figure and hooded eyes gave her a witchlike air, and she seemed wholly unaware of the noise, commotion and smell caused by her numerous dachshunds which were forever on chairs and sofas. Murray was fond of her, though he never felt he knew her well; she had always been very kind to him and often sent useless and inappropriate presents to Martin. Charles was wholly devoted to her and she to him.

After leaving Charles, he went for a few minutes to Dick Bayliss's office and had a talk with him. He could never make himself believe that Dick Bayliss liked him, or indeed did more than tolerate him, but they got on well enough, chiefly, Murray thought, because he liked picking Dick Bayliss's brains and Dick Bayliss enjoyed having them picked. He didn't doubt that Bayliss regarded him as an uneducated barbarian, but in his present buoyancy of mind he felt he didn't care if he did.

He had not spent more than ten minutes with him before Dick Bayliss began to tell him that America's role in world affairs was a wholly sinister one, that America was the arch-enemy and stood in the way of all possible easing of world tensions. Murray longed to be able to say merely, "Don't be silly," and did his best to counter these statements without actually saying it. This view of America, as he was well aware, was apt to be held, sincerely or not, by intellectuals like Dick Bayliss, and on that account, if on no other, he was not sorry not to be one of them. Bayliss was a small man who wore big horn-rimmed spectacles and always made Murray think of a greatly magnified bee. He was slovenly in his dress, and in fact made a cult of untidiness, and Charles had once let drop that he had never got over his disappointment at not being made a Fellow of All Souls. He belonged to a number of clubs whose names and purposes were unknown to most outsiders but whose members were all in some way distinguished and erudite. He had been a member of the firm since its earliest days and was a bachelor. It was rumored that he had a middle-aged German baroness—who was a noted Egyptologist—as a mistress, though no one was prepared to swear to it.

Charles had insisted, as Murray had his heavy suitcase with him, on his borrowing his car to drive home, saying he wouldn't be wanting it till the next morning anyway, and as he said good-by to Miss Purchase, the secretary he shared with Dick Bayliss, and got into Charles's car, he told himself that his trip to America would now have to be pigeonholed and taken out only for his own pleasure. The two women would talk about local happenings, they would not care to hear about a place as remote to them as New York, a city they could read about in the daily papers if they chose to. Murray had had to go there on business; now he was back, and the lawn would be mown and life would resume its normal course, with a man leaving the house each morning and returning to it at night.

When he opened the front door, Sibyl was in the hall polishing a mirror. She liked to do little household tasks at the wrong time of day, or whenever the impulse took her; and as he kissed her cheek she had her polishing cloth in her hand. She could see through the open door, as he came in, that he had come in Charles Kendrick's car and had left it at the front gate, but she made no comment. He saw that she had just paid her weekly visit to the hairdresser. Every golden wave was perfectly set and smooth, and she favored the more elaborate styles. Once, long ago, he had ruffled her hair with both hands just after she had had it set, saying, "Why can't you let it be natural? It's beautiful in its own right," and she had been so furious with him and for so long that he had never interfered with it again. She was now wearing the blue house dress she usually wore in the evening, and a length of blue chiffon was swathed about her neck. The scars on her face she could not hide, those on her neck she could, unless the scarf got out of place. He wished she wouldn't always wear blue, but she considered it the only right color for blondes.

"How is the boy?" he asked. "And how's mother?"

"They're both well. Your mother'll be down as soon as she's finished putting the boy to bed. She took him to the clinic today. They say his physical health's perfect."

She spoke almost with resentment, as if she thought good health wasted in that quarter.

"No improvement otherwise, I suppose?"

"Oh, no. And they say we needn't expect any. Of course your mother is convinced he speaks intelligibly sometimes.

131

He doesn't make sentences, of course, she admits that, but he does seem to get hold of a word now and then. I only got your letter from Washington yesterday. Look, I made a new shade for the lamp. It's pretty, isn't it?"

They were in the living room now, and he wondered how he—and indeed all three of them—could endure that confined little space, which now seemed half its previous size. One corner of the room was taken up by the television set, and the furniture was so arranged as to seat the onlookers squarely in front of it.

"It's a very nice shade. You're getting on."

"I think I have quite a flair," she said. "This is only the third one I've made. I gave the first to Edna and the second one to Mumsie."

She had only lately taken to speaking of her mother in this way. She was inclined, of late years, to make much of her family, as if driven into closer accord with them by the increasing distance between her and Murray. It was true that they rarely saw Mrs. Folsom, though Sibyl wrote to her and received letters from her fairly frequently. Mrs. Folsom would very rarely leave Stoke-on-Trent. She was like a woman who has committed some foolish act she cannot explain, and wishes to hide herself because of it. Mr. Folsom, Sibyl reported, made her very unhappy, and so she chose to live like a rabbit in its burrow, but if that was the way she wanted it, her devoted daughter would just have to put up with it.

Her brother Edgar, Murray had seen only once. He wrote short letters at long intervals and warned his sister not to expect to see him in the near future. After knocking about the world so long, he said, the old country got him down. He didn't care if he never saw England, home and beauty again. Anyone could have the lot as far as he was concerned. Lord Holford Murray had never laid eyes on, nor had Sibyl since her girlhood. Murray wondered if Lord Holford could be another "poor Tom." It seemed probable. All he knew about

132

him was that he was a recluse who was companioned by one old manservant, and lived in what had once been the coach house before the property was sold and parceled out into building lots; also that in his youth he had squandered everything he could get his hands on.

He took his suitcase upstairs, and his mother came out of Martin's room, closing the door softly behind her. He kissed her and she said in her dry, unemotional way that she was glad he was back. She seemed to him older, smaller, softer than when he had kissed her last. Keeping her voice low she told him she had put the boy to bed early because his visits to the clinic always tired him. She thought they frightened him as well.

"I doubt they're doing him little good, poor lad. Will you go in and see him, Murray, maybe in a quarter of an hour? He'll be asleep then."

The little bedroom next to Sibyl's and his own had nothing boyish in it, not a trophy, not a seashell nor a school flag, not even a boy's book. It was like a small hospital room except that over the bed his mother had hung, for some reason of her own, an old yellowed photograph of the vicarage at King's Baddeley. Murray himself, as a boy of about Martin's age, was to be seen cleaning his father's bicycle beside the front door.

Martin was asleep. He fell asleep, as a rule, as soon as his head touched the pillow, and Murray had no wish for him to wake. Asleep he seemed a promising lad, and what was not there could for the moment be ignored. Looking at him Murray realized, with a feeling of guilt, that over the years he had gradually been growing accustomed to what had once been an intolerable grief. So the human creature learns, without conscious effort, he thought, to build its carapace. As he turned away he wondered, as he had often wondered before, how things would have been between Sibyl and himself if their son had been normal. Would they have made something more than tolerable, something good, of their life together?

The accident, presumably, would not have happened, they would have had other children, things would have taken an entirely different course.

He went downstairs again and his mother told him that dinner was ready.

"It's different getting a meal when there's a man in the house," she said, as they sat down. "Sibyl and I don't care what we eat, and Martin has no preferences, poor lad."

Neither of the two women asked him any questions about New York or his visit to Washington, or even about his flights across the Atlantic. What they had needed to know about these things they had got from his letters, though he suspected that in Sibyl's case this lack of any sign of interest was deliberate. She had gradually learned to show indifference toward all that he did. As to his business life, it was too closely connected in her mind with Charles Kendrick to be spoken of without bitterness and dislike. She would never of her own accord make any reference to it.

"What have you been doing?" Murray asked. "Have you seen much of Edna and Hugh?"

"No, not a lot," Sibyl answered, but Mrs. Logan added, "They came to dinner here one night. It was last week. We had roast beef from Chirk's, a really nice tender piece. I think they enjoyed it, don't you, Sibyl?"

"Oh," Sibyl said, "it's a treat for Edna just to eat a meal she hasn't cooked herself. We sat and looked at television afterwards. The Brains Trust was really good that night, and there was a play we all liked."

Had they been to any cinemas? Murray then asked.

"We took Martin to that Walt Disney film," Sibyl said. "They think it's good for him to go sometimes. I don't think he took in anything but he did look at it most of the time; you know, with that vacant stare of his."

"I'm sure he noticed that funny little animal," Mrs. Logan remarked.

134

"It's hard to tell," Murray said.

"I've made some new friends," Sybil then told him. "A couple who live in Merrow Close, named Graham. I've often seen her, and him too sometimes, out shopping, so they've got used to me. You know, it wasn't like meeting people who'd never seen me before. They're quite nice, and she's clever. She draws and paints. I wish I could. She says it takes your mind off everything else."

"Perhaps you can," Murray said. "You've never tried. Buy yourself some painting materials, or shall I get them for you in London?"

"Oh," she said casually, as if the subject no longer interested her, "I suppose I could get them at Shepperton's if I wanted to, but what's the use?"

"I'm sure she could paint if she tried," Mrs. Logan said.

"Please don't speak of me when I'm in the room as 'she,'" Sibyl said sharply. "You know I hate it."

Mrs. Logan hastened to say, "I'm sorry, dear. It just slipped out without my thinking."

"You can speak of Martin in the third person when he's in the room if you like," Sibyl went on, "but I'm not quite an idiot yet."

Murray was accustomed to these little flare-ups and found it best to ignore them. To remonstrate with Sibyl was dangerous.

"What does Graham do?" he asked.

"He's in some sort of stockbroking firm. They did tell me, but I forget. They've got a Jaguar."

It was absurd, he thought, how the mere name of a car brought it all back to him. Once again he was sitting beside Christine driving through Central Park and over to the Hudson.

"At least you can say you've seen the Hudson," she was saying, and he had glanced at the river, dark except for the reflection of the sunset's afterglow and the myriad lights reflected from its banks. Now it was no longer true that he had lost

135

something he had never had; for a brief time he had had it, and the sense of deprivation was a heavy one.

"Ask them in for a drink one evening," he forced himself to say.

"Oh, well, we'll see," she said, but he knew it had been in her mind.

Later when they were upstairs undressing, he said to her, and he had no idea why he said it, "Sibyl, let's go abroad somewhere this year, in September perhaps. Anywhere you like. You haven't been away from Morden for longer than I like to think. Wouldn't you like to go to Paris, and then perhaps to Brittany? Or we could go to Rome. Never mind the expense, we won't think about that. Anyway, we can manage it. It would do us both good to get away."

"You've just been away," she pointed out.

"Yes, but I want you to go."

She was putting on the blue silk dressing gown he had bought for her when she was in the hospital. It was old now, and had been cleaned many times, but she would not part with it. She wore it, he was sure, as a reminder, if he were in danger of needing a reminder.

"I shall never go abroad," she said with finality. "For one thing it wouldn't give either of us any pleasure, and for another, you know very well I can't bear to be among strangers. I'd suffer a hundred times a day."

"Oh, Sibyl," he said, but he spoke gently, "surely you exaggerate. Must you care so terribly what people think? Strangers, who can't possibly matter to you?"

"It's no good talking about it," she answered, "though I suppose suggesting it makes you feel generous. Otherwise you wouldn't do it, knowing how I feel."

"You know very well," he said, "that I would give you any happiness I could."

"That's a word that has nothing to do with me," she re-

136

plied. "And there's something I want to say to you. I've been thinking about it since you've been away. I don't know if you're interested in any other woman but I hope you are, because, naturally, it's all the same to me."

She was at her dressing table now, adjusting a hair net to keep the elaborate waves of her thick blond hair in place. It was a sight he had always disliked, and he averted his eyes.

"Need we talk about that on my first night at home?"

"Why not?" she asked. "We're adults, aren't we? It's something I've been meaning to say for a long time. I suppose I've just been assuming all along that if you wanted to have an affair with someone you would anyway, but it seemed more sensible to say so, that's all."

"Well, let's not give it any thought," he said. "It's time we were in bed and asleep."

She went on, "It's just that if I can't be happy there's no reason why you shouldn't be. That's all I wanted to say. And I'm glad you're back. It's been duller than ever with you away."

"I'm grateful to you for saying so," he told her, and gave her shoulder a little pat.

She got up, holding the dressing gown around her, and the hardness had gone from her face. "You may not think it, but I'd kill the bitterness in me if I could," she told him, and she had never said this before. "The worst of it is, I can't. It's a many-headed monster. You'll just have to put up with it, I'm afraid."

He knew very well he would have to do just that, and there was no need for her to tell him.

"You've every right to be bitter, Sibyl," he said. "Tell me, did the gloves and stockings fit?"

"Well, if I'm to be honest, they were a size too small for me, so I gave them to Edna. I was sure you wouldn't mind."

"I don't mind," he said, "but I'm sorry."

"I'll give you my measurements," she told him, "just in case you go away again."

It was June before a letter came from Christine, and then one day it lay on his desk marked "Personal." When he picked it up his heart was beating as if he had just run up three flights of stairs and he knew then how much his love for this young woman had been growing since the day they had parted in front of the restaurant. He was reluctant to open the letter there and then for fear of interruptions, but he was lunching with Dick Bayliss and a man named Erridge, who was the head of a small firm which published chiefly educational books and had lately launched a new system of shorthand which was meeting with some success. He had tried the system himself and thought so well of it that he had brought it to Charles's attention, suggesting that Atlantic House (London) should, if they could, buy the firm outright. Following this lunch there would be a board meeting. He could, it was true, read it on the underground going home, but that did not seem the best place, nor could he be sure of getting a seat. Better risk interruptions, therefore, and open it now. Greedily, hungrily, he sat down to read.

He had never seen Christine's writing before and was relieved to find that it was first of all easily legible. In fact it was clear, open, even childish. It was written on hotel notepaper, and he wondered for an instant if she were in hiding again as Mrs. Charles Darnay, but this thought was quickly dispelled.

Dear Murray,

Let me say at once that I have not reassumed my disguise. I am just up for the night for a routine checkup, this time with my heart specialist, as I've recently recovered from a rather troublesome bronchial attack. Thank heaven it wasn't caused by any folly of my own! Sam, anticipating the summer, installed air conditioning in my bedroom, which is something I've never wanted myself.

We had a sudden hot spell in May; it was turned on and I caught a cold. Luckily the bronchial attack which followed wasn't as severe as some I've had, and here I am, still alive. As soon as I have written to you I will have a light dinner in my room and go to bed. Sam is in Pittsburgh so couldn't come with me, but Mary Doyle is here and we go home tomorrow. In the end I hadn't the heart to send her away as I'd planned to do, and I am still pretty much under her eye, but she fusses rather less than she used to.

I feel that you and only you have a right to know how things are, and perhaps writing about it to you will help me to discover the truth. I can honestly say, I think, that things are better than they were, though that doesn't mean I don't have to put up a pretty constant fight for such precious independence as I need in order to breathe. In fact I now take a kind of mean pleasure in outwitting both Sam and Mary Doyle. During May—it was a lovely spring—I would pretend I was going to see someone in the neighborhood and instead I would buy a few sandwiches and a bottle of milk and go off in the car to explore the country. This leads to a lot of fibbing—no, to a lot of lying—which I regret, and I am glad of this opportunity of confessing it to you. And, of course, one of these days I shall be found out and Sam will be terribly upset. You see, they still won't let me go anywhere alone, and I do so love being alone! To take some woman friend with me whose mind is on her children and her home, and feels her body ought to be there too, would spoil everything. I have had some wonderful days and intend to go on having them.

I wish you had seen more of Connecticut. Once you get away from the towns it is very beautiful and full of old farms and orchards and crumbling stone walls that are only held together by the wild grapevines. Later in the year the trees will blaze with color and there will be a smell of apples and cider making and the autumn haze will be perfumed by the smoke of bonfires of fallen leaves. It's then that New England is at its very best.

What news have I to tell you? Well, there is this. Lately my mother has been trying to make friends with me, though in a curious way, as you will see. She invites herself to lunch on Sundays and drives here from New York in her enormous Cadillac with a conceited Puerto Rican chauffeur whom Gordon and Maggie heartily dislike. She sits and talks to me and tells me how much she had to put up with from my dear father, in an attempt to win me away from him and from his memory. Why she has suddenly begun to take this interest in me, I don't know. I sit and look at her and wonder what, if anything, I have inherited from her. Nothing, I think, but my conviction that while one lives one should live as fully and consciously as possible, though she and I would go about this in entirely different ways. She fills me with dismay, and a kind of dread. I don't know what she might be able to do to me if she wanted to badly enough. I suppose there is always an invisible umbilical cord between mother and daughter, no matter how little they may love each other, and she doesn't, I am certain, love me. When I was a child and a young girl she did everything to make me unhappy. So these are very trying visits and we are wondering how we can decently put a stop to them, and are much afraid that we can't.

Am I glad I came back? Murray, I don't know. In one way I am because it put an end to Sam's misery, but if I thought that he would be able to remake his life with someone who could make him as confidently happy as he deserves to be, I might not stay. But I am fearful of you know what. My dreams of travel and fresh experience seem as far away as ever. Frederick only goes to the office once or twice a week now, and Sam has taken on more and more of his responsibilities in addition to his own. And this is something you must not tell Charles Kendrick or anyone—Frederick has had another, less serious, attack, though at his age, of course, any such attack is serious. His anxiety to get better and see Atlantic House on a sounder financial basis before he goes is very touching. I need hardly tell you that his anxiety isn't for himself. I think, now that Sam and I are together again, that he is ready to go, although he longs to get to England once more if the doctors will let him.

All this is saddening. One more sadness and then I have finished. Nothing more has ever been heard of my dear, dear Seth. If Sam had notified the police at once—but I'm the last person to blame him for not thinking of it, knowing as I do that his mind was wholly taken up with other matters. I never go out in the car without hoping I may see my beautiful red dog, I never hear a bark at night without instantly thinking, "Can that be Seth? Has he found his way back at last?" I still believe he was stolen. Sam wants me to get another, but of course I cannot bear the thought.

As for the lake and the ducks, they ought to mean a great deal to me and give me comfort, and I am a wretch because it gives me more pleasure to find some little natural lake in the woods that is my own discovery. I don't know why I risk putting you against me like this because I so badly want and need your friendship; yes, I need it, I need it. So bear with me, won't you?

Writing to you is giving me a great and probably selfish satisfaction. I am wondering if writing to me would do the same for you. But it's a pleasure I must do without. Sam is very fond of you, but it might hurt him to know that I have told you so much. One day perhaps I may be able to confess to him that I've given you more of my confidence than perhaps I should have done, and trust that he'll make little of it and forgive me. I told him, by the way, that I was going to write to you, and he said "Give him my love."

All the same, I long to hear from you. Your story has taken hold of me in a way you probably haven't guessed. I've thought about it so much that I believe I've thought myself right into your daily life, and if you can think of me as an invisible companion at your side, you won't be far wrong.

She signed herself, "Yours always, Christine."

He was as shaken by this letter as if he had been close to a dangerous explosion which had left him half stunned and wholly deafened. He did not hear the noise of traffic or the unloading of vans in the street below, nor any sound in the building. As for seeing, he saw nothing but the letter in his hands. He sat in a trance, unable to stir. Only his mind was active, though in trancelike state, fixed upon one thing only —one marvelous thing. She had not, he was sure, meant to tell him, but she had as good as told him that she both loved and needed him. As for him, he knew that he loved her totally, he was entirely overwhelmed now by a single passion, his whole being brimmed with a single emotion. The thing was beyond doubt, beyond argument, beyond reason; he loved Sam's wife. There could be no outcome, no future, no completion and he did not at this stage want or contemplate them. He was entirely possessed by the new, the total experience of loving; total because it was rounded out and made whole by the conviction that he was loved.

His callow and ignorant involvement with Sibyl, his early affection for her, which had been based chiefly on simple sexual attraction plus availability, had never been love or, if it had, it had not been adult love. He had never, after the first few years, mistaken it for adult love. Nor had he mistaken for love what had also been almost entirely sexual and equally due to availability—his five-year-old connection with Irma Brand, Australian-born and divorced from an Australian airman. She had a one-room flat in Chelsea and was the cause of his getting home late about once a week. If Sibyl guessed—and her remarks on the night he had returned from New York made him suppose that she did—she had not troubled her head, nor cared. He had not even been obliged to offer any explanation of why he had kept dinner waiting, or dined in London, a mere apology for any inconvenience he might have caused having sufficed.

But now he knew he would go to see Irma only once more and then put an end to a connection that was on both sides wholly practical, with the minimum of emotional complication. He liked her for her good nature, and because she made him laugh, for she was an actress with an amusing gift for mimicry, though she never got anything but small parts and was often out of work. She would never accept anything from him except an occasional bottle of perfume, but it had to be Balmain, Chanel or Dior. She was fond of and wanted to marry an Australian businessman who had a wife with whom he was unhappy. He was trying to obtain a divorce, but meanwhile he was twelve thousand miles away and she was glad of

Murray's visits. If it had not been for Christine's letter, he knew he would have continued to see Irma. It was one thing to love a woman without a thought of his love being returned; it seemed to him a wholly different thing to have become the object of her love, and he was prepared for any sacrifice, any self-immolation that such a miracle might indicate. The very idea of self-immolation gave him a feeling of calm happiness.

It was a shock when the telephone rang, just beside his elbow. It was Miss Purchase, from her little room next to his, to say that Mr. Bayliss was on the phone and would like to speak to him.

"I say, Murray," Dick Bayliss said, and his speech was a pure distillation of Eton and of Balliol, "I've just been talking to Charles. He's quite shocked at the idea of our lunching Erridge in the purlieus of Soho. He says that in all his forty years of publishing he's never failed to get what he wanted when he took people to lunch at the Savoy Grill. It's a kind of mystique with Charles, and it shows that he wants this thing to go through. One up to you, my boy. You nosed it out. I have to be in the West End this morning, so we'll meet at the Savoy Grill at a quarter to one. Right?"

"Right," said Murray, and Dick Bayliss rang off.

X 🖋

ALL through July and August she
was what she had said she would be, an invisible companion
at his side. So much so that he began to be aware of changes
taking place in him that seemed not to be due to any efforts
of his own will—modifications of character that he had long
ago given up hope of achieving. He found he was growing
more and more indifferent to what he believed other people
thought of him. Christine's letters, intimate, frank, affectionate and now frequent, gave him the feeling of having been,
in every sense of the word, promoted. He became indifferent
to Dick Bayliss's little gibes—his was the kind of wit that is best
displayed at someone else's expense—and to his unconcealed
lack of any desire for his company outside of office hours.
Dick Bayliss, he thought, played the same part in his adult
life that Tom Remenham had played in his youth, but he
was ceasing to care. He was even losing sight of his own
picture of himself as a socially untutored suburbanite, who
carried on his back a repulsive burden of tragedy. He now saw

himself chiefly in relation to Christine, and this could only give him happiness. Nor was this happiness dimmed by any feelings of guilt toward Sam. He could not, even when he tried, summon them up. There was no encroachment, he was certain of that. The terms on which he and Christine met and communicated with each other could not be breathed upon by doubt or criticism.

But with every letter she wrote she seemed to come nearer.

I'm writing this sitting by the lake. I'm so glad you saw it, it makes it still easier to write to you here. The ducks are making their pleasant noise and the day is so hot and still that the reflections hardly quiver and only the ducks themselves disturb its glassy surface.

I'm much the same, no worse, no better, though lately I have been feeling very lifeless. I wonder why it is that I felt a different person when I was with my sister in Mexico, or staying alone at a hotel? I felt alive then. It's all part of my natural contrariness, I suppose, that things that they say I mustn't do seem to do me good.

A week later she wrote:

I'm reading more than ever. It's about all I do now, as I haven't got the energy to go for trips in the car. As I think I told you recently, I've become deeply interested in astronomy, and this is thanks chiefly to your Fred Hoyle, though I've been reading others as well. I love being reduced to nothing at all in the vast scheme of things, or whatever you like to call our universe, and yet at the same time to have the feeling—no, the conviction—that somewhere there's a baffling contradiction, and that we are at one and the same time of no importance at all and all-important. I can't help believing—(at least at moments, not all the time)—that each of us is the center of the universe, and that this is somehow valid. But how? How can this be so, and in what sense? If only I could lay hold of even a glimmering of understanding! Sometimes I feel that as long as there's any life, any consciousness, no matter how simple, left on earth, we all, all exist in it. This sounds naïve, I expect, and I'm

145

sure it is. It's very hard to write these things. I wish you could help me. I'm sure you're much nearer some understanding of the whys of life than I am. You must tell me when we meet—for I am determined that we shall meet.

In August she wrote him a curious letter:

I had a vivid dream the other night, and I do wish it could come true. I dreamt that I was able to be of some help to you, and not only to you but to Sibyl as well. I wonder if she's like my dream? Her eyes were a very vivid blue, and there was something very striking, perhaps even a little formidable about her. At the same time I got an impression of a terrible melancholy and loneliness that she couldn't communicate. But on the whole it was an agreeable dream because in some way I was able to do good. I felt like a goddess descending from a cloud with gifts and blessings. All of which at least shows how much I have been thinking of you. How sad for me that the one person I long to talk to lives three thousand miles away!

At the end of August he received a letter—the envelopes were always typewritten and posted in New York—giving him news he could scarcely credit. She was coming to England.

"I'm making my plans very fast," she wrote, and he could judge her state of excitement by the unevenness of her handwriting:

I'm arriving on September 4th by boat (Sam thinks the sea trip may do me good). He's letting me go for a variety of reasons, the chief one being that I've fallen into a state of lassitude and depression that I can't pull myself out of. My mind beats aimlessly about like a bird in a confined space doing itself nothing but harm. For one thing, Murray, it now seems fairly certain that I shall never have a child, if I'm to believe the doctors. I've always supposed that, given the chance, I would have one quite easily, but that doesn't appear to be the case and the hope I've cherished for so long has vanished. I'm not sleeping and I'm finding the heat very hard to

146

bear. I don't feel like seeing anyone, least of all my mother who for some reason of her own is spending August in New York. I can't even put up with the devotion of the small boy from next door who is my most faithful visitor and whom I've twice sent home in tears. So Sam realizes I have to go away and he's consented to my going to England. He can't come with me but he may fly over later, stay for a while, and bring me back. I've been lucky enough to get a room at the Ritz for a few days, so call for me on the 5th if you possibly can and take me to lunch. I do hope you'll be free! My mother and I stayed at the Ritz once when we spent a few days in London before going on to Paris, and for that reason my recollections of it aren't very happy, but Sam always stays there and wants me to. So please, if you can, meet me in the hall near the side entrance, just by the elevator. I remember it very well because my mother said something so unkind to me there that I burst into tears.

Now I've got more to tell you. I've decided to stay in a furnished house in Surrey for a month or so. It belongs to a cousin of Sam's who married an Englishman and they're spending the summer over here, so it's being lent to me. They say it will be quiet and that their two servants, a married couple, will be kind to me. I hope it isn't far from where you live so that we can meet often. I shall have to have a car, of course, but I can see to that when I get there.

I can't help feeling that four or five days at sea is a terrible waste of time! I'd fly over if I could. Charles Kendrick will know about my coming as soon as you get this, and Sam is telling him that I don't want to be entertained in any way or be a bother to anybody, and that I am very tired. It's only a little more than a week before I'll see you. Think of it!

He could think of little else, but not all his thoughts were happy. The mere fact that she would soon be there in the flesh and as Mrs. Sam Bonner threatened to put a distance between them, and of this he was almost superstitiously afraid. He was now forced to remember, among other things he would prefer to forget, that she was a rich woman able to stay at luxury hotels, hire cars, do anything, in short, that she wished to do. This aspect of her had not, until now, obtruded itself. He feared, and the fear was real and peace-destroying, that there would be nothing left of Mrs. Charles Darnay, who had for a time lived nowhere and had given him, from her isolation and loneliness, a frank, impulsive, almost schoolgirlish affection which, helped on by her letters to him, had grown into love, or something very much like love. He dreaded the discovery, which now seemed to him inevitable, that he had been living in a fragile, prismatic world which her coming might easily wreck. And yet, in spite of this dread, he longed for it with a mounting excitement and intensity.

He was puzzled to know, however, how she could have imagined that there could be any going and coming between the house she would occupy in Surrey and Southview. This seemed to him so totally impossible and even undesirable— for he had no wish that she should actually see the narrowness and bareness of his life—that he thought her, though with all tenderness, a builder of fairy tales to have considered it at all.

Two days after he received this letter, Charles took him out to lunch. He told him that the taking over of Erridge and Company had gone ahead smoothly.

"You did a good thing," he said, "when you brought it to my attention. In its modest way it's a money-maker, and those shorthand books are still selling like hot cakes, and will go on selling. I propose to put Erridge, as I think you know, at the head of the Education Department if the board agrees, and I think it will. Our Education Department badly needs an overhaul, and he's the man to do it. Later, perhaps when Dick Bayliss retires, he can go on the board."

"Is Dick Bayliss really thinking of retiring?" Murray asked.

"Well, not yet, of course, but perhaps in a year or two. His back is giving him a lot of trouble," Charles said. "I think it accounts for his irritability. He wants to devote his time to writing. His book on the Hittites will never be finished as long as he's with us, and he says that when he retires he can

148

write in bed. By the way, did you know that *So Short a Lease* is going to be given the 'Book of the Year' prize? I only heard yesterday. He's very cock-a-hoop about it."

"I hadn't heard," Murray said. "That's excellent. It ought to set Kronkite up, though I don't know that he needs setting up."

"He does not," Charles said. "As conceited a fellow as ever I met. Dick Bayliss never stops reminding me that I wanted to turn the book down. Well, I still don't like it, but the fact is there aren't many novels today that I can work up any real enthusiasm for. You oughtn't to agree with me, you're still a young man. However, I console myself with the thought that better history and biography have never been written."

"Sam prophesied that it would do well in America, too, and it certainly has," Murray remarked.

"Yes, yes, I know, you all guessed better than I did," Charles said. "Don't rub it in. By the way, speaking of Sam, did you happen to meet his wife when you were there? She doesn't go about much, so the chances are you didn't."

"As it happens," Murray said, with a constraint he hoped Charles would not notice, "I did meet her. It was at Frederick Bonner's house one afternoon. She'd called there to see him."

"We none of us know her at all well," Charles said. "I only met her that time when she was taken so ill in Edinburgh and I flew up there to see if I could help. The poor things were on their honeymoon. She very nearly died, and when I saw her she looked like a ghost, though I'm bound to say a very attractive one. I was much taken with her. The general opinion seems to be that she's given Sam more worry than happiness, though I imagine her poor health would account for that. Anyhow, the point is this: she's arriving here Thursday of next week. I thought of giving a dinner party for her, but Sam says she's very tired and only wants to be quiet. Perhaps I can persuade her to have lunch with some of us one day and if so, I hope you'll come."

149

"I will, most certainly," Murray said, and at the same time he wondered how, when the time came, he could avoid something so unbearable and so conducive to self-betrayal. He then said, to change the subject, "How is Aunt Lily? I hope she's well. Please give her my love."

"Lily's very well, barring the arthritis, and busier than ever. The way she gets about is a marvel to me. Just now she's engaged in some experiments with E.S.P., which of course is right up her street. They don't have to prove to me that she has abnormal perceptions. It's a game we often play together. Only last week I chose a card at random out of the pack, kept it in my pocket all day and when I got home that night asked her what it was. She said, 'The nine of spades.' Then she corrected herself and said, 'No, I meant the ten of spades.' It was the ten of spades. She's a wonderful woman. How is your mother, Murray? We never see her nowadays."

"She's well," Murray said. "I'm afraid her time is mostly taken up with Martin. She devotes herself to him completely."

"I know," Charles said, "and what a blessing she does! Give her our love. And how is Sibyl?"

"Oh," Murray said, "she's much the same. She still won't go anywhere. I've given up all hope of persuading her."

"She's a case for a psychiatrist, I suppose," Charles said. "Those scars are much more internal than external. But I suppose she'd never go to one."

"No," Murray said. "I've often discussed it with her. She scoffs at the whole idea."

"You know," Charles said, "Lily and I often feel we're to blame for a good deal because when you first brought her to the house we treated her rather coldly. I've never said this to you before, but we both regret it very much. We had some idea of discouraging you. It was a kind of negative interference, and as I look back it was unfortunate, though well meant. I'm afraid she felt it and has never forgiven us."

150

"She did feel it," Murray said, "but that's all past history now."

"Still," Charles said, "history is history and the effects of it have to be reckoned with. We blame ourselves very much."

Murray could make no answer, and Charles did not pursue the subject.

XI ✍

CHRISTINE, he was sure, had no idea that her asking to be taken to lunch on the day after her arrival presented a difficulty. If they were seen lunching together, say by Charles or possibly Dick Bayliss, who might conceivably have met her on one of his visits to New York, it would cause comment and understandable surprise. It was highly unlikely that they would be seen, but he had to reckon with the possibility. All the same, he decided not to take her to some obscure little place but to order a table at the best restaurant he knew and hope that luck would be with them. He wrote her a letter, "to await arrival" and said he would be at the hotel at a quarter to one. He hesitated for some time over the wording of it, then decided to say what came to him most naturally.

"I still can't convince myself," he wrote, "that I'll actually see you and talk to you in two days' time, but I shall be there, waiting by the lift, and if you don't step out of it I'll know I've simply dreamt the whole thing."

To his regret it was a cool, cloudy day with the prospect of rain. Sibyl had had one of her most wakeful and restless nights and in consequence he had slept badly. When he asked her what had kept her from sleeping, she said, "Oh, it was just one of those nights when I lie awake wishing I'd never been born and regretting every single thing I've ever done."

At breakfast when he inquired, out of habit, what she was planning to do that day, she answered, "Do? What do I ever do? And why should today be different from other days? I'm going to get through it as best I can, I suppose."

It was in his mind that he ought to try to prepare Sibyl and his mother for a possible meeting with Christine, though this still seemed to him an unlikely and undesirable thing. The house she would occupy was about fifteen miles away, at Ifield, and she might, he supposed, decide to pay a visit to Southview. The thought made him nervous and apprehensive. He did not want Sibyl to meet her and feared he knew not what. He said, feeling his way, "You've both heard me speak of Sam Bonner, Frederick Bonner's son."

"The one you went to Paris with once or twice?" Sibyl asked. "Yes. Why, is he over here?"

"No," Murray said, grateful for her help, "but his wife is." He saw his mother glance up at him, briefly. "She hasn't been well, and Sam thought it would be good for her to come. It's been very hot over there this summer, and I gather it's been too much for her."

"What's wrong with her?" Sibyl asked indifferently.

"She had t.b. as a girl, and she's had lung operations and so on. She's been lent a house near Ifield for a while, which isn't so very far from here. It might be a kindness to see something of her or find out if we can help her in any way. Sam Bonner has been a good friend to me."

"I prefer to leave that entirely to you," Sibyl told him. "You know very well how I feel about meeting complete strangers.

153

Do whatever you think you ought to do but please leave me out of it." She then turned to Mrs. Logan. "Perhaps you'd like to meet her, Mrs. L."

Mrs. Logan was helping the boy with his breakfast. He was learning to feed himself a little, but precariously. She answered, "I've no time for visits, Sibyl. Just let me be with Martin. We're always company for each other."

"Well," Murray said, "I only mentioned it in case she asks us to go and see her. She may not, which would simplify matters."

"I suppose you met her in New York," Sibyl said, turning away from the sight of Martin's porridge-smeared chin.

"Yes. I went out to their house in Connecticut. I think I told you about it."

"I've hardly ever met any Americans," Sibyl said, and the subject was then dropped, but Murray felt he had done what he could.

When Christine came out of the elevator he saw, with pleasure, that she was wearing the same neat black suit and lacy white blouse that she had worn at lunch in New York, and that she was again hatless. He guessed that she had done this with deliberate intent, knowing that he would be obsessed, as he was obsessed, by the dread of finding her in some way different. She held out both hands to him, and he heard once again the familiar little clash of coins. Her first words, and she spoke them triumphantly, were "Everything's exactly as I hoped it would be."

He could do no more than stammer, all his gladness in his eyes, "I've got a taxi waiting."

"Good. Then let's get into it quick. I've got so much to say to you."

They went through the revolving doors and out into a light spatter of rain. Instead of waiting under shelter for the com-

154

missionaire to summon the waiting taxi she went out to the pavement and lifted up her face.

"How cool it is!" she said, smiling. "It's so deliciously cool."

When they were in the taxi she took his hand and held it for a moment, tightly, looking out of the window as she did so. When she turned to him he saw that there were tears in her eyes.

"Don't take any notice," she said, with trembling lips. "I'm just so happy to be here, to be away from it all. From my mother, from our dear Sam, from everything. To be free again." She touched her eyes with her handkerchief. "And not least of all, to be with you. I could hardly believe it could happen, and now it has. There, that's over now. Sam was right about the boat. It did me good. I slept well, and last night I never woke once."

"I'm so glad. I grudged every day that you were on that boat, but I don't now. I've been longing for this, Christine, but I've been dreading it too."

"I know that," she said. "But everything's going to be all right. You must trust me, Murray."

"I do. I might have known. You have a way of annihilating time and distance."

She looked at him and smiled. "We won't talk about plans yet. How do you think I look? I've lost five pounds, but that was partly the heat. Now I must put them on again."

"I'd like to see you about double your present weight," he said, and it was the first personal comment he had ever made to her. He had already observed, with a pang of fear, her pallor and the delicate hollow under her chin.

"Oh, not quite double," she said. "Murray, it's been a terrible blank not hearing from you all this time, but you did understand, didn't you?"

"Of course. Your letters were my one delight. You can imagine how I longed to answer them."

"I wish," she said, "I weren't driven into so many deceptions. I think 'driven' is the right word. It's just that we entered so quickly and so deeply into each other's lives, and it's impossible to explain to anyone else just how or why it happened."

He answered, looking down, "I don't think miracles are meant to be explained."

"No," she agreed, "nor shared, when they're the experience of two people. There's another reason why I'm glad I came by boat. I had time to do a lot of thinking. I believe I've succeeded in thinking this strange thing that's happened to us right through to my own satisfaction."

"I haven't even tried," he said, and her words had sent a tremor of delight through him.

"It's even harder for you. Will you trust me to lead this private expedition of ours into no danger? I promise I'll keep my eyes wide open. I've only once gone into anything blindly and that was out of despair."

"Yes," he said, "I know. We'll trust each other."

"And we'll play fair," she said, "and not encroach, but also not allow ourselves to be encroached upon." She smiled at him with a kind of radiance. "We have certain rights, too. Don't you agree, Murray?"

"I do," he said, and he took one of her hands and raised it to his cheek. "I'd die for them," he said.

At the restaurant he did not even glance about him to see if there was anyone there he knew. Again, as at the restaurant in New York, they sat side by side, but this time he felt no shyness, no awkwardness at all. He was completely in his own element, and it was a completely new sensation.

She said she realized it would be difficult for them to meet often while she was in London, but she hoped they could dine together one night.

"The bigger problem is," she said, "how to see each other when I'm at Ifield. But I have a plan and I hope you'll agree

156

to it. And my plan includes Sibyl. I want to know her. Don't think it's conceited of me, but I have an idea I could make her accept me and even like me. In a way, you know, we've got a good deal in common. The biggest obstacle, I imagine, will be to get her to meet me in the first place, but if we could manage that, and I'm sure we can, I believe I could make a friend of her. Do you think that's so impossible?"

"If not impossible," he answered, "very improbable."

"But somehow we *must* persuade her," she insisted, and he knew it was her way to regard obstacles as challenges to her ingenuity and her wits. "You must let me come to your house first, so that I can meet her on her own ground. I want to meet your mother too, and Martin. Then, after that, perhaps you and Sibyl would spend a weekend with me, but we can go into that later."

"Oh, Christine," he said, in a low voice, "it wouldn't work, it wouldn't work."

She ignored this.

"So," she said, "what I'd like to do if you'll let me, would be to come to tea on a Saturday or Sunday, but soon, please."

"Sibyl might go to her room and refuse to come down."

"She might, but somehow I don't believe she would. Anyway, we must try. You'll see why it's so important presently."

"What are you keeping up your sleeve?" he asked, and he knew as he asked it that whatever she wanted him to do he would do, regardless of his own doubts.

She turned her bright and candid eyes upon him.

"Well, now listen and I'll tell you. This is my plan. I want to make Sibyl like me and trust me so that you'll both come with me on a holiday. First to Rome, then to Greece. Murray, I must go to Greece. Suppose I shouldn't survive another winter? I must go, and I want to go with you. And Sibyl, of course, must come too. Was my dream about her true? Isn't she terribly lonely and unhappy? I got such a feeling of *suffering* from it. Was it true?"

157

"It was true," he answered. "It oughtn't to be so, but it is. I mean, it needn't be so. She could have made something of her life; she could even now, but she won't. She never will."

"Well, let me try to help her," she pleaded. "Is that very presumptuous, to think I might?"

"It isn't presumptuous," he said. "It's just that you don't know her."

"But I shall soon. Murray, I've been planning all this for days, weeks. Don't say it's impossible. Don't, please. I've set my heart on it. And there may never be another chance."

The idea was so astonishing, so utterly impossible to visualize that he could only look at her and slowly shake his head.

"You'd have to transform her entirely," he said.

"No," she persisted, "not entirely. I feel she's got caught like a piece of bark in a stream when it meets some obstacle or gets into a backwater, and a touch might set her going again. I've thought about her so much. About the whole dreadful happening. And about Martin. I feel so sorry for her."

There was a moment's silence, then he said, "I don't think that what you want to do is possible."

"Don't *make* obstacles," she pleaded. "At least let's assume it's possible and go ahead. And, Murray, you know I'm a rich woman, don't you? Rich enough to be ashamed of being so rich and doing so little with my money. I subscribe to charities —you know, the usual things—and this trip, this holiday, it's something I long for. You'll help me, won't you? You'll do what you can. All the expenses would be mine, of course. You'd be my guests."

Smiling at her he shook his head. "I couldn't agree to that."

"Well, that could be as you liked. It isn't important."

He saw that she believed in the feasibility of her plan and pitied her because he was so sure it could never be brought about. There were too many reasons why it could not. Looking away from her he said, "Sibyl isn't a stupid woman. She'd want to know why. She'd assume she was merely being used."

"Oh," she cried, "I've thought of that, of course. That would be my job—to make her feel I wanted her, that her coming would give me pleasure. I'm even prepared for the things she's likely to say, the things I'd say if I were Sibyl. What I'm most troubled about is the thought of your mother staying behind with Martin alone. Would that be unkind? Would she mind?"

"She wouldn't mind that at all."

"Then that's one difficulty out of the way."

"And what," he said, "would Charles Kendrick think?"

"There are ways of arranging it so that it needn't surprise him or anyone. You'll think I do nothing but practice deceptions, but if I do, it's out of necessity. If you think it might cause talk, you and Sibyl could go first and I'd follow. We could meet in Rome. That would seem quite natural."

"And Sam?" It had to be asked. "What would you tell Sam?"

"Simply that I've talked to you, that you haven't had a holiday this year, and that we all three think of going to Rome and then Greece. Perhaps I could persuade him to fly to Athens and bring me back. I'd ask him to."

"It all begins to seem at least possible but for one thing," he said. "You'd never get Sibyl to co-operate with you. As to our being your guests, of course I couldn't allow that. We would pay our way. But even suppose the idea were workable, it's getting late in the day to make the arrangements."

"I thought we might leave the first week in October," she said. "Let's say the sixth."

He looked at her and smiled.

"So you'd got as far as that. Well, the whole thing depends on Sibyl. I've no hope at all that you can persuade her."

"At least I shall have a try," she told him. She opened her bag and took out a small diary. She turned over some pages and then showed it to him. He saw that she had underlined October 10 with a red pencil, and had written in ink,

"To Rome with Murray and Sibyl." This made him laugh, but she kept a serious face. She then turned back to September 5. Here she had written, "Lunch with Murray. Disclose plans. Then to Cooks, for bookings and hotels in Rome, Athens." He saw that she had written, under September 7, "Dinner with Murray (?)"

"Yes," he said. "That's quite feasible. We'll do that."

"And that isn't all," she told him and showed him that she had written under the next Sunday but one the words, "Tea with Murray and Sibyl." "That will be my first Sunday in Ifield," she said. "I'll get a good map and you must show me just where you live."

"It's all quite fantastic," he told her. "If it had been proposed by anyone but you I'd say it was utterly impossible. But I ought to warn you that if by some miracle you get Sibyl to agree to going abroad, she might be wretchedly unhappy when she got there, which would spoil it for all of us."

"All right," she said, putting away her diary. "I realize it's a big gamble, but I'm taking it with my eyes open, remember. If it doesn't work, it doesn't, and no one, I hope, will be any the worse. But at least we will have tried." Then she looked at him with a clear, smiling look. "I'm not going to pretend I wouldn't rather go with you alone, just the two of us. But that isn't possible. And if it would give Sibyl any happiness at all and help her to forget things for a while, I'd feel well rewarded."

He took her hand quickly and pressed it and let it go. That happiness, the happiness of going away together and alone, would never be for them. Nor, he was still convinced, would the lesser happiness of going with a third person, and that person Sibyl. He disbelieved in the whole project, but should he try to turn her from it, or let her do what she could?

As she was putting on her gloves before leaving the table, he remembered that he had not yet asked her about Seth. He said, "And the dog? Seth? Did you ever get any news of him?"

160

She turned to him a face suddenly sharpened by pain, made almost ugly by sorrow.

"I was hoping you wouldn't ask that," she said. She dropped her hands in her lap and seemed to let grief and memories of grief overwhelm her. Her lips quivered and for a moment she could say nothing.

"I'm sorry, Christine," he said. "I'm so sorry. Don't tell me now. I ought to have guessed."

"It was another reason," she said, "why I had to get away. He was found, starving, nearly dead. Tied up in an old shed, twenty miles away. Some boys—how can one understand such wickedness?"

"Don't," he pleaded, "don't speak of it any more."

"He died before I could get there. The police didn't dare to move him. They tried to feed him. They did what they could. I went with them to be sure it was Seth. He had just died."

He repeated helplessly, "I'm so sorry."

"I had to tell you sometime." She picked up her bag. "There's no defense against such suffering, is there? Against almost anything else, but not against that. It can't be borne."

He followed her through the restaurant in silence and stopped near the entrance to get his hat and umbrella. Outside she turned to him and held out her hand.

"Wait," he said, "I'll see you into a taxi. It's raining and you've no umbrella."

"I've never owned one in my life," she confessed.

A moment later the meter of the taxi was clicked down and she was gone. It was the end of their third meeting.

He walked back to the office trying to straighten out his thoughts. Joy and the sharpest of apprehensions contended together. He hardly dared think of the immediate future for he could not see at all where all this might lead, what part Sibyl might decide to play, what storms or icy coldnesses might lie ahead. Even supposing that the three of them actually

161

embarked upon this most improbable trip, what would Sibyl feel about the understanding that existed between Christine and himself? Could it be hidden from her? He thought not. What would she think of such a relationship however innocent, however—he searched for a word—however disembodied it might be? She was certain to feel excluded; then would follow resentment, jealousy and mistrust. Here surely, he told himself, he could not be wrong. As soon as she became aware of the deep accord between them, the whole adventure must founder, and founder in bitterness and anger.

That was putting it at its worst. On the other hand, there was the merest chance that, Christine being what she was, it might succeed. Her disarming friendliness, her trick of quickly establishing an easy relationship might work the necessary miracle. And for a while, for a brief while at least, he would see her daily. He made up his mind that he must either take a firm stand at once against everything Christine was proposing—and this might be the wiser course—or withdraw every objection and leave it all to her.

And what, he asked himself, by denying her her wishes would he be safeguarding? If things went wrong, as in all probability they would somewhere go wrong, would any of them be the worse off? What had they to lose? It seemed to him that the answer was, nothing. And this finally decided him. He would give Christine such help as he could and suppress his doubts. He would now try to act as if his household were no different from other households, as if the advent of a stranger were not an almost unheard-of thing, as if even the idea of a trip abroad in the company of a rich young woman who could not travel alone and who had certain claims upon their friendship might not be beyond the limits of possibility.

XII ✐

CHARLES invited Christine to lunch
and she agreed to go. When he asked Murray to join them he
accepted with fewer forebodings than he'd anticipated. He
knew now that he must trust Christine entirely, leaving everything to her skill, a skill that derived from candor, naturalness,
and above all a quick awareness of undertones. He guessed
that a youth spent with a loved father who at all costs was
bent on keeping his home outwardly at least a united one, and
with a mother who constantly threatened such happiness as
there was, must have made her sharply aware of emotional
temperatures, quick to perceive and forestall trouble. He
guessed, too, that she had played a lone hand in this collaboration with her father, that her sister had not helped. It had
made her watchful and observant, sensitive to the feelings of
others; it had helped, he thought, to make her what she was.
It was significant that her father had not long survived her
marriage, though he had urgently promoted it. He knew what
the loss of that adored daughter must have meant to him, and

he could imagine the father's fear that she might have been near to the breaking point.

There were six of them at lunch: Christine, Charles and his wife, Murray, Dick Bayliss and, included at the last minute by Charles to make an even number, Edward Erridge. Christine was placed between Charles and Dick Bayliss, Murray between his Aunt Lily and Erridge. For this arrangement he was grateful. He would not have to talk to Christine unless the conversation became general, and then he need not fear giving anything away. If one or two looks passed between them he felt sure, in his new confidence and happiness, that no one would notice them.

He was all eagerness now for the new revelation, so looked forward to by lovers, the new aspect of his beloved which would be his on seeing her for the first time in the company of others. This would enlarge his knowledge of her and would, he knew, give him occasion for secret pride. She would be the same and not the same; he would catch fresh glimpses of her through the eyes of these four people and, though he knew that the love he felt for her was whole and in a sense complete, his knowledge of her could be added to in an infinity of ways, even though each discovery would only confirm and corroborate what he already, subconsciously, knew.

The weather was still cool, even autumnal, and Christine wore the same red woolen dress in which he had first seen her, but today, as a concession to a more formal occasion, she had put on a tiny black hat, little more than a flat bow which left most of her smooth hair and the shining coil uncovered. She was that rare thing, he thought, a pretty woman who grudged time spent on clothes. He guessed that she bought carefully and then thought as little as possible about what she wore, taking pains, however, to be noticeably neat. Her trimness contrasted amusingly with his Aunt Lily's beads and scarves, her straying hair, her unsuitable hat, the vague, veiled outlines of her stooping figure. But few could fail to apprehend the intelligence behind those hooded eyes, and a mature charm was in all she said and did. She received, like some delicate radar instrument, what others gave out, and no one, as far as Aunt Lily was concerned, gave nothing. Her judgments were rapid and inflexible, though for the most part kind. She had judged Sibyl less as a human being than as a wife for the young man Murray then was. She had foreseen many things. While to Charles Sibyl was merely a young woman who had entirely failed to charm him, his wife had been aware of a discordant spirit, a personality unresponsive to anything but the cruder manifestations of passion, a nature in which there was something violent, harsh and untaught. She had imparted these impressions to Charles; they had then done what they could.

Murray knew these things and he regarded her with respect and affection. She had a foot, he thought, in some other realm, though for the most part she kept her oddnesses to herself and met the people with whom she came in contact on their own ground.

She turned to Murray with a warm smile and said, "I see so little of you. I know you've been to America quite recently, but do come to the flat and dine with us soon, so that we can talk. Would that be possible?"

He answered, not wishing, at present, to be pinned down to any date, that he thought it might be possible later on, and then asked her for news of Celia and Veronica and their families. After giving him the latest report of them she said: "Do you remember how frightened you were of the two girls when you were a lad? What a pity it was. They always liked you so much but they failed to get their liking across to you. You were the shyest young man I ever knew."

"I wouldn't go back to that time for anything on earth," he told her. "It was nearly all of it unhappy. I used to dream about dying young and getting out of it all, leaving a few people—including Celia and Veronica—feeling sorry."

"I know, I know," she said. "But I wouldn't go back to my youth either. It's even worse, you know, to be a shy, awkward girl, and I was all too well aware that young men dreaded being alone with me. You see, I was outrageously plain. Then I met Charles and my whole life was changed. I remember as if it were yesterday my astonishment and incredulity when he said he wanted to marry me. Me! I knew then what it meant to be translated. You know, of course, what I mean —to be conveyed to heaven without death."

He thought he could have told her too what it meant to be translated by love, but he could only smile and say, "Yours is the only perfectly happy marriage I know. No, I know of one other—the Hancocks'."

This led her to ask about Sibyl. "Tell me, is Sibyl still determined never to come to London? Will nothing alter that?"

"Nothing, I'm afraid. She'll only go out in the car, and to the shops in Morden, and to one or two old friends."

"A damaged psyche," she said. "What a terrible thing that is. I wish some joy could come to Sibyl. Joy from any quarter. I think of her often, and of that shocking accident. As if you hadn't your share of sorrow already."

"Yes," he agreed, "I think we already had our share."

"But at least, dear Murray, you're happy at Atlantic House?"

"Oh, entirely, of course. It's more than a job to me. It's a harbor, a refuge. Most of the happiness I've had I owe to Charles."

"One doesn't, in the last analysis, owe happiness to anyone but oneself," she said, "though others may put one in the way of it." She looked across at Christine. "That's an interesting young woman. Not altogether at peace with herself, I should say, but she has resourcefulness, she will always find ways of escaping from what checks or encumbers her. She has remarkable eyes. I remember so well Charles flying up to Edinburgh to try to help Sam when she was so terribly ill,

166

but I've never met her before. Have you met her before?"

"Yes, in New York," he said, and his voice sounded to him unlike his own. "Sam is a very good friend of mine."

"Yes, dear Sam," she said smiling. "I'm afraid I alarm him. He's not used to eccentrics, but I do like him so much. Le vrai bon enfant. She has an enchanting profile, and I like the way her lips are always a little parted, as if in expectation."

"I think she's entirely natural," he said. "I mean, without any affectation at all."

"I think that too. I imagine she's a good deal alone, in spirit, that is to say. Perhaps her poor health would account for it."

When she had turned away to talk to Dick Bayliss he thought over what she had said. He had hardly spoken a word to Christine, but as they all knew him as a reticent man, unlikely to be forthcoming at a lunch table, his failure to try to talk across to her would surprise no one. It was as if he had received an electric shock when she looked at him and said, very clearly, "Murray, do you remember that afternoon at Frederick's house when I showed you that enchanting book on Greece?"

"I do, very well," he answered, his heart beating too fast for comfort. Surely it was indiscreet to call him by his first name before them all.

"Well," she went on, "Mr. Kendrick has seen it too, and he agrees with Frederick about its publication by Atlantic House. Isn't it a pity?"

Wondering what would come next, he agreed that it was.

"I've written to the author," she went on, "to ask if any of the original paintings are for sale. I'm hoping for a reply while I'm here. If I have the luck to get one, I'll try to persuade Sam to let me hang it over the fireplace in the living room. Do you remember, there was a painting by Grandma Moses hanging there?"

"I remember very well," he said, and felt that all eyes were on him. "I also have the impression that you'll have difficulty in persuading Sam to hang it somewhere else."

"Yes," she said, smiling. "She's his favorite painter."

"Those aren't paintings," Dick Bayliss announced. "They're little girls' samplers done in oils."

"Well, at least," Charles objected, "they're not as self-consciously artless as a lot of paintings today. One feels she really saw things that way."

During the talk that followed, in which he took no part, Murray realized that Christine knew perfectly what she was doing and that it could not have been better done. She was building up their acquaintance, putting it on a firm basis before them all. She had let them know he had been to Runnybrook, that they had met at Frederick's house, that they were on first-name terms. She was creating the circumstances needed if they were to join forces for a trip to Rome and Greece, the thing nearest, at this moment, to her heart. She would leave nothing undone that could be done. Next week she might even be able to speak of Sibyl as someone with whom she was on friendly terms. He was ready to believe that she might succeed in these most unlikely plans, that the trip was a possibility, might even become a fact. He could put no limits to what she might accomplish.

Erridge was grateful to him for the part he had played in the take-over of his firm, and showed it. He was a sandy-haired Scot with eyebrows like brushes, over shrewd and humorous blue eyes. Murray did not know him well, but he liked him. He knew he was a graduate of Glasgow University, that he was a philologist—and so had earned the respect of Dick Bayliss—and that he was the father of five children. He knew, too, that Dick Bayliss had been busy making a friend of him. Well, no harm in that, though even as he said this to himself he heard Dick Bayliss say to Charles, referring to some reviewer: "The fellow does his best, but he's simply not educated. Heaven alone knows where he's picked up the odds and ends of learning that appear in his reviews, like plums in a doughy cake—certainly not at any university."

Christine at that moment looked across at Murray and their eyes met and rested on each other until he forced himself to look away. The looks people exchange could, he knew, reveal too much to an observant watcher. Their message is naked, vivid with meanings. He had the impression that his Aunt Lily had caught this look. Well, if she had, there was no kinder woman. She would make of it what her affection for him and her ripe wisdom suggested—not too much, though perhaps not too little.

They were speaking presently of Erridge's shorthand system. Erridge said there was talk of teaching it on television to schools. Lily Kendrick said she thought of learning it herself. "It's good for people of my age to learn something entirely new."

"Bravely spoken," Dick Bayliss said. "Very bravely spoken. I shall do nothing of the sort."

"You've learnt it already, haven't you, Murray?" Christine asked, leaning a little toward him.

"I'm not proficient," he answered. "I worked at it enough to convince myself that it was a first-rate system, and remarkably easy."

"It sounds tempting," Christine said, "but what I want to do now is to learn modern Greek, or enough modern Greek to get along in Greece."

This, Murray thought, was a clever lead, and he wondered how she would develop it.

"Don't bother to learn any Greek the first time you go," Lily Kendrick advised. "Just go. Just go and look and look and come back changed. If you don't come back changed you haven't been to Greece."

"You're not really planning to go, are you?" Charles asked with a look of surprise.

She nodded. "Planning, yes, and longing. That's about as far as it's gone, so far."

"You wouldn't go without Sam, surely?"

"Then I should never go," she replied. "Sam is no sightseer, and besides, he's far too busy."

"You'd better ask Murray's advice," Charles said. "He was there last year."

"You'd do far better to ask mine," Dick Bayliss said, turning squarely to face her, but first throwing a malicious little smile to Murray. "I spent two whole years there after I left Oxford. I even went on some digs. Epidaurus, Crete, Mycenae. I can tell you where to go and what to see. Let me lend you some books."

His fine, thin hair, which always looked unbrushed, made a halo about his big head, but he had taken some pains, Murray had observed, to dress more conventionally than usual. Instead of the rough, misshapen tweeds he usually wore he had put on a flannel suit, and his tie was neatly tied. The magnified eyes behind the big horn-rimmed glasses gleamed at Christine. She had evidently made a conquest. He had an air of clumsy purpose and directness in speaking to her, like a bumblebee charging into a flower.

"I've read such a lot of books," she told him. "Don't, please, lend me any more. Now all I want is to see it for myself."

"Well, at least let me give you some advice. Don't, of course, dream of going alone. Don't join any organized tours either. Just go with one, two, or at the most three others. If you go in the summer, take plenty of enteroviaform with you. Eat cautiously, and don't experiment with strange dishes. Greece has some magnificent ones; learn about them and stick to them. Drink plenty of Greek wine, it's good for you, and don't be afraid of the national apéritif, ouzo. It's an excellent digestive. Look, let me call on you with some maps. It would be enormously exciting for me to outline a trip for you."

"You're exceedingly kind," she said, "but I'm off to the country very soon. And anyway, the whole thing is only a vague idea as yet and may never materialize." Then she smiled at him and said, "If I do go, I promise you'll hear about it."

"Well," he said, undaunted, "let me know in good time. I have excellent friends there, people you ought to meet. Better still, plan your trip for next spring, persuade Sam to come too, and let me be bear-leader. We'd have a lot of fun."

"Then please take the responsibility, first of all," she said, "of persuading Sam. You might succeed where I've failed." She threw Murray a quick glance which he interpreted, gratefully, as meaning, "What a nuisance this man is!" and began putting on her gloves.

"Yes," Lily Kendrick said, "we must send them all back to the office." She was drawing black cotton gloves over her gnarled hands. "Would you care to come with me to an exhibition of pictures in Bond Street, Christine? If so, we'll take a taxi. I'm not overfond of walking."

Christine said she would like to go with her, and so they left. The four men shared a taxi back to the office, Murray and Erridge sitting on the two small seats.

"An absolute charmer, Sam's wife," Bayliss said, his hands planted on his knees. "A rare creature. Highly intelligent, with the good sense to make no parade of it. What an odd pair they must make! Our big football-playing Orson, Sam, and that little willow wand."

"I don't think she looks at all strong," Charles said. "I hope Lily doesn't make her do too much. Lily's energy is phenomenal."

"Shall we have the pleasure of seeing Mrs. Sam again?" Bayliss asked. "Might not a little dinner be planned for her?"

"I think not," Charles said. "She's going to stay in the country—Sam's orders. She needs plenty of rest."

"I take that hard," Bayliss said. "I take it very hard. I

haven't been so charmed with a young woman for years. Why have I been the only one not to meet her before?"

This was clearly addressed to Murray, but before he could reply Charles broke in with a touch of impatience, "I hate to cut short these schoolboy vaporings, Dick, but I'd like you to tell me exactly what you said to Willoughby, as I shall be seeing him in ten minutes. Did you say we'd get his book out in the early spring or did you break it to him that it was more likely to be in our summer list?"

Murray had a letter from Sam the next day, and he put it into his pocket after reading it in case he should feel like showing it to Christine at dinner. Sam had written:

I'm trusting you, and when I say you I mean all of you, to keep an eye on Christine while she's over there, and I'm trusting you, personally, to let me know at once if she needs anything or isn't feeling well. An air-mail letter just now and then would be fine. I know she's happy to be there and I hope everything at Ifield turns out all right. I hope you aren't too far away to go and have a look at her sometimes. I sort of wish she and your wife could get together, but maybe I'm not talking sense at all. Anyhow, it's an idea and I know you'll fix it if it seems a good one. She ought to lie out in the garden as much as she can. When the time came to let her go, I wasn't sure I was going to be able to do it. It came pretty hard.

By the way, you'd better not mention the dog, Seth. I thought she'd go out of her mind with grief. He was tied up in a shed and starved to death. Some crazy kids who meant to claim a reward and then got scared. It was pretty horrible and it strikes me the police were mighty slow.

I'm about up to my eyes in work. Jim is away on holiday and won't be back for a week. Dad is fairly all right, but it's been a long, hot summer and I want to get him out of here for a while, so as soon as Jim gets back I'm taking him to Maine for a little lake fishing. He feels he's putting too much on me and it worries him, but I keep telling him I've got the broadest pair of shoulders this

172

side of the Alleghenies. He wants to go to England if he can, but I want him to get freshened up in Maine first. Maybe I can take him over with me late in October for a short visit and then fetch Christine back before the cold weather starts.

Well, thanks, old man, for anything you can do for Christine, and all my affectionate good wishes,

Yours,
Sam

Before putting the letter into his pocket he sat holding it for a moment, as if by touching it he might receive from it some certainty as to where he stood. Was his conscience as clear as he would like it to be? He could still answer yes. He was not harming Sam; he was depriving him of nothing. What Christine gave to him did not belong to Sam. If they had found a way, and an innocent way, of giving each other happiness on the plane and within the limits that loyalty to Sam imposed, hadn't they at least that right as human beings? A sudden weariness overtook him in the midst of these thoughts, as if the whole thing were beyond him, beyond his judgment or power of assessment, and he slipped the letter into his pocket. He needed Christine's guidance, Christine's assurances, if he was not to worry himself out of this brief joy which was now his.

That evening Christine was in a confident, even triumphant mood. She told him that after leaving Mrs. Kendrick she had gone to a travel agency and made their air reservations for Athens, with a stopover of five days in Rome.

"I can't tell you," she said, "how much I enjoyed doing it. It was the first time, believe it or not, that I'd ever been inside a travel agency. Yes, yes," she said, as he was about to speak, "we'll have an accounting later if you insist, but don't let's talk about it now. I've even arranged for the hire of a car and a driver in Athens. I thought of having one in Rome too, but I think we can rely on taxis there. And, Murray," she

173

said, her eyes alight with anticipation, "I've decided there's no point at all in our going separately. We'll tell Charles and Lily, as they want me to call them, and I'm sure they'll approve. I think I prepared the ground pretty well at lunch."

"It couldn't have been better done," he said. "But remember, there's still Sibyl. Everything probably breaks down at that point. She'll never consent to go."

"Well, if it breaks down we can cancel everything, but I have great hopes. I feel convinced I can make a friend of her. At least I shall do my very best."

"If she agreed to go and failed to enjoy herself, she could utterly spoil it for us," he warned her.

"Then we must see that she does enjoy herself. And if it doesn't work, Murray, what have we to lose? Really, we have nothing at all to lose, have we?"

"I keep telling myself that," he said.

"I have a little plan," she said, and she proceeded to outline it to him. Next week, when he was in London, she would telephone his house and ask Sibyl if she might invite herself to tea, on Sunday. "I'm supposing," she explained, "that she'll find it impossible to say no." She'd then arrange to be there at half past four, but she'd purposely arrive a little early. Would he please be out, and stay out, until half past four, as she wanted to see Sibyl first alone? She wanted at least ten minutes, perhaps fifteen. By that time she'd have failed completely to get on any sort of terms with her or she'd have made some progress. Then he would come in, and after that she'd improvise. They'd both improvise.

"And I'm really eager to see and talk to her," she said, "quite apart from these plans. I feel there's something so tragic about her—no, that's wrong, not tragic, I doubt if she's made for tragedy—but I can picture so clearly the emptiness of her life. Self-imposed, perhaps, but none the less dreadful for that."

174

"But you're right," he said. "Her miseries are self-imposed. She'll never let me forget for one instant what she's been deprived of. It's a part of my punishment. If she were to show a moment's happiness, for that moment, at least, I might feel freed from my guilt."

"I suppose only a saint, or a near-saint, finds the inner happiness that has nothing to do with circumstances," she said. "I've thought about it a great deal. I know, of course, that it's the only sort of happiness that's invulnerable. I suppose one might call it joy. Do you think it can only be found through a religion, or could one find one's own way to it if one tried long enough and hard enough?"

He was aware of such a feeling of oneness with her that he could almost imagine they lived inside the same body. It was as if he had been taken up from his native ground and replanted in hers, putting down roots that were rejoicing in their new vigor.

"I don't see why it need depend on a religion," he said. "Why couldn't one find one's own difficult way to it?"

"But," she went on, pursuing her thoughts, "the desire for it, the need for it, wouldn't that in itself be religious? I think it would. I looked up 'religion' in the Concise Oxford Dictionary one day just to see what was the broadest interpretation they gave to the word. They began with the narrowest —with monastic life—and then they gave the word the widest definition they could, I suppose: 'Human recognition of super-human controlling power, especially of a personal God entitled to obedience.' I wasn't sure I agreed with the word 'entitled' but I did agree with 'controlling power.' There must, there must be one, even if it's only the utterly remote one that made the universe and keeps the stars in their courses."

"And religion," he said, "claims that it can put us into direct touch with that power and that it's a beneficent one."

"Beneficent," she repeated, "that's too anthropomorphic for

175

me. One visualizes a kindly human face, a kindly human hand giving us what's good for us. My father didn't belong to any church, but he was a very religious man, in the sense in which I understand religion. My mother paid lip service to the Episcopal Church and occasionally went. She is the most completely unreligious person I have ever known. She's incapable of a sense of mystery, incapable of awe. But I won't talk about her now. As for myself, so far I can only wholly believe in one law—the law of cause and effect. Which," she said, with a little smile, "is a pretty wonderful law, in my opinion, and at least saves us from a haphazard universe."

"But then," he objected, "aren't you throwing overboard something you value? The sense of mystery and awe?"

"No, because the causes are quite beyond our understanding. It's bound to be a mysterious universe to us—I think it always will be. As someone has said, 'The more we discover the further the mystery recedes.' Do you know why I think I shall never be able to accept the guidance of any religious teaching?"

"Why?" he asked. "I could tell you very briefly what it is in my own case. My reluctance to go to church, except on rare occasions, is a part of my revulsion against my father, and against everything he seemed to me to stand for. What's your reason?"

"I don't want to give up my sense of being on an adventure into life and into death," she told him. "I don't want to give up my curiosity. I feel that to lose my curiosity would be to lose myself, to lose everything. If I joined a religious body I'd have to accept its teachings completely. I'd want to, in fact. Or else, why join? So I prefer to stay outside and be free to wonder to my heart's content. I prefer to accept all the disadvantages of being outside, of being a sort of free-lance Christian and my own mentor and adviser. I prefer that to being mentally shackled, or pressed into a mold."

176

He looked at her sitting beside him, her head bent as if she were studying the design on her plate. Something in her attitude and in the simple black dress she wore was nunlike, and he thought, she's not so far from that either. She's nearer to it than she realizes, and he felt a sudden dread, as if he might lose her to the very thing she questioned. She raised her head and they looked into each other's eyes directly and a little fearfully.

"It's good for us to be together," she said, and he felt she was in search of reassurance. "I'm myself with you. You're yourself with me. It's good for us, isn't it?"

"Yes," he said. "With you I find what I suppose every thing and every creature seeks. Equilibrium; a point at which one comes to rest."

"It's just that," she agreed, and smiled in sudden joy. "Translated into simple, physical terms it's what I felt when I first learned to float, as a child. Sometimes when it was very hot my father used to take me to bathe in the Sound. When I learned to lie stretched out on the water looking up at the sky I was utterly content and at peace. Life was wholly good. And it's wholly good when I'm with you."

He looked at her now with a kind of anguish, as if a knife were being turned in his body. They had both disregarded the dishes placed in front of them, the stir and talk and nearness of other people.

"We're in very great danger, you know," he said in a low voice, and then regretted that he had allowed himself to say it. But she met it quietly and paused to consider it.

"I wonder if we are. I know of course what you're afraid of—of our drifting into what most people in our situation would drift into. But must we? You see, Murray, I'm not what's called a highly sexed woman. There has only been Sam, and I have never felt for him what I imagine one feels when one really loves someone. Perhaps, to use a much-used word,

I'm simply unawakened. What delights me is just this: complete confidence and understanding. We have so much to give each other, we need each other so much. Isn't it possible for us just to be innocently happy? It's possible for me. You must tell me if it's impossible for you."

"It isn't impossible," he said, and his voice was so low he might have been talking to himself. "It's only very difficult. I love you in all the ways there are."

She had heard. He saw a faint color spread over her cheeks.

"So now you've said it."

"But you knew it."

"Yes, I suppose I knew it, just as I knew that I loved you. So now I've said it too." Their hands touched and parted again. "But, Murray, you see I believe that you and I are two people who are really capable of love, and by love I mean the voluntary giving of one's very best to another person. Its object isn't bodily satisfaction, we both know that; it may have that object as well, but it's worthless unless it has a great many other objects. It's only for the sensitive, the imaginative and the intelligent. I doubt if it's for the intellectual. People like Dick Bayliss, for instance, are incapable of it." Her eyes were fixed on his, her face was alight and eager with the message she wanted to impart. "Charles and Lily understand it," she went on. "Sam understands it in his fashion. The tragedy is that I can't give it back to him. But it's rare, it's very rare. It's a seeing, a recognizing; it's something that belongs equally to heart and mind. I'm expressing it badly, but I know I'm speaking to someone who can fill in all I've left unsaid."

He was so moved by her frank admission that she loved him that nothing else, at that moment, seemed important. But if this were so—and he had half known it—to what qualities in him could it be ascribed? This baffled him, unless it were in fact what she had said it was—a recognition. A rec-

178

ognition of far more in him than he himself was aware of. He tried to put this in the form of a question, so much did he need to hear her answer.

"But it's simple," she replied. "I recognized you that first afternoon. I recognized you as the sort of man I could love. It's an emanation, it's something that's given off by people quite unconsciously. It was nothing you actually did or said. Even before you came toward me and took my hand—do you remember kicking my shoes under the sofa at the same time? —I recognized you as my sort of human being. Do you remember when I brought the book and knelt down beside you? I was as sure then as I am now. And in the car, later, driving you through the park, I can't describe to you the wonderful relief of being able to talk to you about Sam and myself, of being able to tell the truth about it all. It was something I had needed desperately. I knew, even then, that you were someone I could be wholly myself with. That, to my mind, is what's meant by falling in love. But it isn't falling; it's being lifted up."

"But what—but what could you have found in me to lift you up? I was as arid and bitter and despondent as a man could well be."

"Oh, Murray, I was aware of a thousand things. Let me tell you just a few. To begin with, I knew a good deal about you from Sam. I knew about the boy, about the accident, I knew that no one ever saw your wife. I could feel repressions in you that matched the repressions in me. I broke yours down by throwing away my own. I talked to you more frankly than I have ever talked to anyone. I can't tell you how that helped me. And I was sure that I could help you. That in itself is a great delight. And the next time we met, when you told me about your life, well, everything I had guessed, everything I'd felt intuitively, was confirmed. I'll tell you one thing more. I knew that I loved you—I can use that word now—partly because of all the qualities and talents in you that have never had a chance to show themselves. Most of all, I think, the talent for love."

He had left his plate almost untouched. He looked at her with a deep and close regard.

"And I have to lose you again," he said, and it was a statement because he dared not make it a question.

"Yes," she answered, and there was not an instant's hesitation, "we have to lose each other again, in the sense I know you mean. When this trip I'm determined on is over, you'll go back to Morden with Sibyl, and I'll go back to Sam, and we'll make the best we can of our lives. I told you I wasn't going blindly into this. But how much better for both of us that we should have had it!"

"Yes," he said, "I assent to that." And he went on: "Nothing in my life had ever led me to think I might meet and know a woman like you. I don't think I guessed there were any. Certainly they hadn't come my way. I suppose there must be some others more or less like you." He smiled at her. "I must assume that you're not unique. And the fact that you exist and that you care about me—well, it ought to keep me content for the rest of my days. But of course it won't. When you go back—I simply don't know how I can bear it."

"We'll both suffer," she said. "I know that, but I'm prepared to pay for this, and you must be prepared too. Now we must eat something, dearest Murray We've let our good dinners get cold."

Later she told him she had a difficult question to ask him. She said she supposed most women would have asked it long ago, but both he and she were inclined to walk delicately. "Do you and Sibyl live together as husband and wife?"

"No," he answered, and could barely keep an inward shudder from becoming an outward one. "No, that's all past and done with. It's nearly seven years since that came to an end."

"But," she said with her clear regard, "surely there's some-

180

one? Didn't you speak of a young woman, an actress? Irma?"

"That's over," he said, "that's finished and done with too."

"But not because of me?" she asked, and at his slight nod of affirmation she cried, "Oh, but you shouldn't have done that."

"Christine," he said, in gentle remonstrance.

There was a little silence, as if a death had been spoken of. Then she said: "Once, during August, when my mother came to see me, she told me she believed I was incapable of love. She told me that was why she was so against my marrying Sam—because she could see I wasn't really in love with him. But that wasn't the reason at all. The real truth was that she was afraid I was going to be happy. To escape was bad enough, to escape and be happy was intolerable. Now that she's convinced I'm not happy she's turned to me with a sort of hunger that frightens me. She feels we belong to a dissatisfied sisterhood and that it ought to bring us together. She's even been trying to make me share her years of unhappiness with my dear father. Well, if she was unhappy it was no fault of his, any more than my failure to be happy is any fault of Sam's. But the thought that my mother and I have that in common terrifies me. I dread being like her in any way. I'm frightened of the natural tendency of daughters, especially as they grow older, to be like their mothers. I want to be grateful for everything, Murray, for my poor health, for my marriage, for life itself. To be wholly and humbly grateful. But it seems that I can't achieve it quite alone. And it seems that with your help and love I can. I can go on fighting to be what I would like to be. Is that pure selfishness? Had I any right at all to involve you in it?"

"I can only answer that," he answered, "by telling you what I hope you know—that my involvement with you is the one good and blessed thing in my life."

In the end he did not think fit to show her Sam's letter. It might have made their evening less than perfect, some sense of guilt, however illogical, might have entered in. They parted without a kiss, without an embrace; only their hands were allowed to meet. His journey back to Morden passed in the luxury of remembrance. He was like a housewife providing against a dreaded famine, locking up first one good, lifesaving thing and then another against an evil day, and he let his thoughts linger on each moment, on each word, with passionate thankfulness, memorizing, preserving, hoarding.

Only his mother was up when he got home.

"You're even later than you said, dear," she remarked. "Sibyl got tired of waiting. She said please to try not to wake her. You know she's had some bad nights lately."

"I'll be as quiet as I can," he said, and kissed her good night. She put out the lights and in the snap of each switch, he thought, there was mild rebuke. His longing for a room of his own became a monster need. He would have given much if he had not been obliged to go into that bedroom with its twin beds, and to see Sibyl's golden head, curled and netted, on her pillow. Please God, he thought, I won't wake her, but as he tiptoed about he saw her open her eyes once and give him a vivid blue glance that seemed to accuse and at the same time to exonerate.

As if I cared, her look seemed to say. Do what you like. Why should I care?

But she did not speak, and soon all was quiet and he was alone with Christine.

XIII ✍

HE came home one evening soon after this and found Sibyl polishing the old silver teapot her mother had given her.

"You're very busy," he remarked. "What's up?"

She went on polishing.

"That friend of yours telephoned today."

"What friend?" But he did not want to seem to dissemble, and asked: "Do you mean Sam Bonner's wife?"

"Yes, that's just who I mean. Mrs. Sam Bonner. She rang up from that house she has in Ifield."

"What did she say?"

"She wants to come to tea on Sunday. Why I don't know. Why on earth should she want to come to tea here?"

"Didn't she say why? I expect she's rather lonely. She probably hasn't any friends nearby."

"That's what she said. She said she wanted to meet me. I don't see why she should want to. Have you told her about me?"

He had to speak to her bent head. "Well, I suppose she knows at least as much as the rest of them. And why shouldn't she want to meet you?"

"I don't want to meet her. I don't want to meet anybody, and you know it perfectly well."

"I hope you didn't say so."

"If I didn't, it was for your sake. I had to tell her she could come, because of Sam Bonner. I shall probably have a headache and stay upstairs. You and your mother can entertain her."

He put the evening paper on the table beside her and looked at the teapot. "You've got a beautiful polish on it. As a matter of fact I think you'd like her." He was choosing his words with care, fearful of saying something that might ruin all Christine's hopes. "She's had a lot to contend with, with illnesses and so on, and she's simple and friendly."

"Is she very American? I mean like a woman in an American film?"

"Not at all, I should think. She's quiet and has a soft voice."

"Well," she said, "it depends on how I feel. I don't suppose she'll stay long."

"About an hour, I suppose."

"Do you think she knows what I look like?" she persisted.

"Oh, Sibyl!" He turned away.

"Does she know about Martin?"

He moved away toward the hall, saying, "I expect Sam has told her something."

"All right," she said, raising her voice, "I'll agree to see her, just this once. But please don't ask her again."

"I didn't ask her. She asked if she might come, or so you just said."

She followed him into the hall, still holding the teapot and polishing cloths. "Well, it seems queer to me. None of the other people in Atlantic House have ever tried to force their way in here." He was going slowly up the stairs now.

184

"Martin's in the kitchen with your mother, if you're looking for him."

"All right," he said, "I'll be down in a minute."

She had not refused to see Christine, for which he was thankful. He had not, so far, blundered. There was hope.

At supper his mother said: "When that friend of yours comes on Sunday, dear, Martin and I will be out. We'll go for a walk, and I'll take him to tea at the Singing Kettle, so you and she and Sibyl can have a pleasant talk."

"Just as you like, Mother. It doesn't matter. She won't stay long, I imagine."

"She spoke nicely on the telephone," his mother went on. "I had a little chat with her before Sibyl came. She likes it where she is, but she says it's a wee bit lonely."

"I dare say it is. We must do what we can for her, for Sam's sake."

As if bored with the subject, Sibyl abruptly changed it. "Do you remember those people I told you about, the Grahams? We talked of asking them in for a drink, but we never did. I've seen him in Morden several times without her. I saw him today. He told me the marriage was breaking up. He's going to take a flat in Wimbledon."

"What was wrong, I wonder?" Murray asked, feeling no interest in these people he had never met, but simulating it for Sibyl's sake. "There were children, weren't there?"

"Only one, a girl of fifteen. He says his wife doesn't take any interest in her home at all. She just wants to paint. I think he'll let her get the divorce on the grounds of adultery."

"Dear me," Mrs. Logan said. "One hears too much of that word nowadays."

"You must have heard it often enough in church," Sibyl retorted. "It oughtn't to shock you."

"The word doesn't shock me, the thing itself does," Mrs. Logan replied. She was cutting up some meat for Martin and feeding it to him piece by piece.

Sibyl gave an impatient shrug. "Where would literature and the drama be without it? There's even plenty of it on television, too. You may as well get used to it."

Mrs. Logan made no reply but said to Martin, "That's a good lad. That's splendid. He has a beautiful appetite, Murray. It's a pleasure to cook for him."

Murray smiled at her and wondered if it made saintliness less saintly to be so in love with the humble task, the daily duty that to others would be irksome or repulsive. Whatever might be the answer to that, she had more than made up for the poverty of the love she had given him as a child. It was not forgotten, the effects had gone too deep, but it was forgiven.

Martin rolled his head and his eyes and made ugly, unintelligible sounds. Sibyl quickly looked away, but Murray forced himself to look directly at his son, forced himself to listen with full attention to that subhuman speech.

"It's all right, dear," Mrs. Logan said. "You've had enough. Grannie understands."

On Sunday he stayed in most of the day, reading the papers and a manuscript that he had brought with him from the office. At a quarter to four he told Sibyl he was going out for a while. He said he wanted to buy some cigarettes.

"But we have plenty in the house," she objected.

"I've taken to smoking a new kind in the office, and I prefer them now. I'll be back soon."

"Don't be long. She'll be here at half past four, and I shouldn't know what to say to her if you weren't here. How does my face look?"

He saw that she had made it up with special care, hiding as well as she could the worst of the scars, those that had cut across and altered her fine, straight nose, and had changed the outline of an eyelid. Liquid powder made the others scarcely visible at a little distance, though she would not believe that this was so. He told her she was looking very well and that he liked her dress, a red and white print.

"Edna gave it to me, in return for that lampshade I made her. It was a little too big for her. I never thought I could wear red."

"It suits you perfectly. And you've made the house look very nice."

She had arranged chrysanthemums and dahlias in the sitting room and had changed the position of the furniture, pushing the television set into a corner so that it no longer dominated the room. In the dining room a cloth had been spread for tea. He said he hoped it had not been too much trouble, and she answered that she hoped she wouldn't have to do it again.

He stayed out until his watch, which he had set by Big Ben, told him it was nearly half past four, then walked quickly home. His heart beat fast when he saw a car at the front gate. She had done precisely what she had said she would do. This was a crucial moment. He let himself in, and could hear voices from the sitting room. He heard Sibyl say, "Here he is now," and the relief in her voice was unconcealed.

The sight of the two women sitting side by side on the sofa struck him as altogether extraordinary. Sibyl and Christine, side by side. It was a near-miracle. They both got up as if released by springs and Christine came toward him, smiling. At the same time he got the impression that she was mentally on tiptoe, overalert, "triggered." He knew that Sibyl had not made things too easy.

"I got here a quarter of an hour too early," Christine said. "I hope Sibyl's forgiven me. I do call you Sibyl, don't I? Murray and I are on first-name terms already. It doesn't take long in America, you know."

As Sibyl did not make the expected reply, Murray asked quickly, "Any trouble finding your way?"

"None at all. I'm a pretty good map reader, and your directions were perfect."

He felt a little chill go down his spine. He had omitted to tell Sibyl that he had sent Christine a little plan, showing the position of the house, but Sibyl spoke before he could. She had gone to the window.

"Isn't that a heavenly car?" she said. "We've never had anything as grand as that at our front gate."

"It's just a hired one," Christine told her. "I learned to drive a Jaguar, so I stick to them. I'll drive over and fetch you to Ifield one day if you'll come. Will you come?"

"I don't know," Sibyl said, turning back from the window. "I don't go anywhere, didn't Murray tell you?"

"Do think about it," Christine urged her. "Anyway, I'll ring you up. I get rather bored just resting and reading and being by myself."

"You can't tell me anything about boredom," Sibyl said. "If it weren't for the television I'd go off my head."

"But don't you ever go to London? To the theater, for instance? You're so near."

"With these scars? Would you want to be seen?"

"Yes," Christine answered. "If I looked like you I'm sure I would. If people saw the scars they would only be sorry."

"Exactly. I can do without people's pity."

"Well, I understand how you feel. I've had to put up with a great deal of it myself. I've spent one third of my waking life in bed."

From the kitchen they could hear the whistling of the kettle. Sibyl said, glad of something to do, "We'll have tea now. Murray, come and carry the tray for me, please. We'll have tea in the dining room. I know it isn't the smart thing to do, but it's easier."

As he followed Sibyl into the kitchen there was time for one quick glance at Christine. She gave him a confident little smile but he thought he saw a look of fatigue beneath it. She had taken on, he guessed, more than she knew, in spite of all his warnings.

188

When they sat down at the table, Christine at once noticed the teapot. "What a beauty! It's Georgian, of course. Do you know the date?"

"Murray looked it up. It's 1780. It's been in my mother's family, and she gave it to me some years ago."

"It would be worth I don't know what in America," Christine said.

"Most of the family silver was sold to pay my uncle's debts," Sibyl informed her. "He's Lord Holford, I don't know if Murray told you. He gambled everything away years ago, the property, the furniture, the pictures, everything. Now he's a recluse and lives in an old coach house on a bit of the estate. He never sees anybody."

"Were the pictures valuable?"

"Not really. They were mostly Victorian, and when he sold them they'd gone out of fashion."

"Tell me more about your family," Christine asked.

"My mother lives in Staffordshire," Sibyl answered, and Murray heard her with some surprise. It was rarely that she talked so freely to a stranger. "She married again after my father's death. Her husband's a horrible man. I don't know why she goes on living with him. My brother's a sailor. I hardly ever see him."

"Did you live in Staffordshire as a girl?"

Sibyl seemed to think she had said enough. She gave Christine a speculative look and refilled her cup.

"I won't tell you any more when Murray's here. He doesn't want to hear it all again."

"If husbands and wives never talked about what the other one already knows, there wouldn't be much conversation," Murray remarked. He wished the little party were safely over. The nervous strain was great.

"Murray's quite right," Christine agreed. "Sam often prefaces what he's about to say with 'Christine must have heard this a hundred times before,' but quite often things come out that are new to me or there are revealing little variations. When will Mrs. Logan and Martin be in? I was hoping to see them."

"Why do you want to see Martin?" Sibyl asked with brusqueness. "You know what he's like, don't you? Is it just morbid curiosity?"

Murray knew that he must make no protest.

"No, it isn't morbid at all," Christine answered, unperturbed. "He's your son, and a big part of your lives. If we're to be friends, as I hope we are, I'd like a small share in your lives. Is that asking too much?" And she looked at Sibyl with a warm and friendly look that was impossible to resist.

"Well, I don't know why you want a share in our lives," Sibyl answered. "We're just unhappy people with nothing to offer. Or I haven't. My life ended seven years ago."

It was best not to reply to this. Christine merely said, "I do wish you'd all come over to Ifield next Sunday. Mrs. Logan and Martin too. Could you come? Would you?"

Murray said Sunday would suit him if Sibyl had no other plans.

"Well, as a matter of fact I have," she said. "I'm lunching out on Sunday with some old friends. I felt I needed a change from Sunday dinner at home." Then she added, reviving Murray's fading hopes, "I could make it Saturday if you like."

"Yes, so could I," Murray said, "if that suits Christine equally well. I won't be going to the office."

"It's all the better," Christine replied. "It's one day sooner. Come a little before one, all of you. I shall look forward to it so much. You'll be my first visitors."

She presently began telling Sibyl about Runnybrook and her life there. She wasn't allowed to live in New York, she said, but she didn't mind that, she preferred the country.

"I believe," she said, "that what divides people most is their feeling—or lack of feeling—for nature. For instance, it might not exist for my mother. The country provides the

190

fruits and vegetables and meats that come to the table; that's its only purpose for her. When we lived on our farm in Connecticut she hated every moment of it. She has never walked a mile in her life. She always refused even to go and look at my father's herd of Jerseys. I was never allowed to own a cat or a dog."

"You don't seem to like her much," Sibyl remarked.

"I'm afraid that's quite true. I don't. And I'm dreading that she may come to England while I'm here. Perhaps it's wrong of me to speak about her so frankly, but I don't think it's wrong of me to feel as I do."

"I suppose she's very rich," Sibyl said.

"Yes, she is. My father was a rich man, you see. She can't even imagine what it's like not to be rich."

"I think if I were rich I'd mind this less," Sibyl said, touching her face. "And I wouldn't feel so shut in and bored. And I'd have more confidence."

Then Christine, with a courage Murray inwardly applauded, seized what she saw as an opportunity. "Tell me, Sibyl. Don't you ever long to go away? To travel? To see foreign countries?"

"In a way I do," Sibyl answered, and Murray was surprised at her admission, "but what's the good? I can't see that I'd be any better off anywhere else. I'd always have to take this with me." Once more she touched her face. "Here at least people have got used to me."

Christine looked from one to the other, her eyes brilliant. "Why not both come with me to Rome, and then Greece? Both of you. I mean it. I'm longing to go, there's nothing I want to do so much, and who knows? I may never have another or a better chance. Here I am, three quarters of the way there already. I can't go alone. Would you come? Would you? Let's think about it. Let's discuss it."

She ignored Sibyl's shake of the head and went on, before she could speak: "It would have to be soon—in a couple of weeks, at the latest. Won't you both come with me? Oh, do, do!"

Sibyl seemed not so much astonished by the suggestion as puzzled and even suspicious. "But how could we? We couldn't, possibly." She looked at Murray for corroboration. "Murray couldn't get away, and besides, we couldn't afford such a trip. It's out of the question. And I'd be wretched among foreigners. No, thank you, we couldn't even think of it."

"I could get away," Murray said, choosing his words carefully. He felt as though his very life, his one hope of living, depended on his and Christine's success or failure. "I haven't had a holiday this year. Why shouldn't we go? You remember I suggested our taking a holiday abroad somewhere after I got back from New York. Why not think this over, Sibyl?"

Sibyl's large blue eyes were fixed on Christine. She made no reply to Murray.

"But you must have lots of friends you could go with," she said. "People who could afford to travel as you'd want to travel. Why us? We'd be no good to you. Except that Murray's been to Greece once. Oh, yes, and Rome too."

"I haven't any friends I'd want to go with," Christine told her. "None at all. And there's no one I'd rather go with than you two. As for the expense, you could pay what you feel you could afford. What's the good of being well off if I can't do more than my share? I haven't any children. I'd love to spend money on a trip like this and not count the cost. We'd spend a few days in Rome, and then go on to Athens. Then we'd go to Delphi and Olympia and Mycenae and Epidaurus, and maybe one or two of the islands if there was time. Oh, Sibyl, I believe you'd enjoy it. You couldn't help enjoying it."

"What do you say, Sibyl?" Murray asked. "There's no reason why we shouldn't go, if you'd agree."

She wasn't, he thought, wholly against the idea. He guessed

192

that it had already made some agreeable inroads into her mind. At the same time he could see that she was puzzled and wary. Her face now took on the closed and stubborn look he knew so well.

"You've planned this between you," she said.

Now everything appeared to be lost. He saw with dreadful certainty that he had been right. He feared, too, that Christine had been too hasty. But his hopes rose again when she laughed. She seemed genuinely amused, as if Sibyl had made a clever guess, as if she herself, or both she and Murray, had been caught out over some trifle.

"In a way you're perfectly right," she said, with disarming frankness. "I did tell Murray when he was in New York how much I wanted to go to Greece. I even had it in my mind as far back as that to ask you both to come with me. Then today, when I met you, I knew I'd been right. I felt sure it would work. If you say you'll come, I'll cable Sam tonight and tell him. You don't know, Sibyl, you don't know what you'd be doing for me."

She was holding her own, he thought, even more than holding her own. Sibyl's look was still cold and speculating, but to his enormous relief she asked, "How long would you want to be away?"

"Oh, perhaps three weeks. Let's plan for three. There'll be so much we'll want to do and see. Would Mrs. Logan mind being left alone as long as that?"

"She wouldn't mind. I'm thinking of myself. Neither of you seem to realize what an ordeal it would be for me."

"Perhaps we'll both forget our disabilities for a little while," Christine suggested. "And I'll do my very best to keep well, and not be a burden to you."

"October's a good time to go," Murray said. "The weather ought to be perfect. The rains don't come till the end of the month, I've been told."

Christine looked from one to the other with delight. "Oh," she cried, "you'll come, you'll come! It's almost too good to be true."

"We haven't said we would," Sibyl warned her.

"No, but I've planted the idea now and I believe it's taken root." She got up, and the other two did the same. "Talk it all over between you. Only we must be quick. There are plenty of things to be done. Have you got a passport, Sibyl?"

"No," Sibyl answered. "I've never been out of England. That'll mean having a photograph taken, which would be horrible. But I'll think it over. If I did go, there'd be times when you'd wish I was back in England. I'm not a good-tempered woman. Ask Murray, he'll tell you."

"You haven't frightened me in the least. And if you decide to come, I'll be in your debt for as long as I live."

"Would we fly?" Sibyl asked.

"As we haven't much time I think it would be best."

"You wouldn't mind, would you, Sibyl?" Murray asked.

She threw him an angry look. "If you two are prepared to fly, why shouldn't I be?"

"Good!" Christine said, and took her handbag from the sofa, where she had left it. "Then may I go ahead and make the arrangements?"

"I suppose so, if you want to. If I change my mind I'll let you know. Anyway, we'll be seeing you next Saturday."

They went out to the gate, and there Christine paused to tell them how to find the house in Ifield. Then, as if she feared Sibyl's doubts might crystallize, she got quickly into the car and drove away. As they turned to go back to the house, Sibyl said, "Well, that was quite a little plot you hatched up between you, but I don't see why I should care if it was."

"I don't see why you call it a plot," Murray said, praying that he might undo nothing that Christine had done. "It would be more accurate to call it a hopeful idea of Christine's."

"I'll still call it a plot, even if I don't mind falling in with

194

it," Sibyl replied. They were in the hall now and she closed the front door and stood there with her back against it. "She's too clever by half, but I don't dislike her, and I can see you're mad keen to go." She went on: "I suppose you'd call her pretty, even though she's so thin. A figure like a French bean. That little brown linen dress with the white collar—I could have made it myself, except that I'm not so easy to fit." She now looked at him with a hard and penetrating look. "Do you want to know why I think I'll go?"

"I hope because it's what you'd like to do," he said.

"I can tell you this much. It isn't for her sake, and it certainly isn't for yours. It's for my own sake. I've decided I want to try what it's like to be among strangers, to be looked at and perhaps stared at. And I prefer to try it in a foreign country."

"It's what I've always wanted you to do."

"Maybe it is, but it's only now I've wanted to do it."

"Anyway," he said, "I'm very, very glad."

"What's more," she told him, "I don't even care if she's in love with you. But you'd be a fool to fall in love with her. That would make a pretty mix-up, wouldn't it? You're such a friend of Sam Bonner's, and you'd never have got put on the board if it hadn't been for him."

"Oh, Sibyl!" he protested, but felt there was nothing more he could safely say. It would have been disastrous to precipitate a quarrel. He went past her, up the stairs.

"All right," she said, raising her voice. "I can still think what I please. That's one privilege I still possess, I suppose. You'd better give me one of your books on Greece, hadn't you? I might as well have some idea of the place."

He said from the landing, "Help yourself to anything you want. You know where they are—on the top shelf of the bookcase. Shall I pick you out one or two?"

"No, thanks. I'll find what I want."

He went into Martin's room and stood for a moment quietly

by the window. He asked himself if he and Christine were not purchasing the delight of spending three weeks in each other's company at too great a price. But there were no scales by which the one thing could be weighed against the other. How else, in their two lifetimes, could such a joy, however precarious, be attained? If Sibyl had refused to consider the idea of the trip, he would perhaps see Christine two or three times more before she returned to America. After that, who could say? Now he had before him the possibility of seeing her every day for a period that seemed to stretch out before his eyes to barely discernible limits. They would see together the places that had given him such delight. It would be his happy, his exquisite privilege to take care of her as if she were his; to take upon himself a precious responsibility he had not dreamed of possessing. Whatever the risks, whatever the drawbacks, he would thankfully accept them. He and Christine would share them and bear them together.

XIV ✐

Dear Sam:

Christine told me about the cable you sent her, giving your consent to this journey of ours and even approving it. You can be sure that I'll do my utmost to make it a happy and successful one, and that Sibyl and I will take good care of Christine. She seems very well, and I think has enjoyed her stay at Ifield. Sibyl and I lunched with her there last week. From now on, until you come to take her home, it will be my agreeable duty to see that she doesn't do too much and that she gets the maximum benefit from our joint holiday. Sibyl has been so shut in for some years past for reasons that I think you know that I was both surprised and delighted when she said she'd like to go. It may be the beginning of the end of her dread of being seen by strangers, and if it is, we will have Christine to thank for it.

Christine will be writing to you frequently, I expect, and I will send reports from time to time. I only wish, Sam, that you could have come with us—[Yes, he thought as he wrote this, that's per-

197

fectly true. I would have liked Sam to come] . . . but your promise to fly to Athens later has delighted us all. I hope the trip to Maine was a success and has done your father a great deal of good. I believe you're due back about the time this gets to New York.

I'm looking forward immensely to seeing Greece again, and I'm deeply grateful, Sam, for the confidence you've placed in me.

All the best, and now for three weeks I shall put publishing worries into cold storage and simply enjoy myself.

Yours ever,
Murray

He had dined with Charles and Lily—Sibyl had been invited but had refused to go—shortly before leaving. Charles had been a little troubled about the wisdom of such a journey for Christine.

"You're taking on a big responsibility. She's a pretty fragile article to have in your luggage. For God's sake see that her enthusiasm for everything Greek doesn't land you in difficulties. Don't let her overdo it."

"I wouldn't myself care to control as ambitious a sightseer as Christine Bonner," his Aunt Lily remarked. "We went to Ifield to see her and I gathered that she means to be pretty thorough. Do ration her strictly."

"I mean to do just that," Murray said. "And remember, we shall be doing it in considerable comfort, with a good car and a good driver. I only wish Sam could have come too."

"Poor old Sam," Charles said. "His anxiety and loving care divided between Christine, Frederick and Atlantic House. It's a lot for one man."

"How was Sibyl persuaded to take such a trip?" Lily Kendrick asked, and he had known she was sure to ask it.

He said it was entirely due to Christine's friendliness and charm. She had succeeded in gaining Sibyl's confidence from their first meeting.

"Quite remarkable," she said, looking at him from under those drooping eyelids.

198

"Dick Bayliss is furious," Charles said. "He says you've stolen a march on him. He was hoping to organize a trip with Christine and Sam next spring."

They were in the plane, flying to Rome. The unbelievable thing had come about. The two women sat together, having agreed to take turns at the window, where Christine now was. He sat just behind Sibyl. A dark, stoutish man who, he surmised, came from some part of the Middle East sat beside him. He was reading Shakespeare.

He had been aware of Sibyl's tension as the plane sped down the runway, but as soon as it was airborne she relaxed and settled herself more comfortably in her seat. Christine was hatless, but Sibyl wore with her navy-blue suit a blue hat with a heavily dotted veil. Presently, to Murray's relief, she took it off and put it up on the rack. He hoped she would not wear it again.

They each had with them a raincoat, a small traveling bag and a large suitcase. He had expected Christine to bring twice as much luggage as they did, but she said it was a matter of pride with her to travel light. She kept beside her, however, a red morocco case that was fairly heavy, and held, she explained, a good many bottles.

"Up to a point," she told them, "I'm my own doctor, and not a bad one either."

Sibyl appeared to take everything for granted. She did not wish to seem untraveled or to show surprise at anything. When Christine pointed out Mont Blanc to her she merely said, "It doesn't look much from here, does it?"

"I'm not sure we have any right to see it from here," Christine said. "It's like observing one of the gods at an embarrassing moment."

Sibyl had provided herself with some Penguins, all of them detective novels, and she presently became absorbed in one. She refused to change seats and Christine continued to sit by

199

the window, looking out at whatever could be seen or reading a guide to Rome. Murray read *The Times* intermittently and looked at the nape of Christine's neck under the coil of hair and what he could see of her profile. The time passed quickly, with lunch intervening, and when they were asked to fasten their seat belts for landing the lapsed time seemed to fold itself away and become nothing. He could have wished it longer. His greed for being within sight of Christine would never, he thought, be satisfied. He could scarcely believe that this coming-to-life that had been his tremendous experience since knowing her could ever have happened in the same degree to anyone else. It was so total a revelation of what was meant by the word "love" that it was comparable to a conversion. His whole mind and heart, his whole attention were now focused on her, had gone out to her entirely, and yet in this going out, which should have left him empty, he had been filled. It was the perfect illustration of the parable of receiving by giving. And there was not any conscious desire in him to receive more than he now had. He did not see how he could contain more. He was happy. It was as if a smoothly running dynamo had been set going in him, lighting up all the dark places of his being. Had he, perhaps, done something comparable for her? Even as he asked himself this question she turned in her seat to look at him, giving him a smile of such delight that quick tears came pricking into his eyes.

She had chosen one of the less expensive hotels in Rome, but as they turned off the Via Vittorio Veneto and drew up at the entrance he wondered if it ought not to have been something humbler and more suited to his means. Then he made up his mind to put such worries out of his thoughts once and for all. He and Christine could settle everything between them and he knew that the larger her share of the expenses the better she would be pleased.

Their bedrooms were on the same floor but not adjoining. The one he and Sibyl were to have looked out on the street, the one offered to Christine overlooked gardens. Sibyl said to the manager, who spoke perfect English, "I'll never be able to sleep in that room. It will be far too noisy. We must have a quiet room like Mrs. Bonner's, overlooking the garden."

The manager said that alas! there were no more rooms on the garden side available.

"But it's perfectly simple," Christine said at once. "We'll change rooms. Mine's a double room too. Unless I'm worrying about something I usually sleep pretty well, and if I don't, I have sleeping pills I can take."

Sibyl promptly agreed to the change-over with a mere, "Well, thanks, it would suit me much better," and Murray knew it would be wiser to accept Christine's offer, though the incident greatly annoyed him. As they were unpacking, Sibyl said with an air of triumph, "It's all very well, but I don't see why I should have to lie awake all night. Sleeping pills make me feel awful."

He refrained from making any comment, and she then asked, "Did you notice how that man, the manager or whatever he was, looked at me? He couldn't help it. I can feel people's eyes settling on me like flies that I can't brush away."

"Try hard not to mind, Sibyl," he said. "After a few days I hope you won't think about it. There'll be too much else to think about."

"Oh, yes," she retorted, "I knew you'd take that complacent tone."

But her resentment did not last, and while Christine rested he took Sibyl for a walk in the Borghese Gardens. The sun was declining in golden splendor, the trunks of the tall pines were gilded with it, and recent rain had brought back all the green of the grass, so that the fatigue of summer had quite gone. He was aware of autumn's richness and sadness but to him at that moment there was a hopefulness in it too, as of a page newly turned and waiting to be written on. The mere thought of Christine resting in the hotel, to be seen again in about two hours' time, gave him a joy so intense that it spread through all his body as if his bloodstream had suddenly received some powerful and vitalizing injection.

He said to Sibyl as they walked, "There's a moon, luckily. Shall we take a taxi tonight and drive to St. Peter's? I'd like you to see it first by moonlight."

She said she thought it a good idea. "I wish we could do all our sightseeing by moonlight. Do you know, by moonlight my scars hardly show at all? I've sometimes taken a hand mirror into the garden and looked at myself, so I know."

He suddenly felt nearer to her; his own happiness had given a new warmth to his pity. He took her hand as they walked.

"Are you glad we came?"

"I don't quite know yet," she answered. "I think so. This place is very beautiful. What are these pines called?"

He said he thought most people called them umbrella pines, though they must have another name.

"That one's good enough for me. I'm not fussy about the names of things. And as you probably know a good deal about Rome, you needn't bother to tell me the names of churches and monuments. I'll know the Colosseum when I see it because I've seen photographs. I was never any good at history. I'm not intelligent like you and Christine."

"What nonsense, Sibyl. But you'll want to see as much as you can, won't you?"

"I'll tell you one place I want to go to," she said. "I've heard about it. It's that villa that belonged to Mussolini's mistress, I forget her name. It's a restaurant now. Couldn't we go there?"

"All right," he answered. "We'll dine there tomorrow night, if that's what you'd like to do."

"Well, it is, and please don't be condescending. I never pretended to be a high-brow."

It was going to be difficult, but at the moment he was too

happy, too exalted, to let himself be troubled. Let her say what she pleased, he would be grateful for any signs of interest or any graciousness she might choose to display.

Later, as the three of them stood waiting for a taxi to take them to dinner in Trastevere, Christine said, "From my bedroom window I could see the moon coming up. Suppose we drive to St. Peter's after dinner and see it first by moonlight? What do you think, Sibyl?"

"I think you and Murray must read each other's minds," she said. "He had exactly the same idea."

Christine merely laughed. "I'm afraid it's a very obvious one. We're in Rome, there's a moon, and the rest follows."

"All right," Sibyl said. "If it's the thing to do, let's do it."

To Murray's relief, Sibyl had no desire to go and see the Catacombs. It would have tired Christine and he was glad of a reason for not going a second time. He tried not to appear to be watching Christine for signs of fatigue. That, he well knew, was what Sam would have done. He made up his mind to trust entirely to her good sense, but he insisted on a good hour's rest after lunch each day before setting out again. At the end of three days' sightseeing, Christine said she was satisfied. All that she had not seen or that she would like to see again must wait for another time. They had looked down on Rome from the Capitoline Hill, from the Janiculum, from the Aventine, from the terrace of the Borghese Gardens. They had been to the Borghese Museum, the Capitoline Museum and the Etruscan Museum, where they had greeted the smiling couple with the unforgettable faces, seated on their tomb. They had seen St. Peter's, the Spanish Steps, Keats' House, the Baths of Caracalla and the Sistine Chapel.

"Even if I never come again," Christine said, "Rome belongs to me now. No one can ever take it away from me."

On the evening before the last day of their stay they discussed where they should go: to Tivoli and Hadrian's Villa

or to Ostia, to see the excavated city? Sibyl expressed a prefer-
ence for Tivoli and Hadrian's Villa. Someone, she said, had
told her that she mustn't miss Tivoli. The others agreed, but
when the morning came Christine telephoned their room to
say that she felt too tired to go. She thought it would be wise
to stay in bed till the late afternoon. Murray was worried and
asked Sibyl to go to her room to make quite sure all was well.
She returned a moment later to report that it was just as
Christine had said; she was merely tired.

"She was in bed, writing letters. She was quite cheerful.
There's nothing to worry about. She makes too much fuss
about her health."

They set off in the car Christine had ordered. On the way,
to fill a long silence, he asked Sibyl who had told her she
must see Tivoli.

"Oh," she answered, "just someone who's been there. The
same person who told me about the villa that had belonged
to Mussolini's mistress. I saw a picture of her somewhere.
She wasn't so very good-looking. I wonder what it is some
women have that makes men want to give them everything;
jewels and cars and houses."

"Acquisitiveness, I expect," he said.

"You know very well it's more than that. Only a few
women seem to have it. I used to think that if anybody could
wear lots of jewelry I could. I think you have to be tall and
blonde to carry it well. You know—ropes of pearls and arms
covered with bracelets. If I were as rich as Christine I'd buy
plenty of jewelry."

"I don't think she cares about it."

"You think she's perfect, don't you?"

Cautiously he said, "I think she has very good taste."

"Meaning that I haven't?" Then before he could reply
she gave a harsh little laugh. "You needn't bother to answer.
To tell you the truth, I really don't care. Bear that in mind,
will you? I honestly don't give a damn."

At that moment a lorry, traveling fast and swerving as it came, forced their driver to take quick evasive action.

"Well," Sibyl said, "if that had hit us it would certainly have finished what you began."

Stifling his anger he replied, "A quick and probably easy way out for both of us."

"Are you looking for a way out?" she asked, and gave him an oddly probing look. He didn't answer her, and they traveled for a long time in silence.

After seeing the gloomy gardens with their multiplication of water jets and spouts—the fantasy, he thought, of a mind seeking distraction, such a garden as a Texas oil millionaire might have dreamed up—they went to lunch at a restaurant with lovely views, and Sibyl drank so much Chianti that she was overcome by sleepiness and said she wanted to go back to Rome.

"I've seen enough," she said. "I don't know anything about Hadrian, and anyway one Roman emperor's just like another to me."

She had not worn her hat and veil since they had been in Rome. At the restaurant when a couple looked at her curiously, she stared back at them with such a hard and challenging look that they quickly turned their eyes away. This, Murray thought, was all to the good. She was learning courage, even if it was of a brassy, almost offensive kind. It was courage, and he welcomed it.

When they reached the hotel he paid the driver and Sibyl went into the lobby ahead of him. When he caught up with her she had some letters in her hand, one of which she gave to him. It was from his mother. The other two she put into her handbag.

"I told Edna not to write," she said. "It only means I'll have to write to her. You go on up if you want to. I'm going out to do a little shopping."

"Are you all right?" he asked. "Do you know your way?"

"Well, I'm only going to walk down the Via Veneto. I could hardly get lost. I want to buy a pair of gloves. I'll be back in half an hour, and then we'd better pack."

He went upstairs and read the letter in their bedroom.

Everything's all right [his mother wrote] though I believe Martin misses you both. As a rule he hardly ever looks out of the window, but yesterday he did several times and I'm sure he was looking for you. He's been a dear boy and no trouble at all except that when we got back from our walk this afternoon he didn't want to come in but held on to the gate with both hands and was quite angry and stubborn. You know I never use force with him and I didn't today, though if I had to I'm sure I'm stronger than he is. After a bit I persuaded him to let go and come into the house. I gave him a good tea and he seemed quite himself again. Now he's fast asleep in bed.

I hope you and Sibyl and Mrs. Bonner are having a lovely time. Your father always disliked Rome because of the Pope, but it must be a beautiful city. I'm not a bit lonely. Mrs. Helger came to tea with me yesterday, so you see I don't lack for company.

Your affectionate mother,

Maud Logan

He felt an impulse to show the letter to Christine. His mother and Martin had not gone to Ifield that day, so she had not seen them. There was a part of his life, therefore, from which she was shut out. As soon as he had thought of going to her room the idea became irresistible. When he knocked softly on her door, afraid that she might be asleep, she opened it herself wearing a dressing gown and with her straight, leaf-brown hair hanging nearly to her waist. He stood and gazed.

"Come in," she said, smiling at him. "Haven't you ever seen anyone with their hair down before?"

"I've so often tried to imagine what it would look like,"

206

he told her, not taking his eyes from it. "Are you feeling rested?"

She closed the door behind him.

"Sit here," she said, taking a little pile of underclothes from a chair. "I feel wonderful. I can hardly wait for tomorrow to come."

She went to the mirror and coiled up her hair while he watched. A twist or two, a few pins, and it was done. The sight of this intimate little performance enchanted him; it seemed to him the most delightful and feminine of acts. He thought he would never cease to see the pretty pose before the mirror; the slim, upraised arms, the simple dressing gown such as a very young girl might have worn, falling in straight lines to her feet, the nimble, expert fingers, so quick about their task. His love and approval were so intense that the pleasure was also a piercing pain.

"I'll go on with my packing," she said. "Was it a good trip?"

He told her about it, and added that Sibyl was now out shopping.

"I came along," he said, "because I thought you might like to read a letter from my mother."

While she read the letter he let his eyes take in greedily all they could of such personal things as would not be packed until the morning. Her old-fashioned bristle hairbrush, little plastic jars and bottles, light for traveling, and on the corner of her dressing table a photograph of the dog, Seth, who had played such a large part in sending her back to Sam. He wore the look a dog is apt to wear on being photographed—full of affection, bonhomie and even of amusement and complicity. Whatever it was that was going on, he was a willing participant, knowing himself to be the center of it all and finding enjoyment in it. She must have glanced up during her reading of the letter and followed the direction of his eyes, for she took up the photograph without a word and handed it to him, replacing it silently when the letter had been read. When she gave him back the letter her eyes looked troubled.

"Murray," she said, "he must be getting quite big. Is it all right for her to have sole charge of him?"

"She insists on it."

"I wonder if it's wise. I wonder if she ought to. You know, you're very like her in one way."

"In what way?" he asked.

"Oh, in the way you shoulder responsibilities. Even responsibilities that aren't rightly yours."

"Tell me what you mean," he asked, but he knew without her telling him.

"I think you know perfectly well what I mean. You must stop feeling responsible for that accident. It's corroding your whole life."

She was fitting some medicine bottles into the red morocco case and her face was averted.

"It was," he said. "It isn't now. Since I've known you I've come to terms with it more."

"It was time," she replied, "and if I've done that much I'm deeply thankful. Murray, I've been thinking about Sibyl a great deal. Do you think this trip is giving her any pleasure at all? I wanted to feel that I was doing as much for her as I was doing for myself. I wanted her to come out of that shell she lives in and be happy for a while. Do you think she's enjoying any of it?"

"In her own way, yes, I think she is. I doubt if she's capable of much enjoyment."

"She isn't jealous or suspicious is she? About us, I mean. I've tried so hard to keep the balance even, to make her feel it's her company I wanted quite as much as yours. And it hasn't been difficult, because I really wanted her to be happy."

"I think she's completely indifferent," he answered, "to whatever she may think we feel for each other."

"I do hope so," she said, "and I don't think we've given her any cause for jealousy, even if she were so inclined." Then she reverted to what he had said earlier. "But I think you're mistaken when you say she isn't capable of much enjoyment. I've come to some conclusions about Sibyl. Shall I tell you what they are?" Without waiting for his reply she went on: "I don't think she gets much pleasure through her eyes or her mind. Very little, I should say. What I think Sibyl longs for, with an almost obsessive longing, is a love affair that would make her forget herself and everything else."

"If you're right," he said, "and you well may be, that only makes her situation still more dreadful."

"You see," she told him, "Sibyl doesn't want love as you and I understand it. If she had wanted it, she might have had it from you. But that's no good to her. She wants something cruder and more violent. All her thoughts seem to move in that direction. She only has to be told that somebody was somebody's mistress or lover for her interest to be aroused at once. Then she comes alive. I've noticed this again and again."

"That's all true," he said. "I know it's true." And then he added, with pity in his voice, "Poor Sibyl, what a ghastly old age she's storing up for herself."

"I can't bear the thought of it," she told him sadly.

"Well," he said, and he spoke with some of his old bitterness, "neither can I bear the thought of my own."

They were both silent. She turned and looked at him, motionless, her arms at her sides. He knew there were words waiting behind those parted lips that he would have given anything to hear. She looked and looked and dared to say nothing. He looked back at her, not daring to break the silence and by breaking it break too much else besides. It was one of those moments of clear and frightening realization. Each knew, overwhelmingly, the desire to make the other's life complete. Their helplessness and pity suddenly appalled them. The pity and the powerlessness demanded that they seize and cling to each other, acting out in unspeakable relief, and need to comfort and be comforted, what could not be spoken. This act, so desperately desired, neither of them dared to precipitate. Only their eyes spoke. He knew it was the moment for flight, that there was nothing braver than to run away. He got up and went quickly to the door. But he could not go without a word, he could not leave in this too-significant silence that neither of them would ever cease to hear. It was better to speak, to say anything at all, to try to get back to where they were before.

"Thank you," he said, "for letting me come in." His voice broke as he added, "Thank you for letting me see you with your hair down."

She quickly put her hands to her cheeks. Over them he saw her eyes glistening with tears.

"Oh, Murray, don't, don't! Remember we have days and days—we have so much—these wonderful weeks together—"

He closed the door softly and went straight to his room. Sibyl had not yet returned. He stood by the window looking out on the garden, trying to control his trembling. Yes, they had days and days, but what was that? In a little over two weeks it would be finished. Everything had gone so well, so temperately, up to now. He had been a fool to go to her room. His mother's letter had been the merest pretext. It must never happen again. To clear his mind and steady himself he sat down and wrote a letter to Sam, telling him they were leaving for Athens tomorrow, that all was well, that Rome had exceeded even Christine's expectations, that Sibyl was losing her dread of being seen by strangers. He begged Sam to come to Athens early enough to stay at least a few days.

"Cable us if you think you can, and we'll make our plans accordingly. Do try. We wish you had been with us here in

Rome. I think you would have enjoyed it as much as we did. All the best, Murray."

As he sealed the letter and stamped it he thought, God help us all. But they must also help themselves, and take no risks. One thing was certain—they would never let Sam down or cause him the least suffering. They would not betray his trust and his innocence. He had few friends, and Sam was one of them. Sam and Charles were the best of them, the only ones who really mattered to him. It was not likely, then, that he would overstep the boundaries he had laid down for Christine and himself. And he could trust Christine. Only they must not try themselves foolishly far.

XV ✍

THE flight to Athens was over a
thick blanket of cloud. The captain told them, however, that
in Athens the weather was clear and that they might even get
a glimpse of the Acropolis as they circled in to land. The dark-
haired, sallow-skinned man from the Middle East, the reader
of Shakespeare, was also on the plane. He sat across the aisle
from Murray this time, and they talked to each other. He told
Murray he was a Syrian, from Damascus, and was making his
tenth visit to Rome and Athens. He spoke English with
pedantic correctness. He was about fifty-five, Murray guessed,
a heavy, calm, slow-moving man, wearing horn-rimmed spectacles and what looked like a Savile Row suit. Apart from the
fact that he wore a large sapphire ring, his dress was wholly
and conventionally British.

"We Syrians," he said, "are deeply conscious of our histori-
cal associations with Rome and Greece. It could hardly be
otherwise. I myself feel very much at home in both places.
I'm afraid it isn't generally realized in Europe or America

that our civilization antedates them both. We are a very old people. A very old people."

"I've never had the opportunity to go to the Middle East," Murray said. "I should like to. It's true, of course, that the Greeks got their alphabet from you?"

"And much else," the Syrian said. "We would prefer, therefore, that many Europeans and Americans did not think of us as barbarians." He smiled as he said it, but Murray could guess that the smile covered painful old wounds. He knew that Christine, who sat by the aisle in front of him, was listening. At that moment her sunglasses slipped off her lap and fell in the aisle. She was unaware of this until the Syrian leaned down to pick them up, half getting out of his seat as he did so.

"Your wife has dropped her glasses," he said, handing them to Murray. "I was afraid they might be trodden on."

Christine at once turned round to thank him.

"How kind of you," she said, and then asked, "Why don't we introduce ourselves? My name is Mrs. Bonner, this is Mr. Logan, and sitting next to me is Mrs. Logan."

The Syrian bowed and said, "I am most happy. My name is Araman, Dr. Araman, from Damascus. I must apologize if I made a mistake."

"Not at all," she said. "It was simply that as we traveled together from London and are traveling together now, I thought it time we made one another's acquaintance."

Sibyl had not acknowledged the introduction; she had merely glanced up and had at once returned to her book. Murray was reminded of a quarrel they had had a few years ago on the subject of the darker-skinned races. A family from Calcutta had for a while rented the house next to theirs in Morden. Sibyl had refused to give them so much as a good morning.

"It's women who feel as you do," he told her during the ensuing argument, "who lost us the Empire."

"Well," she retorted angrily, "if we had to mix with colored

213

people on equal terms in order to keep it, I'm glad we lost it."

Now he no longer had any desire to change her. Let her be what she was. All he asked of her was that she should at least try not to make their life together intolerable.

Christine and Dr. Araman continued to talk. At one point he heard Dr. Araman tell Christine that he was a doctor and specialized in diseases of the lungs, whereupon Christine threw Murray a quick glance to make certain that he had heard. Dr. Araman went on to say that he had his own hospital about eight miles from Damascus.

"I am not a rich man," he told them, "but I have rich friends who have made fortunes in oil. It is good that their money should be put to such a use. There is much tuberculosis among our poor people."

Murray wondered if Christine would speak of her special interest in the subject of diseases of the lungs, but she did not feel, evidently, that this was the right moment for it.

They watched for the break in the clouds that the captain had promised them. Sitting next to Murray was an elderly woman on her way to Istanbul to visit her son and daughter-in-law.

"I would so like just one glimpse of the Acropolis," she said wistfully.

They had their glimpse and Christine's subdued excitement was deeply gratifying to Murray. Thank God, he thought, she's going to have the thing she's longed for, at last. And thank God, I was able to help her to get it.

The car she had ordered for the duration of their stay was at the airport to meet them.

"You certainly know how to do things," Sibyl said, with approval. It was a large, roomy Cadillac and a uniformed chauffeur, a stocky man with a remarkably blue chin, was waiting for them. He told them his name was Pericles. He also informed them, in quite passable English, that he had driven many important English and Americans.

214

"So much the worse for us," Sibyl said, "if he finds out that we're not."

It was the chauffeur who first pointed out to them the Acropolis, hardly discernible now in the gathering dusk. "Most finest place in the world," he told them. "Everyone say so. Parthenon finest building. Built by man with same name as me. Begun 447 B.C. Blown up by Turks 1656. Too bad."

"Oh dear," Christine said, dropping her voice, "let's hope we don't get too much of that."

"If we do," Murray said, "we'll have to have a little talk with him."

On arrival at the hotel they found, to Murray's relief, that both rooms faced inward, on to a large open courtyard. He had been dreading a repetition of what had happened in Rome.

"This place looks pretty expensive," Sibyl said, as they began to unpack. "Are you going to be able to afford it, or is Christine going to pay?"

"No, of course not," he said. "We'll pay our share, so far as we can. Christine insists that the car and chauffeur are her affair. I'm afraid I'll have to agree to that."

"I don't see why not," Sibyl said. "She's welcome to pay for everything as far as I'm concerned. After all, we're only here for her convenience."

"And our own enjoyment, I hope," he added.

"I don't know so much about that. I can think of ways of enjoying myself more."

He did not ask her what these were, nor did he offer any rebuke. Too much was at stake. His whole aim now was to keep Sibyl in a good temper and avoid all possible sources of argument; to spend their time in Greece without a flare-up, without discord. He had had plenty of practice, especially over the past seven years. It ought not to be too difficult now.

Before they set out for the Acropolis next morning there

215

was a heavy shower, but it passed and as they drove up the hill the sun came out again and the clouds dispersed. The brief downpour pleased Christine.

"Now I shall see it," she said, "as it looked in the painting in Paul Riché's book. Did I tell you, Murray, that the originals were all sold? It was a big disappointment."

"What book, what originals?" Sibyl asked, and Christine explained that it was a book about Greece that had been sent her from Paris. She said that Murray had seen it in New York.

"Thanks," Sibyl said with irony. "It's something to have an inkling of what you're talking about."

Christine quickly apologized, saying she was very sorry indeed if she had seemed rude. She thought she had spoken about the book before.

"Oh, it doesn't matter," Sibyl said, "only it's a bit boring being odd man out all the time."

Christine's distress brought tears into her eyes. She put her hand on Sibyl's and cried out, "Oh, Sibyl, if you ever feel that, then I'm wholly to blame. I must be stupid, self-centered and tactless. Please forgive me!"

Murray turned his head and looked out the window, tense with anxiety and shame. It was such incidents as this that he had dreaded. But Sibyl, it seemed, was appeased.

"Oh, it's all right," she said, "don't worry. I'm always apt to be oversensitive. I suppose it's my face."

They had reached the parking place and as they got out of the car two of them felt discomfited and out of tune with the longed-for moment. Sibyl, Murray guessed, had enjoyed herself. She walked ahead of them up the stony incline as if it were her object to get to the top and back as quickly as possible. He briefly took Christine's hand, a silent message conveying his regret and she comforted him with a smile. She said in a low voice, "It's nothing. I've forgotten it. We're here. I'm not afraid of anything now. Not of Sibyl, not of dying, not of anything."

216

The ascent was not easy for her and she paused now and then to get her breath.

"Slowly, slowly," he pleaded. "We've got all day, and we've got other days as well."

"I'll go slowly," she said, "if you'll go ahead with Sibyl. I don't want her to think we're purposely lagging behind."

"I'm past caring what she thinks," he answered, but to please her he caught up with Sibyl. He began telling her what the different buildings were.

"Don't bother," she said. "I know which one's the Parthenon and I'm not going to trouble my head about the others. Why didn't you stay with Christine?"

She was going to exact, he saw, a heavy price for having come. It was no use telling her that they were there, at the very apex of the ancient world, to marvel, to fill their eyes with beauty and to be at peace. She would find her one enjoyment in making things uncomfortable. It was no more than he had expected; in fact so far it had been better than he could have hoped.

In the afternoon, after a rest, they went to the National Museum. Murray took pains to point out to Sibyl, no less than to Christine, the things that had most delighted him the previous year: the happy urchin on his galloping horse; the boy with the goose; Poseidon, the most glorious male figure ever cast in bronze, about to launch his thunderbolt; the Ephebe, the Couros.

"Why so much fuss about men and boys?" Sibyl asked. "Women don't seem to have mattered much, except a few goddesses. They must have had a poor time in those days."

"But weren't they lucky," Christine asked her, "just to have lived among such splendid beings?"

"You could have the lot, as far as I'm concerned," Sibyl said. "I'd settle for one stockbroker in a business suit."

She soon settled herself on a bench and said she'd stay there until they'd seen enough. When they returned she was reading a letter. She put it into her handbag and got up as they approached.

"Well," she said to Christine, "your staying power is remarkably good, it seems to me."

"Yes," Christine said. "As long as I'm looking at things that interest me I want to go on and on, but as soon as I stop I feel as I feel now, pretty well exhausted." She sat down on the bench where Sibyl had been sitting and said, "Just give me two minutes' rest and I'll be all right."

Murray felt a sharp anxiety and remorse. He'd let her do too much, she'd gone beyond her strength. He was thankful when, on their return to the hotel, she said she'd go straight to her room and rest, and that she'd have dinner in bed.

"I've had hundreds of dinners in bed," she said, "but it's still a great treat to me. Tomorrow I'll be ready for anything."

"Can't we take a drive somewhere tomorrow?" Sibyl asked. "It seems a pity to have a car and a driver and just keep him hanging about."

It was agreed that they'd go to Daphne and Eleusis, but not stay too long at either, and then drive along the coast road. Murray stayed behind, at Christine's suggestion, and discussed with the driver their future plans. They had decided that after spending five days in Athens they would set out for Delphi, spending two nights at the hotel there. They would then return to Athens for one night before making a week's trip to the Peloponnese, which would include Olympia, Corinth and Mycenae. The chauffeur approved, saying that all the important English and Americans he had driven had followed much the same program and had invariably said he was the best driver and guide they had ever had.

"We hope to be equally satisfied," Murray said.

As he and Sibyl were dining in the hotel restaurant that evening she said, "I forgot to tell you, Edna's got a friend here she wants me to meet. She's a Greek. She worked at the Air

218

Ministry for a time, as interpreter or something. She's married now and lives in a nice part of Athens. I'd like to go and see her one day."

"Do, by all means," Murray said. "Pericles can take you. Why don't you ring her up?"

"I will. Perhaps tomorrow. Only if I do go, I'll take a taxi. I'd rather be independent."

"Where does she live?"

"Oh, it's a street with an unpronounceable name. The address is upstairs."

She said no more about it and he left it to her to choose her own time for making the visit. She was getting to know her way about. She had provided herself with a map, and while Christine was resting after lunch went out by herself, leaving Murray reading the English papers or writing letters.

"Now that I don't care so much about people looking at me," she said, "I enjoy looking at them. I'd much rather do that than look at old statues or ruined buildings. I've decided I like Athens."

"I'm glad you do," he answered, and felt a twinge of fear that she might say next that she would rather stay in Athens than go to Delphi. But their five-day stay drew near its end and all seemed well.

The day before they were to start for Delphi, Sibyl told him that she had rung up Edna's friend and was going to see her. He asked what her name was.

"Oh, it's something ending in 'opulos.' I can't pronounce it, but I've got it written down. I said I'd go about five this afternoon. She even suggested my staying to dinner, to meet her husband."

"Do by all means if you want to. But wouldn't you like Pericles to take you and bring you back?"

"No, I'll go by taxi, and she said she'd bring me back."

She was ready before four and explained that she wanted to do some shopping first. She wanted to take home a few little presents.

"What about money? Have you got plenty?"

"Well, I'll take a few drachmas off you. I have some, but it might not be enough. If I'm not back by eight you'll know I've stayed on to dinner. Depends how I like her."

He was surprised and pleased by this new independence but surmised that it would not last long. Once back in Morden she would revert to old ways. When she had gone he rang up Christine's room. They had been for a drive that morning to the foot of the Pentelicon and had seen the little church of Ayia Triada. They had lunched on the way home, and then Christine, with the next day's trip in mind, had gone to her room to rest. He told her about Sibyl's excursion and asked if she'd like to drive up to the Acropolis once more. They might sit for a while and look at the view. It was too perfect an afternoon to spend indoors.

"How enterprising of Sibyl," Christine said. "Yes, of course I'd like to come. I'll bring a little traveling rug for us to sit on."

They sat on the steps of the Parthenon looking out over the Attic Plain and the Aegaleus Mountains. It had turned so warm that they were glad to be in the shade of the columns. The distance was washed in a delicate haze, as blue as a flower. Other sightseers moved quietly about, most of them soon turning homeward and vanishing down the hill. Peace and contentment fell on them like a blessing. They felt hushed by it, and by the bliss of being alone.

At last, when she had drunk her fill of quiet, Christine said, "Bless Sibyl for giving us this little time together."

A question that he had never before dreamed of asking her now forced itself to the surface of his mind and took on words. "Christine, do you think you could have been happy married to me? Tell me. I must know."

220

She turned the gentle oval of her face toward him, and her eyes rested on his with such tenderness that he knew the answer before she spoke.

"Of course, Murray. I thought we need never say it. I thought you knew. I love you."

He took her hand and gripped it with violence, a pain she bore without a sign. His own pain was in the first consciousness of guilt toward Sam.

"I had to hear you say it," he said, in his own defense. "If I have to let you go, it helps to be quite certain of what I'm losing. To sacrifice the whole is sometimes easier than to sacrifice a part of the whole. I had to be sure."

"I know, I know," she answered. "It gives a sort of grandeur to renunciation. It makes one feel proud to be able—" she broke off and leaned her forehead against his sleeve. "Oh, words, words! How brave they sound! How can I let you go back to that life you lead? How can I?"

He dared make no reply. He sat unmoving, too conscious of the pressure of her head against his arm to trust himself to speak. Then she drew away and sat upright again.

"Listen, dear Murray. I must bear as best I can the barrenness of our lives. That's my task. But now I want to lighten yours. Living with me is something I don't think you've tried to visualize. Let me tell you about it. Sam has fought through so many illnesses with me, he's had to suffer so many anxieties, that it's now a part of his life. Heaven knows I've rewarded him very poorly for his devotion and even tried to escape from it. But, you see, it happens to be in Sam's nature to love me better ill than well. I don't mean this cruelly; I say it with wonder and awe and admiration. Most men would feel very differently. Even you might in time. No, I know you won't believe it now. When I'm ill, Sam has no doubts. He knows I'm not longing to try my wings somewhere else. I'm his child, his precious, only child. I can't describe how tender he is. Again I don't mean this cruelly, but he's

221

rather more than reconciled to my poor health. That's what I tried to run away from, as you know. Every effort I make to live a normal life tears at his heart. Letting me go on this trip was agony for him. He thinks he wants me to be well and strong, but he's completely reconciled to my not being so. His loving care for me is his *raison d'être*, almost his life's work."

Staring in front of him he broke into this to say, "I believe I could make you well."

"No, no!" she cried. "Don't put such a wicked temptation before my eyes! And don't be deceived by this little time we've had together, these few weeks of good health since I left home. It could end quite suddenly."

She made a gesture, as if to dismiss all such thoughts.

"And anyway, how foolish we are to talk about it, even to imagine for one moment that our love could have any future. We know it couldn't. We've known it and accepted it from the beginning."

"Yes," he said, "of course we know it. Parting is as inevitable as the coming of night. I keep telling myself so. And much good it does."

"Sometimes," she told him sadly, "when I can't sleep, I lie staring at the dark, appalled at my terrible selfishness. It's all my fault, what has happened. I brought it about. If there's been cheating, it's I who have done it. I blame myself entirely."

"Hush," he said gently, "hush. There's no need to talk of blame. Do you imagine for one instant that I regret this? Don't you know that it's all the happiness I've ever had?"

Her eyes filled with sudden tears, and she took a handkerchief out of her bag. "I'm sorry. It's just that I realized to the full what I'd done. My sins are very black. Talk to me, talk to me about something else. Anything."

He took her hand again and held it, calming and reassuring her.

222

"Suppose we had time to visit one of the islands. Which one would you like to go to most?"

She thought she would choose Crete. He put forward the claims of Rhodes. Gradually she grew composed and cheerful again.

"Do you know what I'd like to do more than anything else?" she asked. "This is just folly and childishness, but all the same it's true. I'd like to live here in Greece and never leave it. Everything I see seems to conform to some inner vision of loveliness. Perhaps we were both born with that vision. I'd like to live overlooking the sea, with vines and olive trees nearby. I'd live frugally. Money wouldn't be important here. I'd be content to give most of it away and keep only enough to live on and to buy books with. I could be happy like that."

"If what you're saying is just childishness," he said, "there are two short words you might safely have added."

"With you, with you!" she cried, and put her face briefly against his sleeve. "And now, dear Murray, we ought to go back."

They started down the slope in the light of the setting sun, which gilded every column and broken pediment, glorifying the Propylea still further, gently emblazoning the Temple of Nike and, as they looked back, bathing the Parthenon in a warmer beauty. It gave Christine's pallor a look of health, and turned her hair to copper. He took her arm as they went down. The whole scene gave them such delight that for the moment they were content to be in it and of it and ask for nothing more. He wondered if the feeling they had for each other was as uncommon as he believed it to be, and if so, if it could be due to something within themselves, some specific talent perhaps. In not possessing they seemed to possess, and with the knowledge that they must soon part came the need to grow closer still in spirit. He felt he had undergone an experience of so much depth and power that

223

bodily needs were diminished almost to superfluity. And then, humanly doubting, he asked himself for how long? And might they not regret for the rest of their lives that they had denied themselves the one thing lacking?

As if her thoughts kept in step with his, she asked, "Tell me, does this have meaning and validity for you? It has for me. It's a quotation that often comes to my mind.

> 'Love is most nearly itself
> When here and now cease to matter.' "

"I've no doubt it's true," he told her, "but like most mystical truths it chills to the bone. You have to penetrate to the heart of it to find illumination and warmth. I don't think I can."

She looked up at him with love and sadness; it was as if she had already lost him and yet had never loved or needed him more.

"I think I can," she said. "I think I have."

When they got out of the car at the hotel he told Pericles they would not be wanting him that evening and reminded him that they would be ready to leave for Delphi at ten the next morning.

"Yes, sir," Pericles said. "Pericles never late. No one ever wait for Pericles. All my people say so."

They went to the desk for their keys and Christine found a letter—they came almost daily—from Sam. After hesitating a moment she tore it open and asked him to wait while she glanced through it for news.

"Everything's all right," she reported. "Frederick is much better and he'll be flying to London with Sam. Sam will leave him with Charles and then fly on here." She added with a touch of affectionate amusement, "He says he hopes to spend one day here to see the Acropolis."

224

"One day is something," Murray said. She put the letter into her handbag to reread upstairs.

"If Sibyl isn't back by eight," he said as they went up in the elevator, "we could dine at a small Greek restaurant I know. It's one I found last year. Would you like that?"

She said she would, and as they walked along the corridor to their rooms she said what a surprising thi..g it was that Sibyl had gone off by herself to meet total strangers. It showed a great change in her.

"It may not last," he said, "but at least she'll have tasted independence, and it's all your doing."

They had reached the door of her room.

"The sad thing is," she said, as she opened it, "that I haven't succeeded in making her like me. I believe I've failed completely there."

He knew this was true, and it was more honest not to attempt to deny it. He left her there and went to his room.

By eight Sibyl had not returned, and he knocked on Christine's door. She was ready, and they went down in the elevator together feeling like husband and wife about to have an evening out.

Throughout the evening their talk was carefully matter-of-fact. They felt they had permitted themselves that afternoon on the Acropolis a license to which they had no right, and they did not feel disposed, now, to take advantage of the freedom Sibyl had so surprisingly allowed them. As if to evoke Sam's presence, and in so doing to safeguard them both still further, he said, "It's hard to believe that in just fifteen days Sam will be here."

Her mood of quiet happiness was instantly changed to dismay. She covered her eyes as if to shut out the sight of some black and inexorable calendar.

"Oh, don't, Murray, don't count the days! I've been so careful not to."

"I'm sorry," he hastened to say. "Try to forget it."

225

She dropped her hands and looked at him.

"It's like a piece of precious ice that melts in your grasp. Let's try to think of time simply as Delphi, Olympia, Mycenae and the other places we'll see. If you anchor it to space, it doesn't go so fast. From now on we'll have to guard every moment."

"All the same you're longing for tomorrow to come."

"Yes, I'm longing for that. Did you know we pass the very spot where, according to legend, Oedipus killed Laius, his father?"

"But I know the very place," he told her. "I sat there in the heather last year and ate my lunch. I was on my way back to Athens from Delphi. I got bus rides from time to time, but I walked most of the way."

"Then you must show me where it is. We must make Pericles drive slowly."

They went back to the hotel soon after ten, not wanting Sibyl to come back and find them out. But both keys were in their places, and she had not returned.

When he switched on the light in their room he half expected to see Sibyl's blond head in its silk net, ornamented with rosebuds, on her pillow. He took up from his bedside table a worn volume of Pausanius that Charles had once given him and sat down to read. When he glanced at his traveling clock it was after eleven. He decided to pack, expecting each moment to see Sibyl open the door. He began to feel a little anxious and more than a little guilty. He did not know the names of the people she had gone to see, nor where they lived. She had been so jealous of her newly found independence that she had not wanted to tell him. By twelve o'clock he began to think of taxi accidents, and then the most probable solution occurred to him. They had taken her to a night club. Athens was full of them. There was nothing that Sibyl—now that she had got over her hatred of being seen by strangers—

226

would enjoy more. This seemed so likely that he decided to forget his anxieties and go to bed.

He undressed and presently went to the cupboard where the maid was in the habit of hanging up his pajamas. Beside them hung Sibyl's pale-blue nightgown. He was about to put the pajamas on when his hand touched something that had no right to be there. It made him stand as still as a statue. The soft night air that blew gently in through the window curtains fanned his naked body. He was unaware of anything but the object his hand had touched. It was a letter and it was pinned to the sleeve of his pajamas.

He could not afterwards remember at all clearly what he felt when he found it there. He must, he thought, have experienced a kind of brief mental paralysis caused by shock— the shock of the collision between the violently unexpected and, on the subconscious level but rising instantly into the conscious, an awareness that this thing had been going to occur, a deep-down precognition. Seconds passed during which he made no move, then he stirred, unpinned the letter, and sat down on the bed, still naked, to read it.

It covered several pages and was hurriedly written on hotel paper. It began:

This is good-by, and I hope forever. I'm writing this in what's called the card room where nobody comes in the daytime. Tomorrow before I leave I'll pin it to your pajamas so you'll see it when you go to bed. I'll probably have to do this while you're in the room.

Two days ago when I went out after lunch leaving you reading the papers, I took my passport and return ticket to the travel agency and got myself a seat on the plane leaving for London tomorrow afternoon. They didn't make any fuss about changing it, and anyway there was a cancellation, luckily. I'm not taking anything with me, not even a hairbrush. I've bought a new toothbrush and I put a clean nightie in my handbag. I told them at the booking

227

office that you'd be bringing my luggage later, but you can leave it there for all I care. Len will provide me with everything I want and I mean to start fresh. I never want to see anything that belongs to my old life again and that includes you and your mother and Martin and everyone connected with Atlantic House as well. I'm going to live with Leonard Shawfield Graham—it's a nice name don't you think?—known to me as Len. His wife can get a divorce now on the grounds of adultery with me, and so can you, so keep this letter.

It was funny the way it happened. I used to meet Len and his wife shopping in Morden, mostly on Saturday mornings, and I took a great liking to him. (I never liked her.) He's just my sort of man. You know, a real *man*. He's with a bill-broking firm in the City and makes money. I always thought, right from the start, that he was wasted on her.

Then I met him one day when he was out alone, and he asked me to go for a drive in his new car. (It's a Bentley.) He told me how things were between him and his wife. Then he told me he'd always admired me and said I'd got the best figure he'd ever seen. He said a lot of things I won't repeat, except that he said he didn't care a damn about my scars. Anyone could see I'd been a beauty and I still was. Well, you can guess what that did for me, especially coming from him. We went out again soon after, and on that drive something happened to us. Sitting there in the car—well, it was as if we'd both been set on fire. He took me to an inn and said he wanted a room. He said his wife was feeling ill and wanted to lie down. Well, part of that was true, anyway. We committed adultery that afternoon and whenever we've had the chance since. I've been feeling like a different woman, but as you don't care about me and never have, you haven't even noticed it.

Len's got himself a house in Wimbledon, and he's going to let me buy whatever I want for it. He's already put in a double bed, a few chairs and a table and some kitchen things, and that will do for the moment. He says I've got to get over my sensitiveness about my face, and be quick about it, and no damned nonsense. That's partly why I said I'd go on this trip, though I had other reasons too. I'm more used to being looked at by strangers now, so I suppose it's done me good.

228

I planned to do this from the start if I possibly could. In fact I promised Len I would. It gives me a lot of satisfaction to go off and leave you with Christine Bonner. I knew what you were up to from the first day I met her, and that you only wanted me along for the look of the thing. Well, that was all right with me, even though no decent man would have done it.

I thank heaven I'll never have to see Martin again. No fuss about the custody of the child in this divorce. He's all yours!

Sibyl

P.S. I invented all that about Edna's friend. There wasn't any such person.

Please forward my letters to 12, Upper Marksfield Lane, Wimbledon.

He read it over again, and then a third time. How completely in character it was! She was doing what she would have done at any time during the past seven years if the opportunity had offered. Though she had shunned men during that time, he had known very well that they were her chief interest and that part of her bitterness was that, thanks to the accident, she felt herself to be exiled as a woman.

He shivered and put on his pajamas. He knew he would not fall asleep for a long time, but he put out the lights and got into bed. He thought over every aspect of her leaving him and, remembering back, saw many a sign he had not specially noted at the time. Then he switched his mind to the present. What immediately concerned him now was the problem Sibyl's departure presented to Christine and himself. What should they do? Were they bound to go back to London on the first plane that would take them? Wouldn't it be at least possible for them to go to Delphi tomorrow as planned? Must Christine be deprived of all the joys she had looked forward to for so long? This, it seemed to him, would be nothing less than a tragedy. Need anyone, for the present, know what had happened? Couldn't they make it known in their own time? These questions kept sleep far away, and at

229

last, harassed by problems that kept going round and round in his head as though fixed to a wheel and unable to find positive answers to them, he got up and looked in the drawer of Sibyl's bedside table to see if she had left any sleeping tablets. There was one, and it was lying on a slip of paper that had Sibyl's sprawling writing on it:

"I don't suppose you'll need this but you might. See how thoughtful I am!"

Her planning had been perfect, but not even for the bliss of unconsciousness would he have accepted the sleeping tablet so offered. He threw it and the piece of paper away and got back into bed.

The only decision he came to before finally dropping off to sleep some time after four was to get up early and take the letter to show to Christine. It was the only decision he could make without her.

XVI ✑

He knocked on Christine's door, fully dressed, soon after eight. She called out, "Come in," and he went into the room and closed the door behind him. She was in bed, her breakfast tray on her knees and a bed-jacket about her shoulders. One quick look at his face told her that something had happened. Without speaking he went quickly to the bed and gave her the letter. Her eyes were wide with inquiry but she said not a word until she had read it through. Then she let it drop from her hands.

"What a terrible, terrible letter!"

Her eyes clung to his in an astonishment so great that it seemed to have excluded every other emotion. He nodded without speaking. She said, marveling, "She's there now, at this moment. In that man's house. Probably in that double bed. She's begun a new life. Doesn't it seem to you incredible?"

"I've had all night to think about it."

Her eyes were still fixed on his. "But you knew nothing. You had no idea—"

"I knew nothing at all." He moved to the foot of the bed and stood facing her. "It's the best thing for her. And the best thing for me, though I put that a long way second."

They continued to look at each other and behind this close mutual regard were questions waiting to be asked.

"She's been extraordinarily clever," she said, and she said it with distaste. "Have you had breakfast yet?"

"Yes, in my room an hour ago."

"I've finished mine. Will you take the tray, please, and then sit down and talk to me?"

He did as she asked, and said, "Yes, she's been very clever, but I never underrated her intelligence, such as it was."

"No," she said. "I did, perhaps; I didn't think her capable of this."

"There must have been indications of what was going on," he said, "but I never saw them. She'd met this couple before I went to New York. She spoke about them when I got back, twice at least. She said they weren't getting on. She'd been going out more often—my mother spoke of it, saying what a good thing it was. When you asked us to Ifield, on a Sunday, she said she had an engagement. That was unusual, but she let me think it was with friends of people we know. Other things come to my mind now. Letters she's written and received since we've been here, and said nothing about."

There was a long silence, during which they continued to search each other's eyes. But this amazing happening was beginning to lose its power to shock and astonish. They would talk about it later, and often, but now they accepted it because following closely upon it were new and pressing questions to be considered. He waited for her to speak of them, not wanting to seem eager to reap any advantages from what had occurred. She waited for him, for the same reason. She conquered her reluctance first.

"What are we going to do now?"

He got up, and without answering immediately began to walk up and down the room, his eyes on the floor. Then he paused at the foot of the bed and asked, "Can you see any reason at all why we shouldn't go to Delphi as arranged?" and was glad that he had forced himself to ask it. He caught her swift look of relief and gladness.

"Do you think we could? Oh, Murray, do you really think we could?" Then her expression quickly changed. "No, no, don't listen to me. Don't let me be selfish. I'm almost certain we ought not to go."

He began his pacing again.

"I can't bear you to miss what you've been looking forward to for so long, because of this. I can't bear it. Must we rush back to England by the first plane that can take us?"

"I suppose," she answered, "it's what we would be expected to do, isn't it?"

He parried this with another question. "Need anyone know just when she left? Need they know the day and the hour?"

"I don't see why," she said slowly. "No, I don't see why they should."

"Well, then, why shouldn't we steal just a few days and at least see Delphi? It's unbearable that Sibyl should rob you of that."

Glancing at her he could see anxiety on her smooth forehead, and her eyes were troubled.

"I implore you, Murray, not to consider me and not to let me be selfish. Of course I want to go, desperately, but I feel it would be wiser, somehow, not to go. I don't know what's to be gained by not going, but perhaps something is. I suppose it would be expected of us, as if someone had suddenly died. But don't ask me who would expect it, because I don't know."

He presently stopped his pacing and faced her again.

"Does this strike you as sensible?" he asked. "Suppose we

just leave it to chance? If we can get two seats on the plane now, we'll take them. If we can't, well, so much the better for us. We'll go to Delphi."

Her eyes brightened. "Of course. I'd forgotten we might have to wait. That would settle everything, wouldn't it?"

"I'll go and find out," he said. "As you say, that would settle everything."

She sighed. "I'm wicked enough to hope they'll be booked up for days and days. I'll get up now, but come back and tell me as soon as you can."

He went downstairs, rang up the airline and waited, his heart beating fast. He felt as if his whole happiness depended on the number of people who were wishing to go to England. When the answer came it was even better than he had allowed himself to hope. No seats were available for five days, barring cancellations, and for these there was already a waiting list. He booked the first two that were offered him and said he would bring the tickets in within the next half hour for alteration. As he left the telephone booth he wondered if he ought perhaps to have rung up one or two other airlines, but decided that honor was now satisfied. They had already risked, in a brave gamble, the most valuable days of their lives, and who was likely to ask at some future time if it had not been possible to travel by some other line? No one. Why should they? No one's life was in danger, there was no urgency. Sibyl had chosen to spring this surprise on them, therefore they had cut short their stay by ten days. Surely that was enough.

He went back to Christine's room and she came to the door in her dressing gown. When he told her, her face lit up with an almost childlike joy. It was a reprieve, a gift from the gods, they agreed. She gave him her passport and ticket and he hurried off to his room to get his own.

No one commented on Sibyl's departure the day before. He doubted if it had even been noticed. She had gone out

234

with nothing but her handbag. But he thought it best to tell the manager that his wife had had to return to England and that her suitcase—which he had that morning packed for the first time in their married lives—would be left at the hotel until their return to Athens. He added that they would be requiring the same rooms, or two other rooms, for one night in five days' time. He paid the bills and at a quarter to ten Christine came down. Pericles was already waiting and on being told that the other lady would not be coming with them, seemed to think it of little interest.

In a few minutes they were on their way to Delphi, and as they put more and more miles between them and the events of yesterday they felt reassured about the rightness of what they had done, and the unlooked-for delight of spending these precious days by themselves dispelled any doubts that might have lingered in their minds.

Once Christine said, smiling, "Now you can tell me without the risk of boring Sibyl everything you know about the places we'll pass through."

It was a day of crystalline beauty with a cloudless sky that seemed to promise an indefinite stay. The far blue mountains floated free of the land above a delicate haze, and all was propitious. Cars grew fewer, and there were long stretches of road where they were the only travelers except for occasional shepherds driving sheep or goats. The air became sweet with the scent of heather and, as there had been rain in the night, the earth, too, was perfumed. They lunched at an inn where they drank ouzo and later chose their food from steaming kettles in a fragrant kitchen. This pleased and amused Christine, and, unable to make a choice, she ordered three different dishes and could finish none of them.

They traveled through miles of country thickly covered with tall Mediterranean heath and adorned with little arbutus trees, and they asked Pericles to stop and got out to pick small branches bearing both flower and scarlet fruit. In the clearings there were terraced vineyards, the vines now brilliant in yellow leaf.

Then Pericles suddenly stopped the car in a wild region of low hills and heather and pointed to a place where a barely discernible path converged upon the road, a path that could easily have been missed.

"Here Oedipus," he said, "here Laius. They meet, they fight. Oedipus kill Laius. Long time ago, maybe six, maybe seven thousand years. No one know. Pericles good guide, eh? He remember everything."

They were beginning to grow fond of the squat, blue-chinned man, and though his driving was liable to be over-fast, he drove with skill. They thanked him, and as they got back into the car, Murray said, "I would certainly have missed it. There's nothing to mark the spot." He longed to share with her a magic moment in his life. "That's the very bank I sat on to eat my lunch of rolls and ham, in May last year."

"Oh," she cried, and her whole heart was in it, "how I wish I could have been with you! I think perhaps in a way I was with you."

When she wanted to stop the car and get out and disappear into the heather she said so, and this, to Murray, marked the breaking down of a little barrier caused by her old-fashioned shyness, and he treasured it. It was comparable to the time in Rome when he had first seen her with her hair down. Each little intimacy they attained was precious to him, but warned him anew of the need for caution and made more pressing the necessity of guarding against all that they were bound to guard against. For he was growing more and more certain with each day that passed that nothing but their constant awareness of Sam and their affection for him could keep them apart; and that she was as conscious of this heavy duty as he was. Even if they had made no vows to respect it, both felt that they had; felt bound and chained and manacled. And if they had needed it, there was the thought of Sibyl

236

and her animal-like passion for her new lover to make them feel how desirable it was to keep their love on quite another plane. Their goal must be to attain to the fullest understanding and the highest happiness they could reach, and still be blameless.

It was nearly dark when they reached the hotel. It stood quite alone on high ground that fell away with undulating steepness down, down, miles below to the olive groves that flooded the valley of Pleistos, and in the fading, crepuscular light they could see the distant Gulf of Itea like a dark and tarnished mirror. At the back of the hotel was a terraced garden commanding that incomparable view. They went to look at it before going in to take possession of their rooms, and the sight bathed them in a feeling of calm assurance, as if their futures were truly theirs and rested safely in their own hands. When they were in the lighted hotel lobby, Murray could see from a quick look at Christine's face that, happy though she was to be there, she needed rest and bed. He explained at the reception desk that one member of their party had been obliged to return to England but that no change need be made in their accommodations. He added, looking toward her with a smile, that Mrs. Bonner was very tired and would like her dinner in bed, and she gave him a quick glance of gratitude and acquiescence.

Their rooms were separated by one other room, and Christine came in to see him before starting to unpack.

"Come to the window," she said, drawing back the curtains, "quickly, while there's still some light. I wish we hadn't used up the moon in Rome, it would have been even more welcome here."

They stood looking out at the faint far outlines of the gulf and at the dark and formal shapes of the hills running down into it.

"I thought when I was here before how much I'd like to stay in this hotel," he said. "I little guessed what the next year would bring. I stayed in an inn, in the village. It was dirty and full of fleas. It will be a joy to wake up in the morning and see this."

"Yes," she said. "I'm longing for daylight. Will you lend me your Pausanius? I'd like to read him for a while before I go to sleep."

He told her she should sleep well; they were at the very core and center of the world here, and tomorrow he would show her the Ompholos to prove it. The whole earth would be revolving all through the night with them as its pivot. She smiled and lifted her cheek to him for a good-night kiss. It was their first caress, but it meant no more than she had intended it to mean. She gave him a loving look, said good night and went to her room.

He was in bed by ten, but was haunted between sleep and waking by images of Sibyl as a kind of fury or harpy, bent on revenge. She came and went, always menacing; he dismissed her, and she returned, and behind her, around her and through her he could see the words of her letter, with its ferocity and hate. He made an effort and woke fully, and her image vanished, but he went on thinking about her. He hoped her infatuation would last and that she would get happiness from it, at least for a time. He supposed he would start divorce proceedings as soon as he got back. He lay staring into the dark, trying to picture himself as an injured husband and felt half sickened, half amused. It all began to seem fantastic, a little absurd, and it was hard to believe in it. It seemed to him not improbable that one day a disillusioned, perhaps abandoned Sibyl, whose resurgence of faith in herself had been destroyed, would return to him and ask to be taken back. What his answer would be he did not know, and he debated it a little fearfully. He had pitied her too long to break himself easily of the habit.

One more anxiety now teased his brain. Should he have referred to Christine, when speaking to the manager, as his niece or perhaps his sister? Did it matter? Were such things of any importance nowadays so long as people behaved discreetly? His shut-in life provided him with no answers. Should he have consulted Christine? But it seemed not to have entered her mind that they ought to make use of subterfuges, and he greatly preferred not to. They were friends, not lovers. They were loving friends. Clear consciences, he finally decided, should go far. They would leave matters as they were. He thought of the Ompholos, and what they would see tomorrow, and at last fell asleep, cradled in a dark world of antiquity which, in a few hours, would be blazing with sun and light and beauty.

XVII ✒

Driving to Delphi next morning
under an unbroken canopy of blue, they stopped the car to
get out at the spot from which Riché had painted his picture.
At that moment Murray remembered something he had forgotten the day before; he had meant to point out to her the
headland he had chosen as the spot where he would like to be
buried. But his thoughts had all been of life, not death, and
they were all of life now. He no longer cared to speak of it,
and felt, in fact, a little ashamed of it.

This was a moment which brought past and present together with a kind of elegant neatness, as if binding them
with a ribbon and a bow. The moment when she had knelt
beside his chair, they agreed, marked the beginning of the
sequence of events which had brought them to this spot.
They stood there, their hands touching, feeling a great thankfulness for what they had achieved. Who could have predicted it then?

There was a vast silence about them, all sound seemed

delicately suspended until their ears caught the barely perceptible one made by a small herd of black goats with lyre-shaped horns, quietly cropping the grass not far away. They, and a lad of eight or so who watched them, made perfect foreground figures for the scene beyond. As they turned to go back to the car Christine remarked, with some sadness, "How much easier it is to love poor countries than prosperous ones! Progress seems to go hand in hand with vulgarity in our civilization. Here there's no such thing as vulgarity. If it weren't for Sam, I don't think I would ever leave here."

When they reached Delphi itself she looked about her with rapture, her lips parted, her eyes glowing. It exceeded, she said, anything she had heard, read or imagined.

"If you'll look up," Murray told her, rejoicing in her delight, "you'll see what I've been almost praying you'd see—an eagle circling just below Mount Parnassus. Now it's quite perfect."

They went down arm in arm to the lower Sanctuary of Athena Pronaia and saw the ruins of the Tholos and of the Temple of Apollo, which gave off a dazzling brightness. Christine, beyond speech with pleasure and with the vivid sense of standing where she had so often longed to stand, broke a leafy twig from a wild olive tree and put it in the pocket of her coat, as if she needed tangible reminder that her dream had become reality. They heard a bird's thin, clear, effortless song etched on the silence and looked up to see a robin redbreast perched near the top of the small tree. Christine laughed aloud. "And we call them English robins," she said. "Here I suppose they're called Greek robins. It only needed that song to make the spell of this place complete."

He wouldn't let her stay long there, promising her that they would return the next day, and perhaps the day after, and presently they were climbing the hill to the upper Sanctuary, pausing now and then to rest. He told her she was less breathless than she had been when walking up to the Acropolis, and she said she thought so too.

"I can only suppose," she said, "that happiness agrees with me."

Late in the year as it was, only a few tourists were scattered about the whole wide area, at which they rejoiced. As they went up he showed her the Ompholos, the Rock of the Sibyl, the marble Treasury of the Athenians, the site of the sixteen bronze statues that had once celebrated the victory of Marathon, and then the amphitheater. They agreed that among the many kinds of genius the Greeks had possessed was the genius for places and for placing. Below them, standing on the stage, looking up at them, they saw a dark, heavily built man and recognized Dr. Araman, who had quite clearly already recognized them. They waved to him, and he called up to them, "Can you hear me? I am hardly raising my voice at all. The acoustics here are remarkable."

They said they could hear him perfectly, and he presently came up the steps and sat down next to Christine. He told them he also was staying in the hotel and had seen them arrive the evening before. He was too discreet, or too incurious, to ask what had become of the third member of their party, and began to tell them about the plays he had seen there.

"This place acts as a magnet to me," he said. "Perhaps some of my ancestors were Greek, and came here to consult the Sibyl. I like to think so."

"I suppose you had about a thousand years, more or less, of Hellenism," Murray said.

"Yes, and we are grateful for them."

They learned that Dr. Araman, besides being a specialist in diseases of the lungs, was a scholar and a historian. He told them with a mixture of modesty and pride that he had written a book on ancient Antioch, its founding and its history under the Seleucids. He talked so well that they could not fail to enjoy his company even while hoping that they would not

242

have too much of it during the few precious days remaining to them.

He went with them up to the ancient Stadium and pointed out to Christine the narrow marble slabs set in the earth where the runners had stood waiting for the starting signal. As he had been looking forward to showing her these himself Murray felt a little aggrieved, but catching Christine's eye he saw that she was aware of this, and they smiled at each other. On the way down the hill again, holding to Murray's arm, she said to Dr. Araman: "I was greatly interested on the plane to hear about your hospital and the work you do. As a girl I was tubercular, and I've had lung operations. I expect you've noticed that I'm rather short of breath."

He said he had noticed it. She had not quite recovered from the climb when he sat down beside her in the amphitheater.

"I guessed what your medical history might be," he said, and his face broadened into a warm smile as he added, "but I think you are steadily growing better."

"I suppose I am," she agreed, "but I keep having setbacks—bronchial pneumonia and so on. It's all very boring. That's one reason why I was so anxious to come to Greece. It's been a dream of mine for many years. I hated the thought of dying without having seen something of it."

"Please take very good care not to die," he said gently. "Please believe in your power to live and grow stronger. I think you will, because you have courage." He looked across her at Murray and said, "You should bring her to Damascus this coming winter. I am sure you would both like it, and it would be good for her."

Murray answered with a smile, "There's nothing I'd rather do," and decided to leave it at that. If, in spite of Christine's attempt in the plane to sort out their relationships, he still thought them husband and wife, what did it matter?

243

Dr. Araman had hired a car, so they went back to the hotel by themselves. After lunch and an hour's rest they went to the Museum and looked about them a little fearfully for Dr. Araman, but he was not there.

"I like him so much," Christine said, "but our time is too precious to be shared with anyone."

She fell in love with the bronze statue of the solemn young Charioteer, as he had known she would, and they went back to it several times.

"How much more satisfying than all the gods and goddesses," she said. "I know this boy. Some proud mother's son. A little stupid perhaps, but so brave. I wonder if she saw him win his race. I hope she did. He bridges more than two thousand years for me."

He said, as they finally turned away, "One more lovely thing to share," and she replied, "Yes, for as long as we both shall live." And as she spoke the dreaded time of parting seemed to draw near and to become absolute, and it cast its shadow over them.

While Christine rested in her room before dinner, Murray went for a walk. He kept to the road and strode along taking deep breaths of the pure, thyme-scented air. He tried to look at his future with clear eyes. He could draw some comfort from the fact that life without Sibyl would be infinitely better than life with Sibyl—if he dared regard her departure as permanent. He had not yet begun to count up the advantages his freedom would bring him. He would dispose of the house in Morden, with its hateful memories, and move to London, perhaps find a flat near Kensington Gardens, so that his mother could take the boy for walks there. He would join a club, go to the theater sometimes, perhaps make some friends. Atlantic House would mean to him what it had always meant, and he felt he could discount the rumors that Charles would one day go into politics. Certainly he had never said so to him. In a year or two Dick Bayliss, that thorn in his flesh, would retire, and presumably he would take his place. But in the midst of these thoughts it came to him in the bright, destructive light of self-knowledge that none of these things would matter to him when he was separated from all that could bring him happiness by three thousand miles and every decent principle he possessed. He was destined to be one of those unfortunates, who, having known the best, can never make do with second best, and the future he was planning for himself looked utterly desolate. There was one thing and one thing only that he could do for Christine when the moment of parting came: he could keep from her the full knowledge that this was so.

They woke the next morning to the sound of steadily falling rain. The whole world seemed to have changed overnight. The Gulf of Itea was blotted out by a thick gray curtain of rain and mist and only the immediate foreground, where the steep decline began, was visible. The ground was already saturated, the flowers on the terrace were beaten down and hung their quivering heads miserably. A watery world shut them in. He had planned to take Christine to the Castalian Spring and then back to the upper Sanctuary, but now there was nothing to do but to find a place where they could talk with some privacy. They drew two chairs close to the window in the little bar where they could sit and watch for any signs of clearing.

As if she guessed what had been in his thoughts in the night she began to speak of the incredible thing that had happened two days before and of the effect it would have on his future. They had hardly had time yet to assimilate it, let alone to discuss it with all its implications. Would his mother, she asked, be greatly upset?

He replied that his mother was, after all, a Scot, and possessed a certain resilience and toughness. She had never had an easy life. The divorce, if it came, would distress her most. She looked quickly at him, guessing at once what caused

245

the doubt his words conveyed, and said she prayed that Sibyl's departure would be final, that she would not change her mind.

"I don't know if prayers are answered," she said, "but I shall pray."

He looked out at the streaming rain. "I've prayed hard enough in my time."

She laid her hand lightly on his, knowing what he meant.

"At least he doesn't suffer," she said. "It's you who suffer."

"Less now," he told her. "I'm sorry I spoke of it."

They sat talking until lunchtime and the rain had not once paused or altered the rhythm of its downpour. At lunch they decided that whether it cleared or not they would go to Arachova, the little town of many shops that they had passed through on their way from Athens.

Sibyl was spoken of only once more, when Christine said with some sadness, "I had an affection for her, a quite real affection. I know, because she had the power to hurt me."

As they were getting into the car wearing raincoats and carrying umbrellas borrowed from the hotel, Dr. Araman came hurrying out to them and asked if he might go with them. There was nothing to do, he said, and he was tired of staying indoors. When he heard they were on their way to Arachova he was delighted. He wanted to buy some presents there to take back to his daughters, and said it would be his one chance as he was going to Epidaurus the next day. He went off to fetch his raincoat and Murray said wryly, "This will teach us to talk to people on planes."

Pericles was disgusted with the weather.

"Better in Athens," he said. "Theaters, cinemas, good shops. Here nothing. We go tomorrow, yes?"

They said they would wait and hope for one more good day in Delphi.

The mountain village of Arachova had many small shops

246

that sold local handicrafts, chiefly things woven from wool; gaily colored bags, scarves and rugs of traditional design. As a rule when they drove through a town or village they had to slow down almost to walking pace and keep sounding the horn to clear a way through the male population gathered in the streets, talking, talking. Even today there were groups huddled under awnings or dripping umbrellas, and there was never a woman to be seen among them. When Christine asked what on earth they talked about, Dr. Araman said, "Politics, politics. They have always done it, they always will. It is a feature of Greek life. In Syria it is much the same. And while they talk, the women get on with the work."

They bought a number of things, splashing through puddles as they went from shop to shop, and Christine's shoes were wet through. When they got back to the hotel she hurried to her room to change. Murray took the borrowed umbrellas to the hotel desk, and the manager came smiling up to him. He had a message, he said, for Mrs. Bonner, but he had not had the opportunity of speaking to her before she went to her room. Puzzled that there could be a message, feeling there must be some mistake, Murray asked him what it was.

Still smiling, the manager said how fortunate it was that the room next to Mrs. Bonner's had just been vacated, as he could now give it to Mrs. Gellert, who was arriving the following afternoon.

Murray tried not to show his astonishment, his sense of being completely fogged, as if the manager had been speaking to him in some other language.

He managed to say, "Mrs. Gellert? Mrs. Raymond Gellert? Mrs. Bonner wasn't expecting her. When did you hear this?"

Mrs. Gellert had telephoned from Athens, the manager said, only a few minutes ago. She said she had just arrived from London and asked if her daughter, Mrs. Bonner, was staying there. He said she was. Mrs. Gellert then said she would be coming tomorrow afternoon, and was bringing her maid with her. Fortunately, the manager added, he was able to accommodate them both.

"I see," Murray said. "Thank you. I'll tell Mrs. Bonner."

He went first to his own room, and without changing his muddy shoes, tried to find some reasonable, some plausible explanation for Mrs. Gellert's arrival. Christine had once or twice spoken, with some dread, of the possibility that her mother might come to London. She had evidently done so, and had no doubt learned, from Charles Kendrick perhaps, that Christine had gone to Athens. She had decided to follow her. At the hotel in Athens she had presumably been informed that her daughter was now in Delphi. She no doubt supposed she would be joining a party of three. There was no harm in that, it all seemed natural enough, though it was, as it happened, extremely unfortunate for them and highly awkward. Need he imagine there was more in it than that? He tried to persuade himself that he need not. And if there still was in his mind a faint suspicion, an uncomfortable doubt, he must keep it from Christine.

She opened the door to him wearing her white dressing gown and bedroom slippers. He had more than once been surprised at the speed with which she could change.

"Is anything wrong?" she asked quickly. "Has something happened?"

"Well," he said, "I've just heard from the manager a rather unexpected bit of news."

When he told her what it was she sank down on the bed as if her legs were unable to hold her upright. Her face looked as it might look if she were ill, he thought, strained, pinched, bloodless. It so alarmed him that he sat on the bed beside her and put his arm around her.

"Murray!" she cried, and put both hands to her cheeks. "Murray! What are we going to do?"

He pleaded. "Don't look like that, Christine. What can

248

she do to us? What is there to be afraid of? She can't be such a monster. I'll take care of you."

"What am I afraid of?" she repeated, and he saw unmistakable fear in her eyes. "I'm afraid of her. I always have been afraid of her. She mustn't come here. Or if she does come, we must go. We must go!"

"But, Christine," he gently protested, "we've nothing to be ashamed of. Why should we run away? Leave her to me. I'll deal with her. It can't matter as much as all that."

"She's hunting me down," she said. "She wants to get those dreadful claws in me, in any way she can. You don't know her, you don't know what she does to me. I can't stay here, Murray. You must take me away, out of her reach. Anywhere."

Her vehemence, her frightened looks impressed him. His own instinct was to stay. On the other hand, was it right to subject Christine to an ordeal she so dreaded?

He said quietly, hoping to make less of it all, "I imagine she got to London, heard, probably from Charles, that you were here, and decided to follow. When she got to the hotel in Athens, they told her we'd gone to Delphi. Isn't it all quite simple, really?"

"They told her," she answered with strained intensity, "that two of us had gone to Delphi."

They continued to look at each other, and now he was still less certain that they ought to stay. She had been quicker to grasp the true situation than he had. Mrs. Gellert had no doubt asked questions, she had no doubt obtained facts. It put a different aspect on her pursuit of them. It made it even probable that she was coming with the intention of extricating her daughter from a compromising situation, from some disastrous folly. The thought of having to protest their innocence to this woman of whom he had heard nothing good was, to say the least, displeasing.

"You may be right," he admitted.

249

"Oh, God!" she cried out, "why did she have to come here and ruin our happiness? No one in the world affects me as she does. She brings out the very worst in me. She made my father suffer, it was because of her that Marietta ran away and married the first man she could find; she's been a blighting shadow over all my life. And now, to have her here, looking at us with those hard, unloving eyes, to be subjected to her hateful questions, perhaps accusations—no, Murray, no, I won't see her! Our lovely innocent secret—I'd die to protect it. It's all we have, for the rest of our lives. I won't let her lay her hands on it. I won't, I can't."

She was on the point of breaking into tears, but struggled to keep from doing so.

"Hush, hush," he said gently. "Don't distress yourself, darling. You've convinced me. We'll go. We'll drive to the ferry that crosses the Gulf of Patras. We'll go to Olympia. It's a long way, but we can do it. Then we'll take the road along the Peleponnese Coast back to Athens. If we miss the plane, well, we miss it and we'll take the next. The rush must be over by now. We'll cable Sam as soon as we get to Athens. Now, are you happier?"

She flung both arms about him, quickly and impulsively, and kissed his cheek.

"Oh, bless you, bless you! I was so afraid I couldn't make you see how necessary it is to run away from her. Couldn't we go tonight? There's somewhere we could get to, isn't there? Some hotel?"

But this he would not have.

"Not in this downpour. We'll go tomorrow, as early as you like. I'll go and talk to the manager."

"Of course we'll pay for the two extra nights," she said. "But what will you say? What will you tell him?"

"Simply that we've changed our plans, that we want to see Olympia before we go back to Athens."

"Oh, don't say Olympia, please! She might follow."

250

"Very well. I'll think of something else to say."

"And thank you, thank you!" she cried with touching fervor. "I'm unspeakably grateful."

They had made their decision, rightly or wrongly. He felt sure now that they were right. To have stayed and faced Mrs. Gellert would have been to see all the sweetness of their last days together destroyed, to see crude hands laid upon everything that was precious to them. It was bravest to run away.

The manager was tactful and unsurprised, and made it as easy as possible. Murray mentioned Mycenae, and said it would have been a great pity to go back without seeing it. But of course, the manager said, everyone should see Mycenae. He sent a boy to tell Pericles to have the car ready at eight o'clock.

When Murray told Christine that everything had been arranged and that they would be called with breakfast at seven, her face lost its strained and anxious look and became calm again. A danger had been passed, or at least indefinitely put off. She had already begun to pack her suitcase, and when she lifted her cheek to him for a good-night kiss, she thanked him again for all his goodness to her.

"To be good to you," he said with emotion, "is to be good to myself."

As he closed the door he thought what an artificial barrier it was that they had put between them. His place was with her, comforting and reassuring her. But it was a barrier they had built up with pride and care, to do honor to their special love; it was the tribute they paid to peace of mind and to Sam.

And thinking of Sam and what was due to him, it struck Murray that Christine had probably not written to him since leaving Athens. Until then she had been writing to him every two or three days, but to write from Delphi, unless she were prepared to tell him everything that had happened, or, worse, to omit to tell it, would, he saw, be too difficult. No,

251

she would certainly not have written. Well, he thought, letters were often delayed and Sam would surely not worry too much if he did not hear from her until she cabled him from Athens, giving him the altered date of their return. Explanations could come later.

He went to the window, drew back a curtain and looked out. The rain was still falling precisely as it had fallen all day, splashing up from the lighted terrace, making all the gutters vocal. He dropped the curtain again, wondering how the ancient Greeks had clothed themselves against such weather.

XVIII ✍

THE morning came darkly and reluctantly. There was no change, the rain still fell as it had fallen all through the night. Murray paid the bill and just before eight Christine appeared carrying her traveling case, wearing her raincoat and a scarf tied over her head. They saw Pericles standing in the porch, his very back disconsolate, watching the rain pouring off the roof of the car, streaming down the windows and making little rivers in the driveway. Murray told him they were not going back to Athens but in the other direction—to the ferry that would take them across the Gulf of Patras.

"No good," Pericles said, shaking his head. "Better stay here. Pericles know this road. Very bad in wet weather. Go slow all the way."

"Well," Murray said, "if we have to go slow we will." And then, forgetting caution for the moment, asked, "How long do you think it will take us to get to Olympia?"

He regretted his question as soon as it was spoken, as the

porter, holding an umbrella in case it was needed, stood not far behind.

Pericles shrugged his shoulders. "Maybe ten hours, maybe more. Roads very bad today."

The suitcases were put into the back of the car. Christine got in and Murray, after distributing some tips, followed her. He apologized for the slip he had made, but Christine at once said it didn't matter, she was sure the porter hadn't heard, and anyway his English was poor.

They were soon driving through miles of old olive orchards, a sight that delighted Christine, who would not admit that the sun could have made them more beautiful. It was a vast, dripping, gray-green forest in which the ancient trunks, blackened by the wet, looked like tortured monsters struggling out of the earth.

"I'm so happy at having escaped a nightmare encounter with my mother," she said, "that everything pleases me."

He asked if she had left a message of any sort.

"Yes. I wrote a note last night. I said I had no idea she was coming to Greece and that it was too late for us to change our plans. I ended by saying that perhaps we'd see each other in England, unless she was going home some other way." She sighed. "How I wish she'd marry again! Now she can be a rover. She's free to go anywhere. There's no safety from her."

The road, as it climbed up into the hills, grew progressively worse. The downpour had softened and weakened the outside edges that soon were all that lay between them and precipitous mountainsides. They had to get round endless hairpin bends, and often the narrow road was made narrower still by piles of gravel which had been dumped there for future repairs, work which was doubtless held up by the weather. They could hear Pericles grumbling and cursing under his breath, but he got tired of this after a while and relapsed into gloomy silence, his bullet head sunk between his shoulders. There was no doubt that he strongly disapproved of the journey and of them. He seemed to have cut himself off from them; he was no longer a guide, scarcely even a chauffeur; he was simply a man in a predicament he should never have been asked to get into, and as the car wallowed and slid in the sharp and dangerous bends, they were made to feel this more and more.

When they asked him, some hours later, if there was a place where they could stop for lunch, his answer was "Here in country nobody is, no house, no hotel, nothing."

"All right," Murray said, "we'll do without lunch. But when we are on a level bit of road, stop the car and we'll get a rug out of one of the suitcases. It's getting cold."

The stopping, however, was inadvertent, and came after a sudden lurch and a wail.

"Tire he burst," Pericles said, and got out, throwing them as he did so a look of deep reproach. He had no raincoat and refused to take Murray's, so Murray got out and helped him to jack up the car. Then the bolts of the wheel were found to have rusted and were only unscrewed with difficulty, the two men taking turns with the spanner. Christine got out and vanished up a hillside, and Murray offered up a prayer that she might not get a chill. The spare wheel was at last put on, and Murray got the rug out of Christine's suitcase and in addition found a pair of dry shoes and a sweater. These last he made her put on, for she was shivering with cold. He took off his wet raincoat, put it on the floor of the car and slipped an arm about her.

"Sit as close to me as you can. We'll keep warm this way."

Toward the middle of the afternoon he called to Pericles to stop. They were approaching a small and miserable-looking inn in a hamlet of five or six houses. "Perhaps we can at least get something to drink here," he said. He told Pericles to come with him. The old, bearded innkeeper said he had wine and ouzo. Pericles accepted a glass of wine, and Murray carried two full glasses of ouzo, diluted with very little water, out to the car. They felt warmer after drinking it. Then

255

Pericles, whose heart appeared to have softened toward them, brought out some stale rolls which they all shared. He seemed less bad-tempered when they set off again, but the road grew no better at all. The car lurched and swung, climbed and descended again, until they longed for nothing so much as a stretch of level ground. Then, soon after he had switched on the headlights Pericles pulled up the car with a jerk which almost flung them off the seat. They saw a subsidence on the outer edge of the road, as if a large piece had been bitten out. Pericles threw up his hands and his face expressed an almost comical despair.

"No good. No good Car too big, too heavy. Better we go back."

Murray told him sharply that they had no intention of going back and got out to inspect the cave-in. He picked up all the stones he could find, Pericles helping with no enthusiasm, and tried filling in the gap, but the stones either rolled down the hill or sank treacherously into the mud. He told Pericles to stay beside the car, and went up the hillside to see if he could find a fallen log or two, but frugal peasants had been there before him. He then began to pull up sizable and aromatic shrubs and even broke off small branches of trees, badly scratching his hands, but when he returned to the car he had a good armful of brushwood. He sent Pericles to do likewise and when they had gathered enough they trod it into the mud and piled more and more on the top, making a high and springy bed. Finally Murray felt certain the car could get across, but Pericles was unconvinced and refused to try, so he sent him to stand with Christine on the far side of the cave-in, backed the car down the road a little distance, and then made a quick run, getting across safely. He found this experience wholly agreeable and exhilarating and felt a boyish pleasure in having achieved it under Christine's eyes. She was distressed at the sight of his scratched hands, which she examined in the beam of the headlights, but was unspeakably relieved, she said, that he had saved them from the grim alternatives of spending the night in the car until help came or going back over that dangerous road perhaps as far as the café where they had bought the drinks, as nothing would have induced her to go back farther.

Murray tucked the rug about her knees.

"If only you're none the worse for this," he said. "Promise me you won't get a cold or a chill!"

He continued to hold her close to him and was thankful when she at last fell asleep, her head on his shoulder.

About an hour later, when he had almost despaired of ever reaching the ferry he saw it below them, its lights reflected in the waters of the gulf. They drove fast down the hill, fearing to miss it, and Christine woke and said, "Now our troubles are over."

A few lorries, a number of carts and a great many sheep, goats and donkeys herded by their owners and by frantically barking dogs, were crowding on board. Luck had been with them, Pericles said after talking to the boatmen, as the ferry would not return again for two hours. They pushed their way slowly and cautiously on board, and the gangway was taken up. Soon the car was surrounded by black-mustached men eating grapes and spitting the seeds onto the deck or into the gulf. There was a rank smell of wet animals and wet clothing. Few of the men troubled to avail themselves of such shelter as there was, but let the rain stream down their dramatic brown faces and drip from the potato sacks they wore about their shoulders.

"And none of them will be any the worse for it," Christine said with envy.

As they sat in the car Murray told her that they were not far from Missolonghi, and said he had walked there from the coast the year before in a few hours, returning by bus. He had gone to see the cenotaph erected to Byron.

"How many places there are, covered by this dark night,

257

that I would love to see!" Christine exclaimed, with regret in her voice. She felt for his hand and said, "Tell me you weren't as happy then as you are now."

"I'm as much happier now by comparison with last year," he told her, "as I was then by comparison with the year before. Can I say more than that?"

"It's good enough!" she cried. "Bless you for saying it."

As they crossed the gulf Murray wondered if they ought perhaps to spend the night in Patras, but Pericles was discouraging. The hotels there, he said, were better for sailors than for the sort of people he drove, and Murray came to the conclusion that it would be wisest to push on and be sure of sleeping in a clean, comfortable, modern hotel, and tomorrow when the rain had stopped, as he felt sure it must stop, he would show Christine Olympia. He told her about the effect it had had on him, the sensation he had experienced there of absolute peace, of a well-being beyond his power to express. He had felt that nothing evil had ever happened or could ever happen there, and he longed to discover if it would affect her in the same way.

In less than half an hour they were speeding along level, well-metaled roads, and now, as if it had done the worst it could do, the rain lessened and presently Pericles switched off the windscreen wiper. They went up a small hill covered with pines, and through them they could see the bright lights of a hotel obviously built for the comfort of tourists. It looked so civilized and welcoming after their long cold journey that they were prepared to love it.

Inside it showed itself to be simple almost to bareness. They were given adjoining rooms, practical in their furnishing, almost identical, and each provided with a small bathroom. Murray urged Christine to have a hot bath at once and then to have her dinner in bed, but though she said she would most certainly have a hot bath at once she wanted to dine with him.

They would drink some good, red wine, she said, and celebrate the happy ending to their journey. Her face under the scarf looked white with fatigue, but her eyes pleaded with him so eloquently that he let her have her way.

The hot bath restored and refreshed her, and she was in gay good spirits when they went in to dinner at nine. She had brought with her the red woolen dress she had worn when they first met, and she had put it on tonight for the first time since they had started on their journey. She drank glass for glass with him, and he thought there was something a little strained and feverish in her moments of gaiety as well as in her moments of seriousness. There would be this night and one more night, and that was all that they would have. He knew this was constantly in her thoughts as it was in his.

Among other things to be celebrated, she said once, was their escape from her mother.

"You might like me less if you met her. She's everything I hope I shall never be. If I thought that I'd grow like her I'd rather die."

"Don't exaggerate, my darling," he said, and smiled at her as he said it. "Isn't this becoming a phobia?"

"No, I don't think so. My dislike of her is increased by feelings of guilt, of course. That's bound to be so. I know as well as anyone that a daughter is expected to love her mother." She drank a little wine, and then said, "It's only since knowing you that I've even felt grateful to her for giving me birth. Now I'm truly grateful. That's something on the credit side."

They looked at each other with such clear knowledge of the finality and totality of their love that they dared not sustain the look, and glanced away. There was a moment of silence and then she pushed her nearly empty glass toward him.

"Please," she begged. "It's doing me good and keeping at bay all the things I mustn't think about. Now I'm thinking how wonderfully lucky I am that you're going to show me Olympia tomorrow. I must try not to think how sad it is that you can't show me Mycenae too."

"We'll be thankful for Olympia," he said, "and no Dr. Araman. All the same, I'm strongly tempted to miss the plane and take you to Mycenae too. If it's this quite good claret that's making me want to shed all sense of responsibility, shall we order another bottle?"

"I think it had better be only half a bottle," she said, smiling. When he had ordered it, she asked, "Murray, tell me this if you can. Is one happier, in retrospect, for having had ten years of happiness than one would be if one had only had ten days or ten hours? Or, in the end, is it much the same?"

"I can't answer that," he said. "I've never had the ten years."

"Because," she went on, "qualitatively, no one could possibly have been happier than I have been with you, or than I am at this moment."

"That's a fine long word to use after at least three glasses of wine," he said lightly. For some reason he could not have explained, her brave words had sent a shiver of pure dread down his spine.

"You think I'm tempting the gods," she said quickly. "But I don't care. It's true for me, and I know it's true for you, and I had to say it."

"It's so true that I wouldn't have dared to say it," he told her.

"Shall I tell you," she asked, "what I'm afraid of? And I think it's the only thing I am afraid of. I'm afraid that a time may come for both of us when all this will have blurred and faded. When we'll ask ourselves, 'Did we visit Delphi once or twice?' 'What was the name of that driver we had?' 'How long were we at Olympia?' "

He saw her eyes glisten with sudden tears.

260

"That wouldn't matter," he said, to comfort her. "It's the having had, the having known that will warm us and give us courage."

"Fill my glass once more," she pleaded.

"Only half a glass, darling. I think you should stop now."

"Thank you for the way you take care of me," she said, and now she had got the better of her tears. "It's so tactfully done that I'm hardly aware of it. I will always do what you tell me to do, and I will never deceive you in the smallest thing. Never."

"Nor I you."

"If I'm sometimes deceitful," she said, "it was my mother who taught me to be. I had to have my privacy, my sacred privacy, and she never wanted me to have it; she resented it. But I mustn't talk about her. It's wasting precious moments. Murray, I want to tell you this." Her eyes, that were fixed on his, seemed to shine with a feverish brilliance. "I want you to know that when I go back to my old life, as I must go back, I'm not going to be unhappy. And neither must you be unhappy. For me, to have loved someone as I love you is a revelation. I'm a different person for having experienced it. If you forget everything else I've ever said to you, please remember that. Will you remember it, darling? Especially about my not being unhappy?"

"I will remember it," he said.

"And may I go on talking? I've got more to say. I've learned that from the particular to the general is the rule in love, because having loved you as I do I believe I understand now what's meant by a universal love. And I believe I understand what's meant by the *power* of love. I see now how it could embrace the whole human family and regenerate it, and that nothing else can. Perhaps in time I could even learn to include my mother in this love. But I swear to you, Murray, I swear to you that through loving you my heart and mind have been opened, and this, *this* is going to be my salvation.

261

My salvation and my solace and my comfort. And I pray, I pray that it may be yours too."

She stretched out her hand to him, with the familiar little clash of coins, and he took it and held it, but could not speak. Then their hands quickly parted again as the young clerk who had shown them their rooms, came to the table.

"Excuse me, sir and madam," he said with a little bow. "A lady is on the telephone. She asks to speak to Mrs. Bonner."

Their eyes came together in astonishment and dismay. They could scarcely believe what they heard.

"Did you say that Mrs. Bonner was here?" Murray asked him.

"Yes, sir. The lady is speaking from Delphi, I think."

Murray looked at Christine.

"Would you like me to go and talk to her?" he asked, and he stood up as he spoke.

Her whole aspect had changed in those few seconds. She was grasping the edge of the table with both hands, as if certain of calamity, and the color the wine had brought into her cheeks had drained out of them. He felt a painful concern for her, and an angry resentment against this woman who pursued them.

"I don't know. Could you? Had I better go? Oh, Murray, must we speak to her?"

"I think one of us must," he said. "If you think it had better be you, I'll come with you."

She got up from her chair slowly. "Why is she hunting us like this? Why?"

The young man stood at a little distance from the table, waiting to take them to the telephone booth.

"Come then," Murray said. "We'll go and get it over."

Christine went inside the booth and he stood by the door, holding it open a little in case she might want him. He dreaded the ordeal for her. Mrs. Gellert was by now, he supposed, exceedingly angry, and her effect on Christine was at the

262

best of times deplorable. Even Sam had referred to it more than once.

When Christine spoke her voice had a coldness he had not heard in it before. "Mother? They said you wanted to speak to me. How did you know I was here?"

He could hear Mrs. Gellert's voice but he could not hear what she was saying. Then he saw Christine lean against the side of the booth as if she could barely stand upright and put her left hand over her eyes and forehead as if she were distraught, as at some dreadful news. It flashed into his mind that she might have learned of the sudden death of her sister. That would explain Mrs. Gellert's pursuit of them and Christine's visible distress. Worried, he went into the booth and stood beside her. The scratchy voice went on, and then Christine suddenly turned to him and handed him the receiver. Her face had a look of horror, of pure shock, and as he took the receiver from her he put his left arm about her and held her against his side.

"I can't listen any more," she whispered. "I can't."

He spoke very clearly into the mouthpiece: "Mrs. Gellert, Christine is very much upset by what you have been telling her. Will you tell me about it instead? My name is Murray Logan."

"I supposed it was," Mrs. Gellert said sharply, and though the connection was not good and there were buzzing noises, he heard her well enough. "You should have waited for me in Delphi. I am extremely angry at your running away and behaving in this stupid and inconsiderate fashion. I had a most unpleasant trip through pouring rain to get there only to find you gone, and now I've had great difficulty in tracing you. What I was telling my daughter is this: Sam is arriving in Athens tomorrow afternoon. Your wife has written letters to both Sam and Mr. Kendrick, and for all I know she may have written to Mr. Frederick Bonner as well. I happened to be in London when Mr. Kendrick received his letter. He was very much upset. Naturally he consulted me about it, and I said I would come here right away and find out what could be done. I'm very much shocked and worried by the whole disgraceful affair."

At this point Murray felt obliged to break in. "I'm afraid I don't understand at all," though he was beginning to understand only too well. "What letters from my wife are you referring to?"

"The ones she wrote from Athens to Sam and Mr. Kendrick, and probably Mr. Bonner, telling them what was going on. She was terribly upset, as well she might be, and as all of us are. She said she had to leave because she couldn't endure what she'd had to endure any longer. She's staying with friends somewhere. I think she had a sort of nervous breakdown. Now Mr. Murray—Mr. Logan, I mean—I consider your behavior outrageous, and that my daughter should be involved in all this is of course the worst part of it. Mr. Kendrick didn't actually show me your wife's letter, but he told me the facts. I said I'd come at once and see what I could do."

To Murray it was a lunatic conversation, a nightmare exchange of words, and he saw no hope of establishing any sensible contact with the angry woman in Delphi. He thought that the sooner he could end it the better, both for Christine's sake and for his own. As Mrs. Gellert paused for breath he broke in: "Mrs. Gellert, what my wife appears to have written is quite untrue. I must ask you to believe this. I can and will explain everything. Just a moment, please. Let me finish what I have to say. We're returning to Athens tomorrow in any case, as we've booked seats on the plane back to London the following day. We couldn't get seats sooner. To fill in the time, I took Christine to see Delphi, and we hoped to see Olympia. That is the whole truth."

"Well, I'm sorry, but I can't believe a word you're saying," Mrs. Gellert replied, and he winced from the hard sharpness of her voice. "I see no reason to suppose that your wife was telling lies. However, we'll meet in Athens tomorrow, and I must absolutely insist that you arrive there before Sam does. He's due about five. I must see my daughter before he comes. And you too, I may add."

"I've only one more thing to say," Murray answered, with as much moderation as he could, "and that is that all this concerns only Sam, Christine and myself. The whole thing can quickly be cleared up and it will be."

"I will have plenty to say when I see you," Mrs. Gellert told him piercingly, "and I can't bear to think what Sam must be feeling. I'll be at the Grande Bretagne when you arrive, as I'm leaving here very early and have the shorter distance to go."

She hung up then, and Murray was thankful when the penetrating voice had ceased to trouble his ears. His one desire now was to get Christine to her room as quickly as possible.

"It's all right," he said to her. "Don't worry, my darling. It will be all right. Can you walk to your room?"

"Yes," she said, and stood upright, "but hold my arm, please."

They crossed the lobby, where a few heads turned to follow them, and when they were in the narrow little bedroom Christine sank down on the bed. He sat beside her as he had done in Delphi after bringing her her mother's message, and kept his arm about her.

"I'll be all right in a moment," she said, and her voice was faint and unsteady. "I think I know most of what she was saying, but I'd better hear it from you."

"Wouldn't you rather lie down?"

"No, I'm all right like this. It seems that Sibyl has done the worst she could do."

"I'm afraid she has."

He repeated the conversation he had had with her mother, only leaving out some of her more objectionable words.

265

"It's been in my mind," he said, "that Sibyl had something more up her sleeve. She hinted at it in her letter, but I could never have guessed she would do this."

"I don't think I can forgive her," Christine said slowly. "I don't think I can. Calumny. It's such a vile thing. Poison dropped into the ear. I didn't think she was capable of this."

"We mustn't let it worry us too much, Christine," he said. "By tomorrow night everything will be cleared up. We can trust Sam. His whole idea in coming here as soon as he got Sibyl's letter was to protect you from any talk, and give us both his support. I'm absolutely certain of that."

She said, looking down, "I wish I were as certain. I think he guessed how much I liked you."

"But not to the point of jealousy? You don't mean that?"

"I hope not. Oh, I don't know, I don't know. He gave no sign of it but how can I be sure of anything now?"

He said, with entire conviction, "We can trust Sam."

"And Frederick—he must know, too. Even if she didn't write to him, Sam may have told him why he was leaving so suddenly. Oh, how horrible, how utterly horrible it all is! Everything has been muddied, poisoned!" Tears suddenly spilled down her cheeks.

"No, no!" he cried, and held her closer. "No, they can't spoil it, we won't let them spoil it. Darling, don't despair. As for Frederick, Sam would never have told him. We must trust Sam, we must trust him."

"How could I ever forgive myself if this has done you harm?" she asked, and let her tears fall unchecked. "I could never forgive myself. I'd want to die!"

"Hush," he said, and gently rocked her. "Hush. Must I tell you again that you've given me all the happiness I've ever had?"

She cried out, "But not enough. Not nearly, nearly enough." And she put her hands over her face and bowed her head.

"Please," he begged, "please don't distress yourself, darling. You're only making me more unhappy. Here, wipe your eyes and look at me. Everything will be all right. Try to believe me. I am sure it will."

"But who is going to believe us?" She dropped her hands and looked at him through her tears, not troubling to wipe them away. "Sibyl's leaving us like that—those horrible letters —who will ever believe us? Why should they believe us? Now I see that we should never have run away from Delphi. Perhaps this lovely, innocent happiness of ours has been all wrong from the very beginning. I don't know, I don't know. My mind is utterly confused."

He took the handkerchief from her and wiped away her tears. Above everything he wanted to soothe and calm her.

"Sweetheart," he said, "remember the wine you drank at dinner. And ouzo before that. Enough to confuse anyone a little."

"No, no, it isn't that. It's the feeling that we're trapped, that we've put ourselves into such a position that no one will ever believe what we say. And it's entirely my fault. And even if we could persuade them to believe us, having to explain, having to defend ourselves, to protest our innocence—oh, it's unbearable, it's unbearable. Surely we haven't deserved all this!"

"We haven't deserved it, but we'll have to go through with it all the same. And it won't be as bad as you think, my darling. I put my faith in Sam. We only have to tell him the simple truth. Nothing else matters. Now I want you to go to bed. You've had a long, trying day, even without all this. Will you go to bed now, if I leave you?"

She pleaded, holding to his hand, "Don't go. I don't want you to go. I don't want to be alone."

"Remember the promise you made at dinner."

She released his hand at once.

267

"Yes. Well, then, I will. I'll go to bed." And then she added, looking away from him, "We'll have to give up Olympia tomorrow, of course."

"I'm afraid we must. We ought to make an early start."

She said, sadly and bitterly, "Yes. You'd better order the tumbril for half past eight."

He smiled at her and kissed her cheek.

"I trust we shall keep our heads." He got up, still looking down at her. "Good night, my dear love."

But she did not want him to go yet. "Now that you know what my mother is like, can you still think well of me?"

He answered lightly, "I can't say I feel drawn to her, but perhaps she'll improve on acquaintance."

She threw him a glance in which there was no answering smile, and got up from the bed. As if she could endure the weight of her coiled hair no longer she began slowly drawing out the pins until it cascaded down about her shoulders. Her face looking out from between the curtains it made looked a pale oval of grief.

"Please take a sleeping pill tonight," he said.

"Perhaps I'd better," she answered.

"I'm going out for a few minutes to get some air," he said, "and I'll make the arrangements for tomorrow. Good night, my dearest, and try not to worry about anything at all. If there's any worrying to be done, let me do it for you. Will you promise?"

She nodded, the hairpins in her hand, and was about to speak again, but he said good night and closed the door quickly.

He made arrangements for the morning, and then went out, and immediately the odor of the pines came to him like a blessing and a restorative. For a while he paced about underneath them and presently went down the road that led toward Olympia.

268

There was not a whisper of air stirring. Not a raindrop fell from the black trees. The saturated earth breathed silently, and the white stars looked down with stabbing brilliance. He prayed as he walked—trying not to remember prayers that had not been answered—that Christine would come to no harm through their love for each other. The shock of knowing what Sibyl had done was gradually lessening. He saw it now as still another proof of the fact that in all his dealings with her, ever since the time when he had got her out of her bed, out from under the fallen plaster of the ceiling, he had been unlucky. It was a tragedy that they had ever met. And now it was through her that this innocent idyll had come to near disaster.

Innocent? He was sure it was innocent, in spite of the ugly light now thrown on it. They had wanted to hurt no one. They had sought the comfort and the assuagement of a blameless and tender relationship. It was a brief happiness that, surely, they owed each other and themselves. That Sibyl had used it to revenge herself on him for her seven years of suffering was beside the point. They had accepted the joys of companionship and had faced and accepted the agonies of parting. And now that this was near he wondered if indeed it would prove bearable. He asked himself for the very first time, seriously and urgently, if he could bring himself to ask Sam to give up Christine. His heart beat thickly, heavily, at the thought of it, as if he were contemplating some crude act of violence, a murder even. He had never before allowed himself to consider it as a possibility. Now he did, and he tried to stand at a little distance from himself in order to view the act of asking Sam to give up Christine as if he were watching another man.

The painful beating of his heart, his feeling of repugnance at the thought of demanding from Sam, his good friend, a sacrifice he was not himself prepared to make told him that it was a thing he simply could not do. He could not. Nor could he put another man in his place. What another man might be able to do, he could not do. He was himself, and the thing was impossible for him.

That it would be equally impossible for Christine he never doubted. She had left Sam in order to frighten him into giving her more freedom, in order to make her terms with him. She might even, if he had not capitulated, have refused for a long time to go back to him. But that was something that was between the two of them, something they had had to resolve, though strangely enough it had been resolved in the end with his help—and with Seth's.

Then he asked himself, as he was bound to do, if he were sufficiently considering Christine's happiness. She had admitted that she could have been happy married to him. This was something that he could, if he chose, use as a powerful weapon to overcome his feelings of guilt at the thought of breaking up the marriage. He would need to convince himself that her happiness and health depended on it, and then go forward with righteous feelings, as of a man ending an injustice. He would require her entire collaboration, her deepest assurances that only living with him could bring her peace and contentment, at no matter what cost.

And yet at dinner she had promised him that she was not going to be unhappy. She had begged him to remember it, even if he forgot everything else she had ever said, and she had never been more in earnest. He was certain that she cared too much for Sam to do him this cruelest of injuries. It occurred to him that perhaps a woman like Christine might flinch from hurting a man she had already hurt by insufficiently loving even more than she would flinch from hurting a man she had loved to the point of feeling that in hurting him she was hurting herself.

In any case they were both of them, he and Christine—unluckily, perhaps—sensitive people who were bound to suffer extremely at inflicting pain on someone they cared for.

Christine's part in it might be forgivable. In marriage the hardest blows are given and received. His part in it, looked at from any angle, would be merely despicable. He would need to be made in a different mold in order to do it.

And in addition to this there was one more prohibiting thing. He did not think that either of them could bring themselves to give substance to Sibyl's allegations. It would be too much like deliberately smearing themselves with mud. "No decent man would have done such a thing," Sibyl had said in her letter. No, probably no decent man would. And could they now neatly fit themselves into the role she had accused them of playing? He did not think that they could.

He was not far from Olympia, which lay just below him in the dark, bounded by the sacred wood of Altis and by the shallow river Alpheus. He would go no nearer, he did not want to see it, even by starlight, without Christine. Some exhalation from it seemed to come up to him mixed with the odors of the night, some sweet haunting from its past of more than six hundred continuous years of joy and beauty and peaceful striving. He turned away from it, glad of what it had given him, and walked slowly back up the hill on which the hotel stood. One or two lights went out as he approached. It was getting late.

He had asked himself a question under the stars, the most vital question that had ever arisen in his life, and he had answered it unequivocally. And at the same time he was puzzled to know why his feeling for Sam was so strong as to give him the help he had needed in coming to his decision. He was puzzled to know why it was that when he had had to choose between Sam's happiness and his own he had been able to choose Sam's. Was it some special quality that Sam possessed? Was it his trustfulness and innocence and singleness of mind? The quite unusual quality of his love for Christine? For he was certain that it was not a selfish love. It was Sam's deepest conviction, humbly and religiously held, that it was only through him and his loving tenderness and care that Christine had a future. It was a belief that demanded respect, and it might even be true. It might even be true.

He lingered outside the hotel for a few minutes more, tasting the bitter knowledge that after tomorrow's journey back to Athens he and Christine would be separated by three thousand miles, only to meet, if they met at all, rarely and at long intervals. He tried to visualize how she might change, how, little by little, this meeting of spirits, hearts and minds that had been theirs might come to be for both of them difficult to recall in its wholeness and intensity, causing them to wonder and to question themselves as to its reality.

And the thought of this, the worst that could happen to them, was like a blow in the diaphragm. It made him feel physically sick with pain, for it would mean that there was no truth, no validity in anything, nothing to hold to. He bent over in the dark, his arms crossed at his waist, suffering as much in body as in mind but knowing that the bodily pain at least would pass. His love for Christine, and hers for him, was all that he had. Was it possible that it might lose its actuality, melt away through faulty memory and the years?

His little time had run out, as he had known well enough that it must. Irreversible, implacable, it had run out, and in circumstances that were abominable and unforeseen. He straightened himself and drew a long breath. The thought of Mrs. Gellert was medicinal. He would have her to deal with. He would have to turn her presumptuous and unnecessary anger away from Christine. If toward himself, so much the better; he was quite ready for it. As for the rest, he must learn to bear this grief as he had borne other griefs. It was what he had to do.

He went slowly up the steps and into the lobby, deserted except for the night clerk who was busy making entries in a ledger. He nodded a good night as the man looked up, and went to his room.

As he opened his door he experienced once again, as on the night when his hand had touched Sibyl's letter, the shock of the totally unexpected in violent collision with the subconsciously *known*. In the light of a small bedside lamp Christine was standing as still as a statue, in her girlish white dressing gown that fell straight from neck to feet, her smoothly brushed and shining hair hanging about her shoulders. As his heart recovered from its leap, but still pounded in his ears, she came up to him and looked deeply into his eyes. Then she put her arms closely about him, under his arms, in their first embrace, and said, barely above a whisper, "Now, my darling, my darling, let them think what they please."

XIX ✍

As they drove back to Athens along
the Peleponnese Coast they talked very little, but their hands
were clasped on the seat between them. He had asked her if
she would like to make a detour to see Corinth, but she said
no, and he was glad. If she could not see Olympia, she told
him, she would do without Corinth. She wouldn't even turn
aside, she said with a little smile, to see the site of the ten
thousand courtesans.

He said he had found Corinth disappointing. He would
have been willing to keep his vision of it intact.

"I suppose we'll see the Corinth Canal," she said. "We cross
it, don't we?"

"Yes," he said, "we can't miss that."

After a morning that earlier had been clouded over, the
sun came out and for the rest of the day it reigned in soverign
splendor. Looking out at the countryside she had grown to
love so much, Christine said, "Wherever I happen to be in
Greece I think I'm in the most beautiful place. Except of

274

course that I shall always think Delphi the most beautiful place of all."

She had not referred to last night in any way, and until she did, he felt he could not. The fact that their whole defense was now completely undermined could not, until and unless she spoke of it, be discussed or even mentioned. Until then they could formulate no plans, no policy. He supposed that she too shrank from doing so. It was impossible for him, therefore, to put to her the crude question—and how could it be put otherwise than crudely?—"Do you propose to tell Sam, or not?" He could only be silent on that subject, and keep her hand in his.

He knew, during the long periods when they thought their own thoughts, that she was reliving, as he was, the experience of last night, the sweet and suicidal folly of what they had done. In the morning, soon after daybreak, she had waked and putting her hand against his cheek had spoken in a low voice full of tender sadness, six wholly appropriate words:

" 'And God walked in the garden . . .' "

He had taken her quickly into his arms and had silenced with kisses the mouth that had spoken the words. Above everything it was necessary to have no regrets. It was imperative. Tragedy had been added to their love because both knew now its perfection and completeness. Tragedy enlarged it, but regret could only diminish it.

He had whispered to her, "Promise me never to be sorry. That's the one thing I couldn't bear. Promise me!"

And she had promised, her eyes shining with tears.

It was the moment to re-enact what he had implored her never to regret. But he knew she could not regret it, that their delight in each other, her delight in his power to give her all that she had so far lacked, had brought her life to its peak, to its climax. Her ardent, even feverish responses proved to him that the withholding of all they had to give each other had been as hard for her as for him. The demands they had made

275

on themselves had been cruel ones, yet even so, at the very center of their passion was a feeling of gladness that only Sibyl's outrageous letters, only the belief that they would now be misunderstood and condemned, had finally broken down all barriers. They felt they were two outcasts who owed the world nothing and each other everything, and during all that night and early morning it was as if they had reached some lonely planet on which there was no other life, no other consciousness but theirs.

During her silences, when their only communication was the clasp of their hands and the freighted, eloquent looks she sometimes turned on him, they were supremely aware of their oneness and no words were needed to confirm it. But their little time was slipping away; there were matters that must be talked over between them, and if they kept their voices low there was no danger that Pericles would hear.

When would she speak? he wondered, as the car sped over good roads nearer and nearer to Athens. Was she waiting for him to speak? But he could not be the one to ask, "What are we to do now?" The altered situation in which they found themselves had been brought about by her, by her generous and tender love for him. She had been as unable not to give him all she could as he had been unable to refuse it. The questions that came into his mind seemed one and all to have in them a suggestion of reproach. They were variations of "And now what are we going to do?" He could not utter them. Out of their immense happiness, out of their recollected joy there must come no hint, no smallest suggestion that their difficulties had been increased.

Presently he became aware of something that wholly distracted his mind from these problems. The hand that he was holding had become burning hot. He raised it to his cheek. There was no doubt about it. His already burdened heart now fell like a plummet into regions of pure dread, and his mind instantly flashed back to the evening when the doctor in

276

Morden had warned him, as they stood together in the little living room, of the danger to his unborn child.

"I believe you've got a slight temperature," he said.

"Yes," she agreed. "I think perhaps I have. My head felt rather swimmy when I was dressing this morning. I suppose I may have got a chill yesterday, in spite of all your care of me."

"What can you take?" he asked, hiding his fears.

"I took ten grains of aspirin before I left the hotel. I could take another ten grains now."

"Well," he said, "I think perhaps you'd better."

He asked Pericles, who, this morning, was all smiles and bonhomie, to stop the car, and while Christine took her red leather case on her knees and found the aspirin, he took a flask of hot coffee out of a picnic basket he had asked the people at the hotel to pack for them. She drank a little of the coffee and took the aspirin. She then asked if they might stop for lunch fairly soon.

"When I have a temperature I'm apt to be hungry. It's a peculiarity of mine."

"We'll stop as soon as we can find a good place," he agreed.

Pericles presently turned down a side road where they had a glimpse of a sea of turquoise blue. In spite of having said she was hungry, Christine could eat only part of a buttered roll and drink a little coffee, and he did not press her to eat more. When they set off again she was shivering, and he tucked the rug about her and held her close to him, keeping her hot hand in his. Before long she was asleep, her head on his shoulder. Sleep was what he would have wished for her, and now, left wholly to his thoughts, he told himself that however much his mind shied away from it he had better decide and decide now whether or not they were to conceal from Sam the fact that they had become lovers.

Which was better—or which was worse—to deceive him or to tell him the truth? If he were to tell Sam the truth, which he could do only with Christine's assent, he would at the same time have to ask him to give her up. The one thing followed the other. It was inconceivable that he could tell Sam the truth and then hand Christine back to him with, in effect, no more than a "Sorry, old boy. This is what's happened, but it needn't of course make any difference to you."

No, there could be no question of telling Sam. Therefore the decision he had come to last night must stand. There would be only this difference: that when they asserted that Sibyl's allegations were wholly untrue they would be lying. But they must nevertheless make the assertion.

It was all exceedingly painful, and what was to come would be equally painful to Christine. But the chief obstacle to their surmounting the trials that lay ahead of them would be Mrs. Gellert. Mrs. Gellert would make angry and indignant accusations against which they would have to defend themselves. He did not for a moment believe that Sam would do anything of the sort. Sam would simply wait to be told, and whatever they told him he would accept as true. It was not in Sam's nature to believe anything discreditable of someone he liked and trusted until given proof. Least of all would he be likely to believe it of Christine.

He told himself that at the same time he might as well consider the probable effect of Sibyl's letter on Charles, and on his own situation at Atlantic House. How much would Charles be likely to credit of what Sibyl had written? Surely he was unlikely to be deceived into thinking that she had told the truth. And yet, Charles might argue, if there were no truth in it all, why should she have written such a letter? Might it not be the genuine cry of a deeply hurt and distressed wife? He might conceivably say to himself, or to Aunt Lily, "It's hard to believe this of Murray, but as we all know, such things can and do happen. But Sam's wife! How could he possibly be such a fool? It seems incredible, and yet surely the woman couldn't have invented the whole thing?"

They crossed the Corinth Canal, cut as if by a gigantic

278

knife, and still Christine slept, fatigue and a temperature combining to blot out consciousness. The hand he held was no cooler, her body felt hot against his side. His fear that she might be on the verge of a serious illness was so great that all his problems took second place.

The words kept repeating themselves in his mind: If only you aren't ill, my darling, if only you aren't ill, nothing matters. If she were to be ill, he knew he would be largely responsible. He ought not to have allowed her to persuade him to run away from Delphi. But for that long cold drive over bad roads in pouring rain, this might not have happened.

They were driving through the outskirts of Athens now and still Christine slept as though she had been drugged. In the light of his overwhelming concern for her, Sam's coming seemed providential. It was providential, and whether or not they ought to tell him would now, in all probability, never be discussed. It was purely academic and beside the point. All that mattered now was that she should not be ill.

As they reached the hotel he woke her gently. She opened heavy eyes and asked, "Are we really there? I must have been asleep."

She sat upright and then turned to look at him, aware of his anxiety. "Don't worry, darling," she said. "I run temperatures very easily. I feel quite peaceful now, as if I knew that everything was going to be all right. I'm not worried about anything now. Just help me into the hotel."

Pericles got out their luggage and put it into the hands of the hotel porter. Murray told him to wait; and with Christine holding to his arm they went into the lobby of the hotel. A small, dark, sharp-featured woman who had been sitting close to the entrance got up as she saw them and came toward them. She was bareheaded, carried an enormous handbag and was dressed in a plain, navy-blue suit. It did not take Murray more than a second to guess that she was Mrs. Gellert's maid.

Christine saw her at the same moment. "My mother's

maid," she said in a low voice. "Now I am in their hands."

The woman spoke to her, ignoring Murray entirely. Her French accent had American overtones.

"I've been waiting for you, madame," she said, and it was clear that she had been delegated with authority. "Your mother would like you to come to her room at once. I am to show you the way. Your room is next to hers, and I have your key here." She showed it in her hand.

Christine looked at her as if she saw her from a great distance, as if she hardly understood what she was saying. Then she turned a despairing look on Murray, and did not let go her hold on his arm.

His mind was searching for some way of keeping her there a little longer, against this sharp and sudden assault of the enemy. He knew he could not let her go like this, could not hand her over to this antlike woman, who was clearly in Mrs. Gellert's confidence, without a word.

"Mrs. Bonner isn't feeling at all well," he said, and he spoke with firmness. "She ought to go straight to her room and get into bed. But before she goes I want to speak to her privately. Will you please wait for her by the lift?"

Christine murmured, "Please, Monique. I will be with you in a moment."

The maid said, "Very well, madame," threw him an angry look and walked away, and in Christine's eyes he saw gratitude, relief and supplication, as if she begged him to find words that would take them back to the place where they had been, to speak for both of them before it was too late. Her cheeks were flushed with fever, and she already wore the look of illness. Her lips moved, but no sound came from them, and she took one of his hands in a tight and feverish grasp. Neither knew nor cared if they were watched. She seemed only to be able to implore him with her eyes to narrow the quickly widening distance between them. In this moment of anguish and of loss he was miserably aware of the inadequacy of speech, but he spoke the only words he thought worth speaking at all.

"I will love you till I die," he said, and her face seemed to dissolve before his eyes in mists of his own tears.

"I too," she whispered. And then, with a gratitude that seemed to have her whole being in it, she said, "I thank you with all my heart for giving me so much happiness," and releasing his hands she turned and walked away a little unsteadily to where Monique waited for her.

He could not watch her longer. She seemed now to have crossed a boundary which could never be recrossed. She was on one side of it, with Mrs. Gellert, Sam, Monique and her coming illness, and he was on the other side. She had been wholly his, and now he was dead to her and she to him. He felt, in fact, more dead than alive, as if his spirit had passed out of his body, leaving him a shell. And then he thought that she might be going to die, and at once he knew that he was needed. He must fight for her. If there were any power in love, he must put his to use. He would fight for her, he would not let her die. She would know that he was fighting for her. He could not possibly go back to England now. He would go to some small hotel tomorrow and await events. He must be near at hand.

There was nothing for him to do at this moment but pay and dismiss Pericles, and then go to his room. It was useless to try to imagine what Sam would have to say to him. On the flight from New York to Athens—and he may have seen Charles briefly in London—who could tell what his thoughts had been? In addition to all this he would arrive to find Christine in bed with a high temperature. With a good deal of personal experience of temperatures behind him, Murray guessed Christine's to have mounted to 103. There was nothing to do but wait. He knew that Mrs. Gellert would, if necessary, summon half the doctors in Athens. Then it suddenly occurred to him that there was something he could do for Christine, and at once. He could find out if by any fortunate chance Dr. Araman was back in Athens. If so, he would be staying at the hotel. He rang down to the office and made inquiries. Dr. Araman, he learned, had just returned to the hotel from a trip to Epidaurus. He would not be leaving Athens for Syria for two days. When he rang his room there was no answer, so he left a message with the hall porter that he would like Dr. Araman to telephone him as soon as he came in.

Comforted by the knowledge that Dr. Araman was at hand, he unpacked a few necessary articles and a change of clothes and sat down to await events. Nearly an hour later the telephone rang. It was Monique. She said that Mrs. Gellert would like to see him in her sitting room as soon as possible, and gave the number. He said that he would come at once.

"I will tell madame to expect you immediately," she said, and hung up.

He took a quick look at himself in the glass, brushed his hair and put a clean handkerchief in his pocket. The man in the glass looked no different from the man he had seen daily in the bedroom he had shared with Sibyl in Morden, except that the sun of Rome and Greece had darkened his skin perceptibly. He marveled that otherwise he could see no change, and yet, what a change there was! What an inner transformation! Only he was aware of it, only he, probably, ever would be, for he had no intimates. Only Charles might discern some alteration in him or the too-perceptive Aunt Lily, but no one else.

As he went to Mrs. Gellert's room he hoped she would make him angry, for he thought he could best get through the interview if she did. He recalled Sam's words—"That woman's fallout is really terrific." Now he would experience it for himself.

Monique, the maid, opened the door to him and then went out, closing it behind her. He guessed that she would go and sit with Christine.

282

Mrs. Gellert was seated on a small sofa with her back to the windows, and only her eyes moved as he came in. She gave him a comprehensive look which seemed both to sum him up and to label him as a contemptible and unreliable witness. She was quietly dressed in a neat gray suit and only her hair was instantly noticeable, for it was a pale platinum shade which made no claim to naturalness and was dressed high on her head, giving her the look of an eighteenth-century French-woman of fashion. He saw in her instantly a likeness to Christine; there was no mistaking the fact they were mother and daughter, but Mrs. Gellert's features were both bolder and sharper, and instead of the curved and gently parted lips he loved he saw here a straight and almost lipless line. She indicated an armchair.

"Please sit down, Mr. Logan. We must have a talk." She hurried on, as if to give him no chance to speak, "My daughter is in bed and I hope asleep. A doctor has been to see her, and will come back in an hour. You've somehow allowed her to get a severe chill, and we can't tell what the result will be. I've done everything I can do. My son-in-law's plane has been delayed in Rome, and he won't be arriving before eight, so there's time for you to explain to me exactly how this out-rageous thing has happened."

Yes, he thought, Sam had been right. He was fully aware of the fallout. She had known, too, how to put him on the spot and turn a searchlight on him. He sat down and looked at her steadily. He had already made up his mind how he would deal with her.

"Any explanations that are required, Mrs. Gellert," he said pleasantly, "I would prefer to make to Sam when he comes."

"No doubt," she answered with cutting sharpness, "but I happen to be Christine's mother and I have been put to a great deal of worry and trouble by all this. It's a most dis-graceful affair, and you are entirely responsible. I have every right to learn the facts. You pose, I understand, as a friend of my son-in-law's. You ought to be all the more ashamed of what you have done."

She had made him angry now, but he knew it was wiser not to show it and he answered without a change of tone, "As I told you last night, my wife's accusations were untrue. That's all I propose to say now. I prefer to make full explanations to Sam when he comes."

"But if what your wife wrote in those letters was untrue," she demanded in the shrill and penetrating voice she had used on the telephone, "what on earth possessed her to write them? You really can't persuade me, Mr. Logan, that she was just making it all up. That's asking rather too much."

He said quietly, "I am not asking anything of you, Mrs. Gellert, except that you will be good enough to wait until I have explained matters to Sam. I gather you are not in Christine's confidence. If you were, I might feel differently."

He had touched her, as he had meant to do, in a sensitive place. He thought she deserved it. Her face altered and he saw that she was now on the defensive.

"If my daughter said that, she had no right to say it. Since her father's death we have been very close."

"In that case," he answered, "Christine will no doubt tell you herself all you want to know."

"You know perfectly well," she retorted, "that she's in no fit state to tell me anything now."

"Then I can only suggest that you be patient," he said.

He made a movement as if to get out of his chair, but she was aware now that she had failed to get anywhere with him and that bullying methods would only drive him away. She quickly motioned him to stay where he was.

"Please don't go," she said, and she had somewhat modulated her voice. "I would very much like to talk to you. Do you smoke? There are cigarettes in that box beside you. I don't, myself, but you may."

"No, thank you," he answered, "I won't smoke, but may I ask you, Mrs. Gellert, if you want to talk to me, not to talk as if I were a small boy caught stealing apples?"

"But," she said swiftly, "isn't that just what you have been doing?" Then seeing that he was once more about to get up she made a gesture and said, "You gave me that opening and I took it. I'm sorry. I'll even admit that you're within your rights when you say you must explain to Sam first. But there's one thing I wish you would tell me. I don't demand it, I ask, as any mother would. Is it true that you have fallen in love with my daughter? I presume you have."

"Please," he said, "don't presume anything of the sort. If I say I'm not in love with Christine, you'll choose not to believe me; if I say I am, you'll jump to the conclusion that what my wife said was true."

She looked down at her hands and twisted a very large emerald that was on her little finger.

"So many American women," she said reflectively, "fall in love with Englishmen. It wouldn't astonish me if she had fallen in love with you, though I hope she hasn't. I realize that you're very much her sort of man."

This time he stood up. "I see you're trying to trap me into some sort of admission," he told her. "I really must go now."

She got to her feet too and confronted him. He saw that she was smaller than Christine but, in spite of her smallness, enormously vital and dangerously strong-willed. She was the sort of woman, he thought, who would easily and triumphantly live to be ninety.

"Please don't go," she said. "I ask you to stay. I'm not trying to trap you into anything. I was just thinking aloud. Mr. Logan, I'm prepared to believe that your wife's statements were untrue and I'm prepared to trust you. There are a number of things I want to say to you, but I really can't talk to you standing up."

285

"Thank you," he answered, and sat down again when she did. "What you say is gratifying, but I can't see what's to be gained by continuing this conversation."

"We won't continue it. We'll talk about other things. I wish you'd tell me something about yourself, and about your work at Atlantic House. I'd never even heard of you before, and yet I understand you're one of the directors now."

"Yes," he said, "that is so."

"What a clever and charming man Mr. Kendrick is. I haven't seen him often, but I admire him very much. His wife frightens me. What a queer woman! Does she frighten you?"

"No, not at all. I've known her nearly all my life. She and my mother are cousins."

She said, "I see." It was the same, he thought, as saying, "So that's why you're on the board," but perhaps he was being unfair. She went on: "I rang him up as soon as I got to London for news of Christine. I'd been staying with friends in Newport and I didn't happen to see Sam before I sailed. Mr. Kendrick told me she had gone to Greece with you and your wife, and said he'd like to call on me at the Ritz, where I always stay when I'm in London. When he came he told me about the letter he'd received from your wife, a disquieting letter he very rightly called it, and he asked if I could go to Greece at once and find out what had happened. So although I detest flying I got on the first plane and came here. When I learned from the office downstairs that you'd taken Christine to Delphi, that confirmed my worst suspicions. I got a car and went there as fast as I could, on a horrible wet day, only to find that you'd left in spite of my message. Christine's note told me nothing at all, so I was put to the trouble of ringing up every hotel you might have gone to and finally ran you to earth at Olympia. Now are you surprised that I was angry, and convinced that things were about as bad as they could be?"

"No," he said, "I think it was quite natural, but you might

286

have suspended judgment until you'd seen us. Christine was very much upset by your accusations and reproaches."

"Quite frankly," she said, "I was furious with her. It was a perfectly disgraceful trick to play on her own mother."

"If I may be frank too," he said, "I think you know quite well that Christine has no great affection for you, and I don't believe she would feel as she does without cause."

"That," she cried out, "is impertinent!"

"Very well," he answered, "it's impertinent, but it had to be said. Now will you allow me to go?"

"No," she answered, "no. I refuse to let you go until you hear more. You owe it to me, after what you've said, to hear something about the relations between my daughter and myself, and I propose to tell you."

An emotion that was not anger so much as a passionate need to justify herself showed in her quickened breathing and the nervous movements of her hands. He caught little flashes from the diamonds she wore; from the small ones in her ears, from her rings, from a brooch in the form of a flower cluster that she wore pinned to her jacket. Even her small, high-heeled shoes had tiny paste buckles on them. He suddenly remembered Sam's telling him that she had been voted America's best-dressed woman and he felt a reluctant sort of pity for her because she was what she was—so brittle, so totally unlovable, so palpably jealous of her own daughter.

Nevertheless she had, he saw, not a few tricks in her repertory, for she had visibly softened and was now looking at him as if he were an old and dear friend in whom it was her pleasure to confide.

"The fact is, Mr. Logan," she said, "I've taken a liking to you in spite of the cruel and unjust things you've said to me. You see, the tragedy is that our relationship, Christine's and mine, was poisoned years ago by her father. He worshiped her, he doted on her, and he wanted her wholly to himself. It was deplorable, and to my mind, most unhealthy." Her lips moved sharply, as if with pain. "I was a very unhappy woman. I had two daughters, one of them violent-tempered and headstrong, the other terribly delicate. That one I loved the best, but I was never allowed a share in her affections. I can't begin to tell you what I—what both her father and I—went through with Christine, the struggles we had just to keep her alive, the doctors, the operations, the trips to Florida or New Mexico in search of health for her, the continuous, unending anxiety. Did Christine, during all this time, show me any love or gratitude? Never. It was always her father she turned to, while I was shut out. As she spent so much time indoors or in bed, she became a voracious reader, but if I ever tried to discuss with her what she was reading she would barely answer me. Between them she and her father made me feel an interloper in my own house. And I'd given up everything —New York which I loved and my friends there, my musical interests, my bridge club, everything—to live in the country, which I loathed, because it was supposed to be better for her. It was no wonder that Marietta ran away and got secretly married to an impossible young man. She knew that the whole house revolved about Christine. She's had two divorces since then, and lives in Mexico, but I won't go into her story."

He moved restlessly in his chair, and at once she held up an imperious hand, as if ordering him to stay where he was.

"Please wait. What I'm telling you is for your own good. As Christine grew older I suppose it was natural that she should grow more and more self-centered and selfish. I couldn't bear the thought of marriage for her, for I couldn't see how it could possibly work unless she could find someone who would become her abject slave, as her father had been."

It was time to break in, however brusquely or rudely. He could not sit and listen to her any longer.

"Mrs. Gellert," he said, "I'd rather not hear any more. I'm

devoted to Christine, and what you're saying only angers and antagonizes me still further."

He got up, and at once she too was on her feet.

"So you admit," she cried, "that you're in love with her! You, who pretend to be Sam's friend. So much in love with her that you can't even bear to hear the truth about her. You might just as well admit now that what your wife said was true."

"I will only admit," he told her, "that what you've been saying has thoroughly shocked me, all the more so because at this moment Christine is ill and helpless."

She ignored this as if she had not even heard, or, if she had heard, as if it were entirely beside the point. She looked as if some powerful string in her had been plucked to set her vibrating from head to feet with resentment and bitterness. She seemed to gather up bitterness like a ball to throw in his face.

"Let me tell you this, Mr. Logan," she said, "you may dislike me, and I know you do—Christine will have seen to that —but my advice to you is to have a reconciliation with your wife and leave Christine alone. And I'll tell you why. I love her better than anything in the world, but I know her through and through. She and I are as alike as mother and daughter can be. What I am, she will be if she lives long enough. She has every trait, every characteristic that she despises in me. Yes, despises. I tell you again that if she lives long enough, she'll be exactly as I am."

His anger rang in his ears and sent the blood to his head. He went quickly to the door.

"I think," he said as he opened it, "she would rather die."

He ordered whiskey and soda and a few sandwiches to be sent to his room, as he had no wish to go down to dinner. He could not get Mrs. Gellert's voice out of his ears nor rid himself of her personality. She seemed to have come into the room with him and now pervaded it.

Poor Gellert, he thought, my poor darling Christine! When the whiskey came he half filled a glass, adding a dash of soda. He longed for Sam's arrival. His anxiety about Christine, the strain of waiting, his interview with Mrs. Gellert, tried his nerves unbearably. So despondent did he feel about Christine that he knew he would have given anything—his own life, gladly—if he could have wiped out, conjured away, that flight in the rain from Delphi. What folly it had been! Why had he ever agreed to it? Christine could have locked her door against her mother if need be; he could have dealt with her alone. Whenever he looked back now he could see Christine climbing the hill in the rain, or standing in a downpour with her raincoat held tightly about her and the collar turned up, but her head and feet exposed to the wet, while he drove across the broken road. He could once again feel her shivering against him in the car. And yet, at the same time, he knew how she would deplore his taking the blame for this, too, upon his shoulders. For her sake, and because she would wish it, he must try and see it as fate, as Moira: a thing that had been going to happen to them and therefore had happened. But he found it impossible to discipline his thoughts. If she had been in Sam's care it would not have happened. He would not have taken her to Arachova on a wet day and allowed her to walk through the puddles of the uneven streets. Sam would not have taken her to Olympia in the rain over a road they had been warned against. But that, he argued in his own defense, was one of the things that had contributed to her happiness—that for once she was treated like anyone else, able to take small risks in a normal way. And if they had not fled from Delphi, they would not have known the unforgettable rapture of last night at Olympia. As if his consciousness had suddenly been opened to admit an emanation from hers, he knew, with certainty, that Christine would have changed nothing. Nothing. And this conviction, which he felt he had received directly from her, gave him comfort.

Half an hour later the telephone rang. It was Dr. Araman, and it was an enormous relief to be in touch with him again and hear his voice. His first words were: "How are you, and how is your wife? I hope you are both well and enjoying your trip."

He asked Dr. Araman if he would mind coming to his room, explaining that he could not very well go to Dr. Araman's as he was expecting a telephone call. In a few minutes Dr. Araman was there and his very solidity, together with his calm manner, were reassuring. While Murray was telling him about Christine's illness and making such explanations as were necessary, Dr. Araman made no movement, and his round dark face showed neither surprise nor any confusion on hearing that Mrs. Bonner's husband was expected at any moment and that her mother was already in the hotel.

"Your anxiety is very natural," he said. "She is a delicate woman and every care must be taken. Do you know what doctor is in attendance?"

Murray had to say that he didn't know, that Mrs. Gellert, her mother, had now taken charge, but he said he would find out.

"Don't trouble," Dr. Araman said. "I can easily make inquiries downstairs. I will be at Mrs. Bonner's disposal tonight and tomorrow if I am needed. If a crisis should arise—but I hope it will not—I would even postpone my departure. She is a most charming lady. In any case, of course, I would do what I could."

When he had gone, Murray's anxieties were somewhat eased. Their meeting in the plane, he thought, had been providential, whatever they may have felt about his presence in Delphi. It was providential, it was something on the credit side where so far there were few possible entries. He wrote down Dr. Araman's name and room number to give to Sam later. Whatever emerged from their coming meeting, Sam would be glad that such valuable help was at hand.

Some time after Dr. Araman had gone the telephone rang again. It was just nine o'clock. At the sound of Sam's voice saying "Is that you, Murray?" his heart began to race wildly.

"Hello, Sam. You must have just arrived this minute."

"Yeah, I just checked in. We got held up in Rome. What about my coming up to see you? I haven't seen anybody yet. I could come up right away. I'm down in the lobby now."

"Do please come up, Sam. I'm very anxious to see you."

He put back the receiver and then took several deep slow breaths to try to quiet the beating of his heart. Did Sam want his story first, before hearing Christine's? What pitfalls lay before him? Sam had yet to learn that Christine had a temperature and was in bed. He would have to be the one to tell him. Well, that was right, he would prefer that it should be his responsibility. But how was he to guess what Christine might say, not now, perhaps—though a mere nod could reveal everything—but when she was well again? There was no means of knowing. He only knew that it was best to make no plan at all, to leave what he would decide to say to the needs of the moment. He went to the door and stood waiting for the sound of Sam's footsteps in the hall. Then he opened it.

Sam's greeting was just as usual, the clasp of his hand was precisely what it had always been. And if suspicion, anxiety, mental disquiet were there, they were not to be seen in his face.

"I came right up," he said, dropping his hat on the table. "I didn't stop to see Christine or anything, I was in such a hurry to talk to you."

"I'm glad you did," Murray answered.

"I just want to say," Sam went on, and his words came quickly, "how damned sorry I am about all this. That was a terrible letter your wife wrote to me. Did you know she wrote to me from here, the day after you'd arrived?"

292

"Mrs. Gellert told me. She'd seen Charles."

"She not only wrote one letter, she wrote three of them. God! Has she gone off her head? What could have gotten into her? I never read such a lot of rotten lies and accusations in all my life."

"Yes," Murray said. "Let's have a drink, Sam." He found that he could not at that moment meet Sam's eyes, the confidence he had shown in him was too overwhelming.

"Just a small one," Sam said. "I had one on the plane. So now you've been exposed to Mrs. Gellert, have you? How did that work out?"

"It wasn't too bad," Murray said, busy with the drinks.

"Thanks, old boy, that's enough. What do you think made her do what she did? Your wife, I mean?"

"Oh, I suppose it all began more than seven years ago, when we had that accident. I didn't realize till now how much she must have hated me all this time."

"I thought it had something to do with that," Sam said. "I sort of guessed she'd got right off the beam. Where is she now?"

"As far as I know she's living with another man. She left here to go to him. A man she knows who's getting a divorce and wants to marry her. I was completely taken by surprise." Then he faced Sam, who had just sat down, and said, "But none of this is really important now. What is important is that Christine got a chill two days ago. She's in bed, with a temperature. I hate to have to tell you this, Sam, but I think you ought to go to her as soon as you can. We'll have time to talk later."

Sam got out of his chair with his surprising lightness and quickness of movement, and picked up his hat.

"What sort of temperature? How high?"

"I'd guess about 103. Her mother's taken over, so I don't know exactly. She went to bed as soon as we got here, somewhere around four-thirty. We'd been to Olympia." He hesi-

293

tated and then said, "You know, Sam, she was eager to see as much as she could."

Sam nodded. "Of course she'd want to see what she could. Why shouldn't she? I'll get along now."

"There's a Syrian doctor in the hotel," Murray said, and handed him the slip of paper. "We met him on the plane. He's a specialist. He runs a hospital for diseases of the lungs in Damascus. I thought it might be a good idea to get in touch with him."

Sam looked at it and put it in his pocket.

"Gosh! This is bad luck," he said, with a worried frown. "She'd been so well. She said she'd never felt better. Well, I'll be giving you a ring later."

When he had gone Murray took the glass he had prepared for Sam, which Sam had not touched, and drank it himself. The meeting which he had been dreading ever since hearing that Sam was on his way was now over. He had had confidence in Sam, but he had never anticipated that he would not ask him a single question. Sam's extraordinary trust in him left him quite confounded, utterly grateful and deeply humbled. He would not have believed it possible that Sam would not ask for a single assurance that Sibyl's accusations had been lies. His eyes misted over with tears. He wished he had deserved such trust, he wished it had been possible to deserve it. He lay down on the bed with his arms over his head and shut his eyes. He must have fallen into a profound sleep, for the ringing of the telephone woke him. It was nearly twelve.

"The news isn't too good," Sam said, and his plaintive voice gave to his words an extra dimension of gloom. "It looks like developing into pneumonia, and you know what that means with Christine. I got that Syrian doctor and I'm glad I did. He and the other doctor—his name's Meletis as near as I can get it—have had a consultation and they've decided to take her off to the hospital. God! I'm thankful I got here

294

when I did. Sorry if I woke you up. I'll report again tomorrow."

Murray undressed and got into bed, but now he could not sleep. He would have given anything to have been at the hospital with Sam, to be near at hand, to know at once of any improvement, to be at least within Christine's orbit. He realized that she might become delirious, that she might call for him, that she might speak of things they would neither of them want spoken of. The very night before she had been in his arms. But although this, if it happened, might be a cruel and a tragic thing, it seemed of no importance at all beside the fact of her illness. Nothing mattered but for her to get well.

He got out of bed and knelt down to pray. He was on his knees for a long time, fumbling his unaccustomed way through improvisations that were made up of both confessions and entreaties, but were chiefly entreaties. He begged for Christine's life until he felt emptied of words, emptied even of the power of supplication. When he got up from his knees he felt not so much that he had been heard as that a burden that was too heavy for him had been eased.

The first person to ring him in the morning was Mrs. Gellert, and remembering how they had parted, he was amazed. She was speaking from the hospital, she said. They were very much worried about Christine. Her chest condition was bad, but all that could be done was being done. Of course she wished that they were at home, in an American hospital, but it was a blessing that Sam was there. He knew Christine a great deal better than the doctors did.

"I had a little talk with Sam," she said, "and I realize I owe you an apology. I'd like to make one now. Are you leaving today?"

"No," he said. "I canceled my booking. I won't go until Christine is better."

"In that case, why not lunch with me? What with all the

worry and annoyance I've been through, and the fact that you made me so thoroughly angry, I said things I ought not to have said. I'd like to explain a little."

He asked her to excuse him. He said he felt he had to be alone. He would lunch by himself at a small restaurant he knew.

"Well, if that's the way you feel, perhaps another day. Good-by."

He went to the restaurant to which he had taken Christine. It had been a happy evening, with Sibyl, as they thought, dining with friends and enjoying her new self-confidence. Sitting at the same table where they had sat before he knew even more surely than he had known outside the hotel in Olympia that, however deeply and wholly he and Christine loved each other, he could not have broken up her marriage. Sam's generosity of mind, the wholeness and sincerity of his liking and trust, made it impossible. He told himself that his sins against Sam were many, but there was one thing that could be set against them—that he had made the greatest sacrifice he could make.

He tried to divert his thoughts from their anxieties about Christine by thinking about her mother. What an extraordinary woman, and what an extraordinary outburst! Was it possible that even with Christine lying ill it had still been jealousy that had caused it? She had tried to establish herself in his mind as a woman who had suffered much and unfairly at her daughter's hands. For what purpose? For the purpose, he supposed, of trying to eradicate any unfavorable opinions he might have gathered about her from Christine. And there was also, of course, the fact that she believed Christine to have embarked upon a love affair from which she might derive a happiness that she herself envied, and had never had. Was this delicate daughter who had opposed and gently thwarted her over so many years to have *everything*?

His mind, sharpened by the crowding experiences of recent

296

weeks, now suddenly perceived that Sibyl had been actuated, at least in part, by a similar resentment; the resentment felt by a strong, healthy woman against a delicate, invalidish woman who, in spite of her disabilities, triumphs. Sibyl, of course, had had a double motive, perhaps several motives, but he felt sure that one of them had been her feeling that Christine had taken an unfair advantage of her charm and her frail health to arouse men's chivalry, a chivalry that her own scars had not, she felt, won for her.

He could almost smile at his past ignorance, his past simplicity and inexperience. Since the day in New York when Christine had astonished him by getting him to talk freely about himself, he had learned much, he had been breaking out of the shell or chrysalis that had enclosed him. From noninvolvement he had passed to an involvement he could never have imagined, from dullness to awareness. And, he now said to himself, surely a heightened awareness is the goal of every thinking creature. What else were we born for? And what else is love? He made a vow, as he sat there at the table where she had once sat beside him, that even if he was never to see her again, this growing and expanding awareness would be a continuing process, and he longed, above everything, to go to her now and tell her that it would.

He thought of all the questions she had asked. He could illumine nothing for her, she was by far the more fully aware of the two, but he knew that together they would have comforted each other for their ignorance and perhaps would gradually have grown in stature, like children stretched on tiptoe at a knothole in a fence too high for them.

He did not leave to go to a cheaper hotel, for he could not cut himself off from news. And Sam was more than glad of his company.

"For God's sake don't leave me alone with Mrs. Gellert," he begged. "Charles doesn't often make mistakes, but he certainly made one this time when he asked her to come here. You'd hardly believe it, but that woman is eaten up with jealousy of Christine even now. It burns her up that Christine is getting everybody's attention and she isn't getting anybody's. I try to keep her out of Christine's room as much as I can. I kept her out today and unless Christine's a lot better I'll keep her out tomorrow too."

He asked Sam once if he'd like a quick run up to the Acropolis. It need only take half an hour.

"God, no!" Sam exclaimed. "I can see as much as I want to from the window in Christine's room at the hospital. No, sir, I'm doing no sightseeing unless I can do it with that girl."

The subject of the letters now seemed to be closed. Sam made no further reference to Sibyl. The whole thing already seemed to have faded out, lost in the general anxiety.

The news was a little better, then it was a little worse. Then it was a good deal worse. He only saw Sam now late at night, when he would come back to the hotel for a few hours' sleep.

One night he said he was not coming back. He would snatch a few minutes sleep in an armchair in the waiting room. Already his clothes hung on him loosely, his whole face sagged. Murray sometimes wondered which of them suffered most. He kept to his room, fearful of missing any news and wanting to keep out of Mrs. Gellert's way. There was a third reason, and that was that he felt a desperate need of prayer.

On the fifth day at about four o'clock Sam knocked on his door and came in. He flung himself exhausted into a chair and at the sight of his haggard, miserable face Murray knew what he might expect to hear.

"It looks as if we are going to lose this fight," Sam said. His whole body began to shake and he put his bent arm over his face like a child. Murray went to him and put a hand on his shoulder.

"She can't be going to die, Sam," he said. "She can't be."

"This time," Sam said, his voice muffled by his sleeve, "she

298

isn't putting up a fight. She used to help me. She used to fight back. Not this time."

Murray could find no words to say. He stood bleakly, feeling frozen, his hand on Sam's shoulder. He felt as if he were exposed, naked, to an icy wind out beyond the world; as if he had lost his foothold on the world and was alone, falling into outer space. He closed his eyes, sickened by the sense of falling.

"She wants to see you," he heard Sam say.

He made a great effort to get back, to find a foothold again, and repeated, dully, "She wants to see me?"

"She said so just now. We'd better go. The car's waiting. Dr. Araman's there and Dr. Meletis. God! They've had five doctors and they can't do a damned thing!"

They went down together, two men enclosed in their own private and incommunicable tragedies. When they reached the hospital Sam said he would wait downstairs. He told Murray where to go.

"They'll only let you stay a minute," he said.

So this was how he was going to see her again.

He knocked too softly to be heard and knocked again. A nurse opened the door to him. He saw Christine stretched out quite straight in her narrow white bed, and the two doctors were on either side of her. As he came forward Dr. Araman turned toward him and gave him a look of pity and sorrow. A tentlike affair had just been moved aside and the room was terrifying in its blank orderliness, as if Christine had already died and everything had been tidied away. Her hair was in two braids which lay on either side of the pale oval of her face, and she was breathing with great difficulty. The two doctors moved toward the window together.

Her eyes were open and he saw that she was conscious, but she seemed very remote. Then her eyes moved to meet his. They looked at each other, and he thought he saw on her face the faintest of smiles. He bent his head and lightly touched her forehead with his lips. She whispered something and he bent his head again. He could hear quite distinctly what she was saying.

"I ask you to try to be happy. It's a wonderful thing to have been given life."

"I will try, my darling."

"It's true what you said to me? That last thing?"

"It is true."

"I'm glad."

Her eyes closed; then she opened them and said, a little more faintly than before, "Good-by, for now."

He straightened himself and looked down at her. Her eyes were closed again. There was nothing to wait for or to expect. He went out of the room quickly, afraid that Dr. Araman might follow and try to speak to him. Finding that he did not, he halted for a few seconds in the corridor and then went down and into the waiting room. He could not utter a word. Sam looked at him and said, "Take the car and then send it back."

He took the car back to the hotel.

So it was Christine who, at her request, was to be buried in Greece. She had said she did not want to leave it, and now she would not.

He felt that he had been permitted for a while to see with a new and rare clarity, and now, in spite of his promise to Christine, it seemed to him that he was destined to live for the rest of his life in a twilit world.

XX ✒

He did not go back to the office until ten days later. When, a few days before, he had rung up Charles, Charles had said, "Take your time, take your time. You've been through a very sad experience. Why not turn up next Monday, and when you do, come straight to me?"

There seemed to be no change in Charles, who welcomed him with his usual friendliness and urbanity. With his fresh, slightly sun-tanned complexion, his pleasant blue eyes, his becomingly whitened hair, he seemed to come from another world, a world where nothing could ever go very wrong. Yet Murray knew that he had taken Sam's loss very much to heart.

"It was good of you, my boy, to write to me," Charles began, "and now that I've seen Sam I think I've got the whole affair quite straight. I gather it was a tactical error on my part to have sent Christine's mother out there, but, well, I really didn't know what to think or what to do, and she arrived at what seemed an opportune moment. I hear she's back in New York now. Sam says that her idea of mourning was to abstain from going to the Paris dress shows."

"I think that seems in character," Murray said.

"You didn't stay for the funeral," Charles remarked.

"No," Murray replied. "Sam seemed to want it to be quite private. I came straight home."

"That was astonishing news about Sibyl," Charles said. "I suppose those letters were a sort of farewell gift to you. What do you think her future will be? Will the man marry her?"

"She believes so," Murray said. "None of it has any interest for me, but I suppose I must go ahead and get a divorce."

"I think you must. I gather that you have a completely factual letter from her."

"Yes. She admitted adultery and asked me to use what she wrote as evidence."

"I'd like you to go and see my old friend Roderick Glaisonby, and let his firm handle it for you. You can safely leave it entirely in their hands."

"I'll probably do that," Murray said.

"Well, you can rely on Glaisonby. He's first-rate." Charles picked up a paper knife and began turning it about in his fingers.

Murray was aware of an unusual constraint in his manner. To break a silence, he said, "I imagine there are pretty heavy arrears of work for me to attend to."

"I shouldn't worry too much about that," Charles said. "Everything can be taken care of." Then he turned about in his chair, dropping the paper knife on his desk, and faced Murray squarely. "It's no good putting these things off, I suppose," he said with a sigh. "I have some rather bad news for you, my boy. I'm afraid we shall have to put an end to your connection with Atlantic House. I can't tell you how much I regret it."

302

After an instant's stunned silence, Murray said, "But why? Because of all this?"

"You see the trouble is that your wife not only wrote to Sam and me, but to Frederick as well. I expect Sam told you. Well, Frederick is a large-hearted, large-minded man, and I have always known him to be a just man, but you must remember that he's a sick man too, and that letter hit him just where it could hurt him most. It hit him through Sam and Christine. Not only that, but the villain of the piece—and I'm afraid he believed most of it at first—was not only a member of the firm, but an Englishman. Well, a Britisher; I forgot you were born over the border. Now, you know what Frederick's like. You know how chivalrously and tenderly he loves and admires this country. That a citizen of Great Britain should have been the cause of what looked like disaster to Sam, and Sam's marriage, was more than he could bear. It seemed to him utterly shocking. It amazes me that when he opened Sibyl's letter he didn't have a third heart attack. I conclude that he was too angry. So, you see, there was that in it too, the feeling of having been stabbed in the back by someone he specially liked and trusted. Sam tried his hardest to persuade him that it was just a pack of lies written by a spiteful woman, but—well, I'd better read you some extracts from his latest letter, written in his own hand, and a shaky hand at that."

He picked up a letter from his desk and glanced down the first page.

There's been a lot of mud thrown and some of it is bound to stick. The Atlantic House team has never been involved, from the very earliest days, in any scandal. I don't even remember a single unpleasant rumor in connection with any of them, and that's the way I want it to be as long as I'm alive. It's extremely displeasing to me to know that one of us, a member of the board especially, and someone with whom Sam has been on friendly terms, has been involved in this. I'm afraid he'll have to resign. I feel very strongly about it, and I hope you will give me your fullest support. I can never forget that he was, indirectly if you like, the cause of Christine's death. Pay him whatever compensation you think just and right, but ask for his resignation. I couldn't meet him face to face again. I would find it too difficult and too painful.

He laid the letter down.

"I see," Murray said.

"I'm sorrier than I can possibly say, my boy. I've known you nearly all your life and Lily and I are both very fond of you. To me it's a sad personal loss. But really, compared with Sam's tragedy, is it such a serious matter?"

Murray made no reply.

"With your experience," Charles went on, "you oughtn't to have any difficulty in joining some other firm. As a matter of fact I spoke to Herman Shaeffer about you the other day. He seemed definitely interested. Why don't you write to him?"

"I will write to him," Murray said, "and of course I offer my resignation now, and I'll write you a formal letter tonight."

They both stood up, and Charles put a hand on Murray's shoulder.

"I'll have to let you go now, my boy. I have an appointment. Keep in touch with me. And remember you'll always have the warmest of welcomes from Lily and me. I'll tell you a curious thing. Lily fervently hoped that something would happen to prevent your going to Greece. She had a kind of presentiment. She spoke of it more than once."

Murray could not trust himself to make any comment on this. He merely shook Charles's hand and went to the office he shared with Dick Bayliss. He hoped he would find Dick Bayliss out, and he was. He felt no bitterness toward anyone. He was sure that Charles had done what he could. There was only the feeling of shock and of loss, and there was the pain of knowing that he had to begin, when he was most depleted, a fresh chapter.

He had guessed that Sam would want to see him before going back to New York. The next day when he was in the office collecting the last of his papers, Sam telephoned.

"I've got to see you before I go. I'm at the Ritz. When could we meet?"

"Any time," Murray said. "What about this afternoon? I could come along about four-thirty."

Sam said that would suit him, gave him the room number, and told him to come right up.

He knew that Sam wanted to tell him he was sorry about his resignation, but he felt certain that there were other things he would want to say as well; things it would be painful for him to hear. He felt no reluctance to meet this or any other ordeal. He was anesthetized by sorrow. Christine's death had purged him of all personal anxieties. Even the pain of leaving Atlantic House was dulled and diminished by it.

He avoided the side door, where he had once met her, and went up in one of the main elevators. When he knocked, Sam called out, "Come right in," and he opened the door. It was a hotel sitting room furnished in the French style, bare of a single personal belonging. There was not even a book to be seen, and a vase of carnations, a white card still dangling, was pushed aside into a dark corner.

Sam's handshake was not the same. It was briefer and less firm and Murray guessed that this had a special significance. Sam looked wretched, his eyes were still rimmed with red and the flesh under them was baggy. He wore a black tie very carelessly tied.

"Want a drink?" Sam asked. "I'll order it up if you do."

"No, thanks, Sam."

305

"Tea, then? I always forget about tea."

"No, thanks. Not even tea."

"O.K. We'll just talk. Sit down. God! How I hate hotel sitting rooms!"

They sat facing each other, and then Sam said, "I'm sorry about your resignation. I wanted to tell you so and try to explain how Dad felt."

"There's no need to, Sam. I understand perfectly. What's more, I think your father is quite right."

"All the same," Sam said, "he thought a lot of you. Well, I don't give him a great deal longer to live. It seems I've got to lose everything and everybody I love. If it weren't that I've still got Atlantic House, I guess I'd just about go off my head."

"I'm thankful you have it."

"Do you remember," Sam asked after a moment's silence, "that Sunday you came to the house and we walked down to the lake to look at the ducks? That seems a hell of a long time ago."

"It seems an age."

"All the same, it's a day I'll always remember. I'll always remember telling you about Christine and why she'd gone away. It was lucky I did because thanks to you we had six months of happiness. I did, anyhow. I don't think I was ever happier, and I'll always be grateful to you for that."

"Don't thank me, Sam. I don't deserve any thanks."

"Well, I'm not forgetting. Things were temporarily in a bad way and you helped us both."

He got out of his chair, walked to the window and returned. He wore his sorrow as a child does, for all to see. It would not have been like Sam to try to conceal the fact that he was suffering.

"Murray, there's something that's going to be pretty tough for me to talk about and pretty tough for you to hear, but

306

I've got to tell you and we'd better get it over with now. No, you sit still. I'll just walk about. It's easier that way.

"When Christine was delirious she talked about you. Sometimes I'd go away so as not to hear. It was too much like eavesdropping. She kept thinking you were there with her, not me. God! I wish I hadn't had to know, but maybe it's better that I do know because it explains a lot. I could feel she was fighting to get away, as if everything was too much for her. I never flattered myself that Christine really loved me but I loved her so much that most of the time I could forget it. I just wanted to live for her; I wanted to give her a future. That was what my life was about."

Murray sat silent, his elbow on the arm of his chair and his hand over his eyes.

"If I'd stopped to think things out," Sam went on, and sometimes his voice came from near at hand and sometimes from a little distance, "I'd have guessed that she'd have to love someone someday. It seems to be something none of us can do without. I guess it was bound to happen, and it did, and it happened to be you. I'm not blaming you in any way at all. You had no more idea she was going to love you than I had. And if I know my darling Christine, once it had happened she had to try to make things go the way she wanted them to go. I can pretty well guess that the whole idea of the trip to Greece was her idea and that she planned it without a single wrong intent."

Murray sat without moving. He knew that Sam had not finished yet.

"Well, maybe that was something that had to happen," Sam went on, "and I don't believe Christine would have left me because of it. In fact I know she wouldn't. I know her so well that I haven't got a single doubt. She'd have stayed."

"Yes," Murray said. "She would have stayed."

"She'd have stayed," Sam repeated. "She knew what she

307

meant to me and we'd have come through it the way people can if they want to enough. So I don't hold that against you."

There was nothing Murray felt he could say and there was a silence during which Sam continued to walk up and down. Then he stopped in front of Murray's chair and when he spoke again his voice had altered.

"That's finished with," he said. "That's over and done with, but why in God's name couldn't you have looked after her properly? Why in God's name did you have to take her over a road that was under repair and pretty dangerous at the best of times? And in the pouring rain, and the temperature down below fifty? Dr. Araman knows that road and he said it was terrible in heavy rain. And why in God's name did you have to take her to that damn town up in the hills where she got her feet wet? Araman said it might have started then. Why the hell? Do you realize she'd have been with me now if it hadn't been for you? Oh, what's the good of talking? It's done, it's done; it's happened and nothing's going to bring her back, but it's something I can't ever forget. I can't get it out of my mind. If Dad hadn't asked for your resignation I'd have had to get out of Atlantic House myself and let Jim Hancock take over. Because I can't ever see you again. I'm sorry, but that's the way it is. I can't possibly ever see you again."

Murray had taken his hand down from his eyes and was looking at Sam, but Sam avoided looking at him.

"I understand perfectly," Murray said. "I shall never forgive myself for not taking better care of her. There's nothing more to be said."

"No," Sam replied, "there's nothing more to be said. I guess this had better be good-by." And he still kept his eyes averted.

Murray got up. On the opposite wall was a large gilt French mirror and he saw in it a face he hardly recognized as his own.

308

"I'll go now," he said. "Good-by, Sam."

Sam turned away toward the window and his whole body sagged with grief. Murray picked up his hat and went to the door. It was best to open it quickly and then close it quickly behind him, with Sam on one side of it and himself on the other. The closing was final, and he knew that nothing else was possible.

Set in Electra
Format by Seamus Byrne
Manufactured by American Book–Stratford Press, Inc.
Published by HARPER & BROTHERS, New York